PRAISE FOR MICHELLE FRANCES

'Brilliantly twisty, a sharp, sinister and addictive read'
Sunday Mirror

'I was blown away. *The Girlfriend* is the most marvellous psychological thriller'
Jilly Cooper

'Tension oozes from the pages'
i newspaper

'A fab debut with two twisted women at its core'
Prima

'Utterly compulsive reading'
Jenny Blackhurst

'An original and chilling portrayal of twisted relationships'
Debbie Howells

'A fantastic psychological thriller . . . We couldn't put it down'
Take a Break

'Taut and suspenseful'
Heat

SISTERS

Michelle Frances has worked in television drama as a producer and script editor for several years, both for the independent sector and the BBC. *Sisters* is her fourth novel, following *The Girlfriend, The Temp* and *The Daughter.*

ALSO BY MICHELLE FRANCES

The Girlfriend
The Temp
The Daughter

SISTERS

MICHELLE FRANCES

PAN BOOKS

First published 2020 by Pan Books
an imprint of Pan Macmillan
The Smithson, 6 Briset Street, London EC1M 5NR
Associated companies throughout the world
www.panmacmillan.com

ISBN 978-1-5098-7717-1

3 5 7 9 8 6 4 2

A CIP catalogue record for this book is available from the British Library.

Typeset in Sabon LT Std by Palimpsest Book Production Ltd, Falkirk, Stirlingshire
Printed and bound by CPI Group (UK) Ltd, Croydon, CR0 4YY

For Leila. You couldn't ask for a nicer sister.

PROLOGUE

Christmas Eve 2017

As Ellie got off the train at Redhill station, laden down with her overnight case and a bag full of gifts, she was immediately caught in a gust of freezing wind, laced with sleet. She grimaced and pulled her cashmere scarf closer to her neck, not just to keep herself warm, but also to stop the scarf from getting ruined by the atrocious weather. Thank God she'd treated herself and bought it. It had cost a small fortune but on days like today it was well worth the investment. If she'd gone away for Christmas, like she had in the summer on a birthday treat to herself in the form of a two-week holiday to the Maldives, she wouldn't have needed a cashmere scarf. But the credit card balance was looking a little high, to the point of starting to give her sleepless nights. Her plan had been to pay it off with the pay rise once she'd been offered the trainee teacher job at the school where she worked. Instead, Ellie was still smarting from the rejection she'd received only the previous week.

Ellie sighed as she put her ticket through the barrier machine. Leaving the station, she looked up at the busy road and contemplated the twenty-minute walk to her childhood home. The sleet was getting heavier, large droplets of frozen water attacking her. She walked over to the taxi rank and got into the first one. Sod the expense, this was an emergency.

Abby glanced at her watch – she was late. She'd sent a guilty text to her mother, Susanna, to apologize: she'd had to stay on at the office and finish off some reports. She hadn't really needed to, but she was so used to working all hours that she felt anxious when she wasn't, a feeling exacerbated by the knowledge that she was going to her mother's house for Christmas Day. Abby saw it as a feat of endurance.

She'd managed to duck out of it for the last few years, citing either a work trip or, once, so as not to hurt her mother's feelings, she'd pretended that friends had invited her over, when in actual fact she'd spent the day alone in her flat. They'd sent texts wishing each other a happy Christmas. Her sister Ellie had taken a selfie of herself and Susanna with paper hats on, arms around each other, saying they missed her. Abby thought it unlikely.

As she walked up the road to her mother's house she saw the familiar black gate, the lights on in the windows. She knew Ellie would already be there, her sister and mother gossiping over glasses of wine, heads bent conspiratorially. Whenever Abby came into the room, she always felt as if she was ruining their moment, as if she was guiltily tolerated. It was only thirty-six hours, Abby reminded herself as she fixed on a bright smile. She rang the bell, resolving to make an effort.

The door opened but instead of her mother, it was Ellie standing there. It was ridiculous but Abby immediately felt slighted, as if her mother couldn't be bothered to welcome her.

'You look wet,' said Ellie.

The sleet was still pelting Abby but Ellie made no move to shift aside.

'Well, let me in then,' said Abby, as she stepped into the house and shook off her coat.

'You should ask Mum for a key,' said Ellie.

Abby didn't feel as if she should have to. Ellie seemed to have had hers for years without ever having had to ask.

Her sister was glowing, as usual. Ellie leaned over to kiss her on the cheek.

'Nice to see you,' she said, and Abby felt the soft warmth of Ellie's skin, smelled the high-quality shampoo in her lustrous blonde waves, just as she caught sight of her own reflection in the hall mirror: red nose and sleet-flattened hair.

Ellie had always been the one to draw the looks. On the rare occasions the two of them went out together, Abby felt very much in Ellie's shadow, the invisible girl, while men fluttered around her sister like hummingbirds around nectar. She told herself it didn't matter, that the men wouldn't be the type she'd go for anyway, but when it happened every single time, it couldn't help but bug her. And then there was that time Ellie had stepped well over the line, just after that boat trip they'd been on. Abby felt herself start to simmer and quickly put the resentment to the back of her mind. Now was not the moment to rake up old animosity.

'It's been a while,' said Ellie dryly, and Abby was immediately reminded of how her sister had emailed some time ago suggesting they meet for dinner one night. Abby tried to remember all the conferences and board meetings that had taken place since then and thought it might have been back in the autumn. *That was months ago*, she realized and felt a pang of guilt.

'Ah, Abby, it's you,' said Susanna, appearing from the kitchen with a glass of wine in her hand.

Who else would it be? thought Abby.

'Hi, Mum. Thanks for having us.'

Susanna waved a hand in a gesture of generosity. 'Oh, it's a pleasure. You know I like to spend Christmas with my daughters.' She beamed, but her eye contact was with Ellie, Abby noticed.

More wine was poured and a shop-prepared shepherd's pie pulled out of the oven. They ate, catching up on news. Ellie had a colleague whom she didn't much like, a woman called Zoe, who'd recently been promoted to trainee teacher.

'What's wrong with her?' asked Abby.

'She's all targets and plans,' said Ellie. 'Teaching doesn't come parcelled up like that.'

Abby secretly thought targets sounded like a good thing, but recognized she knew very little about teaching.

'And she's hardly been at the school – only a year. She doesn't understand the kids yet, not properly.'

Her sister was clearly disgruntled. Abby decided to rally. 'You should have gone for it yourself. You've worked as a teaching assistant there for years, haven't you? And aren't you covering loads of lessons single-handedly? Must have masses of experience over this new girl. I bet if you'd applied for the job you would have wiped the floor with her.'

Silence descended. Abby looked up from her dinner, saw her mother and sister watching her. Suddenly it dawned.

'Oh. Sorry, I didn't know.'

'I didn't want to just put it in an email,' said Ellie pointedly. 'I never know if you read them.'

Abby felt a wash of shame. She knew Ellie was talking about the fact they were meant to have met up. Abby had never replied.

'Sorry,' she said. 'Work . . . there's been a few changes,' she stumbled, evasively. 'It's kept me more occupied than usual.'

'What changes?' asked Susanna.

'Sorry?'

'You said there were changes?'

She had, damn it. Why hadn't she thought before opening her big mouth? And now they were both looking at her again.

'I, er . . . I had a promotion.'

'Oh right,' said Ellie. 'What kind of promotion?'

'I've, er . . . I've been made a director.' Abby knew she sounded apologetic, and it rankled. She was over the moon about her new role, had worked so hard for it.

'Congratulations,' said Ellie eventually.

'Thank you.'

'Yes, congratulations, Abby. That's great,' said her mother breezily. 'Now, who's for dessert?'

Abby knew she wasn't a child anymore and didn't need her mother's approval, but it still stung.

When does that feeling of longing for parental endorsement go away? she wondered as she lay in bed that night, the first to go up as she was so exhausted. She was a fool. There she was, a successful business leader on a huge salary, but she still couldn't shake the feeling that at home she was very much second best. Worse, it still had the power to wound her deeply.

'Merry Christmas!' they all chorused to each other the next morning. The sleet had turned to snow overnight and the unexpected surprise of a thick blanket of white over the garden seemed to bring in a sensation of newness, of starting afresh. Susanna popped a bottle of champagne and poured them each a Buck's Fizz.

'Right, presents!' declared Ellie, as she moved into the living room and pulled two gifts from under the tree. She handed one to Abby, then sat back with a huge smile on her face, impatient for her sister to open it.

Abby undid the fabric bow and peeled off the beautiful paper to find a jewellery box. Inside was a bangle made of hammered gold. It was so elegant and stylish, Abby gasped. She instantly fell in love with it, but found it hard to accept. She was worried.

'You like it?' asked Ellie, pleased.

'It's beautiful,' said Abby.

She saw Ellie was looking at her expectantly. There was nowhere to hide. Abby retrieved her gifts from under the tree and handed one to Ellie. The smile on her sister's face died as she removed the wrapping paper.

'It's a calendar,' said Ellie.

'An academic one,' said Abby. 'I thought it would be useful . . . you know, with you being at school. September to September.' Her sister's face was so crestfallen, Abby could barely look. Then Ellie found the other item in the package.

'And a pen,' she said.

Abby nodded. When she'd bought it, she'd been really pleased with it. It wasn't a Montblanc or anything like that but it was a fancy rollerball, in a blue and chrome casing. She looked down at her bangle. It was clear their gifts were wildly different in value. Abby's guilt rendered her silent for a moment and then she suddenly found herself getting annoyed.

'I thought we had a budget,' she said.

'What?' said Ellie.

'I sent an email. Twenty pounds each. I'm sure I did.'

'Well, sorry if I didn't get your memo on having a tight Christmas.'

'It's not tight,' said Abby hotly. 'It's . . .' She was at a loss as to what to say. She could see that to some people it might seem miserly, but actually too much was spent at Christmas anyway; it was all so horribly commercial. 'It's sensible,' she declared.

Ellie choked on her Buck's Fizz. 'OK, good. As long as we're being sensible.'

'You know what I mean.'

'Now, now, girls,' said Susanna, holding up the champagne bottle. 'Anyone for a top-up?'

'I just don't see the point of spending loads of money on something people don't really want,' said Abby.

Ellie slowly put her glass down on the side table. Her hand was shaking. 'First of all,' she started quietly, 'you take the time to think of something people *do* want, maybe by spending more time with them so you actually get to know them. And what is wrong with spending a bit of money? Especially if you're being paid a whole stack of it!' Her eyes were blazing with hurt and accusation.

Abby resented other people having opinions on how she should spend her salary, the expectation that because she was well paid, she should disburse her cash at a higher than average level. Well, it was none of Ellie's business. Abby had a strict budget and she was going to stick to it.

'I'm sorry you didn't get the email,' she said, 'and I'm sorry I hurt your feelings.' She cleared her throat, wanted to set the record straight. 'But actually, I did put quite a lot of thought into your present.'

'It's a calendar!' said Ellie. 'To help me organize my school year! Oh God, now I sound like a spoiled bitch. I'm upset. There, I know it's vulgar, crass beyond belief to discuss this, but I really can't quite believe it. Next you'll be telling me the pen is to do my marking.'

Abby opened her mouth but then thought better of it and closed it again. She lowered her eyes.

Ellie's jaw dropped. 'Good God. No, I don't want to hear it. *Seriously?*'

'Please don't . . .' said Susanna.

'Do you have any idea how much I earn?' said Ellie. 'Do you? Twenty grand a year! I bet that's your annual bonus, isn't it?'

Actually, it was about a third of her annual bonus, but Abby wisely kept that to herself.

'And yet, I still don't get a decent Christmas present, even though I like to think the one I got you is quite special.' Ellie, suddenly deflated, slumped down on the sofa. 'Oh, never mind.' An unhealthy silence filled the room.

After a while, Abby cleared her throat. 'I might go out for a bit of fresh air. Just five minutes.' Nobody said anything so she went into the hall, donned her coat and boots and, grabbing her sister's key on the hall table, she stepped outside.

As Abby walked on the untouched snow, she wondered how she was going to get through the rest of the day. She genuinely hadn't meant to hurt her sister's feelings – the whole thing had been a huge misunderstanding (she must check her sent box to see if her budget email actually went) – but at the same time, she couldn't help feeling a bit resentful. What was the big deal, anyway? Her sister always had to make such drama out of everything. It always had to be about Ellie.

By the time she had traipsed over much of her childhood

stomping ground, she'd calmed down. The unexpected beauty of the snow, and the way the bright blue sky made her gaze upwards with a smile on her face, had lifted her spirits. Nothing could be that bad, she decided, and she resolved to apologize fully when she got back to the house. Better than that she'd finally sort out that dinner invitation Ellie had sent all those weeks ago. She felt a pang of shame then at having overlooked it for so long, but now was the time to make amends.

Abby nervously made her way back up the front path and let herself in. Christmas music was playing loudly from the kitchen. She hung up her coat and put her boots to dry next to the radiator. She took a deep breath and, before her resolve left her, went to join them.

Her mother and Ellie were huddled together at the table with their backs to her, poring enthusiastically over Ellie's laptop. Neither seemed to hear her come in. Abby was about to announce her arrival when she caught a glimpse of the image on the screen – a beach somewhere.

Suddenly they realized she was there and Susanna guiltily minimized the tab.

'What's that?' asked Abby, furious that her voice sounded so small and hurt.

'We were just looking at places to go,' stumbled Susanna. She gave a big smile. 'Nice walk?'

'Go?' repeated Abby.

Ellie looked awkward. 'Mum and I were thinking about a couple of days away somewhere. You know, a European break.'

'Oh yes? When?'

'Um . . . probably March time, escape the cold. We were, er . . .' Ellie looked at Susanna. 'We were going to ask you to come but thought you were probably busy. You know, with work. But you're more than welcome to join us,' she added brightly.

Except Abby knew she wasn't. In fact, if she hadn't walked in on them at that exact moment, she would have known nothing about it.

'I'll check my diary,' she lied, 'but I do think March is quite full . . . a new contract we're negotiating.'

Ellie smiled. 'You see, always working. You should take a break every now and then.'

'You're right,' said Abby. Suddenly she thought she was going to burst into tears. It shocked her. She made some excuse and went into the living room where she made a gargantuan effort not to cry. It was too shameful, too weak. She couldn't let them see how upset she was.

Ellie and Mum. Mum and Ellie. That was how it had always been. It was lonely being the third wheel of the family. What had her sister got that had made their mother fall in love with her, right from as early as Abby could remember? Abby knew that whenever Ellie walked in the door, her mother's face lit up like the golden star on top of the Christmas tree, and no matter how long she lived, nor what she did, Abby knew she would never, ever have that same impact.

She got through the rest of the day as best she could and left early the next morning. As she sat on the train home, she realized she hadn't sorted the dinner date with Ellie.

ONE

Nineteen months later

As the taxi climbed into the wooded hills just outside Portoferraio, Ellie stared out of the window, wrestling with what she could see. This Italian jewel of an island – still green even though it was nearly the end of July, where she could glimpse the glittering Tyrrhenian Sea through palms and pines – this was where she would be spending the next six weeks in a rare break from her relentlessly demanding job as a teaching assistant for rowdy adolescents. A job that had morphed into actually taking the responsibility for teaching them, as the usual staff member had been signed off indefinitely with stress. This place was a paradise and would be a balm to soothe her overburdened mind and soul, six weeks of utter escapism, if only one thing wasn't bugging her: this was where her sister now spent the entire fifty-two weeks of *her* year. Because Abby had moved to the island of Elba, just off the coast of Tuscany, three months ago. She had, in fact, retired here.

Retired. Just thinking the word made Ellie's insides ripple with resentment. Abby could now live her life as she chose, never work again, frolic in the sunshine – what was it she said she'd recently taken up? Paddle-boarding, that was it. She could drift carefree across that sparkling sea for the next forty-odd years if she so wanted because Abby had achieved something remarkable: she had retired at the age of thirty-six.

Ellie would be thirty-six herself in three years' time but the notion of retirement made her laugh out loud – bitterly and with a sense that she still had three decades of a jail sentence to see out.

The taxi wound its way into a pretty medieval village where cats basked on flagstones and the elderly cackled into their espressos as they sat outside a cafe. The smell of thyme and broom drifted through the open window. And the light! It seemed to cast a spell over everything, rendering her speechless with its beauty. Ellie had recently tried to introduce some romance into her Year Eights' geography lesson, telling them the legend of Venus, who had risen from the waves, causing seven precious stones to fall from her tiara, which tumbled into the sea to create the seven islands off the Tuscan coast. Which one was Elba? she wondered. The forest gleam of an emerald? The deep azure of a sapphire? Or a perfectly cut diamond that reflected a kaleidoscope of colours?

They pulled up outside a villa and Ellie sat up. So this was Abby's house. It wasn't palatial, and it didn't draw much attention in looks. Ellie had pictured something resembling holiday-brochure utopia. She should have known better; Abby was never one to splash the cash. In fact, this house seemed modest, ordinary even, with just a few token decorations. Two small pots either side of the front door held a single red geranium plant each, and an apricot bougainvillea blended humbly into the ochre walls. This was where Abby lived with her new husband, whom Ellie had never met.

The front door opened and Abby appeared, hand raised to shade her eyes from the sun. Ellie hadn't seen her for nineteen months but nothing had changed. She still wore the same old faded denim skirt she'd had for a decade, topped by a cheap T-shirt.

Ellie got out of the car and took her suitcase from the driver as he heaved it out of the boot. Once she'd paid him, she turned to face her sister properly. The last time they'd seen each other, tensions had been high. Now they had a chance to start again. Time to form a proper sisterly bond.

TWO

Abby watched as her younger sister stepped out of the cab. The sun was directly behind Ellie and lit up her long, wavy blonde hair, making it glow as it caught in the breeze. Her legs were visible through her white summer dress, the sun outlining their length and shapeliness. Abby shielded her eyes, noting the admiring look the taxi driver cast in Ellie's direction, feeling the familiar tug of inferiority. She self-consciously touched her own mousy, straight hair, surreptitiously tried to fluff out its thinness, an automatic tic that had begun in childhood.

Ellie was walking towards her then and Abby smiled broadly. At the threshold, both sisters stood for a moment before going in for an air kiss, with a light brush of a hand on a shoulder.

'Come in,' said Abby, leading Ellie through the hall into the kitchen. 'Would you like a drink?' she asked, opening the fridge and pulling out a bottle of local lemonade. She'd bought it specially, thinking Ellie would like it.

Ellie nodded. 'Thank you.'

'Good journey?'

'Yes, fine. It's a beautiful island,' she declared generously.

Abby smiled. As she poured some lemonade into three glasses, she heard the thunder of bare feet come running down the stairs.

'*Ciao! Benvenuta!*' exclaimed her husband as he entered the room, immediately clasping Ellie on her upper arms and kissing her on both cheeks. Abby couldn't help but notice Ellie's instantly warm smile, saw Matteo's fingers on her sister's bare skin. Her husband still had that 'just woken up' look about him as he'd been on shift the previous night. He'd thrown on a pair of shorts and a T-shirt, the only thing he ever wore when he was out of his police uniform, and his clothes emphasized his tanned, muscular arms and thighs. He was one of those lucky people who were effortlessly sexy. *Bit like my sister*, she thought.

She handed her husband and sister a glass of lemonade and lifted her own. 'I'm really glad you could come,' she said to Ellie, thinking she ought to say something welcoming and polite.

'Thanks for inviting me.'

'To the holidays!' said Matteo enthusiastically, and they all clinked glasses and laughed.

Abby saw Ellie's eyes slide across to the kitchen wall tiles, a quizzical look appearing on her sister's face at the squares of wafer-thin plastic hanging off them. They looked like strange, peeling layers, as if the tiles were shedding a clear skin.

'Cling film,' said Matteo, amused. 'Abby thinks we should reuse it. So she washes it and sticks it on the tiles to dry.'

And why not? thought Abby. *There's nothing wrong with the cling film, so why not save money?*

'Was she always this thrifty?' Matteo asked Ellie, as he came over to kiss his wife.

'Yes,' said Ellie. 'Ever since she got her first pay packet.'

Abby listened for a note of rancour in her sister's voice but heard none. She was starting to feel claustrophobic.

'I thought we could go for a swim,' she said, finishing her drink. 'Why don't I give you a quick tour and show you your room, and once you're settled in, put your swimsuit on and I'll meet you on the patio.' She looked at Ellie and smiled. 'Fancy it?'

Abby led her sister across the patio away from the house rather than round the front towards the car. Ellie was puzzled. 'There's a path back here,' explained Abby, crossing the terraced garden. She indicated just beyond a languid, low-level pine to a set of steep steps that seemed to beckon enticingly and then disappeared out of view. Abby felt her sister stall momentarily, but when she looked back, Ellie quickly smiled and, hoisting her bag onto her shoulder, followed her down the steps. Matteo was already at the bottom, laying out towels on a rocky shelf at the edge of which lapped the crystal-clear Tyrrhenian Sea.

Ellie stared. 'Is this yours? I mean, is it private?'

'Er . . . yeah.'

'Wow. Your own beach.'

'It's not a beach,' said Abby.

'Next you'll have your own boat.'

Abby saw Ellie's gaze move around the rocks to a simple mooring, off which was tied a small boat.

'Oh. You already do.'

Abby pulled off her clothes, turning self-consciously so Ellie didn't see her shoulder. Underneath she was wearing an old bikini.

'Coming in?' she asked, and her sister nodded and slipped out of her dress. They both plunged into the blissfully cool water and, as they surfaced Abby gazed around her. It was a view she loved. They could see for miles, the sea stretching out in an endlessly winking blue. Abby sometimes wondered if it moved her soul so much because she'd spent fifteen years in an office in the City of London with no outside window, getting very little natural light and, in winter, never seeing daylight at all.

They swam for a while, then Matteo said he was going to go out further, but the girls preferred to warm themselves in the sun. They lay back on their towels, welcoming the heat on their skin. Ellie had been quiet during the swim and, as they sunbathed and the minutes ticked by silently, Abby felt herself grow nervous, sensing the awkwardness between them. It wasn't altogether unsurprising. When Abby had emailed the invitation, back in June, it was a spur of the moment thing that had been sent out of guilt for refusing to help her sister in what was, frankly, a ludicrous request. She hoped Ellie had got over it by now, or at least seen that it had been impossible.

'How's work?' asked Abby.

'Hideous.'

'Oh. Why?'

'The usual. No money for the school to buy textbooks for the ungrateful bastard teenagers who don't want them anyway. And yet, we still have to get the results. It's a bit like being a potato farmer but you have to dig the field by hand and you spend the entire growing season battling floods and poor top soil.'

Abby smiled. 'Are you likening your students to spuds?'

'Not all of them.'

'Do you hate it?'

Ellie paused. 'There are moments of satisfaction, especially when you see a kid's eyes light up. But mostly, it's tough.'

'Ever fancy a change?'

'To what?'

'I don't know. Anything.'

'I was never the high-flyer. Not like you.'

Abby bit her lip. It was true, Ellie had struggled at school. Ever since she'd fallen ill, aged five. There had been recurring bouts of nausea and diarrhoea, which led to time off school. *Lots* of time off school. It had also affected her thinking. Sometimes she'd been confused, had looked at them in puzzlement when asked simple questions, such as what she wanted for breakfast. As the doctors had searched for a diagnosis, months had passed and Ellie had fallen behind in her learning. Their mother, Susanna, had decided she was best off home-schooled for a while, something that had made Abby seethe with resentment—

'I can't ask you the same question anymore,' said Ellie, interrupting her thoughts.

'What's that?'

'"How's work?"'

'No.'

'So, how's retirement? It's been, what – three and a half months now?'

Abby paused, knew she was on sensitive ground. But still, she didn't want to lie. 'Nice. Relaxing.'

'Is that it?'

'Well, no. I mean, I realize I'm very lucky . . .'

'Yep.'

'But sometimes I feel like it's such a contrast to what I was doing before, it feels odd. Alien.' Ellie was silent and Abby knew she'd annoyed her. 'I'm not complaining.'

'Good.'

'It's just going from fourteen-hour days to nothing . . .'

'You're not alone, you know. With your fourteen-hour days. Lots of us work ridiculous hours. Many for less pay. Some of us can barely keep it together. Make ends meet.'

Abby's skin prickled with irritation and the guilt resurfaced. So Ellie hadn't got over it. She wondered about bringing it up but knew instantly it would kill this reunion stone dead and so she kept silent. When she'd received the email from her sister earlier in the year (after months of silence) she'd been rendered speechless. Ellie had written with a request for a loan so she could buy a place to live rather than rent. Abby had been astounded at the notion Ellie thought she could just lay her hands on a hundred and twenty thousand pounds for a deposit. Even if she could, she didn't believe in paying through the nose for a tiny Victorian conversion flat just because it was in a 'cool' part of town.

'I decided to save my money, not spend it. For *years*.'

'If I had any left over to save, I would.'

Abby sighed. 'You do, Ellie.'

'I don't.'

'Still living in South Wimbledon?' Her sister's lack of response confirmed she was. 'Why don't you pack in the London rent and move further out – Coulsdon in Surrey, for example? It'll probably cost you less than half.'

'Never heard of it. And anyway, I need to be near school, especially with the hours I do.'

'It's in zone six. Still a doable commute. Look, I don't want this to become an argument. Can't we just try to get on? Put everything else aside and just enjoy some time together?'

Abby saw her sister shift on her towel, trying to get comfortable.

'Bit hard, isn't it?' said Ellie.

'You get used to it,' replied Abby, clipped. She was not in the mood to hear her sister's digs at the lack of sunbeds.

Matteo swam back up to the rock and pulled himself out of the water. He shook his head, sending sparkling drops flying into the air. Abby looked up at him towering over them both, the sun lighting the water droplets running down his body. What was it with Italian men and their insistence on wearing tight swimwear? Nice for her, but . . .

She glanced over at Ellie in her yellow bikini and noticed, not for the first time, how it clung to the roundness of her perfect bottom and brushed against her pert breasts. She tried to see if her sister had noticed Matteo's near-naked body, but Ellie was starting to get up.

'I might just go back to the house,' she said. 'Get some more sun cream.'

As Abby watched Ellie stalk up the steps, in what she knew to be barely suppressed anger, she felt a pang of anxiety.

Damn her guilty conscience. Not for the first time since she'd sent it, Abby was regretting her invitation. She was beginning to think the next six weeks with her sister might be the longest of her life.

THREE

As Ellie reached the top of the steps and Abby's modest house came back into view, she felt as if it were mocking her for her earlier dismissive thoughts. It wasn't about the house at all; it was about the house's *position*, with its own goddamn path down to a private platform, from where you could swim in your own private bit of sea. Anytime you wanted. It was just another thing to add to Abby's perfect, lucky life.

She stepped into the cool of the villa and took a long, deep breath. She had to stop letting everything that Abby had, and that she didn't have, get to her. But it was hard when every day back home was a struggle, when she'd have to lug a bag full of marking home every evening – and, no, she couldn't move to that place in Surrey that she'd already forgotten the name of, because the idea of carrying a ton of books back and forth on public transport made her want to cry. Even more so lately, after her recent bombshell. Something she hadn't told anyone about yet. Truth was, she couldn't bear to. She was always so tired, so very, very tired. And if she had to spend three hours a night marking essays written by teenagers who spent more time thinking up japes such as drawing a box halfway through their work with a 'Tick here if read so far' message, than they did putting any effort into the *actual content*, then why shouldn't she treat herself to a nice bottle of wine to ease her through her evening? She deserved it. As she did the new yellow bikini for this much-needed holiday. And the gym membership so she could get out of the flat on the freezing, dark winter weekends, and the occasional massage to relieve the tension in her shoulders, and any of the other small treats she gave herself just to be able to get through the relentless uphill battle of the weeks.

Screw Abby and her judgemental attitude. It was easy to save if you could put enough away to actually make a difference; if you could envisage a goal that might be achieved within your own lifetime. It was even more galling that Abby was suggesting places she, Ellie, could live when Abby had refused to use some of her fortune to help her own sister get on the property ladder.

Ellie had been stunned when she'd received the point-blank refusal from Abby, without even a suggestion that they might discuss it. It had burned even more because Abby, being that bit older, had managed to get her own place over a decade ago. She'd had a decent job straight from graduation and during the recession of 2008, when prices had tumbled, she'd bought her first flat. At the time, Ellie had been earning next to nothing as a trainee teaching assistant and, even if she'd had a deposit saved, she wouldn't have been given a mortgage on her tiny salary. Over the years Ellie had watched as the goal of being a homeowner had drifted ever further out of reach, with prices rising far higher than her pay. Of course, the value of Abby's flat was also rising and Ellie had googled its worth one dark, miserable evening at home in her rented apartment. In two years it was worth over a hundred thousand pounds more than what Abby had paid for it. *One hundred thousand pounds!* Abby had acquired all that money by doing sweet nothing. Ellie had been so depressed at this sense of being left behind that she'd booked a weekend away in Istanbul to cheer herself up. It had been a much-longed-for dose of sunshine during a grey February half-term.

Ellie knew Abby still had that flat (now worth double what she'd paid for it), and she rented it out. To some poor mug just like herself, forced to line someone else's pockets, as they couldn't afford their own home.

Engulfed by resentment, Ellie poured herself a glass of cool water from the kitchen tap and drank half of it back. If she wasn't going to go mad with envy during her stay with her sister she had to get a grip.

She placed the glass down on the worktop and climbed the stairs to go and get the sun cream. Then she would return to the swim platform, poised and calm. Dignified.

She paused outside the first room upstairs, which Abby had said was her and Matteo's bedroom. She peeked inside, her eyes briefly lingering with curiosity over the light, airy room with its rustic furniture. Abby wouldn't waste money on a decent dressing table or wardrobe. There was a simple wooden double bed with white covers and a chair with what looked like Matteo's uniform tossed on it.

There was another room next door that Abby hadn't shown her, and the door was shut. She opened it to find a small box room, in which an easel had been erected. Resting on it was a half-finished acrylic – amateur, obviously – a seascape drawn from the platform at the bottom of the steps. Ellie cocked her head as she looked at it – it had an earnest quality to it; the colours were too bright but it tried hard. Other canvases lay stacked against the wall, nearly all of them of the house, the garden and the sea view from the platform. Ellie wondered who'd painted them – Matteo or Abby – and then she saw the little signature in the bottom right-hand corner: 'AM'. For a moment she wondered who that was, but then remembered that Abby was no longer a Miss Spencer like herself, but for three months now had been a Mrs Morelli – *Signora* Morelli. Ellie hadn't been invited to the wedding – nor had their mother – as Abby had somehow persuaded Matteo she wanted something small and private, and they'd surprised Ellie and Susanna with an email and a photo of the happy couple outside Portoferraio town hall.

Ellie had been shocked. Not so much that her sister had got married on the quiet, but how much it had hurt. When they were small, all Ellie had wanted was for Abby to play with her, to make up games together in the garden, pretend they both had imaginary pet dogs that they could take for a walk around the small lawn, but Abby was always aloof, would go off and do her own thing. This continued as they got older, Abby always seemingly with her eye on some private goal, something Ellie knew nothing about. Abby would be building a den in her room, an idea that she hadn't shared with Ellie; she would arrange to go to a friend's house for tea when Ellie was hoping to ask her about her new make-up; she'd come back to say she'd passed her driving test when Ellie hadn't even known she'd applied for it; and, of course, the biggest betrayal was the years and years she'd spent saving and investing, never once sharing her goal or her financial savvy with her sister. Then out of the blue – wham! – Abby announced she was leaving the workforce forever. *See you later, sucker* – that was the message she seemed to be sending, while Ellie had been left abandoned and feeling like an inadequate fool.

You'd think she would have become used to it, hardened herself to the hurt, but one memory was still imprinted on her brain and, even after twenty-two years, it had the power to move her.

Ellie had been in the first year of secondary school, a place she found isolating after her sporadic primary education. She'd been placed in the bottom set in every subject; the years of missed schooling had taken their toll, and she felt slow-witted and ashamed of not being anywhere near her older sister's league. One group of girls in particular noticed this fact. There were three of them who went around in a pack, two lesser bitches flanking the ringleader, and they would mock her for her stupidity. When Ellie had been found crying her eyes out, hiding behind the temporary classroom block, and Abby had extracted a name, Ellie had followed her sister from a safe distance back to the playground, wondering what on earth Abby was going to do.

She was rewarded by seeing Abby punch the ringleader on the nose. All hell had broken loose: blood and screams and a rapidly ballooning crowd.

Three big things changed after that: the nose was broken and would forever have a kink, Abby was suspended for a week, and the bullies never touched Ellie again. But the one thing she really wanted to change still didn't happen. Abby was just as aloof and it had hurt even more because deep down Ellie now knew that, on some level, her big sister cared for her.

She suspected she knew why there had always been a distance between them: Ellie was their mother's favourite, something that was never said aloud but was blatantly clear. In fact, Susanna had paid little attention to Abby's successes, as she'd been so preoccupied with Ellie's childhood illness, the doctors and hospital appointments, the constant care. If Abby did well in her exams at school, she was told not to speak of it, for fear that it would make Ellie feel inferior. The same if Abby achieved something sporty – Ellie had suffered from so much sickness, it was 'unfair' to 'flaunt' it in Ellie's face.

Ellie had felt guilty for being so sick and blamed herself for Abby's upset, but was often too ill to have the energy to try and make it any different. As they grew older, Ellie watched the gap between them widen, and even when the illness seemed to abate, years had gone by and she never caught up. Abby did so much more, achieved so much more, and Ellie's confidence slowly disintegrated.

She looked again at the paintings. These, at least, were

no masterpieces, and she was just turning to leave the room when her eye caught something.

She stopped. Frowned at the small bookcase in the corner of the room. Then she kneeled down in front of it, her heart racing.

There, on the very bottom shelf, was a collection of children's books. Not just any old children's books but first editions: *The Hobbit*, *Where the Wild Things Are*, *The Wizard of Oz* and an extensive collection of Roald Dahl including *Charlie and the Chocolate Factory*. They were worth thousands of pounds.

Hand trembling, she reached out and touched them, hurt and confused by the sight of them. Not wanting to believe how they had come to be placed on a bookshelf here, in Abby's house.

FOUR

1994

Ellie was sitting on the bottom step of the stairs, her shoe-clad feet planted on the hall floor, trying to imagine them sticking to the wooden floorboards, growing roots so she didn't have to leave. Her and Abby's suitcase was upright by the front door and, if she turned her head she could just see through into the living room where her sister was kneeling on the sofa, leaning over the back so she could watch out of the rain-pelted window for the car.

Her mother was scarce, doing something busy in the kitchen, as she always did on these occasions. Ellie still didn't quite understand why she never accompanied them on their trips to Grandma and Grandad's, except that Susanna had said that she had had a 'falling-out' with her parents over 'Daddy' years before. Ellie couldn't even ask 'Daddy' to explain more as he had left before she was born.

'It's here,' Abby called through flatly and climbed down off the sofa, just as the large silver car pulled up and her grandparents' driver, Harold, who had worked for them for two decades, climbed out.

Susanna appeared from the kitchen. Saw their downcast faces.

'Come on, it's not that bad.'

'It's horrible, Mummy,' Ellie burst out. 'They are always asking us questions. Questions, questions, questions!' She felt on the verge of tears.

'What musical instruments are you learning? What are your grades like? Why don't you ever wear dresses?' intoned Abby, as the doorbell rang.

'It's only twice a year,' pleaded Susanna. 'It's not too much to ask, is it?'

'And their house is so big,' continued Ellie. 'And full of breakable things! I'm scared of breaking something like last time. They were so cross. They said it cost thirty hundred pounds.'

'*Three* hundred,' corrected Abby, and Ellie felt humiliated. She always got things wrong. 'For a vase,' added Abby incredulously.

'But it's nice to have lovely things, isn't it?' said Susanna. She spoke carefully. 'Just think. Some of those things might be yours one day. They're your only grandparents. It's important to get to know them. And it's only for a week.'

Ellie, already feeling desperately homesick, couldn't bear it any longer. She flung herself at her mother and burst into tears. 'I don't want to go. Don't make me – please, Mummy. What if I get ill again?' she suddenly wailed.

She felt her mother's strong arms embrace her but then they loosened their grip and the familiar, comforting warmth was taken away.

'You won't get ill. You've been so much better the last few weeks. Now, Abby, why don't you let Harold in and you can be on your way?'

Ellie and Abby sat in the back of the cavernous car, their seat belts unable to keep their small bodies from sliding around on the leather seats as Harold navigated the rain-slicked roads. Ellie pressed her nose up against the window, trying to keep the image of her mother in her mind, her kind face getting smaller and smaller as they'd driven away. The journey wasn't long, as their grandparents lived in Weybridge, just a few miles away. However, despite the short distance, the two houses could not be more different.

Grandma and Grandad lived in a place called St George's Hill, which, when she was five, Ellie had thought might also harbour dragons. But now she was eight, she realized this was a ludicrous notion and, in fact, it only housed very rich people. Grandma Kathleen and Grandad Robert's place was a large, flat-fronted mansion with pillars either side of the imposing front door. Whenever she arrived, Ellie felt as if the dozens of windows were staring at her, or there was someone hiding behind the balustrade that ran around the top of the house. Grandma was waiting at the top of the steps as the car pulled into the enormous drive and Ellie scrambled out, knowing her grandmother was already scrutinizing her.

She felt intimidated here – her grandmother set great store by the acquisition of knowledge and would turn each and every conversation into a test. 'What's the capital of Peru?' she'd ask, when she found Ellie gazing up at a picture of Paddington Bear on the landing (an original artwork, Grandma said), or 'How much milk would you have left if I poured you a quarter of a pint from this bottle?' when she was so dying of thirst she couldn't even think straight. Even if she could, she wouldn't have been able to answer. Ellie was always pitiful at answering the questions. She'd missed so much school from being ill. She was back in a classroom at the moment but had spent lots of time having lessons with Mummy at home. She'd loved having her mother all to herself, especially as they didn't really do much work but would often go to the park instead and she would sometimes even buy her an ice cream, something she had to keep secret from Abby. Also, being at home meant that she got a break from the children who teased her. Some of the really mean ones called her 'Illie': 'Hey, Illie, why are you at school? Illie, are you going to be sick?' It made her want to cry. But the worst thing about being ill was having to go to see doctors all the time. They asked so many questions and made her lie on a bed and poked her tummy and put a needle in her arm and stole half her blood and she was worried she wouldn't ever get it back, even though they said she'd grow more. She hated it. She'd even had to go to hospital where they asked even more questions. Most of them Mummy answered, thank goodness.

'How long did your journey take?'

Her grandmother was asking her a question already, looking at her pointedly as if she were her teacher at school, and Ellie felt her insides curl up in fear as she didn't yet know how to tell the time. She didn't know anything much, not like Abby. She couldn't even read properly and was well aware she was on the bottom table in school for maths, English *and* spelling, even though the teacher gave them different names like 'Badger' table for spelling and 'Triangle' table for maths.

Grandma was waiting for an answer. She was always dressed nicely, with lots of scarves, even indoors, whereas Ellie and Abby had hardly anything new. Their mum had new things too but she said that was because she worked in a boutique and she had to look nice, so the owners sold the clothes to her cheaply. If Grandma was rich, and they were poor, then Ellie wondered why she didn't give them some of her money.

'Thirty-three minutes,' said Abby, as she walked past and Ellie felt herself go weak with relief.

'I was asking Eleanor, not you,' said Grandma.

Days consisted of hanging around the house or the garden – their grandmother seldom took them anywhere and their grandfather worked until late at night. He had a business importing wine and they only really saw him at the weekend. He would call them into his study and ask them to read aloud to him, something else that Ellie failed dismally at, and so he'd taken to only asking Abby.

As today was a wet day, there was no going outside. They were expected to entertain themselves with board games;

TV was strictly off limits. Abby decided to take herself up to her room and Ellie followed, but Abby closed her door firmly. Ellie sighed, knowing this was an emphatic 'do not disturb' message. She wandered back downstairs, listening out in the large silent house that she still sometimes got lost in. She could hear a far-off hoover, which was the cleaner doing her daily rounds. At the foot of the stairs Ellie could see into the drawing room where her grandmother was sitting in a small armchair, her heels up on a footstool as she read her newspaper. A cup and saucer lay on the side table. Ellie knew from experience not to disturb her grandmother during her mid-morning 'downtime' and so she slunk away. She found herself outside the library and peered inside. It was a room she avoided as it intimidated her – all those books she couldn't read – but this time something caught her eye. A butterfly was trapped inside, fluttering futilely against the windowpane. Ellie watched as it withdrew a distance, took a small circle and then headed back to the window, desperate to get out to the air it must have sensed outside.

She ran in and pushed a chair against the wall in front of the window, then climbed up so she could reach the catch. She opened the window and watched as the butterfly made its bid for freedom, her heart leaping as it escaped, and then she tried to keep sight of it until eventually it disappeared from view.

Ellie turned away from the window and sat in the chair, swinging her legs. The time went so slowly here, painfully eked out minutes and hours. She suddenly missed her mum so much it hurt. Her feet abruptly stopped swinging and she felt tears form, something she tried to stop as Grandma said tears were for babies and people who couldn't articulate themselves well, except she didn't know what that meant. She looked around and on her right was a small case with a glass front, inside which were yet more books. On the spine of one of them a word caught her eye. A word that she could actually read very well.

Chocolate.

She slid to the floor and opened the case. Pulled out the book, which was old. The front cover was nearly filled with a picture of a large bar of chocolate with the corner bitten out, an image that made her salivate. A ghost-like boy's head was beaming underneath it and sitting on the boy's arm was a man in a top hat. The book was called *Charlie and the Chocolate Factory*, written by someone whose name she couldn't read.

Ellie opened it up. For no other reason than that she had nothing else to do, she started to read the first page, and before she knew it she'd got to the bottom and was turning it over. She finished that one too, and the next, and the next, until she sat up and felt the thickness of the pages she'd turned and was shocked and delighted to be able to squish a significant amount of paper between her thumb and fore-finger. It was a most unusual feeling but she didn't stop to think about it too long as she wanted to know if this boy Charlie was going to find a Golden Ticket. She read on, stumbling in places, but something about this story kept her turning the pages, until she heard the gong in the hall that meant it was lunchtime. She was astonished. How could it be lunchtime already? Time never went this fast. And she didn't want to go and sit in the large dining room with the loud ticking clock and answer questions from her grandmother, she wanted to find out what was going to happen to Augustus Gloop now he'd put his face in the river of chocolate.

Ellie knew better than to disobey the gong and she struggled through lunch and the questions and being told she was using the wrong cutlery, but for the first time she didn't feel like crying into her plate. All she could think about was going back to the library and reading the book.

Which, the minute lunch was over, was exactly what she did. Once she'd completed the story, breathless with wonder, desperate to go to Willy Wonka's factory herself, she was wistful for grandparents just like Charlie's who all shared a bed together and were kind and funny, instead of what she'd been given: one strict, one absent. She pulled out another book from the cabinet. This one was called *The Magic Finger*.

She was just about to start it when something struck her so wondrous, so impossible, that for a moment she forgot to breathe.

She'd just read her first ever book. The whole thing. With no help from anyone.

FIVE

Oh shit, oh shit, oh shit. Abby stopped in the doorway when she saw Ellie leafing through *Charlie and the Chocolate Factory*. At that moment, Ellie looked up and Abby was struck by the hurt and anger in her sister's eyes.

'Why do you have this?' asked Ellie, raising the book aloft.

Oh God, why did I forget to move them?

'This was Grandad's, wasn't it?' Ellie indicated the bookcase. 'They all were.'

'Yes.'

'So why are they on your shelf?'

'He . . . left them to me.'

'In his *will*?' asked Ellie, incredulous.

'Yes,' repeated Abby.

'But . . . why you? I mean, he didn't leave me anything.'

Abby felt a flicker of irritation. Ellie sounded so pitiful – the victim. Again. It wasn't her fault their grandfather had singled her out.

'He gave them to me because . . . he thought they would be safer.'

'They're here on a bookshelf, hardly kept at a controlled temperature under glass.'

Ellie was staring at her and Abby wilted under her gaze. 'Not like that . . .'

'How do you mean, then?'

'He wanted them kept in the family.' Abby bit her lip as her sister's face contorted in growing disbelief. She was unsure if the message had sunk in. 'Forever,' she added for emphasis.

Ellie was crushed. 'He thought I'd sell them?'

'Well, wouldn't you?'

'No!' Ellie stood abruptly, tears pricking at her eyes. 'I loved these books. These books were my friends when you never bothered to spend any time with me. When you hated me.'

'I never hated you.'

'Yes, you did. You hated the fact I got all Mum's attention when I was small. That my illness took her away from you.'

'You're wrong—'

'It was obvious! And you weren't even that bothered by *Charlie and the Chocolate Factory*. When I tried to tell you I'd read it, you just said *you'd* read it when you were *six*!'

Abby looked chastised. 'Yes, I might have said that but . . .' She took a deep breath. Maybe now was the time. Maybe she should speak up. 'Ellie, there's something you need to understand—'

'What, that you're always trying to stab me in the back?'

'There'll be no stabbing while I'm here, thank you very much.' A woman's voice cut through the argument.

Abby spun around. Her mouth dropped as she saw the

familiar slight frame, the cropped blonde wavy hair framing the petite face. 'You're not supposed to be here until Wednesday!'

'Charmed, I'm sure,' said Susanna. 'And I'm very happy to see you too, dear daughter.'

SIX

'Oh my word, look at this *terrace*! It's sublime!' Susanna was breathless with delight as she gazed out across the sun-bleached flagstones, the olive and lemon trees, the large wooden table under a pagoda that was bursting with semi-ripe vines.

Abby watched her with an element of suspicion. She was unused to approval from her mother.

'And the view! My God, it's like gazing out onto heaven itself.' Her face was enraptured and she pushed her sunglasses onto the top of her head. 'You've done so well. Clever, clever girl to find all this.'

Her mother turned and smiled at her, waiting for a response, but Abby deliberately didn't meet her gaze. She sensed her mother's hurt, felt her falter and, out of the corner of her eye, saw Susanna turn back to the view, embarrassed by her daughter's snub.

Ellie was sitting away from them, alone in a small wicker chair, sipping silently at a glass of wine. Her face gave nothing away but Abby knew she was still fuming. She also knew their mother's lavish praise of the house was fuelling Ellie's jealousy.

Matteo appeared from inside and handed a glass of wine to his mother-in-law.

'And this husband,' said Susanna. 'He's entirely wonderful.'

'*Salute!*' said Matteo, clinking her glass with his own. 'It's so great to meet you at last.'

Abby watched as Matteo, knowing she hadn't wanted to invite Susanna to their wedding, took it all in his stride. *Except he still doesn't know the real reason why I didn't want Mum here*, she thought.

'And you're a policeman, you say? Must be very reassuring for Abby. To think, she had no expectations on that singles' holiday, and she was right. But in the end it was lucky that she got mugged, otherwise you two would never have met.'

Abby stiffened and immediately saw her sister sit up in surprise. It hadn't been something she'd talked to Ellie about. When it had happened, a year ago now, Ellie had been away on some long-haul trip, and by the time she'd come back, Abby had buried it.

'The main thing is she was OK,' said Matteo.

'I know. I was beside myself when I heard about it.'

'I need to start dinner,' said Abby, turning away.

'I'll help,' piped up Susanna, following her back inside to the kitchen. 'What can I do?' she asked brightly.

'Start chopping the salad,' said Abby, pointing at the pile of vegetables on the side.

Abby busied herself with the pasta and they worked in silence for a while. Abby knew her mother had offered to help as she wanted to talk privately, but was obviously taking her time, avoiding the elephant in the room. Abby sliced an onion, fried it in the pan and added herbs, garlic and tomatoes, all the while her irritation building. Her mother wasn't even supposed to be here yet. This was meant to be time for just her and Ellie.

After her impromptu invitation, Abby had wanted to write again to retract it but it was too late: Ellie emailed to say she'd booked the flights. Then her mother had got wind of Ellie's trip and had invited herself along too. It was impossible to say no, but Abby knew what it was like when the two of them were together, knew she'd be the third wheel, and so *specifically and clearly* asked her mother to come two days later.

'I know why you've come here early,' Abby suddenly said, unable to take the silence anymore.

Susanna smiled. 'You always were a know-all, that was your problem. But in fact, I just came early as I really wanted to see my girls. Although, judging by the argument when I arrived, I'm not too sure how you're getting on. Surely you've buried the hatchet by now? You just have to accept that you're two very different people and learn to get along.'

'We're getting on just fine,' said Abby through gritted teeth. Outside they could hear Ellie laughing, seemingly brought out of her slump by Matteo. Abby stopped chopping to listen. Ellie's laugh grated on her nerves. *What is she doing? Always so flirty, getting men eating out of her hand.*

'Well, *they* certainly seem to be,' said Susanna, cocking her head and smiling with approval.

Abby stopped still. She flashed a look to her mother but Susanna, slicing up tomatoes, didn't notice.

'You could be nicer to her, you know,' said Susanna. She turned to face Abby. 'I'm sorry for what happened when she was young. For not spending enough time with you. I feel like I'm responsible for your relationship now.'

Abby's mouth dropped open in utter astonishment. Her mother was *apologizing*? It was far too little, too late. She furiously stirred the pasta on the hob.

'Are you going to tell her?' asked Abby, a brittle edge to her voice.

'Tell who?' Ellie walked into the kitchen, empty glass in hand.

Abby spun around, heart racing. Neither she nor Susanna said a word.

'What's going on?' asked Ellie, a puzzled frown appearing on her face.

Abby's voice felt strangled in her throat – should she speak up? 'We thought it would be nice to go to the beach tomorrow,' she said. 'Maybe get some lunch there.'

'Yes, it would be lovely to explore,' said Susanna. 'What do you think?'

Ellie was watching them both strangely but then nodded. 'Sure, why not?'

There was a moment's silence, then Abby smiled. 'Great!' she said. 'I'll just go and set the table. Will you serve up, Mum?'

Susanna nodded and Abby left the room.

After she'd gone, Susanna exchanged a look with her

other daughter. She shrugged and smiled reassuringly, putting on her best 'it's Abby, you know what she can be like' face.

'You want a hand?' asked Ellie.

'It's fine, darling. You go and take a seat and I'll bring it out in a minute.'

Susanna waited until her daughter had left, then exhaled deeply. It wasn't enough. She breathed in again. In, out. In, out. *In. Out.* Finally, when she had composed herself, she turned her attention to the dinner.

SEVEN

'Ta da!' said Susanna as she carried through plates of pasta and salad, placing them on the old table on the terrace. More wine was poured and Abby pulled in her wooden chair, bleached soft by the sun. She had made sure she was next to her husband, with Ellie opposite her. Her mother she had placed furthest away.

'This is delicious,' said Susanna. 'I never knew you could cook like this, Abby.'

And yet I'm thirty-six years old, thought Abby. *Time enough to have found out.*

'Matteo is a very lucky man,' joked Susanna.

Abby's nerves grated again. 'We share the cooking,' she said.

'Ah, a thoroughly modern relationship,' said Susanna. 'So come on, Matteo, spill. Was it Abby's skills in the kitchen that drew you to her?'

Matteo turned to Abby and she saw that look in his deep brown eyes, the one that made her belly fire up with warmth. If she had to describe it, it was something between pride and admiration, and it made her melt and fall in love with him all over again.

'Actually, it was her legs,' said Matteo.

Abby snorted and tapped him on the hand.

'Seriously?' asked Susanna, surprised.

Abby frowned; what did her mother mean? What was wrong with her legs?

'I mean, she has lovely legs, bit like myself. But are you teasing me?'

'It was in the hospital where I first fell for her. After the accident.'

'She was a damsel in distress!' exclaimed Susanna.

'The nurses told me she hadn't had any visitors . . .'

'What, you felt sorry for me?' asked Abby, put out.

'Only because I knew you were in a foreign country and it would be hard for your friends and family to see you. Their loss was my gain. I faked at least one reason to have to come back and interview you.' Matteo smiled and Abby touched his hand again. 'Then, of course, when she went back to the UK, it was hard to get hold of her.' Matteo turned to Ellie and Susanna. 'She works so hard!'

Abby saw her sister paste on a polite smile.

'Worked,' corrected Ellie.

Matteo nodded. 'She understands my long, erratic hours. The need to stay behind in the office every now and then to get everything prepared to catch the bad guy.'

'So you like being a policeman?' asked Susanna.

'Every day is different.'

'But come on, the proposal,' said Susanna, tapping the table with her fingers in anticipation. 'What made you pop the question?'

'Mum,' admonished Abby.

'It's OK,' said Matteo. 'I just knew she was the woman for me. With Abby, I never feel lonely. But I was worried. I never thought she'd say yes, give up her career to come out here.'

'No, must have been hard to leave rain-soaked concrete London to move to this star-studded land,' said Ellie dryly, waving a hand up at the night sky.

'It's still a big deal,' pointed out Susanna. 'And you, Abby?'

'What about me?'

'I think your mother wants to know why you decided I was the man of your dreams,' teased Matteo.

'I could rely on him,' said Abby.

'That's not very romantic!' exclaimed Susanna.

'I disagree. It's one of the most important things.'

'I didn't say it wasn't important. But there's also . . . well . . . *romance*.'

Matteo grinned. 'Susanna. I am *Italian*.' He waved a hand. 'Anyway, enough about us. What about you, Ellie? Are you dating?'

Ellie placed her fork primly on her plate. 'Not at the moment.' She stood, started to stack the empty plates. 'I'll clear away,' she said.

'I'll give you a hand,' said Abby, taking some of the dishes.

Susanna went to get up as well but Matteo stopped her by pouring some more wine into her glass and insisting she stay at the table. 'I want to know about your life back in

London,' he said. 'Tell me about your job. Abby tells me you work in a clothes shop.'

Thank God for Matteo, thought Abby as she walked away, even though he was unaware of the favour he'd just done her. She wanted a moment alone with Ellie, something that Susanna seemed determined wasn't going to happen.

She followed her sister into the kitchen, started to rinse the dirty plates before placing them in the dishwasher. 'I was thinking it would be nice to go on a boat trip tomorrow. What do you think?'

Ellie handed her another plate. Shrugged. 'Sure, why not? Mum would enjoy that too.'

'I was thinking just you and me,' said Abby quickly.

'Oh. Seems a bit mean to leave Mum out?'

'It's not like that. I was just thinking we could go early. Before the beach. You know what Mum's like; she doesn't rise till mid-morning if she doesn't have to. We'll be back by the time she gets up.'

Ellie paused for a moment, plate mid-air. 'OK. Why not?'

Abby smiled with relief. 'Great! Only . . . don't mention it, will you? Otherwise she'll only feel like she's obliged to come. I don't want her to miss out on her lie-in.'

Ellie looked at her suspiciously for a moment, but Abby held her gaze and then the moment passed.

EIGHT

It had been a relief to shut the bedroom door that night. Retire to the privacy of her room with just her husband for company. Abby finished brushing her teeth and came from the en suite into the bedroom where Matteo was tidying away his police uniform – discarded in the early hours when he'd come in from his night shift. She got into bed, enjoying watching her naked husband as he went about his domestic duties. He put his jacket and trousers on a hanger, punched in the code on the safe that was in the wardrobe and put away his police-issue gun, then leaped dramatically onto the bed, making Abby smile.

'So, finally I get to meet your family.'

Abby braced herself, waiting for criticism.

'They're nice,' he said, smiling as he noticed her reticence.

'Yeah?'

'I think your mother believes I am some sort of hero. That you call the police and I rescue you from the big bad world.'

'She's just caught up in the romantic idea of it all. She's lonely. Has been for a long time. I think all her life she's been hankering after a strong man to look after her.'

'Your father wasn't that man, no?'

'Danny? I seriously doubt it. She hardly ever talked about him, but from what I understand, he was charming but flighty. Her parents didn't approve and when she ran off with him, they cut her off.'

Matteo turned to face her. 'You didn't tell your mother how it really happened that night.'

'No . . .'

'And your sister didn't even know about it.'

Abby looked apologetic. When she'd spoken to Susanna about the mugging she'd deliberately underplayed it, relayed only the facts. A man had put a knife to her back; another had run off with her bag. Matteo had handled the case and he was the only person who really understood what had happened to her. 'Thanks for not saying anything.'

Sensing her discomfort, he kissed her. 'Families, eh? Why is your mother here early? I thought it was supposed to be you and Ellie for two days.'

'It was.'

'What did you have planned with your sister?'

Abby shrugged, non-committal. 'Nothing much. Just hanging out, you know.'

Matteo wrapped his arms around her and fixed his eyes on hers. 'So, what's the big secret?'

Abby faltered. 'What do you mean?'

'I think it is obvious. There is something, a history, in your family. The way everyone was a little bit on edge tonight; because you don't really talk about them so much.

And trust me, I was as happy as you to have a nothing wedding—'

'Nothing?' exclaimed Abby, in light protest.

'You know what I mean. No fuss. But I do not know of any girl in Italy who would do the same.'

Abby wondered about telling him then. It would be so nice to confide in this man who filled her heart in a way she'd been searching for since childhood. To confess everything she'd been shouldering for so many years.

She looked at him. 'I will tell you. Just not now.'

'Why not now?'

Abby ran her fingers lightly over his chest. She knew exactly how to distract him. 'Because I'd rather be doing something else instead,' she said as she kissed him softly on the lips.

NINE

The sound of the crickets had faded as the night had worn on and now – Ellie turned her head very slowly towards the clock on the bedside cabinet – at three a.m., they were almost silent. She shifted her head back, wincing as the pain throbbed behind her temples. It had only been a couple of glasses of wine. It didn't seem fair that she had such a pounding headache.

Maybe it was the stresses of the day that had exacerbated everything. Seeing her sister again for the first time in ages. Seeing her house. And her husband. Abby had rarely had time for boyfriends when she was in London – she'd worked all the time. Matteo seemed quite a catch and Ellie had been surprised. He was easy to talk to and good-looking – how could she help but notice the latter when he'd been standing in front of her at the sea in all his near-naked glory?

Abby was also on edge and now, with Susanna here, she'd got worse. Ellie didn't know why Abby always had to be so cool towards their mother – carrying her childhood resentments around like a pile of rocks on her shoulders. OK, so Susanna had had less time for Abby when they were young, but she had been pretty preoccupied. And now Susanna was trying so hard with Abby, had been so complimentary about the house, but Abby had just blanked her. It had felt a little weird, in fact, her mother being so attentive to her big sister. Usually it was her, Ellie, who got all the affection.

And then there was that strange conversation in the kitchen earlier. For a moment Ellie had thought her sister and her mother were keeping something from her. She'd gone along with the explanation about a visit to the beach the next day but they'd seemed cagey and she felt there was more to it.

Argh, tomorrow! There was this boat trip too, something she had to be up early for. At this rate, with no sleep and now feeling nauseous, she was going to miss out. Maybe a glass of water would help.

Ellie quietly got out of bed and padded down the stairs to the kitchen. She held a beaker under the tap, drank, and then rubbed the cool glass against her forehead. Outside the window she could see the full moon over the front garden, the pine trees lit with a ghostly glow. Something dark flitted across the window and she jumped, then it happened again and she saw it was a bat. Now she'd seen one, she saw many, crossing the sky as they searched for insects. What a beautiful place this was. And it was all Abby's. Ellie stopped herself; she didn't want to go there again; hours of boiling resentment would put paid to any hope of sleep.

She turned and went back upstairs. As she walked across the landing she instantly knew what would relax her. She stopped. Listened. The house was silent. Very carefully she opened the door of what she'd dubbed the 'painting room' and went inside. Tucking the copy of *Charlie and the Chocolate Factory* under her arm, she made her way back to her room.

Door firmly closed, she got into bed with her stolen comfort. She opened the book at random and started to read, instantly transported back to childhood where the warmth and friendship of Charlie's world soothed her. After a few minutes her eyelids started drooping. Ellie closed the book and, leaning over the side of the bed, she hesitated a moment – *should she?* She felt somehow as if it was rightfully hers.

Ellie pulled out her suitcase that was stowed underneath the bed. Tucking the book into the front pocket, she zipped it up, before pushing the suitcase back under. She lay against the pillows and within minutes was asleep.

TEN

Abby knocked softly on Ellie's bedroom door. After a few seconds it opened and Ellie's still sleep-creased face appeared.

'Ready?' whispered Abby.

Her sister nodded and they crept down the stairs and then outside onto the terrace. Abby loved this time of day, when it was still early and there was a lingering freshness from the night, not yet burned away by the sun. She led Ellie down the steps to the boat and held it tight against the little jetty while her sister stepped gingerly on board.

'Are you sure about this?' asked Ellie.

Abby laughed. 'It's just a bit of rowing. We won't go far; out a bit and then around the peninsula.'

'Where's Matteo?'

'We don't need a man's help,' said Abby firmly. 'You and I will manage perfectly well on our own.'

'That's not what I meant,' said Ellie, not altogether convincingly, as Abby started to untie the rope.

'He's asleep. Still recovering from his night shifts.'

'Wait! Girls, wait!'

Abby looked up in dismay, heart plummeting as she saw a figure in a kaftan running down the steps.

'For God's sake,' she muttered under her breath.

'Mum!' called Ellie.

Both girls watched as Susanna made it to the platform, slightly out of breath.

'It's not like you to be up this early,' said Ellie.

'No, well, I happened to get up for the bathroom and I looked out of the window and saw you two heading down the steps. Thought I'd see what you were up to.'

Why can't she just leave us alone for a bit? thought Abby angrily.

'We're going on a boat trip,' said Ellie.

There was a lull where Abby knew that Ellie was waiting for her to extend the invitation to Susanna. She knew she should but she couldn't quite form the words quickly enough.

'I'm sure there's room for you too,' said Ellie.

Abby could feel her sister's eyes boring into her. 'Course,' she agreed.

'Well, only if I'm not in the way,' said Susanna.

Abby gritted her teeth and held the boat steady as Susanna got in and went to sit on the bench next to Ellie. Abby stepped into the boat herself, then pushed them away from the rocks with an oar before starting to row out to sea.

'It's utterly glorious,' breathed Susanna, transfixed by the early morning sun on the water.

For a moment Abby forgot her bad mood. It *was* glorious. A gentle breeze stroked their skin and filled their mouths and lungs with a holiday saltiness. The sea glistened, the odd lively wave slapping against the boat and splashing their arms and legs. The sun would dry off the water almost instantly. It was as if nature itself wanted to play with them. Abby continued to row, the water from the blades dripping and catching in the light with each stroke.

'Can we swim?' asked Ellie, entranced.

'Course. I'll stay here, though, with the boat.' Abby waited while her sister took off her shorts and top, revealing the same yellow bikini she'd had on the day before.

'Geronimo!' shouted Ellie as she leaped into the sea. Abby held on to the oars as the boat settled and smiled as her sister's head popped up from under the water, her hair slicked back.

'It's actually warm!' exclaimed Ellie, and she started to swim out in long leisurely breast strokes.

'Are you going in, Mum?' asked Abby.

'Oh no, not for me.' Susanna settled herself onto the bench.

Abby suddenly felt the presence of her mother, just inches from herself, disproportionately irritating. Ever since Susanna had arrived in Elba, she was always there, everywhere Abby turned, and she was finding it suffocating.

Susanna caught the expression on Abby's face. 'Sorry if I barged in on something.'

'You didn't,' lied Abby.

Her mother smiled gently. 'Really? Only it doesn't look that way. You should have said; I'd have stayed on the shore. Sat on the rocks and watched you both.'

Abby felt her ire rising. 'That's not what you wanted at

all so don't try and pretend it was. You were determined to come on this boat trip.'

'Is that why you planned it early? So I'd miss it?'

Abby's stomach twisted in shame. She couldn't bring herself to deny it so she gazed out at Ellie, who had turned back and was swimming towards them again.

'You don't want me alone with Ellie. What do you think I'm going to do, Mum?' Abby had a dangerous, goading note to her voice.

'I'm just not sure I can trust you, that's all.'

'Trust? You want to talk about trust?'

'You can be very hurtful sometimes, Abby,' said Susanna.

For God's sake! Abby felt a flash of anger. She didn't dare say anything; instead she grabbed hold of the oars and started to row vehemently towards Ellie. She only slowed her pace as she came alongside her sister. Then she held the boat steady as Ellie hauled herself back on board.

'Everything all right?' asked Ellie, as she looked between her mother and sister.

'Everything's wonderful,' smiled Susanna. 'Abby and I were just chatting about breakfast.'

Back at the house, Ellie decided to take a wander into the village. Abby was fixing some food for everyone, and Susanna was tired from the early start and had returned to bed for a lie-in after all, so Ellie sneaked out on her own.

It was only a short stroll down to the village and when

Ellie arrived she was delighted to see it was market day. She wandered amongst the stalls piled high with the best of the season's produce: fat melons; soft fuzzy peaches; ripe, bulbous plum tomatoes. Another stall was filled with a mind-boggling range of cheeses: everything from milky-white mozzarella to creamy blue-veined gorgonzola. The smell of breads filled the air and Ellie bought a rosemary-studded focaccia to take back to the house. As she walked along the lanes, the sun now high in the sky, she wondered how she'd find her sister and mother. There had definitely been an atmosphere on the boat when she'd come back from her swim. It was the second time since she'd arrived that she'd interrupted them only to sense they were hiding something from her.

Ellie came into the house and took the bread to the kitchen.

'That looks nice,' said Abby, taking it from her. 'You have fun?'

'It was great. I could have bought loads more.'

'Oh Ellie, focaccia! My favourite,' said Susanna as she entered the kitchen.

'Right, I think we've missed breakfast,' said Abby. 'This is lunch. Hungry?'

Ellie nodded and was about to take plates of hams and cheeses outside when Abby suddenly spoke.

'Oh, by the way, you haven't seen *Charlie and the Chocolate Factory*, have you? Only it's not on the shelf.'

Ellie froze. Oh God, she'd done that thing last night. Put it in her suitcase in a fit of pique.

She turned to Abby, smiled. 'Yes, I borrowed it last night when I couldn't sleep. I'll go and get it.'

Ellie made her way quickly upstairs. She'd dive into her room, retrieve the book and hand it back to Abby. As she went into her bedroom she quietly pushed the door to behind her. Then she scurried over to the bed, pulled out her suitcase and undid the zip on the front pocket.

'What are you doing?' asked a voice from behind her.

Ellie spun around to see Abby in the doorway, a look of disquiet on her face.

'Just getting the book,' said Ellie, awkwardly holding it up.

'It was in your suitcase.'

'Yes.'

'Why?'

Ellie struggled to think but could see no way out. 'Oh, for God's sake, Abby, will you stop talking to me like I'm a recalcitrant schoolgirl. I was annoyed, OK? I was pretending it was mine for a bit. I was going to put it back.'

Abby was quiet for a moment and Ellie took the opportunity to stand up, brush herself down. 'There,' she said, holding out the book.

Abby didn't take it. 'Were you?' she asked. 'Or if I hadn't noticed it wasn't on the bookshelf, would you have kept it?'

'No! Course not.'

Her denial hung in the air, mocking both of them.

Abby nodded. 'You should have it.'

'What? No! It's yours. Take it back.'

'You keep it.'

'I don't want it,' insisted Ellie, brandishing the book, but Abby was already halfway out the door.

'I just came up to see if you wanted coffee or tea,' she said.

'Coffee. Please,' said Ellie.

Abby nodded, then left. Ellie looked at the book in her hand, her precious childhood book that was now hers, and suddenly felt as if she'd never quite love it in the same way again.

The day had an awkwardness to it after that, even as Matteo joined them, and the three women decided to postpone their trip to the beach. The sun made them lazy, they said, which wasn't altogether untrue, and they spent the afternoon alternately on the terrace and the swim platform. After a simple supper, both Ellie and Susanna claimed an early night.

ELEVEN

Ellie lay in bed the next morning, dozing as she heard her sister get up. When she finally surfaced, as she shut her bedroom door, her mother came out of her own room just behind her. Something about the timing made Ellie think that Susanna had been waiting for her to leave her room.

Everyone was on best behaviour over breakfast: polite requests were made to pass the butter, attention paid as to who needed their coffee topping up. It was decided they'd make the trip to the beach. Matteo was unable to join them as he'd promised a friend he'd help him fix his boat.

The drive and the excitement of the destination temporarily pushed the tension into the background; everyone had a veneer of optimism to hide behind. The front of good feeling continued as they gasped at the turquoise and gold beauty of the beach and settled onto sunbeds.

The sun bore down on them as they dozed and read their books. After a while, Abby sat up.

'Anyone for a swim?' she asked.

Ellie was in the shade, under a palm tree, and was content to stay there. She looked across at her mother who was in direct heat and was turning a little pink and perspiring.

'Maybe in a minute,' said Susanna, pulling her longing eyes from the water.

Ellie frowned; it seemed obvious her mother would benefit from cooling off but Ellie had the distinct impression she hadn't wanted to go with Abby. Ellie watched Abby get up from her sunbed and wade out into the crystal-clear water, shades of aquamarine flecked with patches of darker blue where small rocks lay on the seabed. On the back of Abby's right shoulder was a scar about two inches long. Ellie had noticed it the day before, when they'd swum at the house, but hadn't asked about it, as Abby had seemed self-conscious.

Susanna leaned up on one elbow. 'Shall we get some lunch in a bit? We could try one of the restaurants along the beach.'

Ellie nodded but felt a flurry of disquiet. She had to be careful on this trip and not eat out too often. Funds were tight; in fact, she was trying to manage a substantial debt on her credit cards. Nearly eighteen thousand pounds, as it happened. She tried to pay off a little every month but the interest was greedy, eating into her deposits. It was something that made her feel sick if she dwelled on it too much, so she didn't.

After Abby's swim, they packed up their things and wandered along the seafront, checking out the restaurant menus.

'This one looks nice,' said Abby, stopping outside a cafe. Ellie wasn't so sure – it seemed a little basic and had plastic tables and chairs, and she knew in the heat those chairs would be sticking to the backs of her thighs.

'Or the next one along?' she suggested. Ellie walked on a few metres and looked at the menu board. A little more expensive but you'd get the *quality* and the whole experience would be so much more enjoyable. She'd be able to relax, to let go of some of the tension in her shoulders, and wasn't that the whole point of this holiday? Life was for enjoying – you could get run over by a bus tomorrow. Also, she noted with pleasure, this one had fabric cushions on the chair seats.

They ordered and sat back, gazing out at the sea. Then Susanna rummaged in her bag, pulled out her phone. She held it up to Abby and Ellie.

'Smile!'

'Mum!' protested Ellie lightly, but it was no good and Susanna got her picture.

'Oh, I could stay here forever,' said Susanna, sighing and taking a long drink from a glass of iced water.

Ellie saw Abby rip off a piece of bread and dip it in olive oil, her face expressionless.

'Think you might cramp Abby's style, Mum,' she said. 'She is a newly-wed after all.'

'Of course. It's been so nice to finally meet Matteo. I can understand why you wanted to keep him to yourself for so long.' She put down her glass. 'Isn't this lovely? The three of us being here. Getting on. It's important, you know, that we make the most of the good times.'

'What are you going on about?' asked Ellie.

'Nothing. Just being sentimental. Enjoying seeing my children spend some time together. Nothing should get between two sisters, you must always remember that.'

Abby was stony-faced but then the food arrived, breaking the moment.

Ellie thought that her sister seemed quiet during lunch. Then Susanna got up to use the bathroom and it was just the two of them, sitting back, eyes drawn again to the sparkling Tyrrhenian Sea. A group of young men in swimwear walked along the beach, bronzed, oiled bodies gleaming in the sunshine.

'Nice view,' said Ellie and Abby couldn't help but smile.

Ellie pondered at how so many Italian men seemed to beat their English counterparts in the looks department. She wondered if they treated their women well; Matteo certainly seemed to dote on Abby – little touches to her knee, a whisper in her ear, a sense of looking out for her. Ellie felt another glint of envy. Her own love life was littered with the carcasses of disasters, the latest being a six-month relationship with a married man. She hadn't known he was married when she'd met him at the gym. He'd asked her out for a coffee after a class and they were sleeping together by the end of the week. He worked in something to do with technical design at a local company, a career that had impressed her, and he would take her out for dinner at least twice a week, always in her part of London as he said he didn't want her travelling home alone late at night, or needing to get up early in the morning just to get to work. What she'd perceived as chivalry was actually his avoidance of admitting that his home in north London was filled with a wife and two children, and therefore it wasn't really convenient to invite her back there.

It had hurt like hell when she'd discovered his deception – and it was humiliating too. She'd told friends about him – although not Abby, thank goodness. The truth was, she'd been saving that one up, something she could finally compete with Abby on. She'd been looking forward to dropping it casually into conversation; thank God she hadn't got around to mentioning him. She still cringed at the potential shame of having to explain to her big sister that she'd failed so mightily in her choice of boyfriend. Especially with Abby so perfectly married. Matteo had fallen into her lap – a chance meeting that was worthy of a Hollywood plotline. Ellie was reminded again of her sister's mugging, of how Abby had kept it to herself.

'Was it here, in Elba? Where you met Matteo?'

Abby waited a moment before she answered. 'No. In Florence. That's where Matteo was working at the time.'

'What happened?'

'I don't really want to talk about it.'

'You told Mum.'

'That was the hospital. They called her. She was next of kin.'

'Is that how you got your scar? From your attacker?'

Abby stiffened. 'I said I don't want to talk about it.'

Ellie could feel her irritation rising. Why was her sister always so stubbornly secretive?

'Why not?'

'What?'

'You never tell me anything. Anything big you do in your life, you keep from me. I didn't even know you were getting married.'

'It was a spur of the moment thing.'

'So spur of the moment you couldn't even pick up the phone? What, Matteo proposed, the priest was waiting and the dress was about to be turned back into rags?'

Abby didn't answer.

'And now you have this new secret. Something else you won't tell me.'

'I don't know what you're talking about.'

'I'm not stupid. I've seen you whispering with Mum.' Ellie paused. Whatever it was, she knew it would make her feel inferior and she'd rather just know and get it over and done with. 'What is it you've done now? What big thing have you got to announce?'

To Ellie's frustration, Abby was saved from answering as Susanna breezed back up to the table, followed by the waitress, who placed the bill on the cloth. Abby picked it up and started making mental calculations.

'OK . . . so I had the mushroom pizza, Mum you were the artichoke and a lemonade and Ellie—'

'Can't we just split it three ways?' Irritation burning, Ellie stared at her sister.

'I suppose . . . it's just . . .'

'What?'

'Nothing,' said Abby graciously. 'It doesn't matter that some people ordered more drinks.'

'Oh, for God's sake!'

'What's up now?'

Ellie gritted her teeth. 'You're so . . . *tight*.'

'I'm frugal!'

'I'm not just talking about the money! It's everything! You're so tightly wound, so not relaxed! And look around you!' Ellie waved her arm towards the beach. 'You're in the most perfect place with the most perfect life—'

'It's not as straightforward as you think.'

'No? You want to swap?'

'I needed to escape.'

'Don't we all.'

'It was more than that.' Abby looked at her uneasily. 'I've needed to escape ever since I was small—'

'I've settled up, girls.' Susanna was standing next to the table, smiling carefully at them. Ellie had been so irritated she hadn't even seen her mother leave. 'Just popped to the till,' continued Susanna, 'while you were,' she lowered her voice, '*arguing*.'

Abby started to protest, to get out her purse, and in exasperation, Ellie flounced out of the restaurant.

TWELVE

They drove back to the villa in strained silence. The car was unbearably hot; black seats burned bare skin and, even with the windows fully down, only a blast of warm air filled the car as it wound its way over the shimmering tarmac. Feeling faint from the heat, Ellie found herself smouldering at Abby further – *she's got enough money, why can't she get a car where the air conditioning actually works?*

She was first out and didn't wait for Abby to open the front door but unlatched the side gate and made her way around the back to the terrace. As she approached, a lizard stopped dead on the flagstones. The sun beat down. The leaves on the lemon trees in the large terracotta pots were utterly still. Ellie felt a rivulet of sweat trickle down her lower back. She heard the patio doors slide open behind her. Her shoulders stiffened.

'Are you all right? Ellie?'

It was her mother. Her voice was soft, gentle and full of understanding, and it triggered neuron pathways that had been set when she was a child, sick and reliant on her rock of a mother. Embarrassingly, Ellie felt herself well up. She quickly brushed away the tears.

Susanna came out and walked over to her, resting a hand on her shoulder. 'Why don't I get you a drink?' she said and then went back inside.

Ellie looked down at the lizard. It was still there, not even an eyelid blinking. The sun was burning her shoulders and she half thought about moving into some shade. She heard footsteps behind her and turned – she was so thirsty – but it was Abby standing there, not her mother. Abby crossed the terrace until she was standing next to her.

'I know you think I have everything I could ever want . . . a charmed life . . .' said Abby. 'But you could have the same too.'

'Oh, pur-lease,' said Ellie.

'But you *could*.'

'I was not given the gifts you were, Abby. Or if I was, they were stunted in childhood.'

'No, but that's the point. All those years you felt your illness was holding you back—'

'It *was* holding me back. I was too ill to learn. It affected everything. Whereas you – you were able to do whatever you wanted. You just . . . took off, and I was left on the sidelines. No Girl Scouts, no trampoline club, no going to friends' houses to play, half the time not even any school . . . just a struggle, everything a struggle. You didn't even look back over your shoulder. Thank God for Mum. She understood, not just that I was ill, but what it was doing to me.'

Abby was watching her, a contorted look on her face. *Maybe some of this is finally getting through*, thought Ellie.

'Mum didn't care what it was doing to you,' said Abby.

Ellie thought she'd misheard. 'What?'

'She's a liar. She's been lying to you for years.'

Ice clinked in a jug. Both girls turned to see Susanna framed in the doorway, a tray in her hands filled with glasses and iced water, her face white.

'*Really*, Abby? You're going to try to claim *that*?' she said.

Ellie looked from her mother to her sister. 'What's going on?'

'This mother of ours is not the tender, caring soul you think,' said Abby.

'Stop that right now, Abigail,' said Susanna, walking towards them, the tray still in her hands.

'You were ill because she *made* you ill,' said Abby.

'You are a wicked, wicked girl. How dare you spout such lies.'

'She poisoned you. For years.'

A loud crash splintered the air; glass shattered and water spilled across the darkening flagstones. Stunned, Ellie looked down. The lizard darted off into the dry undergrowth. Ellie kept her eyes on the space where it had been, trying to understand what she'd just heard, but her mind was spinning with thoughts of alarm and disbelief. She raised her head.

'Mum?' she said in a small voice, a child seeking reassurance.

'Your sister is lying,' said Susanna. She reached out a distant hand but Ellie felt herself pull back.

'I saw her,' said Abby.

Ellie's eyes bulged in horror.

'When I was nine.'

Susanna scoffed. 'This is utter rubbish. Do you want to know the real truth?' she said to Ellie, stepping her way through the broken glass towards her. Ellie saw her mother's foot catch on a shard, saw her wince, blood seeping onto the stones, but Susanna hardly seemed to notice, she just kept coming at her.

'Don't come near me.'

Susanna smiled. 'Don't be silly.'

'I said don't come near me.'

'You need to listen to me.'

Susanna was still approaching, making bloody footprints on the ground, her arms outstretched. The heat was searing Ellie's head and it was all too much, too hot, too bright, and as her mother went to touch her, Ellie pushed her back and Susanna stumbled; her foot already in pain and her step unsteady, she lost her balance, and with a small cry she fell and her head hit the terrace with a loud *crack*.

THIRTEEN

Abby stared at her mother lying on the ground, unable to fully take in what had just happened.

Beside her, Ellie was dumbstruck. Shock contorted her face, her hands over her eyes, fingers splayed.

Abby moved over to where Susanna lay on the terrace. She bent down.

'Mum?'

There was no answer. Her mother was so still. Hands trembling, Abby went to pick up Susanna's limp wrist. She placed her fingers tentatively on the space under her mother's thumb. She frowned, not immediately finding what she was searching for. *Her hands just wouldn't stop shaking.* Then a trickle of blood began to form under her mother's head. Slowly, slowly it spread, creeping, edging its way along the paving. Abby's eyes widened in horror. The pressure she had on her mother's wrist instantly weakened and her hand fell from her grasp as the realization kicked in.

She couldn't find a pulse. Susanna was dead.

Slowly, Abby stood up, her shivering hands hanging by her side. She turned to Ellie who was now crouched into a ball, sitting back on her haunches, muttering to herself.

Abby could make out, 'Oh God, oh God, oh God.' Ellie looked up at her, a terrified question in her eyes, and Abby gave an imperceptible shake of the head. Her sister froze and then seemed to visibly crumple. She looked so small to Abby, so vulnerable, so utterly paralysed with fear. Just like she had as a child. A memory roared into her head. Ellie coming into her bedroom, frail and wan from throwing up, and asking if Abby would play dollies with her.

Abby suddenly felt an overwhelming surge of panic. She grabbed Ellie's hand, even as her sister barely seemed to register it, and pulled her into the house. She sat her on the sofa with barked instructions not to move, unsure if Ellie was hearing her. Then Abby raced upstairs and, pulling a holdall from her wardrobe, she started stuffing it with clothes. She was about to turn away when she saw the safe. She punched in the code and the door swung open. Her passport lay on one side and she grabbed it. At the back of the safe was Matteo's gun. Abby froze. Her panic was overriding everything other than a primal knowledge that she had to be prepared for any eventuality. Her hand reflexively closed over the weapon and she threw it in the bag.

Then she went into Ellie's room and searched urgently for her suitcase. Finding it under the bed, she pulled it out and opening the wardrobe and the drawers, she filled it with some essentials, then carried both bags down the stairs, the suitcase banging against the banisters. She took them out the front and chucked them into the boot of her car. She went back inside and grabbed Ellie's hand again.

'Come with me,' she said, and Ellie followed her to the front of the villa and allowed herself to be put in the car. Abby buckled both of them in, then started the engine and drove away.

FOURTEEN

She didn't know where she was going. She didn't even know what she was going to do. There was only one thing clear in her mind: get her sister away.

Abby drove fast, propelled by an urgency she had no control over, a sensation that had no boundaries of thought or logic.

She knew there was a ferry crossing to the mainland in fifteen minutes and they had to be on it. She bought tickets at the terminal and drove the car onto the lower deck. Ellie was still numb, unseeing, unaware. As the ship's ramps rose up and it began its journey across the sea towards the Tuscan coastline, Abby took Ellie up to the on-board cafe and bought her the strongest coffee she could get.

She got one for herself too and they sat at a table outside, Abby choosing the one furthest from the other passengers. She took hold of her espresso cup, added two sachets of sugar and downed it in one. She blinked and swallowed, waiting for the drink to shock her into a state of clarity.

'Now you,' she instructed Ellie, who was sitting staring at nothing, her coffee untouched.

Ellie's glazed eyes moved across to Abby and she seemed

to understand what Abby was saying. She looked down, was surprised to see a coffee there and lifted the cup to her lips. She drank some, wincing at the bitterness.

'All of it,' said Abby, adding sugar to Ellie's coffee too, then watching as her sister tipped her head back until the cup was empty. Ellie put it back on the saucer as Abby sat tensely, waiting for a reaction, and then Ellie crumpled.

'Mum,' she wailed, tears beginning to roll down her cheeks. 'What have I done?'

'Pull yourself together,' whispered Abby quickly, glancing over her shoulder to see if anyone was watching.

'We've left her,' Ellie wailed again.

'Shush.'

'But she's all on her own. We didn't even call an ambulance.'

'It was too late.'

'But what if it wasn't?'

'I checked.'

'But what if there was somethi—'

'I CHECKED,' snapped Abby and Ellie recoiled. Abby took a deep breath. 'Sorry. I didn't mean to shout.' She glanced around again but it was noisy up on the outer deck; the engine and the waves had drowned out her voice and no one was looking.

'I . . . I . . .' Ellie faltered, couldn't seem to bring herself to speak. 'Jesus, I killed her.'

'Don't ever say that again.'

'But I did, I—'

Abby took hold of Ellie's hands across the table, held

them tight. 'It was an *accident*,' she said. Ellie's eyes were brimming over again; guilt and fear made her break Abby's gaze.

'Look at me,' said Abby firmly, but Ellie wouldn't. '*Look at me*,' instructed Abby, giving a sharp shake to her sister's hands until she raised her eyes. 'It was an accident,' repeated Abby. 'An accident, an accident. Not deliberate. Not like what she did to you.' They sat there for a few moments, neither saying anything. Then Ellie slowly pulled her hands away as she looked around her, taking in the endless blue horizon, seeming to notice for the first time that she was on a ferry. 'Where are we going?'

'I don't know. A trip. We need some time. I need to figure it all out. What the best thing is to do.'

'What about Matteo?' asked Ellie.

Abby grimaced. She was well aware he'd be home later and he'd find Susanna on the terrace. As awful as it was, Abby had no idea what she could do about it. It was another problem on top of everything else and she just couldn't deal with it right now.

'I don't know,' she repeated.

The journey was short and within another fifteen minutes, passengers were being asked to return to their cars. Abby led Ellie downstairs and the girls waited silently while the ferry docked, before taking their turn to drive off.

Abby headed into Piombino town and parked up in a busy district, leaving Ellie in the car. She told her to wait and then crossed the road to a bank. Taking a deep breath to compose herself, she stepped into its air-conditioned interior. She went up to the first available cashier and smiled at the woman in her uniform shirt of white and green stripes.

'I need to withdraw some money,' she said in her stilted Italian.

'How much would you like?' asked the cashier.

Abby placed her bank card on the counter. 'The maximum possible, please.'

The cashier asked her to place her card in the reader and enter her PIN, which Abby duly did. The cashier viewed her screen and then wrote a number down on a piece of paper and pushed it under the window. 'This is your balance.'

Abby didn't need to look at it. She knew exactly how much she had in the account. She suddenly wanted out of there, didn't like leaving Ellie so long, didn't like drawing attention to herself. 'So how much can I take out?'

'Well, usually for sums over two thousand euros, we ask for advance notice, just so we have the cash available,' started the cashier.

'I need more,' said Abby. She forced a light smile. 'Whatever you can do.'

'OK,' said the cashier slowly. Abby smiled again, as casually as she could. *I mustn't seem weird*, she swiftly reminded herself. They agreed on a figure, Abby produced her passport and then she waited while the cashier counted the notes, mentally urging her to hurry up. *Keep calm, keep calm.* Eventually it was done and with an envelope of euros padding out her bag, she hurried back to the car.

'Let's go,' she said to Ellie, starting the engine. She needed to get away. The experience in the bank had left her guilty, nervous, feeling like a fugitive. A heavy responsibility suddenly weighed on her shoulders, its load crushing her. She felt her heart race, had to fight for breath.

'Are you OK?' asked Ellie.

I have to be, thought Abby. *But I need time to think. To fix this.*

'Give me your phone,' she said to Ellie.

Her sister looked at her quizzically but did as she was bid. Leaving the engine running, Abby got out of the car and strode up the road. She took Ellie's phone and, with a quick check that no one was watching, dumped it in a bin. Then, with reluctance, she took her own out of her battered old handbag and did the same thing. The money would pinpoint them here anyway. But nothing else. Not for a while. Not while she worked out what to do.

Going back to the car, she got in and drove away.

FIFTEEN

Every now and then Ellie would glimpse the Tyrrhenian Sea from the car window, and every time she did, somewhere she registered it was further away, until she suddenly realized she could no longer see it at all. She made herself sit up and pay some attention for the first time in what felt like hours. She looked out of the window – properly – and saw they had long ago left the town and were deep in the Tuscan hills. The road was quiet and, as they climbed, Ellie could see olive groves and vineyards for miles and, at a distance, the occasional hilltop village, its russet roofs glowing in the late afternoon sun. The horizon was punctuated with the stately height of cypress trees that cast growing shadows across the landscape.

'Where are we?' Ellie asked.

'Heading north,' said Abby.

Ellie looked over at her sister, with her hands fixed firmly on the wheel, her gaze set ahead. She was leading, as ever, had made all the decisions ever since . . . Ellie shuddered. It had all been so quick, such a blur, that part of her didn't think it was real.

Then a picture flashed into her mind – her mother's

closed eyes as she lay on the patio. Everything quiet, everything still, and then slowly came the blood. The horror of that deep red trickle would stay in her nightmares forever. Her mother. Her dear, darling mother. The woman she loved so much. *The woman who poisoned me as a child.*

The agony of grief that had been hurtling through her at an unstoppable speed was suddenly halted. Ellie was speared by confusion and a need to understand.

She tried to think back all those years, tried to remember scenarios, moments, meetings with doctors, anything to ground what Abby had said, to make sense of it, realize it for herself, but all she could recall was her mother's tenderness.

'What did she do?' she started tentatively. 'When you saw her that time. What did Mum do?'

Abby glanced across. 'She was pouring liquid paracetamol into your food.'

'Oh my God.' Ellie was silent for a moment. 'Are you sure?'

'Yes.'

'How old was I?'

'Six.' said Abby.

Ellie calculated. 'And you were nine.' *Still quite young. Maybe Abby made a mistake.*

'Can you tell me exactly what happened?'

'It was a school day. You were in the living room, lying on the sofa, unwell. You hadn't been to school that day. Mum was in the kitchen, making dinner. She thought I was outside, playing in the street, but I'd come in for a snack.

I was starving. You remember the blue fruit bowl that she used to keep on the counter by the kitchen door?'

Ellie nodded. It had had white flowers painted around the outside.

'I was getting an apple and I saw her with the medicine bottle. She had her back to me and was measuring it out into the small plastic spoon, then tipping it into a plate of casserole. Then she stirred it in. I remember being puzzled because whenever I'd had medicine, she'd just given it to me straight from the spoon. I must have made a noise because she swung around and I'll never forget the look on her face. She was panicked, then she became angry, really angry. I asked her what she was doing and she just looked at me with the apple in my hand and told me to put it back – it was dinner time and I shouldn't just help myself without asking.'

Ellie took all this in. 'Did she still give me the food?'

'Yes. Well, I assumed so. Later, when she said goodnight to me in my room, she told me it was a special medicine. Just for you. I said I thought it was the normal one, you know, the one I'd have too if I got a temperature or something, but she said I'd been mistaken. It was something the doctor had prescribed just for you and you wouldn't like the taste so she put it in your food. And I wasn't to tell you or you wouldn't eat your dinner and then you wouldn't get better.'

'Did you believe her?'

'I had to. What else could I have thought? I was a child myself.'

'But this was years ago. Maybe you didn't understand – you were young. Maybe it *was* something the doctors prescribed,' said Ellie.

Abby shook her head, took a deep breath. 'I heard something on the radio back in the spring. About mothers harming their children. It reminded me of what I'd seen all that time ago. And I started to think about it. I called Mum, confronted her. She tried to deny it of course. Said you were sick and needed the paracetamol. It was pretty clear she was lying – she got so flustered, and it just didn't add up. And there was your constant sickness, the diarrhoea, your confusion, your yellowed skin. I kept on at her and so then she tried to play it down. Said it hadn't happened that often. Sometimes she would give you enough medicine to keep you off school, but she was careful not to make it too much. She said she didn't want you to have any long-term damage.'

It was almost too much to hear. 'What?' Ellie asked, anguished.

'She was worried about liver damage,' said Abby. 'I know, I know, it seems nuts. So Mum would make you ill, then she'd reduce the dose a few days before you saw the doctors so they couldn't trace it. I checked it out online. Seems if any overdose is staggered over a long period, paracetamol tests are impossible to interpret and they can be normal.' Abby sighed. 'Mum insisted I never say anything to you. I thought you had a right to know and she should tell you herself. She rang me a few days before your trip out here, pleaded with me again not to say anything.'

Ellie was silent as she took it all in. A lump was stuck in her throat and it was a while before she could talk.

'I was ill for another two years. Until I was eight. Is that how long she was giving it to me?' She was suddenly flooded with memories and didn't see Abby glance away awkwardly.

'God, the sickness,' continued Ellie. 'That's what I hated the most. The nausea. I would dread it. And the missing out. I always felt like I'd just be watching everyone else have fun, feeling like the outsider.' Her voice cracked. 'The only thing that made it remotely bearable was having Mum. The way she looked after me. I felt like she loved me so much.'

'She did. You know that you were her favourite.'

Ellie scoffed. 'Funny way of showing it.'

'She doted on you. Trust me, I remember. It was always about you.' Abby paused. 'I know it's hard to understand but I think she needed you. Couldn't stand it when you started school and left her alone.'

'All kids leave their mothers when they start school!'

'I know but . . . Dad had also left her. And her parents. I asked Grandma once why Mum never came on the visits with us. She said Mum had betrayed them and it wasn't something she could forgive. Did they ever speak to her again after she ran off with Dad?'

Ellie shrugged but she didn't think so. She wanted to know for certain, wanted to ask questions that would take away some of the shock. She wanted to ask her mother. Ellie was suddenly overwhelmed with a crushing sense of abandonment as she realized she'd never know the whole truth.

My mum hurt me. The thought kept on going round and round in her mind. And yet the loss was almost unbearable; Ellie couldn't reconcile the two different people in her head: the one who'd deliberately made her ill with the one who'd been so supportive, who'd encouraged her when she was low – right on into adulthood, even as Abby was racing ahead in life. Her mother – that beautiful, wonderful woman who'd been by her side her whole life – was dead, and it was her fault.

'I'm sorry,' said Abby.

'What for?'

'If I'd said something, told a teacher or something . . .'

Ellie stiffened. As much as she wanted to lay some of the blame at Abby's feet, she couldn't really. She had to remember that Abby had been a child too.

'You were only nine. You couldn't have understood.'

'I was then,' said Abby quietly.

Ellie looked at her sharply. 'What do you mean?'

'I saw her again.'

A deep, sickening feeling was nestling in Ellie's stomach. 'When?'

'Two years later. When I'd just started secondary school. When you were eight.'

Ellie's mouth dropped open. 'You what?'

'I'm so sorry. I said to Mum it didn't seem right. I told her I didn't like it. She thought I was going to tell someone.'

'And did you?'

'No. I had no idea of the enormity, the severity of what she was doing. I was a kid. And anyway, she told me it would stop.'

'*What?* And you believed her?'

'Well, yes. I mean, she did. Stop.'

'But how did you know she would? What if she'd carried on? Maybe she kept on poisoning me and you didn't even know?'

'I'm sure she didn't. You got better, you stopped going to the doctor's—'

'But that's not the point! I was already damaged. I needed help.' Ellie was shouting now, crying with despair. 'I thought I was stupid. That I'd never catch up. I thought I'd get ill again. I *always* thought that. Don't you see? I could've been different! If you'd said something!' She rained her fists down on Abby's shoulder.

'Stop it!' said Abby, trying to simultaneously push Ellie's hands away and hold on to the steering wheel. 'I'm sorry!'

Ellie heard the apology but instead of soothing her, it inflamed her further. There was something so inadequate about those words, something that was so disproportionate to the years of misery that she'd suffered. She continued to rain blows down on Abby. 'You just carried on, looking out for yourself. But what about me? I could've been *differen—*'

The noise was like an explosion, the deafening bang of flattened steel. Ellie lunged forward, the seat belt slicing across her shoulder, and her face hit the white pillow with a force that winded her, and then everything was quiet.

She lay there for a moment, gulping for breath, panicking

that she couldn't take in any oxygen; then, as the airbag deflated, her lungs seemed to regain control.

'Shit!' said Abby, unbuckling and wrestling with her door.

Ellie looked up and through the broken windscreen saw stones strewn across the bonnet. The car was on the wrong side of the road, a disintegrated wall splattered over it. She extricated herself from her seat, went outside to join Abby. The whole front end on the driver's side was crunched in, a tangle of steel and exposed innards. The two sisters gazed at it.

'That looks bad,' said Ellie.

'You reckon?' snapped Abby. 'What the hell did you think you were doing, attacking me like that?'

'I'm sorry.'

Abby cut her a fierce look and went back to the car. Ellie watched as her sister brushed the broken glass off the driver's seat, then got in and attempted to start the engine. It turned over sluggishly, then not at all.

'Brilliant,' said Abby, smacking the steering wheel. 'Just brilliant.'

Ellie walked over and stood next to Abby by the driver's side. 'I said I was sorry.'

'Sorry isn't going to make this car start!'

'You've cut yourself,' said Ellie, pointing at her sister's hand. 'Here.' She pulled out a pack of cosmetic wipes from her bag, peeled one off and handed it through the open window to Abby. Abby hesitated, then took it and dabbed at her hand. The cut wasn't deep and was already clotting.

'Why do you buy these things when water does just as good a job?' said Abby, of the wipe.

Ellie bristled; she knew what was coming. 'Because you never know when you might be in a car crash and a bottle of water isn't readily available?'

'It's another example,' said Abby, still dabbing, 'of not being smart with your money.'

For God's sake! Ellie could feel the irritation rising up in her. Even now, right here, straight after an accident, Abby could put her down. She wrestled to find a comeback, but could think of none.

'Give it back.'

Abby looked up. 'What?'

Ellie held out her hand. 'Give it back.'

'What, this?' Abby was waving the soiled wipe in disbelief.

'Yes, if you don't like it, you don't have to have it.' Ellie leaned over to grab it but Abby pulled away.

'You're not serious.'

'Deadly.'

'Don't be stupid.'

'That wipe saved your bacon and all you can do is . . . *complain* and not recognize when spending a few quid can actually have a profound effect on your life.'

Abby was trying not to smile. 'Profound?'

'You know what I mean.' Ellie pulled a face at her sister. Then sighed; it was all too exhausting. 'What do we do now?'

Abby considered. 'The car's fucked,' she said.

'Yes,' agreed Ellie.

Abby got out and, shutting the driver's door, she looked up and down the road. Then she walked to the back of the car. She popped the boot and took out the holdall and suitcase she'd put in there earlier.

'I guess we walk,' said Abby. 'See if we can find a village or something.'

Ellie nodded, then the two sisters, the late sun on their backs, continued along the road.

SIXTEEN

'I think I can see a house,' said Ellie, pointing up ahead. They had been going for forty minutes and she was ready for a break. Her right leg was tingling with pins and needles and she knew she needed to rest before it became too difficult to walk.

'Hallelujah,' said Abby. She strode on ahead, Ellie following, and within a few minutes they had crossed a small stone bridge into a hamlet where a smattering of houses led to a restaurant. Peering in at the windows, they saw it was closed, the chairs stacked up on the tables. Abby gazed around the streets. It was quiet. They were in that no-man's-land time that fell post lunch and before the day's heat had waned. Then they saw a movement in the distance. A figure walked across what looked like a garage forecourt, weaving between several cars before disappearing into a hut-like office.

'Bingo,' said Abby softly.

The girls headed over. Abby tucked her bag behind a wall and placed Ellie's suitcase next to it. 'Don't want any awkward questions,' she said. Then she went over to the office and opened the door. Ellie stayed outside and, sitting on the wall, she rubbed her leg, trying to ease the numbness.

She gazed around the forecourt. There were only a dozen or so cars, mostly Fiats, although a black Alfa Romeo Spider had pride of place right at the front of the plot. It gleamed in the sunshine – a car that had attitude. There was a sign propped up on the dashboard that was visible through the windscreen. It was for hire at an astronomical amount. Ellie felt the butterflies dance in her belly. They needed a new vehicle but would Abby be expecting them to go halves? Ellie could never afford that kind of money. She turned her back and, leaving the wall, went to look at the Fiats. They were all for rent and nearly all standard 500s. One was a convertible; a white roof was pushed back against the red bodywork. Ellie peered inside: the red paintwork continued on the dash too – and the seats were upholstered in white leather. *Wouldn't burn my bum on those*, she thought, as Abby came outside with the proprietor of the business, a late-middle-aged Italian man with salt-and-pepper curly hair and a rotund belly. He saw Ellie over by the open-top Fiat and stopped for a moment, then brightened, his day markedly improved. He headed over.

'This is our best car for you,' he said to Abby in his accented English. 'Perfect for two ladies.'

Abby glanced at the cardboard sign in the windscreen. 'But it's more expensive than the other 500s,' she said. 'And seeing as I'm paying . . .'

Ellie ignored the barb, secretly relieved she wasn't expected to contribute.

'Ah, but you have the roof,' exclaimed the car dealer.

'I don't need the roof,' said Abby.

'Everyone needs a roof,' said Ellie.

'You like it, no?' said the dealer, conspiratorially to Ellie.

'It's gorgeous,' she replied wistfully.

'We don't need it,' repeated Abby. 'It's spending money we don't need to spend.'

Ellie and the dealer exchanged a glance and Ellie shrugged.

'Advertisers tell you that you need the wind in your hair. I just need to get from A to B,' said Abby.

'Jeez, live a little,' said Ellie, under her breath.

'What about that blue one there?' asked Abby, pointing at another car further along the forecourt, an ordinary Fiat 500 without an open roof.

'That one is gone,' said the dealer.

'It's right there.'

'I mean, it is reserved.'

'OK, that white one next to it.'

'Also reserved.'

Abby frowned. 'The green one? I suppose that is reserved too?'

'I'm afraid so,' said the dealer gravely. He gave a surreptitious wink to Ellie, who pretended not to see.

Abby let out a sound of frustration. 'This is . . . extortion,' she seethed.

The dealer looked apologetic. 'I can do little discount,' he said and, looking at Ellie, added, 'especially for two such lovely ladies.'

*

'At least the weather's nice,' said Ellie, tilting her face towards the sky and closing her eyes, suddenly feeling utterly exhausted. As she did so, an image of her mother's body on the terrace came into her mind and, sickened, she quickly opened her eyes again. They were behind the wheel in the red Fiat, top down, cruising through the Tuscan countryside.

'He robbed me,' said Abby.

'You heard what he said – it was the only one.'

'He was lying. All because you wanted this one.'

'You think?' Ellie tutted. 'That's naughty.' She hid a small smile. 'Lucky I didn't go all gooey over the Spider.'

The light was fading. As the sky darkened, sunless and foreboding, the guilt and the sadness stalked Ellie with a vengeance. She stared out of the window, watching her mother's last day fade into black. Beside her, Abby shifted uncomfortably. It was becoming clear they needed to stop – Ellie had noticed for some time now that Abby was tiring. And anyway, they couldn't just keep on driving – they had no idea of where they were heading. As they came into the next village, Abby said what Ellie was thinking.

'Maybe we should find a place to stay for the night. Figure out what to do.'

They booked themselves into a B & B just off the village square, then took a table in the small dining room for dinner. There were only two other guests there, a young backpacking couple from Germany who hunkered up together poring over guidebooks.

Ellie and Abby sat as far away from them as they could. Ellie spoke first, before Abby could say anything. 'I need to turn myself in.'

'What? No!'

'But there's no other way. And I deserve it.'

'You do not,' said Abby emphatically, keeping her voice low. 'Are you forgetting what she did to you?'

'Doesn't mean I needed to do what I did,' said Ellie, upset. 'Push her like that.'

Abby rested her hand on her sister's across the table. 'You didn't mean for that to happen,' she said. 'You didn't go out of your way to hurt her.'

'No, but—'

'It was an *accident*.'

A tear rolled down Ellie's cheek and she quickly wiped it away. Abby glanced around the room, made sure the backpackers weren't watching.

'Maybe it could look just like that. An accident,' said Abby carefully.

'What are you getting at?'

'Maybe Susanna didn't want to come to the Tuscan mainland with us on our little sightseeing trip, maybe she opted to stay at home.' Abby shrugged. 'She fell and hit her head.'

Ellie gasped. 'We can't say that!'

'I realize there is the problem with the three glasses.' Ellie looked blank. 'On the tray,' explained Abby. 'The police will find broken shards from three glasses, not one.'

'Oh God,' said Ellie, her face in her hands.

'Did she grab you in any way?'

'No. What . . . you're thinking self-defence?'

Abby deflated. 'I was, but . . .'

'What?'

'Well, we ran. It doesn't look great.'

'But . . .'

'I know, that was my idea. But I . . . I panicked. I wanted to get you away.'

'But if we'd stayed . . .'

'You'd still be going to prison.'

Ellie's eyes widened in shock.

'Yes, prison,' repeated Abby. 'There's no beating around the bush here, it's manslaughter.'

'Oh jeez,' said Ellie, her voice cracking.

'Now come on. Don't do that, don't cry,' said Abby urgently. 'Stop it, people will see.'

Ellie got a tissue, blew her nose.

'If anyone should have gone to prison, it's her for what she did to you. Just you remember that.'

'So what do we do?' asked Ellie helplessly.

'I don't know,' said Abby. Ellie started to crumple again. 'I'll think of something,' Abby added quickly. 'Let's sleep on it. I'll think of something.'

SEVENTEEN

Matteo was surprised to see no lights on in his house as he pulled up outside. Helping his friend fix his boat had taken a little longer than he'd thought and he had expected to find his wife and her family at home. They were meant to all be having dinner together – he'd brought back some fish that his friend had caught. It was then he noticed that Abby's car wasn't there. Perturbed, he checked his watch – it was getting late. They would have left the beach hours ago.

He let himself in and listened out but the house was silent. Throwing his keys in the dish on the hall table, he went to put the fish in the fridge. The motor hummed and whirred and he stood there for a moment, wondering where his wife could be. He moved through the house towards the living room, which was also dark. As he entered, he switched on the light.

Matteo yelled out in fright. Sitting on a chair was Susanna. But not the woman he'd seen that morning. Her face was burned red by the sun; her hair was dishevelled. Then he saw she had a tissue in her hands, blotted with blood.

She looked up at him, an expression of consternation on her face.

'Are you OK?' he asked, growing more disconcerted as he now noticed her hair was matted with dried blood. He walked over to her but she held up a hand to make him stop. Confused, he did so, and that was when he saw the terrace through the patio doors: it was strewn with broken glass and a patch was stained dark.

Matteo started. 'What's happened? Where's Abby?'

'Gone,' said Susanna.

'Gone where?'

'You need to call the police.'

'But—'

'Oh, I know, you *are* the police,' said Susanna. 'But not even you can handle this.'

'You're hurt,' said Matteo, walking towards her again.

'Stay away from me!' Susanna said sharply. 'And call them. It's in your own and your wife's best interests.'

Matteo slowly pulled his phone from his pocket and did as she bid. A cold, ugly fear gripped him as he dialled.

EIGHTEEN

'I do not need to go to hospital,' Susanna said imperiously to the paramedic, who had tended to the cut on the back of her head. 'Nothing and no one will persuade me to, so you might as well leave me alone. I'm perfectly fine now, thanks to your medical assistance.' She gave a brief but thankful smile for their application of steri-strips to the gash she'd sustained when she fell onto the broken glass. They'd said she needed stiches but she had no intention of leaving the house. 'I just need time to rest and heal.'

And talk to these police people, added Susanna in her head, as she looked up at the two Carabinieri hovering at the side of the room, a man and a woman. She winced as she did so: her head was a ball of pain from the fall – and she had a lump the size of an egg to go along with her cut.

Eventually the paramedics were persuaded to leave and the Carabinieri sat either side of her. They'd been speaking in Italian to Matteo and, although she couldn't understand the words, she'd thought by their body language that he had claimed ignorance of the day's events. Susanna stretched a hand out towards the side table and the policeman who'd introduced himself as Captain Santini understood and handed over the glass of water. She sipped at it delicately through a straw. When she had finished, he took it from her and placed it back on the table.

'If you would like to tell us what happened,' said Lieutenant Colonel Baroni, in English. As the senior officer, she was leading the questioning. Susanna wondered if she had children. Whether they got on. If she did, they'd be young; Baroni was only in her thirties. Susanna felt a wave of sadness. Her own daughters had never been friends, not really. There had been too much jealousy, too much rivalry, for years.

The captain, tasked with writing down everything they were saying, was poised with a pen and notebook. Susanna took a deep breath.

'We had gone for a lovely lunch,' she started, 'after our trip to the beach. Except that Abby and Ellie seemed tense around each other. They have a history – don't all sisters?' she said. 'Except, their relationship is more complicated than most.' She glanced up at Matteo, saw he was watching her intently.

'When we got back, Ellie was upset. She went out onto the terrace . . .' Susanna waved a hand towards the patio doors. 'I went to get some water for us all and when I came back from the kitchen, Abby was here too.' Susanna stopped. Took a breath. 'Abby has always resented Ellie, ever since she was born. Oldest child syndrome. Found she had to share her mother with a new baby. And then, when Ellie was only five years old, she became ill. Quite severely ill. It lasted for several years. I was beside myself.' Susanna's voice began to break with anguish. 'The doctors couldn't find out what was wrong, and then . . .' She trailed off.

'Please continue,' prompted Lieutenant Colonel Baroni.

'Sorry,' said Susanna. She inhaled. 'I eventually discovered what it was. Why Ellie had been so very ill.' She looked up at Baroni. 'Her sister hated her so much she had been poisoning her.'

NINETEEN

Matteo was looking at her, dumbfounded. *Let him look*, thought Susanna, *he needs to hear this.*

He shook his head and gave a disbelieving laugh. 'What did you just say?'

Susanna's head dropped; it was hard enough to say the first time, and then Baroni spoke sharply to Matteo in Italian. It was clear she was telling him to be quiet.

'How did you get your injury?' Baroni asked Susanna.

'Well, when I got the drinks for us all and came back outside I could see Abby was upsetting Ellie. You have to understand that Ellie knew nothing about what her sister had done to her. When she was a child, I thought it best not to tell her, and then after Abby left home at eighteen . . . well, so much time had passed. Why bring it all up again? I was so relieved when Abby moved to Italy as I thought the distance would be good for Ellie. She always wanted to be close to Abby, you see, but Abby would push her away.' Susanna checked herself. 'Sorry, I've gone off on a tangent. Ellie told me that Abby had invited her out here to Elba and I was immediately on alert – it was so out of character. I phoned Abby and asked her why she'd invited

Ellie over and she said something about wanting to make amends. I didn't believe a word of it. Why now? I asked her why she'd want to do that to a sister she couldn't stand.'

'And what did she say?' asked the lieutenant.

'She told me the animosity was years ago. Wanted to start afresh now she'd moved out here. I still didn't believe her but I thought my energy was better used seeing for myself. So I suggested that I come too. Abby agreed but I was to arrive a couple of days after Ellie. Then last week Abby rang me. Begged me not to tell Ellie about what she'd done to her little sister when they were children. I've kept it secret for years – I've felt guilty about that too – and it did occur to me that if Abby wanted a clean slate, then maybe it was a good idea for her to explain what she'd done. But she insisted on keeping it quiet. She got quite upset with me about it.' Susanna sighed. 'I didn't like the sound of any of it. That's why I came here a couple of days early. I was wary of Abby being alone with Ellie.'

'You still haven't explained the injury,' said Baroni, pointing at Susanna's head.

'This is all complete rubbish,' said Matteo, unable to contain his frustration anymore. 'Sorry, Susanna, but Abby's not some child abuser. She asked her sister here because she genuinely wanted to get closer to her.'

'She has a history of lying,' said Susanna quietly. 'When I brought the drinks out on the terrace, I could see she'd upset Ellie. Then she told her' – Susanna looked visibly shaken, placed a hand on her chest – 'that Ellie had been poisoned as a child but that I had done it. I couldn't believe it. All those years I'd protected her and then she did that. Lied about me like that. I could see Ellie was distraught and I went to her but she was so traumatized she pushed me away. I fell and must have blacked out. Cut my head on the broken glass.'

Lieutenant Baroni took all this in. Susanna saw Matteo shake his head in disbelief.

'Where is she now?' asked Baroni. 'Where are both of your daughters?'

'I don't know,' said Susanna hopelessly. 'They're not here and Abby's car is gone. I'm guessing Abby took Ellie somewhere.'

'Any idea where?'

'No. I mean, I've only just arrived. I don't know the island or where Abby would go.' Susanna looked up at Matteo for assistance.

'Are you trying to suggest she's gone on the run?' he asked incredulously.

'Well, she didn't stay and help me,' replied Susanna. 'Might as well have left me for dead.'

Matteo stood. 'I'm going to be late for work,' he said and went out of the room.

Susanna heard him go upstairs. She turned to Lieutenant Baroni. 'We need to find them. I'm worried about what Abby might do to Ellie.'

'You think that she still might harm her?'

'I'm convinced of it. She's psychologically damaged, has

an obsessive personality – controlling almost. She did nothing but work until she was able to retire early. But even coming out here hasn't made her let go of Ellie. She's always hated her, hated the bond Ellie and I have. Something that ironically Abby made even stronger by causing Ellie's illness.' Susanna paused. 'That must have hurt a lot.'

Susanna got her bag from the floor and found her phone. She turned the screen to face the police, so they could see the photo she'd pulled up. Captain Santini's eyes widened, as he made no attempt to hide his interest.

'Yes,' said Susanna, clipped. 'She's beautiful. Something else Abby resented about her.'

Baroni frowned at Santini's lack of respect. She'd never worked with him before but she'd been distantly aware of his reputation. He was known for his violent undertone – nothing that would get him into trouble, but there had been rumours of him breaking the rules with prisoners when no one was looking. Baroni had been dismayed when he'd been assigned to the investigation with her. She'd requested an alternative officer but her boss, irritated by her challenging his authority (not for the first time), had refused.

Matteo, now changed into his uniform, had come back into the room. He seemed agitated.

'Are you leaving for work now?' asked Susanna.

'No,' he said. 'I can't.' He ran his hand through his hair, seemed unsure of what to do.

'I thought you said you were going to be late?' said Susanna.

Matteo paused. 'My gun is missing from the safe.'

The room fell silent.

Susanna felt goosebumps run up her arms. 'Who knew the code?' she asked quietly.

Matteo was wrestling with himself. 'OK, so, yes, Abby did too,' he said defensively. 'But it doesn't mean she took my gun.'

He wasn't convinced, Susanna could tell. She shifted her eyes over to the police and was relieved to see they were taking her concerns a whole lot more seriously. She also saw Santini's look of relish. This investigation had clearly just stepped up a gear.

TWENTY

The farmer drove his tractor along the road, enjoying the quiet warmth of the evening. The sun had almost set and if he looked up into the hills to his right, he could see his olive groves becoming blanketed by the dark. It gave him a sense of well-being, of the right order of things. Soon he would be home where his wife would have a hearty stew on the table, which he would enjoy with a glass of Sangiovese.

As he rounded the corner, he clocked something in the shadowy road up ahead. He frowned; it looked like a car, abandoned. He approached, stopping just before the vehicle. Switching off his engine, he climbed down and walked over to the car. He saw the wall and whistled. This land belonged to his neighbour, Antonio, who would be most disgruntled at the amount of damage to his wall. This section would need rebuilding completely! The farmer checked up and down the road – night was coming and drivers wouldn't see the deserted car in the dark. He took his phone out of his pocket and dialled for the police.

TWENTY-ONE

'Their phones are going straight to voicemail,' said Lieutenant Baroni. 'We'll check the ferry records – see if Abby's car was registered with any of them.'

'You think they've left the island?' asked Susanna.

'It's possible. Can you show us their rooms?'

'Why?'

'They're looking for bodies,' said Matteo. 'They'll search the whole house.'

Susanna looked from Matteo to Baroni, aghast. 'You think they're here? Ellie's here?'

'We don't know anything yet,' said Baroni with a reprimanding look at Matteo. 'But if we could see their rooms . . . ?'

Susanna stood and led the way upstairs. The Carabinieri followed, with Matteo bringing up the rear. Susanna stopped outside Abby's room first but, aware Matteo was behind her, didn't like to encroach any further.

The lieutenant had no such qualms and stepped forward. 'Have any of her clothes gone?' she asked.

Matteo uncrossed his arms and went over to the wardrobe, looking inside. 'I think so. A few.'

'Anything else you notice?'

'No.'

Susanna watched from the doorway as the police moved around the room, looking on shelves, opening drawers. Captain Santini moved over to the bed, began to rummage around the bedside cabinet. From the top, he picked up the book Abby must have been reading, turned it upside down and flicked through it, but nothing fell out. He opened the drawer and pulled out a couple more books and a bundle of envelopes.

Santini separated the envelopes from the books and, taking one off the top, tossed the rest on the bed.

'Hey!' protested Matteo.

Santini smiled smugly at Matteo, at his look of indignation. He opened the envelope. 'It is from you?'

'Nothing in there is useful. Written a year ago. After we'd first met.'

Santini shrugged and began to read, a smirk on his face.

'We should still check,' said Lieutenant Baroni, plucking the letter from her colleague's hands. She pocketed the envelopes, much to Matteo's frustration, and Susanna braced herself, as it looked as if he was about to object, when Captain Santini spoke again.

'Well, what do we have here?'

He was crouched on the floor, the door of the cupboard underneath the cabinet open. In his hand was a small yellow plastic container.

'What's that?' Susanna asked, frowning. She couldn't read the label on the front from the other side of the room.

Baroni took the bottle from her colleague. 'Weedkiller,' she said.

Susanna started. 'Oh my God.'

'What?' exclaimed Matteo.

'Any idea why your wife would keep weedkiller hidden in her bedroom?' asked Baroni.

Matteo was struggling to answer; confusion riddled his face. 'I don't know how that got there. It wouldn't be Abby . . .'

'Who would it be?' asked Baroni matter-of-factly.

'I don't know . . . It doesn't make sense.'

Susanna was beginning to feel sorry for him, but then a sudden thought made itself present in her mind.

'Ellie was ill,' she said breathlessly. 'Night before last. She was feeling terribly unwell.'

She looked up at the bottle of weedkiller with its glaring yellow packaging. 'You have to find them,' she urged the police. She started to cry, the salty tears irritating the sunburn on her face. 'Please. You have to find them.'

Matteo took a deep breath, tried to restore calm. 'This doesn't prove anything.'

The lieutenant's phone rang. She answered. '*Pronto*.'

She spoke in Italian and Susanna was unable to follow the conversation, but she watched Matteo's face, saw the shadow cross it.

'What's happened?' she asked quickly.

Lieutenant Baroni hung up. 'Abby's car has been found. On the mainland. It's damaged, crashed into a wall.'

Susanna cried out, a sound of anguish. 'Oh my God. Ellie, is she OK?'

'There was no one at the scene,' said the lieutenant. 'I think it's of the highest importance that we find your daughters as soon as possible.'

TWENTY-TWO

Lieutenant Colonel Baroni watched as the pickup truck winched Abby Morelli's car up onto the ramps. Night had fallen and the crash site was lit by the forensic team lights. Numerous moths and bugs flitted in the beams, suicidal as they hurtled themselves at the piercing brightness. The car would be checked over thoroughly but Baroni had already flashed her torch over the seats. There were no bodies. A small amount of blood on the driver's seat but that was it. She looked up at the torches flaring through the olive groves, could hear the sounds of the dogs as they strained at their leads. Were the women out there somewhere, perhaps having wandered off from the scene to get help? Or had one tried to escape from the other and failed, now lying dead and bloodied under an olive tree? Somehow she sensed not. Baroni's instincts told her these women had gone in the direction of the road. She looked into the darkness, the same way that the car had been facing. In her gut she felt the two sisters had continued on the same course. She called over to Captain Santini and they got back into their patrol car.

*

Standing outside the ochre-painted house, Baroni knocked for a second time. Santini was standing next to her, his whole body hyper with impatience. He raised an arm, about to hammer on the door again, but she flashed him a look and he sulkily pulled back. Inside she could hear the sounds of people in for the evening – and a woman's voice calling out to her husband to answer the door as she was cooking.

A few seconds later the door did open and Baroni was faced with a portly middle-aged man. She introduced herself and the glowering captain by her side, apologized for disturbing him that evening, then confirmed with the man that he owned the garage on the edge of the village. She clocked his slightly nervous, shifty stance when she mentioned his premises, but focused on Signoras Morelli and Spencer.

'Did two women in their thirties visit your garage today?' She supplemented her question with a photograph of the two sisters that she had got from the mother's phone.

He glanced down at it and scratched his head. Squinted as if he couldn't quite make it out. Baroni bit back her frustration, prayed Santini would keep his cool.

'Well?'

He pulled a face, sucked in his cheeks. Frowned as he kept on looking at the phone.

If he doesn't answer me in the next ten seconds, thought Baroni, narrowing her eyes, *I'm going to have him investigated for whatever minor misdemeanour he's hiding; fiddling the books most likely. That's got to be at least six seconds*, she thought, mentally counting. *Seven, eight, ni—*

'*Si*, I recognize them.'

She smiled. Just before the bell! Luckily for him.

'What did they come in for?'

'To rent a car.'

'I need the vehicle type and registration plate,' said Baroni, and after the dealer had got the information, she and Captain Santini left.

TWENTY-THREE

Susanna had been awake most of the night. She lay in her bed as the light crept around the edges of the blinds, feeling her heart sink at what she knew was going to be another hot day. She'd need to stay inside; in fact, would probably have to do so for a couple of days. Her skin was still sore from lying out on the patio in the full sun the previous afternoon and her head was pounding.

She slowly swung her legs off the bed and onto the floor. She needed to get to the bathroom and, carefully pulling a towel around her for modesty, she quietly opened the door and crossed over the landing. She locked the bathroom door behind her, relieved not to have seen Matteo.

As she turned, she caught sight of her face in the mirror. It was still red, one side brighter than the other from where it had taken the full force of the sun as it had lowered across the sky. Her hair was still matted and her scalp was sore from the fall. She tentatively raised a hand to touch the wound, felt the skin raised from swelling. Tears clogged her throat but she kept them back; no point feeling sorry for herself. She stared, seeing an ugly woman in front of her. Maybe she should have gone to the hospital after all. But it had been important – no, *essential* – to tell the police about Abby and the danger Ellie was in. She'd needed to do that before attending to her own injuries. Whatever sacrifice it was to herself, it was worth it.

TWENTY-FOUR

From her bed Abby stared through the crack in the curtains at the bright Tuscan sky. The window was open and a gentle breeze lifted the fabric every now and then, revealing glimpses of the hills, shrouded in an early morning blue haze. It was still cool but the brightness of the sun told Abby that, as the day progressed, it would be another scorcher.

With a sense of unease, Abby wondered if her car had been found yet, and what was going on back at her home in Elba. She felt a pang for Matteo that threatened to undo her and tears began to gather in the corners of her eyes. What must he have thought when he came home the previous day? She looked longingly at the phone at the side of the bed but knew she couldn't call him. Not yet.

Abby quietly got up so as not to wake Ellie. She showered away the fitful night's sleep, then as she got dressed she checked the time – it was early, not quite seven. But that meant it wouldn't be long before the buffet downstairs opened, and she could kill for a cup of coffee.

Leaving Ellie asleep, Abby padded quietly down the stairs. In the dining room, the tables from the night before were remade with fresh linen. All stood empty. A long table running down the side of the room was filled with breads, pastries, cheese and cereal. Abby's nose twitched at the smell of coffee and she poured herself a cup and added milk. As she took a sip, the owner of the *pensione* came in with a plate of fresh figs, which he placed on the table. He wished her a *buongiorno* before leaving again.

Abby's attention was drawn to the corner of the room, where a TV was mounted on the wall. It was switched on; a stylishly dressed pair of presenters sat on a sofa, hosting a breakfast news show. She listened to the musical inflections of their language – her Italian was improving but she was still a long way off being fluent. They seemed to be discussing a political issue but she couldn't quite make it all out. Then they took a pause before launching into the next item. Eyes fixed to the screen, Abby almost dropped her cup in horror. She was looking at her own face, Ellie by her side. A fixed smile on their faces as they obeyed Susanna's request to have their photo taken in the restaurant they'd had lunch in only the day before. The newsreader was saying they were missing, that they had left Elba sometime yesterday afternoon and the police wanted to talk to them.

Abby flung her cup onto the nearest table and raced upstairs. She burst into the room just as Ellie was surfacing.

'What's happened?' asked Ellie, still half asleep, nervous at Abby's anxiety.

'We need to leave,' said Abby, starting to stuff Ellie's

things back into her suitcase. She threw over a dress, which Ellie caught. 'Get dressed.'

'What? Can't I have a shower first?'

'There's no time.'

'It won't take long.'

Abby turned and looked at her sister. 'Now, Ellie. We need to leave now. We're on TV,' she said through clenched teeth. 'The owner of the *pensione* is down there – it'll only take a couple of seconds for him to recognize us. That's if he hasn't already and called the police.'

Ellie's eyes widened in fear. 'Oh my God.'

Abby got her own bag and quickly filled it with her things. Ellie, now dressed, was simultaneously shoving her feet into her sandals and flinging her hair up into a ponytail.

The two sisters walked silently down the stairs, bags in hand. Halfway down they could see the *pensione* owner working at the reception desk. The minute they reached the bottom of the staircase, he'd spot them.

Abby waited, unsure of what to do, and then the owner's wife called him from the kitchen. He got up and left the desk.

'Now,' said Abby, hurrying down the rest of the stairs. Ellie followed and they ran for the front door and across the car park to the car.

'Hey!' shouted a voice, and Abby turned to see the *pensione* owner coming after them. 'You need to pay! *Pagate!*'

'Get in, get in!' yelled Abby and she flung their bags in the back as Ellie clambered into the car. Abby started the engine as the *pensione* owner's fingers were grasping at the door handle. Petrified, she wrenched the car into gear and, just as the door began to open, she pulled away in a cloud of dust.

TWENTY-FIVE

'What else did they say?' asked Ellie. She looked anxiously over at the speedometer and wished Abby would slow down a bit.

'I didn't hear anything else. Just that we had gone missing and the police wanted to talk to us urgently.'

'Do you think the guy back there, at the *pensione*, do you think he heard the news?'

'If he hadn't, it's only a matter of time.'

Ellie stretched out her right leg; it still felt numb from the day before and she rubbed the muscles in her thigh.

'You OK?' asked Abby, glancing across.

'Just a bit sore. Must be from the accident,' Ellie said briefly, before changing the subject. 'Where are we going?'

'Don't know,' admitted Abby.

'You do realize we've run again?'

Abby bit her lip. 'Yeah.'

'Makes me look even more guilty.'

'You think we should've stayed? Handed ourselves in?'

'Not "ourselves". Me. I'm the one who pushed her.'

'I drove the car. I'm an accessory.'

Ellie looked across at her sister. 'Funny, isn't it?'

'What?'

'All those years I wanted to spend time with you and you wouldn't let me. Now look at us.'

'Yeah, well, you were annoying,' said Abby.

'I was not!'

'Were to me. You couldn't do a thing wrong. Mum only ever cared about you and your needs.'

'I was *ill*,' said Ellie. 'As you well knew,' she added tartly. She looked over at Abby, who was making a point of concentrating on the road. *Probably avoiding the conversation*, Ellie thought. *Well, I want to have it.*

'I always felt guilty, you know. That Mum seemed to . . .'

'Yes?'

'Prefer me. I used to feel sorry for you but at the same time I loved her attention. Loved her.' She shook her head. 'So screwed up.'

'Yes. But not you.'

'So how much did you hate me?' asked Ellie.

'It wasn't like that,' said Abby, not altogether convincingly.

Ellie raised an eyebrow. 'Come on, I want to know.'

'No, you don't.'

'Let's have it out. Here. Clear the air. It's been hanging over us for, what . . . twenty-eight years?'

They were approaching a small village and Abby slowed the car. 'I think we should get some food,' she said as they passed a bakery. She turned into a side road and parked up. Without waiting for Ellie, she got out of the car.

Ellie exhaled, exasperated. She waited, drumming her

fingers on the dashboard until Abby came back around the corner, hands clutching full paper bags and a bottle of water under each arm.

'Here,' said Abby, handing over one of the bags.

The smell coming from inside was intoxicating, but Ellie snatched both bags from Abby and held them out of reach.

'No,' she said firmly. 'Not until you tell me.'

Abby laughed, unsure. 'Are you serious?'

Ellie moved the bags even further away.

'OK . . .' said Abby. 'Well, sometimes I used to pretend the milk you were pouring on your cornflakes was bleach. Then you'd die and be out of the way and Mum would finally pay me some attention.'

Ellie's jaw dropped. 'Oh my God. That's horrific.'

'I was young. Eight.'

'You wanted me dead?'

'Don't all children wish their siblings dead at one point or another?'

'No!'

'Course they do. You just don't remember.'

Abby wiggled her fingers and, still stunned, Ellie wordlessly handed over the paper bag of food.

'That's the wrong one, said Abby. '*That's* yours.'

'Oh,' Ellie said, and handed Abby the other bag.

As Abby started the car, she looked over. 'Come on,' she insisted, 'you should eat.'

Ellie looked into her own bag. She realized she was starving and, as they drove away, she pulled out the pastry and took a big bite.

TWENTY-SIX

1991

Abby dragged her feet as she followed Oscar's mum down the street. She didn't like it when other people picked her up from school, and she especially didn't like Oscar's mum because she was mean to her dog. She looked at the dog now, at it stopping to do a wee on the pavement, and Oscar's mum was yanking its lead, telling it to 'bloody hurry up', and the poor dog was practically choking, still trying to get its wee out.

Oscar's mum must have seen her look of disapproval because she glared at her and Abby's eyes fell to the ground. Oscar was running on ahead, pretending to shoot at the cars as they drove by. Abby felt angry with him, at the way how he was completely oblivious to how his mother was treating his pet. She briefly wondered about faking a sprained ankle or something, just to buy the dog a bit of time, but knew it would make Oscar's mum even angrier.

'Can we get a bloody move on,' said Oscar's mum, only this time it seemed to be directed at her, and Abby knew she was an irritation, an inconvenience in this woman's life.

Someone different had brought her home every day this week as Ellie was ill and off school. Susanna had been unable to leave the house, as Ellie was always being sick. If she'd had a dad, he would've been able to get her, but she hadn't seen her dad since she was two – or at least that was the age her mother had told her she was when her dad had deserted them all for some 'rich floozy'. Abby wasn't really sure what a floozy was and, in fact, it sounded quite nice. The word had a sort of breezy, floating quality to it. But it was clear from her mother's bitter look of disappointment that a floozy was not a good thing.

Abby hiked up her backpack and strode on after Oscar's mum, the dog now having relieved itself. At least it was Friday, so she didn't need to be palmed off on anyone tomorrow. And it had been a good Friday, thought Abby, smiling to herself. She had a special surprise that she couldn't wait to share with her mum. This was a big one: something really cool that she was convinced would make her mum proud.

They turned the corner into her street and Abby ran on ahead until she got to her house. She lifted the door knocker and hammered it down loudly, both desperate to get away from Oscar's mother and excited to be home and share her secret with her mum.

Her mother opened the door with a frown. 'Abby, for heaven's sake, Ellie's just fallen asleep.'

Abby deflated – how was she supposed to know? – and she silently went into the house while her mother passed the obligatory small talk with Oscar's mum.

As Abby went into the living room she saw her little sister lying on the sofa looking very tired and a bit yellow. A bucket was on the floor beside her. Ellie lifted her head when Abby came in, smiled at her.

'Have you been sick?' asked Abby.

'Five times,' said Ellie.

Abby's eyes widened in awe. This was a new record. The last time Ellie was ill, back when it was snowing, she'd been sick a lot but the most was four times in one day.

'Don't disturb her, Abby.'

Her mother had come into the room and Abby was reminded of the secret she had. She excitedly shrugged her school bag off her shoulders so she could get out what was inside. Her mother went over to Ellie, laid a tender hand on her forehead.

'Do you want Abby to leave the room?' asked Susanna.

Abby halted a moment, hurt. Was she about to be thrown out? But Ellie shook her head. Now Abby had found what she was looking for and she thrust a piece of paper at her mother.

'Mummy, look!' she beamed. 'I got a Head Teacher's Award.'

Her mother glanced across at the certificate but didn't take it. It was *for working hard on her fractions in maths this week*, and it was her third award that year, an exceptional milestone that was celebrated at school with a mention in assembly, and you had to stand up and all the other children clapped you.

The sound of retching interrupted them: Ellie was vomiting into the bucket.

'Out of the way, Abby!' snapped her mother and Abby found herself pushed aside. She watched as her mum held back Ellie's hair and rubbed her back as she threw up nothing more than bile.

Abby waited for the episode to subside and, when it did, Ellie lay back on the sofa, exhausted. *Now Mummy will look at my certificate*, thought Abby, but her mother sat on the sofa next to Ellie, her back to her eldest daughter.

After a few moments it dawned on Abby that her mother wasn't going to turn around – that she'd forgotten all about the certificate. Abby stood there for a moment, engulfed with shame, unsure of what to do. She quietly turned to leave the room. At the doorway she looked back again – just in case – but her mother hadn't even noticed she'd left. Ellie saw her leave, though, and offered up a weak smile, but Abby cut her a look and walked out of the room.

Later that night, Abby lay in her bed listening to the sound of her mother's voice in the next room. She was reading Ellie a story and Abby knew if she went in there, her mother would be lying in Ellie's bed with her, one arm holding the book, the other around her sister. Abby also knew that when her mother had finished she'd come into her room to say goodnight, but she wouldn't read to *her*, not even if Abby asked her to. Her mum always said she could read by herself now and it was Ellie who was having to miss school and needed the help. Except Abby knew that

Susanna had always read to Ellie, even when she hadn't been ill. That was back when Abby was only small, but then her mother's excuse was that Abby would learn quicker if she read herself. Tears pricked as the resentment erupted in her stomach. *Ellie always gets what she wants, always has Mum's attention.*

In that moment Abby had never felt more alone. She put her book down because the tears were making it impossible to see the pages. Angrily, she wiped them away and yearned to be grown-up. It scared her how long away it was – years and years – so she pushed that to the back of her mind and instead thought about how, once she was an adult, she would be able to look after herself and not need anyone. Not even her mother.

TWENTY-SEVEN

Matteo answered his front door to find Lieutenant Colonel Baroni and Captain Santini standing there in the morning sunshine.

'Have you found them?' he immediately asked.

'Yes and no,' said Baroni. 'Can we come in?'

Matteo led them into his kitchen and offered a drink, which they declined. He wanted them to get on with what they had to say. He was about to call in Susanna, who was sitting in the cool of the living room, alternating between reading her magazine and dozing off, but they said they wanted to speak to him first.

'Has Abby called you?' asked Baroni.

'No.'

'You are sure?'

'Of course I'm sure.'

'You understand that you need to tell us if Abby calls you, either on your mobile or here at the house?'

She is really pushing her luck, thought Matteo. He was tired. He had eventually got to work the previous night and had to explain to his superior officer that he suspected his wife had taken his gun. The other part of the story, the part he hadn't admitted to Baroni and Susanna, was that although he'd locked it away, as per the 'custody of weapons' procedure, he'd made a fatal error of judgement.

He'd left the gun loaded.

His boss's face had fallen. He'd had no choice but to hit Matteo with what he'd been dreading. *I'm suspending you from duty with immediate effect.*

It had been a long night and Matteo desperately needed sleep, but Lieutenant Baroni was looking fresh and determined. He wondered if she knew about his mistake with the gun.

'So you've been suspended?' she said, with what he thought was a strong note of disapproval.

He refused to rise to the bait. So she knew. Had to, really, seeing as she was in charge of this investigation.

'Where are Abby's letters?' he asked, pouring himself a coffee. Stupid, really, if he wanted to go to sleep soon, but he felt as if he needed to sharpen his mind for whatever might be coming next.

'We'll return them to you as soon as we can,' she said, and Matteo felt himself get irritated by the stock phrases. He knew he was being fobbed off, damn it. Worse, she knew he knew. He met her cool eyes. She was treating him like a member of the public.

Santini, who had been silent until now, spoke. 'He hasn't answered the question.'

Matteo stiffened. He looked at Santini, saw an expression in his eyes that he didn't like. This was a man who enjoyed his position of authority, who likely abused it. Matteo tried to remember what the question was but was too tired, and anyway, this Santini was winding him up.

'You *understand*,' said Santini, in a patronizing tone, 'that you need to *tell* us if Abby *calls* you.'

Who is this total idiot? thought Matteo. He was about to retort when Susanna came into the room.

'I thought I heard voices,' she said urgently. 'What's going on? Have you found them?'

'Signora Spencer, we have some news of your daughters,' said Lieutenant Colonel Baroni. 'We know they stayed in a *pensione* in Barga last night. This is a small town in central Tuscany,' she explained. 'However, they left very early this morning.'

Susanna clutched her chest in relief. 'Oh my God. So they're OK? Ellie's OK?'

'They appear to be.'

'Where are they now?'

'We don't know. Your daughters stayed at the *pensione* under false names, which of course meant their identification was delayed and consequently gave them time to get away. But we know what vehicle they are driving and we are looking for them.'

Susanna's earlier relief evaporated. 'So they could be anywhere.'

'How are they surviving?' Matteo asked the lieutenant coolly.

'Abby withdrew a significant amount of money yesterday. Ten thousand euros.'

Susanna's eyes widened. 'She always was Miss Money-bags.'

'Which makes it all the more concerning that she didn't pay the *pensione* owner for the night's stay. In fact, both she and Ellie ran out on him this morning, not even stopping when he chased them.'

'Why would they do that?' asked Matteo.

'We don't know for certain. It's possible they thought they had been recognized. They were clearly in a hurry to get away.'

'We know they don't have their mobiles with them as we were able to track these to a street bin near the bank where Abby withdrew the cash. I would like to reassure you that we're very concerned for the safety of your daughters and we're doing everything we can to find them.'

The Carabinieri left soon after and, feeling utterly exhausted, Matteo went outside to the terrace and collapsed into a chair. He couldn't understand what was happening, how his wife whom he loved had suddenly become a person he didn't recognize. Hearing a sound behind him, he looked up. Susanna was standing in the patio doorway, staying in the safety of the shade.

'I know it's hard,' she said, 'to hear these terrible things about Abby. Trust me, as a mother it's hard to hear them too, but I have had a little longer to get used to it.'

She paused, waiting to see if he was going to speak, but he didn't know what to say.

'I just wanted to say how very sorry I am,' she said softly, before turning to go back inside.

Matteo stayed on the terrace, staring up at the sky, knowing he should go to bed, knowing sleep would be impossible.

Susanna watched Matteo from the shelter of the living room and knew he'd be struggling to take everything in. It was hard to learn that the person you fell in love with was in actual fact going to let you down. Become someone who would lie to you and betray you. She knew this from personal experience. Susanna shook her head in sympathy, then moved out of the room and went upstairs. She closed her bedroom door softly behind her and went over to the window that looked out over the terrace. Matteo was still there, sitting in the chair. Making sure her window was shut, Susanna picked her phone up from the bedside table.

TWENTY-EIGHT

It was easy to allow herself to become preoccupied with the task of driving. When Abby had to keep her eyes fixed on the road, slow at tight bends, change gear, check mirrors, she didn't have time to think about anything else. All she had to do was keep moving ahead.

Abby had followed the curve of Italy's coastline, heading west. They had long since left behind the Tuscan hills and the road signs had been changing for a while. New cities were posted: Genoa, Sanremo, Monaco, Nice. They'd deliberately stuck to the smaller roads and Abby knew that when she got to France there was no real border control; she would be able to drive through.

Except she also knew she wouldn't be able to avoid cameras. There may not be passport checks, but automatic number plate recognition for every vehicle that went across the border would be routine. And there was nothing she could do about it.

Ellie had been silent for much of the journey. Abby had glanced over every now and then and seen she was just watching the landscape slide by, not really paying any attention. As they got to the French border, however, Ellie sat up in shock as she realized where they were.

'Just relax and don't say anything stupid,' said Abby anxiously as they slowed to the speed limit. Up ahead was a police station. Armed officials stood on either side of the road, patrolling the vehicles that drove past. Would their number plate ping on the system? Would one of the officers raise a hand and force them to stop? Sweat beaded on her upper lip but she didn't want to draw attention to herself by wiping it away.

Abby tried to look nonchalant as she passed the police officers. A few seconds later they crossed into France. Abby realized she'd been holding her breath and exhaled loudly.

'Can I speak now?' asked Ellie, through gritted teeth.

Abby glanced behind in her mirror, saw the police station receding into the distance. 'Sure.'

'Where are we going? I mean, we can't just keep on driving.'

Abby didn't need to look at her sister to know she was about to kick off. It seemed safer not to answer.

'What next? Spain? Portugal? We keep on going until we fall off the edge of Europe into the Atlantic?'

Again, Abby didn't answer.

'We need to stop!' Ellie smacked her hand on the dashboard for emphasis.

'And do what?' said Abby.

'I don't know. Something! Anything!'

'Neither of those suggestions are particularly detailed, or helpful.'

'You always were patronizing.'

Abby looked taken aback. 'Who, me?'

'Yes, you! Always thinking you're better.'

'I don't.'

'Could have fooled me.'

Abby was trying to keep her patience. 'Look, I don't know what to do for the best. I've never been in this . . . situation before.'

'What do you mean by that?'

'What?'

'*Situation*.'

'You know.'

'I want you to say it.'

'Seriously?' asked Abby, exasperated.

'Yes. Go on, say it.'

'Oh, for God's sake. Where my sister has killed my mother!'

Ellie took a sharp intake of breath. 'Well, thanks very much. You . . . you're so heartless. Always were. Got no feeling.'

'Maybe I had it squeezed out of me as a child by a mother who didn't care.'

Abby suddenly took a left turn, heading south towards the French coast. Somehow she felt better about changing the road she was on every now and then. She looked up in her mirrors, just to check she was alone, but instead of the reassurance of an empty road, her heart began to race.

'*Shit!*' she said, swiftly followed by an urgent, 'Don't look behind.'

Ellie, who had half turned her head, stopped in alarm. 'What is it?'

'Police. Behind us.'

'Oh my God! Are they here for us?'

'I don't know. *Shit.*' They were nearing a roundabout where there were three other exits – a two in three chance of losing them. Abby slowed and did a perfect manoeuvre at the first exit, heading for a small town. Then she surreptitiously checked her mirrors again.

'Have they gone?' asked Ellie nervously.

'No.'

'But they're French police, right? Not Italian?'

'Jesus, Ellie, you think they'll forget about us? You think they don't have *translators*?'

'All right, no need to be so bloody superior.'

They were nearing the town now and Abby did her best to keep calm. *Just a little further. Don't look suspicious.* She continued until she came to the town centre, and then casually turned down a side street.

'I don't believe it,' she said.

Ellie glanced in her side mirror, started at what she saw. 'They're still following us, Abby. What do we do?'

'It's OK. Keep calm.' She could feel the sweat pooling on her back. Her palms were slippery on the steering wheel as she turned again. *Please don't let them follow*, she prayed, and as her eyes flicked to the mirror she almost cried with relief when she saw them drive on.

'Have they gone?' asked Ellie.

Abby pulled over. She lifted herself from her seat and peered out the back of the car, just to be sure. 'Thank God.' She turned back around and saw Ellie was slumped in her seat, her forehead resting against the dashboard, her hands protectively over her head. After a moment, Abby saw her sister's shoulders heaving. Then the sounds came and Ellie was openly weeping – deep, inconsolable sobs that caught in her throat.

Abby tentatively placed a hand on her shoulder. 'It's OK. They've gone now.'

But Ellie kept on crying. Abby tightened her grip, turned it into an awkward one-armed hug. To her surprise, Ellie lifted her face from the dashboard, her eyes red and streaming with tears, and in them Abby caught a raw, unrestrained grief. Ellie put her arms around Abby's neck, clung to her.

'I miss her, Abby, I miss her so much.'

A bolt of realization froze Abby for a moment. *Susanna*. Then she held her little sister, feeling the shuddering, great rifts of grief escaping from her body. They stayed there a while, parked up on the edge of a small square, neither of them noticing the man watching from the bench by the fountain.

Crying was normal, it was acceptable, especially after everything Ellie had gone through, but there was a limit, thought Abby, and just as she was starting to think that it had been going on long enough, and she was mentally phrasing a pep talk, Ellie peeled herself away and apologized.

Abby handed her a tissue. 'Don't be silly. There's nothing to be sorry for.'

'I think it's all been a lot to contend with . . .'

Ellie looked so down, Abby squeezed her hand. She glanced up the street, saw a *boulangerie*.

'I think we could both do with a strong coffee, don't you?'

Ellie nodded and Abby jumped out of the car. 'I'll be back in a minute,' she said, and crossed the road into the little shop.

Ellie watched her sister disappear into the *boulangerie* and suddenly felt a desperate need to stretch her own legs. She'd been in the car for hours and, tugging at the door handle, she stepped out with a sense of freedom and relief. It felt good to walk, as she headed over to the little square, where she dipped her hands in the fountain and looked up at a cherub above her head, who poured water from his stone urn.

The water was cool and clear and Ellie felt a strong urge to splash some on her face and neck. She scooped up the water and sighed as it soothed her hot, reddened eyes.

'It's meant to have healing properties.'

Ellie swung round, wiping away the water dripping from her face. A man, dressed in Lycra, was sitting on the bench, his forearms resting on his thighs as he watched her. A bike was propped against the side of the seat.

Her first thought was whether or not he was talking to her, but a quick glance around confirmed that he was.

'Healing in what way?'

The man held up his phone. 'Anyway you like, according to this website. Flu, sprained ankle . . . broken heart.'

Ellie was distracted from trying to place his accent (*Norwegian? Swedish?*) by his last comment. Had he seen her crying? Probably. Was that what he thought was wrong with her? Broken heart? She was too drained to care. She looked a little closer at him; he was young, younger than her, she thought, although not by much. She noticed his biceps and quads. He was fit.

She nodded at his bike. 'You on a trip?'

'Pilgrimage.'

'Seriously?'

'Of sorts. I've cycled down from Oslo.' (*So, Norwegian then*, thought Ellie.) 'I'm following the Méditerranée a Vélo cycle route across southern France.'

'Why?'

'Because it's so scenic. And safer than the motorway.'

'No, I mean, why are you crossing southern France? What's the pilgrimage?'

He smiled at her then, a fleeting, sad smile, she thought, before it vanished.

'That's not the pilgrimage.'

'I'm confused.'

'That's just a cool cycle ride. The pilgrimage is across northern Spain. The Camino de Santiago. I get a train to the start of the trail.'

'Oh right,' said Ellie, not really following.

The man moved up on the bench and patted the space next to him. 'I'm Fredrik.'

Ellie hesitated, but then thought, *Might as well be friendly.* 'Ellie,' she replied, as she sat next to him. He really was extremely good-looking. Even though he was sitting down she could tell by the length of his legs that he was tall. There was a clear tan line where his shorts had ridden up – from all those days of cycling, she thought. And his blue eyes shone in creases that went from tan to white, depending on whether or not he was smiling.

'So, what's your story?' he asked.

Ellie pondered. 'Just on a little road trip.'

'Yeah?'

'Yeah. Thought I'd explore a bit of southern France.'

'Which bits?'

Suddenly she couldn't think. She smiled blankly at him while she tried to remember some place, any place – good God, she was a *teacher!* She shrugged. 'Any bits.'

He was amused. 'Sorry,' he said, 'none of my business.'

'No,' said Ellie.

'You don't have to tell me if you're an international bank robber.'

'No, I don't.'

'Or a spy.'

'As then I'd have to kill you.'

He laughed. 'So let's just say you wanted to get out and about for the hell of it. Take in the scenery.'

'Exactly.'

He was smiling in a way that told Ellie he was deeply intrigued by her story.

'Seems like we're both on a pilgrimage,' he said.

Ellie opened her mouth to correct him but then decided against it.

'I'm hoping mine helps me get a little perspective. Kind of handy when life throws some curveballs at you.' He paused, searched her face. 'You know what I mean?'

Ellie nodded. He was curious, maybe even suspected that something was up, but he wasn't going to ask and she was relieved. And his words were kind, but he had no idea of the extent of the mess she was in. She was unable to see how she might ever be able to come to terms with what had happened to her over the last twenty-four hours.

'Which way are you headed?' asked Fredrik.

Ellie pointed in the direction the car was facing. 'That way.'

'West?'

She looked at him, impressed. How could he tell so quickly?

He held up his phone in confession. 'Compass app. Been checking my route.'

'Cheat. So, what about you? Where's next?'

He leaned closer to her and pointed across the square, where a road ran off. 'That way. Two hours and forty kilometres later I'll be in Antibes.'

'Antibes,' sighed Ellie. 'Impressionist heaven.'

Fredrik looked at his bike. 'If only it were a tandem . . .'

She laughed.

'There's a lady over there who looks quite fierce,' said Fredrik, nudging her shoulder.

She turned to see Abby had just come out of the *boulangerie*, two coffees in her hands, and was looking over at them suspiciously.

'My sister,' she said, and was suddenly aware that the lightness she'd briefly felt was rapidly evaporating. She had an urge to do something reckless, just get on the back of this man's bike and disappear to Antibes, but of course this was a fantasy.

'If you give me your number, I could send you a picture? Picasso Museum by the sea?'

Ellie turned to face him, taken aback.

He held up an apologetic hand. 'Or not. Didn't mean to step out of line.'

She could sense Abby approaching, and her sister's encroaching presence was overbearing. In a matter of minutes they'd be back in the car going who knew where with Abby calling all the shots, and Ellie wanted to grab hold of a lifeline. She rattled off her number, and watched as Fredrik typed it into his phone, just as Abby arrived.

'One cappuccino,' she said, handing over one of the drinks.

'Thanks,' said Ellie.

'Who's this?'

'Fredrik. From Norway. Cycling across France.'

'That's great. We need to get going,' said Abby brusquely before turning and heading back to the car.

Ellie sighed. 'Sorry about her. She's . . . got a lot on her mind.'

'Ellie!' called Abby sharply.

'Jeez.' Ellie stood, held out her hand. 'It was very nice to meet you.' Fredrik stood too, keeping hold of her hand, then seemed to make a sudden decision and leaned in and kissed her cheek.

'You too. Hope it's not as serious as you think.'

Ellie held his gaze. 'Hope you find your perspective.'

'Ellie!'

Ellie rolled her eyes but turned and headed towards Abby, who was sitting in the car, engine running. As she made her way across the square, she looked back at Fredrik who, she was pleased to see, watched her all the way.

'Finally!' said Abby, pulling away as Ellie belted up.

'I wasn't that long,' said Ellie, breaking into a smile as she turned and waved to Fredrik. Then Abby left the square and she could see him no more.

'Oh!' she exclaimed.

'What?'

She'd given Fredrik her number but she no longer had her phone! What an idiot. She'd completely forgotten Abby had ditched it. Did she explain? Taking one look at her sister, she thought it best not to. Ellie felt a sadness cloud over her; seemed she wouldn't get any pictures of Antibes after all.

'Nothing. Just spilled some coffee,' she said, brushing away an imaginary spot off her dress.

'So, what was all that about? He rescuing a damsel in distress?'

'We were just talking. Passing the time of day.'

'You do realize it's probably better not to speak to anyone. Let alone cosy up to some strange man.'

Ellie paused, then levelled her gaze at her sister. 'Oh, I see what this is about.'

'What does that mean?'

'You. Being all huffy. Not liking the fact I'm . . .'

'What?' goaded Abby.

'I can't help it if some men are attracted to me, Abby.'

'You make it sound as if that little encounter there was nothing to do with you.'

'Fredrik asked me over to the bench, actually.'

'You were *flirting*.'

'Oh, for God's sake.'

'It's like you can't help yourself.'

'Are we really still going on about this? It was years ago. You two had broken up.'

'Only because you decided you wanted him for yourself.'

Not true, thought Ellie angrily. There had been a man – Jon – whom Abby had been dating. They'd all been so young, and she had been insensitive, but Abby and Jon weren't dating when Jon had asked her, Ellie, out. She glanced across; God, her big sister looked so self-righteous.

'You know, when the police got to your house, they wouldn't know,' said Ellie.

'Wouldn't know what?'

'If it was me or you.'

'What . . . ?'

'Who pushed Mum. No one saw. Could've been you.'

It had the desired effect. Abby was furious, but could do

nothing other than continue driving. 'You want to walk?' she managed.

Ellie gave a tiny smile. 'I'm just saying.' She turned her head and looked out of the window. Didn't want to rub it in too much.

Sorry, Mum, she offered up in her head. *But sometimes she drives me so mad . . .*

TWENTY-NINE

1993

The long metal spike glinted in the bright overhead lights and Ellie whimpered as it pierced the tender inside of her elbow, a place that had been punctured so many times she felt the accumulative effect of what seemed like a thousand needle jabs. She knew she wasn't supposed to cry, she was supposed to be 'brave' and 'not make a fuss,' but it stung and she could see the blood – her blood – filling the vial, and it made her feel as if something was wrong with her, so very wrong, and the tears were more from fear than pain. She turned her head into her mother's arm and wept, knowing she had no control over what these people were doing to her body, and then the nurse said it was all finished and she was sticking a plaster over where the needle had been. Ellie watched weakly as the nurse wrote on sticky labels and attached them to several vials of her blood.

'Mummy?' she asked, turning to Susanna.

Her mother smiled. 'Yes?'

'Am I going to die?'

Ellie saw her mother's face contract in a strange way,

almost as if she had forgotten to breathe or something, and then she smiled her biggest smile and said, 'Don't be silly.' Ellie didn't know whether to believe her or not. She knew dying was what happened to really ill people and you stopped moving – a bit like the bird that flew into the window a few days ago with a loud bang, even though it was only a tiny little thing. It fell onto the patio on its back with its stick-like legs up in the air. Her mum had put on a pair of rubber gloves and picked it up, holding it at a distance, then she'd put it in the rubbish bin. Ellie had been sad about it lost there in amongst all the stinky rubbish in the dark and hoped that even though it was dead it wasn't too scared.

They caught the bus home and Ellie found herself alone while her mum went into the kitchen to make some lunch. She sat on the sofa feeling the plaster pull at her skin and hated it because it reminded her of how she was different. The patio doors were open and she got up and stood on the sill, rocking her feet back and forth until a sound drew her into the garden, pulling her like a magnet.

A distant collective laughter: four hundred children in a playground on their lunch break, playing, shouting, screaming. Ellie strained to hear the detail – the rules of the games they were enacting, the chants from the skipping songs – but as with every other time she'd come out here to try and be a part of it, she was just too far away. Usually she liked to stay outside to listen and imagine herself in the playground, running in a game of Tag so fast she'd never get caught, but today it made her feel trapped in her tiny square of a garden where she couldn't see over the hedge, and she was feeling so angry she went back inside and lay on the floor.

It wasn't fair. She hated being ill, hated the sickness, the doctors, the needles. She hated being alone at home when all the other children got to go to school and play and have fun. She hated everything.

As she tipped her head listlessly to one side she spied something under the sofa: a pile of books she'd shoved under there the day before, books her mother had made her get from the library. She hadn't wanted to pick out any but Susanna had got cross and told her to hurry up, so she'd just taken the top four from the pile. Ellie thrust an arm through the dust, retrieved the one nearest to her and pulled it closer. There wasn't much point really and she didn't know why she was doing it except that there was nothing better to do. There it lay, close to her cheek. She didn't bother opening it up; instead she stared at the picture on the front: a map.

Her mother came into the room.

'What are you doing on the floor?' asked Susanna, bustling over and holding out a hand, but Ellie refused to take it.

Susanna glanced down at the book. '*Atlas*,' she read, '*A journey around Europe's Biggest, Tallest, Longest*.' She picked it up, flicked it open. 'Ooh, Hungary. Home to the Danube, Europe's second-longest river. Fun fact: the Danube passes through ten countries.'

Ellie was barely listening; she could still hear the playground joy filtering in through the patio doors.

Susanna turned to another page. 'Spain,' she read. 'Home to the Alhambra, a royal palace.'

The word 'palace' filtered into Ellie's consciousness. She liked palaces. And princesses.

'The Sultana's Garden, one of the oldest surviving Moorish gardens,' read Susanna.

Hmm, though Ellie. *A garden where they grow sultanas.* She liked sultanas. More than raisins. They were squidgier.

'Oh, and what's this?' said Susanna, moving her finger across the page. 'The Vixía Herbeira cliffs. Six hundred and twenty-one metres high. Wow,' she exclaimed, 'it says here that's nearly six times the height of the White Cliffs of Dover!'

Ellie didn't know about the White Cliffs of Dover but her mother's voice held enough excitement for her to sit up. She peered over at the book and Susanna turned it so the photograph was facing her. Ellie's eyes widened; it was so high! She felt a flutter in her belly and pulled the book closer.

'*If you don't go while alive, you must go after death, goes the saying*,' read Susanna.

'What does that mean, Mummy?'

'It's probably a legend or something. It must mean it's so good, you absolutely mustn't miss it.'

Ellie nodded and thought for a moment. 'One day, when I'm better, can I go there?'

'Of course,' said Susanna. 'You can go wherever you like.' Her mother handed her the book. 'You keep on looking while I check the macaroni cheese.'

As Susanna left the room, Ellie looked back at the cliffs.

The image stirred her again, something strong and powerful that she found hard to describe, but one thing she did know for certain was that she liked how it made her feel. And then it came to her. The feeling was escape.

She flicked through more pages, unable to read much of the text, but it mattered less now. It was the pictures that spoke to her, that transported her and took her away from her lonely place in the living room.

One day, Ellie thought, she would go to these places in this book. When the book was due back at the library, Ellie asked if they could keep it for longer. It was renewed. Again and again.

THIRTY

They drove through the heat of the middle of the day, the roof down as they stuck to the minor roads that jumped in and around the coast for much of the Côte d'Azur, skirting around Monaco, Nice, Cannes, places whose very names conjured up glamour and allure. In another time, it would have been the perfect adventure, cruising through some of the most beautiful places in France, except Abby and Ellie had to avoid the towns themselves, only occasionally getting a distant glimpse of shiny dense high-rises and luxury villas perched on cliffs. Between the towns they would travel along narrow roads lined with maquis, roads that would bend to dramatically reveal a hidden cove, flanked by palms and rocks, everything bathed in the bright Mediterranean light.

Ellie's eyelids began to droop. She was feeling so sleepy; in fact, her whole body ached with fatigue. She forced her eyes open and, for a moment, the view of the coast on her left was partly missing. The sea appeared to suddenly cut off, right at the periphery of her field of vision. Alarmed, she blinked, but her sight stubbornly wouldn't adjust. She closed her eyes, waited a few seconds, then slowly opened them. Gradually, as she kept her head very still, the images went back to normal. She sat still for a moment, unsettled.

'Are you OK?' asked Abby. 'You look a bit pale.'

Ellie carefully shifted her gaze to her sister. 'Yeah. Think so. Everything just got a bit weird there for a minute.'

'Probably need some food,' said Abby. 'We'll find a place to stop.'

'We need to find help,' said Ellie. 'We can't just keep on driving.'

'I know but . . .' Abby's voice suddenly took on an edge of excitement.

'What?'

'I have a friend, back in London. He's a lawyer. Criminal.'

Ellie sat up. 'How come you didn't mention him before?'

'I've only just remembered him. It's been a year since we were in touch.'

How could you forget a friend like that, right now? thought Ellie. Her sister clocked the look on her face.

'Sorry, OK? I've had a lot on my mind. When we stop for food, I'll get a phone as well. Jamie might be able to make this whole nightmare a little bit easier to manage.'

'Like how?'

'I don't know, give us some advice maybe. It's worth a try. He's a good guy.'

They had moved inland and Abby saw a sign for a retail park. They pulled off at the roundabout and headed towards the mammoth shopping area, parking up outside an electrical store.

'I'll get a pay-as-you-go,' said Abby. She nodded at another huge shop further along. 'Then we can go to the supermarket.'

Ellie watched as Abby went through the sliding glass doors of the phone shop and then could see her no more. She stretched out her numb legs, and knew she needed to get out of the car. As she put her foot down on the tarmac, her leg unexpectedly gave way and she grabbed hold of the car door to steady herself. Ellie took a moment to recover and, leaning against the door, she looked across at the phone shop. She'd like to buy a phone herself but knew her credit card would almost certainly be declined. Even if she did buy one, she wouldn't be able to give Fredrik the new number. That moment had gone. She wondered where he was on his cycle route. They must have passed him long ago, unknowingly been mere miles from a tall, blond Norwegian man peddling through the French countryside. Perhaps he had stopped for lunch. He was sitting in a village square like the one she'd met him in, eating a baguette. She wondered if he'd thought about her at all since they'd parted that morning.

She sighed and gazed around at the soulless car park. A few shoppers pushed giant trolleys from the supermarket, laden with food. Cars pulled in and out of spaces, their occupants on the hunt for new electricals or sofas. To the side of the phone shop was a row of plastic cubicles, each with a payphone in it. They were all empty, as of course no one really used public phones anymore. It was then that Ellie had the idea. She'd call her old mobile, see if Fredrik had rung her and left a message. It was unlikely – after all, only a few hours had passed – but it gave her something to do while she was waiting for Abby.

She walked across the car park and, digging some change out of her purse, she dialled her own number. It went straight to voicemail and she intercepted the recorded message by typing in her access code. To her delight the automated voice informed her she had two new messages. She contained her hope – they were most likely her bank telling her she needed to get in touch about her overdraft.

'*Message one*,' said the automated voice, '*received today at twelve forty-seven p.m.*' That was only an hour ago, thought Ellie. Her heart leaped as the message kicked in.

'Hey, Ellie, it's Fredrik. We met this morning, at the fountain. I just wanted to say hi again. I'm sitting on a bench, a different one with a different view. I'm at the top of some hills and the road is snaking back down in a switchback all the way to the sea. It's a shame you're not here as well. Anyway, it would be great if you wanted to call.' As he relayed off his number, Ellie frantically scrabbled around in her bag for a pen and paper and wrote it down. *He rang, he rang!* Her heart sang and she mentally checked her change – she probably had enough to call him back, although maybe she could try the phone shop after all, see if she might be able to swing it with her card. She carefully saved Fredrik's message, following the robotic instructions in her ear.

'*Message two*,' continued the voice, '*received today at ten seventeen a.m.*' This would be the bank one, thought

Ellie, but she was so euphoric from Fredrik's call, she didn't care.

'Ellie, it's me. Your mum. You need to call me as soon as you get this. Don't tell Abby.'

Ellie was vaguely aware of the ground reaching up, or was she falling? Then everything blacked out.

THIRTY-ONE

She came around to a blurry hand waving in front of her face. Ellie, eyes half open, saw two identical middle-aged women looking at her with concern in their eyes. As she blinked, the two women morphed into one and this woman was babbling to her in French.

Confused, Ellie tried to make sense of where she was. Her legs were splayed awkwardly and she instinctively pulled her skirt down so it covered her. *What am I doing on the ground?* Feeling vulnerable, she tried to get up but her head began to spin. The woman helped her but Ellie could only manage as far as sitting before she had to rest her back against the wall, as she tried to contain an onset of nausea.

'*Merci*,' she managed weakly to the woman, who on hearing Ellie's poor command of her language immediately switched to English.

'Are you OK? I saw you faint.' She fussed and held out a bottle of water that Ellie took automatically. She drank, just as the woman was insisting. Then in a swift, breathless moment, she remembered.

Her mother had left her a message. Her *dead* mother.

It couldn't be, thought Ellie. It's madness. Her brain scrambled for some logical explanation – triumphantly relieved when she reasoned that the call must have been made *before* the accident.

But the relief was short-lived. Ellie remembered. The message had been left at quarter past ten that morning. Susanna had died on the terrace of Abby's house yesterday. Ellie thought hard. Was it definitely her mum's voice she'd heard? Yes, she was certain she'd recognize it anywhere.

'Shall I call a doctor?' the woman asked in her heavily accented English.

Ellie plastered on a smile of what she hoped was reassurance. 'No, thank you. I'm fine. I think it must have been the heat.'

She let the woman help her to her feet and, steadying herself against the wall, she brushed herself down.

Her mother had called her.

She started to walk back towards the car, the woman still insisting on staying with her. Ellie could see Abby making her way over, a plastic bag in her hand with the phone shop's logo on it. She was frowning at Ellie and quickened her pace.

'What happened?' Abby asked as she hurried up to them.

Abby was staring at her and Ellie felt her pulse quicken. She closed her eyes a moment, still bewildered. Aware she was being watched by her sister, she lifted her head, tried to rearrange her features into something resembling normality. 'Nothing. Just passed out for a moment. Overheated. This nice lady helped me out.'

'You look as white as a sheet,' said Abby, placing a hand on her arm. She turned to the lady. 'Thank you so much. I'm her sister. I'll take care of her.'

'She needs to drink,' said the French woman.

'Absolutely,' said Abby. 'And some shade.'

While they discussed her recuperation, Ellie indicated the hypermarket. 'I think I might just use the bathroom,' she said.

She went to head off but Abby said a swift goodbye to the French woman and then was by her side, insisting on escorting her. Ellie's head was still spinning and she wanted to be alone, to think. *Mum said not to tell Abby she'd called.* None of it made any sense.

As they hit the wall of air conditioning inside the shop, Ellie knew what she had to do.

'Abby, is there any chance you could get me something to eat?' She waved towards the maze of aisles. 'I've got a pounding headache. I think some food will help.'

'Are you sure? I don't want to leave you.'

Ellie smiled. 'I'll be fine.' She spoke as firmly as she could. 'I'm just going to use the ladies, then I'll wait for you by those seats.' She pointed to a row of bright green plastic seating just around the corner from the supermarket entrance. Next to them she could see a payphone.

'OK. I'll be as quick as I can,' said Abby.

'Honestly, don't rush,' said Ellie. She went towards the toilets and looked back to see Abby go through the turnstile into the shopping area. As soon as Abby had been swallowed up by one of the aisles, Ellie doubled back on herself and hurried towards the public phone. Hands shaking, she dialled her mother's number. It rang for three rings, four, five, and Ellie thought she'd imagined it, the whole message – it was her mind playing tricks on her, some sort of response to her grief and shock – when suddenly—

'Hello?'

Ellie felt the room spin. 'Mum?' she whispered.

'Ellie! Oh my God, it's really you. Are you all right? Are you hurt?'

'No . . . I'm fine.'

'I can't believe you're there. You're alive. Thank God.'

Ellie shook her head. 'Of course I'm alive.' She felt a surge of relief, of joy. 'It's you who . . . We thought something awful had happened, Mum. When you fell. We thought . . . Abby said you'd died.'

There was a silence at the other end of the phone.

'She did?' her mother said eventually.

'Yes. I mean, we both thought it. It was so *terrible* and . . . well, then Abby told me to get in the car. We've been driving—'

'Ellie, listen to me carefully. Are you listening?'

'Yes.'

'This is a hard thing to say but you need to know. Your sister . . . Abby is a very damaged individual. What she was telling you, yesterday, when we were on the terrace. That awful accusation.' Ellie heard her mother take a breath. 'It wasn't me who poisoned you, Ellie. It was Abby.'

THIRTY-TWO

Ellie grabbed the wall. Her mind felt as if it was splintering into a million pieces.

'What?'

Her mother was speaking deliberately slowly. 'I realize this will be hard to take in. But you must believe me. Abby is the one who poisoned you when you were children.'

Ellie was struggling to absorb it all. 'But she said it was you.'

'She was lying. You must try and understand.' Ellie could hear her mother's strained patience. 'Abby resented you from the day you were born. She still resents you. I'm incredibly worried about her state of mind, about her capacity for lying.'

'Lying?'

'Ellie, you said she told you I was dead.'

'Well, yes, but that was what she thought . . .' protested Ellie.

'And why did she think that? What made her come to that conclusion?'

'She took your pulse . . . Oh my God,' said Ellie, the bottom suddenly falling out of her world.

'Did *you* take my pulse?' asked Susanna.

'No,' whispered Ellie.

'And now she's driven you somewhere. Where are you, Ellie?'

Ellie rested her forehead against the side of the wall. She couldn't process all of this. And then, through the shop's interior glass windows, she could see Abby in the queue at the checkout. It was her sister's turn to be served.

'She's coming.'

'Coming *where*?'

'I'm in a supermarket,' blurted Ellie. 'Abby's getting food.'

'Do not tell her we've spoken,' said Susanna. 'If she knows I'm alive, she'll know I've told you the truth. For God's sake, don't tell her, Ellie.'

'I'm . . . I need to go.'

'Call me back. You need to call me back as soon as you can. And don't take anything she gives you. Promise me,' urged Susanna.

Ellie saw Abby finish packing the shopping, saw her hand over some cash.

'Ellie? Ellie! Are you there? Promise me!'

'I'll call you, Mum. As soon as I can.' And then Ellie hung up. She moved away from the phone to the green plastic seats. She sat down, her world now tipped on another axis.

'Here,' said Abby, as she approached. In her hand were two tablets. 'I got you these.'

Ellie started and looked up at her sister, as if seeing her for the first time.

'Are you OK?' asked Abby. 'I knew I shouldn't have left you.' She put the two tablets into Ellie's hand. Passed her a bottle of water. 'Take them.'

'What are they?' asked Ellie faintly.

'They'll make you feel better.'

Ellie looked down. Had she seen Abby push the tablets out of a blister pack? She was suddenly aware she hadn't. She stared at them.

An alarm sounded in the shop, loud and aggressive, catching their attention. Someone's purchase had set off the sensors at the exit and they had their bag open, letting the security guard check it.

Ellie dropped the tablets on the floor. They bounced a short distance from her. Quickly, she shifted her foot so that she covered them up, then took a swig of water, just as Abby turned back around. Seeing Ellie swallow, Abby smiled approvingly. 'Good. Are you OK to get going?'

Ellie nodded and stood up. She sensed the hardness of the tablets under her shoe and, as she lowered her weight onto them, felt them crumble to dust.

THIRTY-THREE

Ellie sat motionless in the car, aware of Abby busying beside her, putting the shopping bag on the back seat, breaking off some baguette and taking out a wheel of cheese. She tore open a bag of plastic cutlery, spread some of the camembert on the bread and handed it over.

Ellie viewed it distantly.

'Eat,' instructed Abby, and Ellie took the sandwich her sister proffered.

'The man in the phone shop set this up so it's good to go,' said Abby, taking the new phone out of the bag.

Ellie watched as her sister pushed a few buttons.

'I've got an old email here somewhere, from Jamie's work account. I'm sure it has his mobile on it. Bingo!' said Abby triumphantly, and she dialled. While the phone was ringing, she looked sternly over at Ellie and indicated the baguette.

Ellie looked down at the crusty bread with its creamy filling. Abby, phone to her ear, was watching her expectantly. Ellie slowly lifted the bread to her mouth, waiting for Abby to turn away, but she didn't. There was nowhere else for her jaw to go but down and she bit into the baguette, the cheese oozing through her teeth. She started chewing, the mouthful seeming to last forever, then she swallowed, forcing it down her throat.

Abby tutted and Ellie looked up to see her sister mouth, 'Answerphone.'

'Hi, Jamie, it's Abby Spencer,' she said in a bright voice. 'It's been a while . . . I'm actually in a bit of a fix over something and could do with some advice. Please could you call me?' She paused. 'As soon as you can,' she added, the urgency finally breaking into her voice. She left her number and hung up.

'He'll call back,' she said, only it seemed more to reassure herself than anything. Then she leaned over the back again, got something else out of the shopping bag.

'Here,' she said, handing Ellie a road map. 'This'll make it easier to follow the minor roads; keep us off radar.'

Ellie took it wordlessly.

'Are you sure you're OK?' asked Abby, frowning.

Ellie mentally shook herself. She had to get a grip. 'Fine,' she muttered. She opened the map and located where they were.

'We just have to buy some time until Jamie calls us back,' said Abby, pulling away from the car park.

Do we? Mum isn't dead after all, thought Ellie. *But then, maybe Abby already knows that.* What if she'd pretended that she couldn't feel their mother's pulse? Lied about her being dead? She stole a glance at her sister. Was she a pathological liar?

'Where am I going?' asked Abby as they came to a roundabout.

Ellie looked down at the map. *Keep to the minor roads.* 'Third exit.'

Abby continued driving. 'Ellie, what do you know about this stuff?'

'What stuff?'

'Avoiding the police. Not getting caught. We've just been in that shopping centre. Must be CCTV everywhere. Except, of course, they don't know where we are.'

Ellie's stomach lurched. The payphone she'd just called her mother from – Susanna would now have a record of it on her mobile. She felt certain the police would be able to trace their location.

'Nothing,' she said. 'I don't know anything.'

'OK. We just keep driving for as long as possible. Until we can speak to Jamie.'

And then what? thought Ellie anxiously. What would happen next? Who was Jamie, anyway? Had her sister actually called a Jamie? Did he even exist? Her mind was blurring with uncertainty as she tried to still the fear growing in her stomach. But there was one thing she knew for sure. Her mother had sounded genuinely scared on the phone.

THIRTY-FOUR

1993

Snap! went the girl's gum as she popped it against her teeth. Then she chewed, oblivious to the noises she was making, oblivious to anything, including Abby, who was sitting on a seat in the reception area of East Surrey Radio, staring at this exotic being with pink hair and black fingernails. She had her nose pierced and also, Abby had noticed, wide-eyed, when the girl had stood to reach a file behind the desk, her *belly button*. There was something about this receptionist girl that Abby admired: her obvious independence, her freedom to do what she wanted.

Seeing this girl was the only upside of being here. Abby hadn't wanted to come. She wasn't allowed in the recording studio and had to sit out here with nothing to do. She'd begged to be allowed to stay at home by herself but her mum had refused. 'Not until secondary school,' she'd said. Abby couldn't wait: only one more year.

The radio was on, loud, and The Bluebells finished singing 'Young At Heart'.

'So, back to our guests, Ellie Spencer and her mum,

Susanna,' said the jaunty DJ. 'So, tell me, Ellie, what would it mean for you to go to Disneyland?'

Abby heard Ellie inhale, breathless with anticipation.

'It would be amazing.'

'It certainly would,' said the DJ. 'And this little girl, who has been sick for the last two years, would have a dream come true.'

It's my dream too, thought Abby, indignant. She hadn't dared believe it when her mum said people had started to raise money for a holiday because Ellie was so ill. The local paper had run an article and the school had had a bake sale. *Disneyland!* It had been her secret dream for years and she wanted to go so much it hurt.

'Mum,' said the DJ, 'how much do you think she deserves it?'

'Oh, she's so brave,' said Susanna. 'She never complains.'

That's a lie.

'And she's been through so much. I've lost count of the number of hospital visits she's had.'

'We have a caller,' announced the DJ. 'Christine, from Reigate. Go ahead, Christine.'

'I just wanted to say I think she's marvellous. I've been listening to your show and I can't believe how that poor girl has coped. And her mother too, it's almost unbearable. And to think they still don't know what it is. To have that sort of illness hanging over you with no end in sight . . . Well, I want to help so I'm giving the last three hundred you need for your holiday fund.'

Collective gasps around the radio station: Susanna and

the DJ in the studio harmonized with Abby and the girl receptionist, who was finally shaken out of her self-absorption.

'That is amazing!' exclaimed the DJ.

'Thank you so much,' said Susanna, her voice cracking with emotion.

'I hope you and Ellie have the most wonderful time,' said the woman. 'You both deserve it.'

What about me? thought Abby, swallowing the lump in her throat. She listened hard but at no point did her mother, her sister or the DJ mention there was another person in this family, currently banished to the reception area, who wanted to go to Disneyland more than life itself.

'Of course it's enough for you as well, Abby,' said Susanna on the bus home. 'What a silly thing to think.'

Abby was hurt. It wasn't that silly. Ellie got everything she wanted. She was ill, and it wasn't that unusual for Abby herself to be an afterthought. But she brushed that aside as she began to fill with a warm glow. *Disneyland, I'm going to Disneyland*, she thought, and she was suddenly overcome with happiness and excitement. *Magic Kingdom! The Typhoon Lagoon!*

'Well, what do you say?' said Susanna.

Abby, brought out of her thoughts, blinked, confused.

'You should be thanking your sister. It's only because of her that this has happened.'

Abby could hear the disapproval in her mother's voice. She leaned over to Ellie and awkwardly hugged her.

'Thanks,' she mumbled. Then she said it again, a bit louder, just in case she was reprimanded. It didn't matter. Disneyland was the single best, most amazing thing to happen in her life, ever. It made up for everything. It meant she even forgave Ellie for monopolizing family life ever since she was born.

Three weeks before they were due to fly, Ellie fell ill again. Susanna was up in the night with her, helping her through her vomiting. Abby lay in bed listening until it subsided and then, when Ellie had quietened, she drifted back to sleep.

The next morning, Susanna sat both of them down for a chat.

'Girls, I know this is going to be disappointing and I'm really sorry, but we're not going to be able to go to Disneyland.'

Ellie promptly burst into tears.

Stricken, Abby looked at her mother – was it true? But she could tell by Susanna's face that it was. She suddenly felt as if her insides had been crushed. She wanted to cry too, to wail and throw herself onto the floor in the hollowed-out little ball that she now felt as if she'd become. But Susanna was busy comforting Ellie and Abby knew if she kicked off too, there would be little sympathy. She'd seen the dark shadows under her mother's eyes that morning. So she was forced to keep her devastation to herself.

'Hush, hush,' said Susanna, stroking Ellie's hair. 'It's not all bad. I'm going to change the tickets to *Euro* Disney just for a couple of days.' She beamed. 'It's brand new. Much better than silly old Florida. Plus, it's much closer to home if you get poorly, which I think is really important, especially as you've not been well.' She paused for effect, on the cusp of a big announcement. 'In fact, we're going to have *two* holidays.'

Ellie finally stopped crying, looked up at her mother in intrigue. Abby narrowed her eyes.

'After Euro Disney, we're going to a resort in Greece for ten whole days!' said Susanna. 'Where there's a swimming pool with a slide and a spa for Mummy.'

Abby saw the hidden relief on her mother's face and knew that this new plan, this place in Greece, was somewhere her mother liked very much.

'What's a spa?' Ellie asked.

'It's a place where I can get a massage and possibly some beauty treatments while you two girls have loads of fun in the kids' club,' said Susanna. 'Where they'll have ice cream,' she added, tapping Ellie on the nose.

Abby knew when she was being sold an idea and slipped out of the room. She went upstairs and lay on her bed where she mourned the loss of a trip she had yearned for with all of her heart. And her mother knew it too. Abby understood that Susanna had taken Disney away from her for something Susanna wanted more. Abby's sense of self-worth plummeted that night. She understood fully where she stood in the pecking order of her family.

'Can I go to the slide pool now?' asked Abby, as she stood dripping in front of her mother, who was lying on a sunbed in her bikini. Abby had been in this shallow dipping pool for what felt like hours at her mother's behest, so she could 'stay with Ellie'. Ellie was nervous of the slide pool, but that was mostly because their mum kept saying things like 'I'm not sure if it's right for you, Ellie,' and 'It's very high, I wouldn't like you getting dizzy,' and so they'd stayed here forever, Ellie splashing about in the shallows, while their mum dozed.

Just a little way along from them was a lady Mum had met the day before. The lady, Miriam, was on holiday with her husband. They didn't have children and so Miriam spent a lot of time in the spa, and she would come back talking of massages and treatments and hold out her fingernails for Susanna to admire. When she'd heard why they were there she'd given Ellie what Abby secretly called the Super Sorry look – when adults made their eyes go all gooey and thrust out their bottom lip in sympathy. 'Poor little thing,' she'd said, and she'd told other people as well because later, in the restaurant, Abby had overheard someone say, 'That's the sick girl,' and she'd looked up to see Miriam nudge another woman and they were both looking in their direction.

'Not now,' said Susanna, stretching out lazily. 'Honestly, this is such a beautiful pool here, why do you want to go running off? Ellie's happy here, play with her.'

Abby watched as her mother closed her eyes again and knew it was pointless arguing. She went to sit at the edge of the pool, her legs dangling in the water, and wriggled her toes, watching as the refraction made her feet seem bigger.

From a distance she could hear the exhilarated screams of other children flying down the blue slide into the pool. She'd seen it every time they'd walked through the resort, her eyes on stalks. It was the best pool she could ever have imagined; the slide went through a tunnel and a loop until it finally deposited you into a deep lagoon.

A sound from behind caught her attention. A little snore. Abby turned and looked at her mother. Her eyes were closed, her sun hat pulled down over her forehead. Her mouth was ever so slightly open as she breathed deeply and Abby knew she'd fallen asleep. She looked across at Ellie, who was standing in the shallows, her neon orange armbands on, scooping a bucket into the pool then pouring it out again.

Abby went over to her sister and took her hand. 'Shall we go and see the other pool?'

Ellie looked at her in doubt. 'You mean the slide one?'

'Yes. It'll be fun, just me and you,' said Abby. 'We can play mermaids.'

Ellie's eyes lit up. Abby knew she'd been aching for them to play together.

'Really?'

'Course. Come on.' Abby led Ellie down the palm-lined pathways through the resort to the bigger pool. This was where most of the other children were and Abby looked up in wonder as she saw a young boy come hurtling down the slide, his mouth open in fear and excitement.

'I'm going to be a mermaid with a purple tail,' said Ellie excitedly. 'What about you?'

'I'm just going to have one go on the slide first,' said Abby and Ellie was immediately alarmed.

'But—'

'Don't worry, you don't have to. You can stay here and watch. Can you touch the bottom?'

'Only just,' said Ellie, her feet on tiptoes, the water up to her chin.

Abby knew she'd only be a few minutes, that's all it would take to have one go. She pointed to an area of water a bit further out. 'That can be our mermaid cave. We'll play when I get back. In two minutes.' She didn't wait for a response, but ran off towards the slide and started to climb the steps. At the top, she looked down at her sister, saw her playing where she'd left her. Then the green light in front of her flashed on and it was her turn. She pushed off, hurtling through the tubes, tipping at the corners in an adrenaline rush that finished with a bubble immersion as she fell deep into the pool.

She kicked herself upwards, utterly delighted. It was the best, most exhilarating thing she'd done in a very long time. She looked over to where she'd left Ellie, contemplating whether she could sneak in another go.

Ellie wasn't there.

A commotion was going on a little further into the pool, where it was deeper, where their make-believe mermaid cave was. Abby saw a lifeguard dive into the water. She kept watching and saw him pull her sister from under the surface. She swam towards them, saw him haul Ellie's small body out onto the tiles. She looked on in fear as the lifeguard shook her sister, then turned her over on her side where suddenly she vomited.

Again, thought Abby.

Her mother was furious, so much so that she could barely speak to her. Abby hung back a short distance from the sunbed, ostracized from the group, her sister wrapped in a fluffy towel with a large ice cream, their mother fussing over her, and Miriam too. Neither adult would meet her eye.

Ellie meekly held up the ice cream. 'Would you like a lick, Abby?'

Abby shook her head, mumbled a 'no thank you' for appearances' sake, hiding her fury and upset.

Miriam was murmuring something to her mother. Abby's ears pricked up. 'I'd gone for a walk, that's when I saw her. Yes . . . well, I don't know . . . It was just a little bit odd. She seemed to know it was too deep but still . . . I'm sure she only meant to be away for a few minutes. It was just an awful accident.'

Abby pretended not to hear. She walked away to the edge of the water where she sat on her haunches and contemplated how much simpler life would be without a little sister.

The rest of the holiday passed by in some agony for Abby. She knew she was being punished by being mostly ignored and she tried not to cry about it. Her mother never challenged her over the trip to the slide pool and Abby sometimes wondered what she really thought. On the last day, Abby and Ellie had to stay in the room for a couple of hours while Susanna packed. Ellie was colouring on the floor by the window, and Abby lay on her bed and watched as Susanna took the things from the bathroom and placed them in the case. She held up a bottle of children's paracetamol and shook it with a frown.

'Oh.' It was a small sound, escaping from her lips.

'What's wrong?' asked Abby.

'I thought we had more, that's all. I'll have to get some when we get home.'

She placed it in the case and continued to pack. Halfway through the flight home, Ellie began to get sick again.

THIRTY-FIVE

Matteo woke to the sound of a loud banging. He started, taking a moment to realize he was still in the chair on the terrace. He looked at his watch and was astounded to see that several hours had passed since he'd come outside this morning. So he'd managed to sleep after all. He quickly rubbed his eyes and went to see who was knocking on his front door loudly, with purpose.

Susanna had got there first. Walking into his hallway was Lieutenant Baroni, pulling off her sunglasses. Behind her, Captain Santini followed.

'Can we come in?' asked Baroni.

Matteo shrugged. They already were.

'We wanted to let you know that the car Abby and Ellie are in has come up on automatic number plate recognition,' said Baroni.

'Where?' asked Matteo.

'Crossing the border into France.'

Still groggy with sleep, Matteo rubbed his forehead. Stared at Baroni with incredulity. 'Seriously? And this is the first time it's pinged on the system?'

Baroni was unfazed. 'They've obviously been taking the minor roads, keeping away from the town centres.'

'So what now? Have the French police taken charge of this?'

'The investigation is still with the Carabinieri,' said Baroni. 'It's an *inseguimento in atto*. Pursuit in progress,' she translated for Susanna. She looked at them both. 'Have either of you heard from them?'

'Thank God you're here. I was about to call the police station,' said Susanna. 'I've just got off the phone to Ellie.'

'You did?' asked Matteo, stunned. 'Why didn't you wake me?'

'Go on,' said Baroni, ignoring Matteo.

'We couldn't talk long. But she's all right; at least, she said she's not hurt. She's with Abby and she seemed scared. I told her about Abby's history, about how she lied. Look, the number she called me from is on my call history.' Susanna reached for her phone.

'What about Abby?' asked Matteo. 'Is Abby OK?'

'I have no idea,' said Susanna with distaste. 'She was shopping.'

Baroni handed Susanna's phone to Santini. 'We'll get this number checked. Did Ellie say where they were going?'

'No . . . She was in a hurry to hang up. She said that Abby was coming, seemed very anxious about it.' Susanna paused. 'Ellie thought I was dead. That's why they ran. Abby told her I was dead and persuaded her to go on the run.' She looked up at Baroni. 'Ellie said she'd call me again. As soon as she could.'

'That's good,' said Baroni. 'Does she trust you?'

Susanna looked surprised. 'Yes. At least I think so. Despite the fact her sister's been trying to turn her against me.'

Baroni nodded. 'And I think that she will trust the police, yes? Then we ask her to persuade Abby to drive to a certain place. Somewhere we can meet them.' Baroni held out her card. 'My direct line. You need to call me as soon as she rings you.' She turned to Matteo. 'Have you heard from your wife?'

He straightened, indignant. 'No. Or I would have said.'

Santini stepped forward, pushed his chest out. 'The detective is just doing her job. You just answer the questions.'

Matteo looked at him all puffed up with self-importance. High on his own authority. He laughed.

'Is something funny?' snapped Santini, stepping even closer to Matteo.

'Yeah,' said Matteo.

Santini shoved Matteo in the chest. 'You fuc—'

'Stop!' yelled Baroni, pulling her partner off. She spoke calmly. 'If Abby calls, I am asking you not to tell her that her mother is alive. If Abby is dangerous, as Susanna suggests, it could make her act irrationally.' She pointed at the card in Susanna's hand. 'If either of them ring, call me. Do not wait.'

They turned to go and Matteo watched as Susanna let them out of his house. He didn't wait for her to come back into the room; instead, he returned to the terrace. He stood with the sun burning down on him, unable to understand how his life had been turned upside down in such a short space of time. His wife was missing. On the run with his sister-in-law. And Abby had his gun. He breathed deeply a moment, searched his soul. Would Abby use it? Was Ellie in danger? He'd have unequivocally said no only twenty-four hours ago, would have laughed the suggestion off, incredulous. But now he didn't know what to think.

He heard Susanna come to the patio doors behind him and he turned around. She stood in the safety of the room and he was aware she was trapped there – she wouldn't come out to him in the heat, not with her sunburn. This gave him a sense of relief.

'I'm just going for a lie-down,' said Susanna, 'but I have my phone with me.'

He nodded and watched as Susanna turned away. Why hadn't she woken him after Ellie had called? He could have laid his hands on Baroni's number immediately; Susanna would have known that.

Matteo waited a while, long enough for Susanna to get upstairs and settle, close her eyes. Then he quietly re-entered the house. He looked around the living room, paid attention to things he'd not really noticed before, such as Abby's books on the shelf. He ran his finger across the spines, tried to see if he could see any personal papers tucked in between. He moved to the bureau at the side of the room, opened the doors. He rummaged through folders, carefully indexed, papers meticulously filed, and then underneath them all, he found a small grey book: an address book. He flicked through, the names meaning nothing. People from Abby's life before he met her.

Then at 'G', his finger stopped. Abby had made an entry: Grandma. Next to it was an address – and a phone number.

THIRTY-SIX

Ellie went over and over it again in her head. She stared out the window as they drove through the French countryside, trying to make sense of her mother's stark warning. She scoured her memory for recollections of childhood that might throw some light on what Abby was supposed to have done. Had her sister had access to her food? Had she insisted Ellie eat something? But Ellie couldn't remember. It seemed one of them had hurt her, though, and she wasn't sure which of the two was easier to stomach: her mother, who was currently several hundred miles away, or Abby, next to her in the car.

Ellie didn't know if she should be afraid or not. And then suddenly, exhausted by the uncertainty, she let out a hysterical bark of laughter. Surely Abby wasn't about to do away with her in broad daylight? Careful, risk-averse Abby? It didn't seem possible. Whatever her mother claimed.

'What's so funny?' asked Abby.

Ellie tried to get a grip on her mania. 'Nothing.' She saw Abby look over at her oddly. Ellie was certain Abby was about to question her further, and she was desperately trying to think of ways to change the subject when the French landscape did just that for her.

'It's more beautiful than I even imagined it would be,' she gasped. The fields had morphed into wet plains that were criss-crossed with reeds of the palest green. On either side of the road were vast swathes of rippling shallow water that held on to the reflections of the clouds.

'What is this place?' asked Abby, looking around in awe.

'It's the Camargue,' said Ellie and then both girls saw a flamboyance of pink flamingos, some wading, some resting on a wide sandbank.

'Oh my God, look!' said Abby, eyes wide as she stared across the lagoon at the birds. She was so enraptured, Ellie couldn't help but smile.

'Anyone would think you hadn't been away before,' she said.

'Well, I haven't. Not really.'

'You live in Elba.'

'I know. And I went to Florence. But that's about it.'

Ellie frowned. 'That can't be right. What about all those work trips? Mum used to say you went to the Middle East a lot – Doha, Dubai. And Hong Kong . . . I'm sure she mentioned Hong Kong.'

'Yeah, I did. But as you say, that was work.'

'But surely you explored?'

'Not really. A plane, an airport, a conference room and a hotel. Then straight home again.'

Ellie still didn't understand. 'But what about holidays? You had holidays, right?'

'I got twenty-five days' leave a year.'

'And?'

'I sold them.'

'Pardon?'

'Back to the company. They had a scheme where you could sell most of your leave if you wanted. So I did and then I invested the money.'

Ellie was staring at Abby, mouth agape. 'You voluntarily gave your leave back to the company so you could work even longer?'

'It was a good deal.'

'Didn't you ever feel as if . . .'

'What?'

'You were missing out?'

'On holidays?'

'On *life*!' exclaimed Ellie. 'All those places to explore and people to meet. All those adventures you've never had.'

Abby bristled. 'I did OK, thanks. Not everyone can say they've retired in their thirties.'

'No, they can't,' murmured Ellie. 'So, what made you want to?'

Abby was silent for a moment. 'It was always about feeling safe. I never felt Mum had my back in the way she had yours. I wanted to set myself up for life, then I could go and enjoy it.'

'And are you?'

'What?'

'You know. Enjoying it.'

'Course!'

'That didn't sound very convincing.'

'It's just getting used to another lifestyle, that's all. There's lots of time to fill.'

'Whereas before you had no time. Did you ever go out? You know, an evening's entertainment?'

'Course I did!'

'You'd allow yourself to spend money on drinks?'

Abby rolled her eyes. 'It's very simple. You stick to a budget.'

'Hmm,' said Ellie. 'Let me paint you a picture. You're in a bar, having a great time with your friends. You've all done equal rounds, right, fair and square? As I can't imagine that not happening. It's only nine o'clock and the budget is spent. It's your round again. You don't want to go home. What do you do?'

'I'd drink water.'

'Oh my God.'

'It was the only way.'

A group of white horses waded through the water up ahead, their tails flicking. The girls watched as the straggler suddenly ran to catch up with the rest, its coat catching in the sunlight.

'They remind me of the horses in Andalucía,' said Ellie. 'So elegant.'

'The dancing ones?'

'Yes.'

'When did you go there?'

Ellie pondered. 'Can't remember. It might have been twenty sixteen, after I learned to sail around the Greek islands. No, it was twenty seventeen. The same year I saw the Northern Lights in Lapland.'

'You've done some travelling.'

'I love it. I love being somewhere different, the sense of freedom.' Ellie looked at her sister. 'Is there nowhere you've yearned to go?'

Abby thought. 'Do you remember . . . when we were little, we were supposed to go to Disneyland?'

Ellie nodded. 'Yes.'

'Well, I'd never wanted anything more in my life. I would cry myself to sleep every night after it got cancelled.'

The horses suddenly galloped off in unison, a flock of white birds wheeling overhead, their cries intermingling with the splashing from the horses.

This sort of thing was priceless, thought Ellie, an experience that was worth more than money. Wasn't it? She wondered exactly how much Abby had gained through her sacrifices. What value her sister had put on missing encounters like these.

'How much are you worth?' she asked.

Abby did a double take. 'Pardon?'

'Money. How much have you got? To the nearest fifty thousand,' added Ellie, 'to make it easier.'

'I'm not telling you that!'

'Why not?'

'It's none of your business.'

'That is true,' said Ellie, 'but what harm can it do to tell me? Is it really that big a secret? Personally, I think it might inspire me. Let me know what my big sister can achieve from nothing and maybe it'll reform my spending habits.'

Abby pulled a face. *As judgemental as ever*, thought Ellie but she refused to buckle.

'A hundred grand?' she persisted, teasingly. *It had to be more, surely.*

'I'm not having this conversation.'

'Two? Three? Go on, you can say. Maybe even five. Five hundred thousand pounds. That should last a while, shouldn't it? I don't really know how it works – do you live off the interest? Then you wouldn't need to spend any of it. You could keep going forever. What's the interest on five hundred K? Maybe not so much. So is it more? Six? Se—'

'Two million.'

'What?' Ellie's mouth dropped open.

'Two,' said Abby. 'Million,' she repeated. 'Seeing as you wanted to know.'

'Two million pounds?' Ellie closed her mouth. She was finding it hard to breathe, as if a great lump of rock had been placed on her chest. Two million was more than she would ever see over the course of her entire lifetime. She suddenly felt very small, very foolish.

'It's not that much,' said Abby quickly. 'Not compared to what some of my bosses were doing. And don't even get me started on some of my City worker friends.'

Ellie gave a pained smile. 'Sure. Not that much,' she echoed.

'I went without for years.' Abby gave a small laugh. 'Baked beans for weeks. And don't forget it's got to last me the rest of my life.'

Oh, poor you. Needing to stretch out two million pounds. However will you survive? Ellie thought bitterly, and then stopped herself. There was no point. And she'd asked for it by starting the conversation. *Two million pounds!* The amount kept reverberating through her brain, like a deranged wind-up toy spinning out of control. *Two million pounds! Two million pounds!* There were three of them in the car now: herself, Abby and, between them, a giant swag bag, large enough to suffocate her. She thought of her eighteen-thousand-pound credit card debt, a bill that she found impossible to pay off. Abby could make it disappear in a heartbeat.

Ellie stared out of the window again, seeing the salt marshes, the delicate flamingos. She thought of all those wonderful holidays she'd had that Abby had sacrificed. All those good times. The experiences, the memories. She still had those.

Suddenly they didn't seem as special anymore.

THIRTY-SEVEN

1999

The new careers teacher was called Mr James. He'd only just started but was already immensely popular with both the girls and boys. He was young, much younger than the crusty old staff who'd been around so long they had a faded quality, like the desks in their classrooms which had spent too many years by the window being bleached by the sun. No, Mr James was good-looking and vibrant. He joked around with the kids; he wore chinos instead of ancient Marks and Spencer's trousers that disappeared under a middle-aged gut. He would be interested when you had something to say and he could talk about whether Manchester United were going to win the treble and sing along to Fatboy Slim's 'Praise You' without ever embarrassing himself.

Ellie was only vaguely aware of Mr James as she'd not had any interaction with him yet. Towards the middle of the summer term, however, he was tasked with talking to each of the Year Eight pupils about their options, with a view to helping them decide which subjects to study for their

GCSEs to help them get on the right road for their career interests. Ellie didn't yet know what she wanted to do when she left school and, in any event, she already had a resigned sense of pessimism for what she might be able to achieve. It was hard to believe in yourself when you were in the bottom set for every subject. Ellie had no illusion about how the teachers perceived her and the other kids in her set: the staff were only interested in getting them over the very minimal line to keep the school numbers from alerting Ofsted.

She knocked on Mr James's door with little enthusiasm.

'Come!' was the cheery instruction from inside and she walked into his room, instantly noticing the scent of after-shave, something that evoked crashing waves on a deserted beach. Mr James smiled his twinkly smile and indicated she should sit in the chair on the other side of the desk to him. He leaned over and held out his hand.

'We haven't met yet,' he said. 'Mr James.'

'Ellie Spencer,' she said, unsure of quite how to take this new-style friendly teacher who oozed positivity.

'I've heard about you,' said Mr James. Ellie's smile dropped. Heavy-hearted, she prepared herself for the conversation about the importance of focusing on maths and English and gaining a pass in at least these two subjects.

But Mr James was still buoyant. 'Yes, a number of teachers have been singing your praises.'

Have they? thought Ellie, puzzled.

'So, any thoughts on your GCSE options? You should be thinking ahead to your A Levels, university – maybe

Oxbridge. From what I hear, you're already on that track. I'm going to start up a new scheme here,' continued Mr James, 'for those who show potential for Oxbridge. There are lots of hoops to jump through to get somewhere so prestigious and I want to be able to prepare students as much as possible.' He smiled at her. 'So, what are your thoughts?'

For a brief, magical moment, Ellie felt as if Mr James was her fairy godfather. This teacher, who exuded passion, was interested in her and was waving a wand and promising to send her to the ball. For a brief, magical moment she believed what he was saying, that she was special, she was capable, she was bright.

'What does Mr Cummins say about you choosing history?' asked Mr James.

'I don't have Mr Cummins, I have Miss Short.'

Ellie watched as Mr James's face began to deflate, like a balloon with a leak, its air slowly dissipating. He knew Miss Short took the lower sets.

'Sorry . . . I don't understand.' He looked down at his desk and then he found her file. He froze as his eyes scanned over it and a red blush crept up his neck.

'I . . . er . . . I think I might have got the wrong end of the stick.' He pushed his hand through his hair, looked back up at her, tried to regain his composure. 'I had a conversation this morning, with the deputy . . . I think I may have got my names mixed up.' He shook his head, perplexed. 'Although I was sure she said Spencer.'

The poisonous snake uncurled itself from the stones in the pit of her stomach. It reminded her it was there every so often. It was a snake whose venom was inferiority and bitterness. Ellie wondered whether to put Mr James out of his misery.

'She was probably talking about Abby Spencer,' she said.

Mr James lit up, as the light bulb switched on. 'Abby. Yes, that was it. Sorry.'

'It's all right. You're new.'

'Not sure who Abby is,' joked Mr James, waving a hand in pretend dismissal.

'She's my sister,' said Ellie, looking him right in the eye. 'She's in Year Eleven.'

This time the blush flooded his entire face.

At the end of the day, after the bell rang, Ellie was a bit later than the other kids as she'd lost a textbook that she needed to take home for her homework. As she walked down the quietening corridors, past the staffroom, she overheard Mr James talking with the deputy, heard her name mentioned.

'I felt really bad,' said Mr James. 'I had no idea. Must be awful for her, her sister being so brilliant and she not even average.'

Ellie stopped in her tracks, feeling as if someone had just punched her in the gut. The snake unleashed another dose of venom and her throat thickened up with hurt. Tears threatened. She put her head down, set her jaw firm and left the school as quickly and as invisibly as she could.

Three words reverberated around her head all the way home.

Not even average.

THIRTY-EIGHT

The shadows were so long now they were beginning to stretch far into the landscape. In an hour or so they'd melt away altogether, swallowed up by the night. The growing lateness of the day had slowly changed the atmosphere inside the little Fiat, not least because as the hours had slipped away, Abby's phone still hadn't rung. Neither of the girls had yet mentioned the lack of a response from Jamie, the criminal lawyer, but as time ticked on, each of them became a little more agitated, a little more desperate.

Ellie, one finger constantly on the map, knew they were just outside the hilltop town of Carcassonne. Up in the distance she could see the fortified wall that snaked around the medieval city, its honey-coloured stone lit up for the night. She wondered what Abby would do as they got closer – would she suggest they stop or would she ask Ellie for directions that took them beyond the town? They passed another sign, this one saying they were only five kilometres away and, exhausted, Ellie felt an overwhelming urge to head for civilization, pull in somewhere and rest.

'Time to change it up a bit?' she asked Abby, who sighed with relief.

'I thought you'd never ask,' said her sister. 'I'll keep going until we get to the town and then let's swap.'

Ellie frowned. 'Swap?'

'Yes. I have been driving for pretty much the entire day.'

'You mean you want me to get behind the wheel?'

'It's not too much to ask, is it?'

'It is, actually.'

'Flipping heck, Ellie, I'm knackered. You could at least give me a bit of a break.'

'I can't drive,' said Ellie.

'*What?*'

'Never had the need to learn.' She shrugged. 'Lived in London or its suburbs my entire life. Trains and tubes got me everywhere I needed to get to.'

'Are you kidding me?'

'Nope.'

'So what now?'

'I guess we stop. Find somewhere to stay the night,' said Ellie. Abby glanced across, frustrated, but could put up no argument.

From the back seat of the car came a sound. Two high-pitched beeps, muffled by a handbag.

The girls locked eyes – Jamie! – and Ellie reached over to grab Abby's bag and retrieve her phone.

'Don't!' snapped Abby.

Stung by her sister's sharp tone, Ellie stopped midway between the back and front seats, with the bag hanging from her fingers. 'But—'

'Leave it.'

'It might be Jamie,' said Ellie, puzzled. 'In fact, it probably is. Who else is going to have your number? I'll just check—'

'I'll look in a minute.' Abby tried to neutralize her outburst. 'We're almost there anyway.'

Ellie dropped the bag back on the seat and flung her hands up in surrender. 'OK, whatever you want.' She shifted back in her seat and stared out of the windscreen, aware of Abby glancing over to her, trying to gauge her mood.

'Sorry. Didn't mean to snap,' said Abby. 'I just don't like people going through my bag.'

'You mean me.'

'No, not you,' said Abby in an overly bright voice.

God, she sounds so fake, thought Ellie.

'Except you might have been trying to steal some of my millions,' said Abby with a forced grin.

It was a punch to the gut. Ellie stared at her, mouth agape. 'I beg your pardon?'

Abby immediately realized she'd overstepped the mark. 'I was joking. I didn't mean— Sorry. I was trying to make light of it.'

'How dare you?' Ellie took a sharp intake of breath. 'My God, you have a really low opinion of me, don't you?'

'No—'

'Well, I'm sorry you're having to fund this . . . escapade, but I don't have two million in the bank.'

'That's not it at all . . . OK, it was in bad taste. Crap joke. Not even a joke—'

'Let's just get one thing straight. I may be broke but I would never, ever stoop so low as to steal from you.'

'Not even a first edition book,' mumbled Abby under her breath.

'What?' demanded Ellie furiously, unsure if she'd heard right.

'Nothing.' A sign loomed up above for a bed and breakfast. Abby suddenly turned sharply off the road into the gravel driveway and she stopped the car outside a tired stone building with a large peeling wooden door. Rusty railings of julienne balconies clung to the exterior walls and two cracked pots filled with half-dead plants flanked the entrance.

'Yes, this looks perfect,' said Abby decisively. She got out of the car and retrieved her bag from the back seat, and Ellie watched as she checked her phone. 'It's from the phone company,' said Abby, the hope in her eyes fading. 'A special offer on an upgrade.'

Ellie gave a tight nod, then wordlessly walked into the B & B.

They hurriedly ate before the dining room closed, then Abby decided to return to the room to shower.

Ellie saw her opportunity. 'I'll be up in a few minutes,' she said, 'after I've finished my coffee.'

She watched as Abby left the dining room and mentally counted to fifty. Then she placed the coffee cup back on the saucer and headed out of the room. As she approached the reception area she glanced towards the stairs but they were empty; Abby had long gone.

'*Excusez-moi?*' she asked the woman on the desk, a fierce *madame* with her grey hair in a chignon. 'Is there a payphone I can use?'

'Over there,' replied the woman, indicating what looked like a dusty cupboard.

'*Merci*,' said Ellie, but she stayed at the desk. 'Um, I need the call to be private.'

'I do not listen,' said Madame, affronted.

'No . . . I mean, is there a way to hide the number when you dial?'

Madame was looking at her. Then, just when Ellie felt she couldn't bear the scrutiny a second longer, Madame ripped a piece of paper off a block pad on the desk and wrote some numbers on it. 'You dial this first,' she said.

Ellie went over to the payphone and inserted some coins. Carefully, she dialled. As the phone rang, she glanced in her purse. There were only a few euros left. Maybe, after she'd called her mother, she'd ring Fredrik. It would be nice to hear his voice.

'Hello?'

'Mum, it's Ellie.'

'Ellie! Where are you?'

'It doesn't matter.'

'Of course it does. We need to get you safe.'

'Have you told the police we've spoken?'

'Is that a problem?'

'No . . . I don't know. Look, I just don't get it. How did Abby poison me? She was a child! How on earth would she even get the stuff?'

'She took it out of the medicine cupboard.'

'But surely you noticed the level in the bottle going down?'

'She smashed one once. Pretended it was full so I would buy another. Another time she stole some. From the chemist on the corner – you remember?'

It was on a parade of shops on the way to school; Ellie could picture it now, with its windows crammed with beauty products and the queues of people waiting in line to get their prescriptions, keeping the staff busy. Perhaps distracting them so much that they wouldn't notice child shoplifters.

'But how did she give it to me?'

'You remember your sister's job was to set the table? I always used to insist you drank milk with your meals. You were ill so often I worried you weren't getting enough nutrients. Abby would put out the drinks. One day, when you were about eight years old, I caught her spooning liquid paracetamol into your milk.' Susanna's voice was catching with emotion. 'I stopped her immediately. I'm so sorry I didn't notice anything earlier. She'd been doing it for years.'

Ellie shook her head, her mind whirring. 'Seriously?'

'Yes. I promise you, I'm not lying.'

'But Mum, she has no reason to hate me. She's got everything! She's a multi-millionaire, for God's sake.'

'Is she?' gasped Susanna in wonder. 'I knew she was wealthy, but I didn't reali—'

'Mum, you're missing the point,' said Ellie, frustrated. 'I

don't see how Abby would want to harm me.' Uncomfortable, she paused. 'Which means . . .'

'It was me?' retorted Susanna sharply. 'It would do you well to remember that she wasn't a multi-millionaire when she was nine years old. She disliked you from the moment you were born. You took me away from her. You have to try and imagine what it's like for an only child to suddenly get a sibling. She used to constantly ask me when your mother was coming to take you home. I had to explain that you *were* home, and she would go off into these awful tantrums. She'd stop breathing, turn blue. Even when she got older, she could never accept you.'

Ellie was suddenly hit with an overwhelming sense of exhaustion. She leaned against the wall, tried to breathe evenly.

'Are you OK?' Susanna had suddenly realized Ellie hadn't been responding.

'Just feeling a bit dizzy.'

'You're unwell?'

The beeps suddenly sounded in Ellie's ear. She fumbled for her purse, slotted in her last coins.

'I've been a bit off-colour.'

'Oh . . .' It was a small word, spoken with dread.

'Mum . . .'

'Has she given you anything?'

There it was again. The fear that blew a cold wind right through her.

'Ellie?' Susanna's tone was sharp.

'Mum, stop. Please.'

Her mother's voice hardened. 'Look, there's something you need to know. She has a gun.'

Ellie stopped still. 'A what?'

'Go and look in her things if you don't believe me.'

'Sorry, did you just say she has a gun?'

'Yes, a gun! A bloody gun!'

'But what would she have that for?'

'I keep telling you, Ellie, she hates you.'

'But she has all that money. That free life.'

'Money does not buy you happi—'

Ellie heard a click in her ear. The call had dropped out. She looked at the display on the phone – her balance had run down to zero. Ellie slowly replaced the receiver.

Her sister had a *gun*?

THIRTY-NINE

Ellie slowly walked back through reception, not even noticing Madame look up as she passed the desk. She climbed the stairs, her mind racing. Surely it couldn't be true? *A gun.* She couldn't conceive of such an idea. It didn't seem real; it was a mistake, some sort of madness. She got to the second floor, to the door of their room, and opened it.

The shower was running. Ellie listened to the sound of the water. On Abby's bed was her travel bag. Ellie hesitated a moment, then went over. Tentatively, she unzipped the bag and, with a sense of treachery, put her hands inside. She felt only the softness of clothes, nothing hard. She checked the inside pocket too but it was empty. She zipped the bag back up.

Ellie looked around. There was a chair on the other side of the room, tucked away in the corner. On it was draped Abby's clothes, those she'd been wearing that day. And poking out from underneath a T-shirt was Abby's battered blue leather handbag.

With a jolt, Ellie remembered how she'd lifted that same bag off the back seat of the car earlier, and how Abby had snapped at her to leave it.

It must be in the handbag.

She stepped over to Abby's side of the room and, pushing the clothes aside, she opened it. The thick envelope of cash lay on the top. Ellie slowly lifted it and then recoiled.

Cold hard metal gleamed up at her. It had an energy, even though it was a stationary object, a brutality that made her shudder.

Ellie suddenly heard the shower turn off. Panicked, she shoved the envelope of money back on top of the gun and, fingers scrabbling, zipped up the bag, then ran over to her side of the room.

The bathroom door opened. Abby stepped out, wrapped in a towel. 'All right?' she said.

Ellie smiled as casually, as normally as she could. Her mouth felt strange, as if the muscles couldn't quite form the right expression.

'I'm going to give Jamie another call,' said Abby, 'then I'm going to turn the phone off. Just in case. Don't want anyone picking up where we are.'

'You mean the police?'

'Yes. I don't know how they'd track us to the retail park but I don't want to take the risk. We can switch it back on in the morning, to check for messages.'

Ellie nodded.

'You OK?' asked Abby.

She smiled quickly. 'Fine.'

Ellie watched agitatedly as Abby went over to the chair. Her sister opened her bag. Ellie stared as she saw Abby's hands disappear into its depths to retrieve her phone. She looked at her sister's face. *She knows there's a gun in there*, thought Ellie, *and she doesn't even flinch*. Abby looked up then, caught Ellie watching, and Ellie quickly turned away.

Abby made the call but, by the look on her face, Ellie knew she'd got the answerphone again. Her sister left a brief message, then put on a fresh T-shirt and climbed into bed.

'Are you sure you're all right?' she said.

Ellie snapped to, realized she was rooted to the spot.

'Yeah, sure.' Her head felt heavy with tiredness. She undressed and stiffly got into bed. Her legs would hardly move and she had to lift them to turn on her side, her back to Abby.

'Night,' said Abby, switching off her light.

'Night,' Ellie replied.

She lay there in the dark, rigid with fear and uncertainty. *Mum was right.* Ellie felt hyper-aware of her surroundings. She heard Abby shift in bed and stiffened with fright. Was her sister getting up? My God, was she, Ellie, even safe in this room with her? But then she heard Abby settle back down again. Heart hammering, Ellie tried to think. But she was so tired. *Stay awake*, she instructed herself firmly. *Do not fall asleep.* She suddenly knew what to do. She had to wait until Abby fell asleep and then creep back downstairs. Call Susanna and tell her where they were. This had gone on long enough – Ellie mentally kicked herself for not believing her mother sooner. If she'd listened, she could have avoided this situation; she might not have been lying here in the pitch black, afraid of what her sister might do.

Her eyelids drooped and Ellie forced them back open. *Stay awake!* It wouldn't be long, Abby was tired too, Ellie knew. She just had to wait long enough for Abby to fall asleep and then . . . what? *Call!* Yes, she had to make a call. She could do it. She felt herself drifting and pinched her leg. To her alarm she couldn't feel anything. She pinched again, harder. There, that was better, she was awake now. Wasn't she? Ellie sensed her mind might be wandering but she was too tired to chase it, to bring it back under her control. *So, so tired.*

FORTY

Abby lay in her bed listening to the sound of her sister breathing as she slept. She knew she should sleep too but there was too much on her mind.

There were several ways this little venture could play out and Abby didn't know yet where it was going. There were two things she was certain about: the first was that she had to finally put an end to a lifetime's unhappiness, remove the thorn that had been forever in her side. The second was that whatever the final scenario turned out to be, Abby was aware she'd need Jamie's help. It wasn't beyond her understanding that there was a looming possibility of a custodial sentence somewhere down the line. It had to be avoided at all costs and she knew this was something Jamie was notoriously good at. His reputation as a defence lawyer was second to none.

That's if it ever got to that. Abby was determined that this would not end up in any court.

She sighed and turned her mind to more pleasant thoughts. A smile came to her lips as she remembered the extraordinary discovery of the afternoon. The Camargue had been so beautiful, breathtakingly so. She'd never experienced anything like it and it would stay in her memory forever. The light, the glorious light on the pink wings of the flamingos and the grey-and-white horses. And their sense of freedom. Those horses were in their own utopia, away from humans, able to do as they pleased. A calm, simple life with no one to rely on for their survival.

It was all Abby had ever wanted for herself and she knew her extreme sacrifices had bought her independence, freedom from her mother. But she hadn't actually planned on retiring quite so young. She'd originally thought of reducing her hours, maybe even finding another job. Of living her life more fully, taking a holiday, trying out new places, new experiences. Maybe even going out for dinner once in a while. Instead she'd stopped altogether and hidden herself away on a tiny, albeit beautiful island, where she couldn't get out of the habit of scrimping and saving, just to make certain she'd have enough to last her until old age – which was half a century away. Perhaps even longer. No, the decision to retire had been sudden, unexpected. It had come out of fear.

FORTY-ONE

2018

The placard held up by the rep in arrivals read *Someone Special Singles' Holidays* in bold black letters and Abby cringed. If it had been possible for her to turn back around and head through baggage reclaim to the plane, she might have done just that, but then she would've had to explain to her boss how she ended up not taking a holiday after all and he would go on at her and HR would send some officious email and it was all too much hassle. It wasn't even really a holiday, it was a long weekend, Friday to Monday, and she'd picked that weekend purposely as the Monday was a bank holiday, which meant she only spent one day's leave. (She wasn't allowed to sell them all, there were regulations against it, but she certainly wanted to max out her allowance.)

She walked over to the beaming man with the sign and was directed to a minibus outside Florence airport. As she stepped on board her heart sank further as she noted a collection of . . . she didn't want to say oddballs – that was unkind. In any event, she was there too, but it was becoming clear to her that people who booked a singles' weekend were not necessarily busy high-flyers looking to make like-minded new friends.

Abby took a seat in an empty row, nodding hellos at those she passed. One or two of the girls looked at her with a sharp eye of appraisal, clearly summing up the competition, and all of the men's gazes were open and hopeful.

As she sat down, the man opposite, dressed in a black T-shirt and ripped black jeans, leaned across the aisle.

'Hi, I'm Sean.'

She shook his outstretched hand, noting it was slightly sweaty. 'Abby.'

'What do you do?'

Flipping heck, it was one hell of an opening question. No warm-up at all, and the way he'd said it, it sounded like a test. Abby had the distinct impression she was about to be defined by her job.

'Business analyst.'

His eyes remained blank, then he quickly covered with a knowing smile. 'Cool.'

You have no idea what that is, thought Abby.

'You?' she asked.

'I'm a music producer,' he said faux-casually as he attempted to cross his leg and rest an ankle on the other knee, but he was hampered by the tight leg room and had to drop it to the floor again.

'Oh yes? What kind of music?'

'Bit of grime, garage, jungle. Some hip hop. I did Shanga Weed's debut – you heard of them?'

She shook her head. 'Sorry.'

He looked downcast. Or was it relieved? She couldn't tell. But then another female boarder, a not unattractive blonde who cast her eyes over the bus looking for a seat, took his attention. Sean was about to indicate the space next to him when she slid into one at the front. *Did she just swerve him?* thought Abby, hiding a smile.

The blonde was the last to board and the rep opened with his effervescent welcome as the bus drove off. Sean took up where the rep finished, non-stop jabber the entire journey to the hotel, and Abby began to wish she'd had the foresight of the blonde woman and eyed up the seating arrangements with a little more nous.

There were a number of excursions organized that they were encouraged to sign up to – *all included in the price!* the rep kept enthusiastically reminding them – and later that day, after the welcome drinks, Abby found herself, along with about eleven others, following the rep around the highlights of Florence. They explored the Piazza della Signoria, taking in the Uffizi and the Palazzo Vecchio, outside which stood the vast copy of Michelangelo's *David*. Abby was happy to hang back and listen and wonder at the genuinely magnificent buildings. She found she was even beginning to enjoy herself. As they gazed upwards at a spectacularly painted dome, or marvelled at a statue, Abby was increasingly aware of Sean zoning in on the blonde girl from the bus again, always within two feet of her, gesturing, talking. Even when Blondie moved away he managed to find her again, always at her shoulder. Abby amused herself as she noted how, as much as Blondie continuously batted him away, he kept coming back for more.

The afternoon wore on and they stopped outside a *gelateria* in another picturesque square, where, unable to decide between chocolate and cherry, Abby went for both.

'Lucky you don't have to watch your figure,' said Sean, grinning as she took her first lick.

He was proud of his 'compliment', Abby could see. She really couldn't be bothered to explain to him how objectifying his comment was and, looking around for the blonde girl, Abby saw she was talking animatedly to another man from their group.

So Sean had finally been elbowed away and now she, Abby, was next in line for conquest. She started to wander off but, to her dismay, Sean followed. He made a beeline for her at dinner too and she had to endure two hours of how difficult it was handling 'creative types' in the music 'biz'. Eventually she could stand it no more and went to bed. Served her right for being amused by poor Blondie being trailed earlier.

Sean had the uncanny knack of knowing when she would be in the hotel dining room for breakfast, and had also signed up for the morning excursion to the Duomo, like herself. By late afternoon, Abby had had enough. She let the rep know she was going off on her own, declining Sean's offer of company as politely as possible, and when he wouldn't take no for an answer, she waited until he'd stepped behind a pillar at another grand church and made a run for it.

The sudden freedom made her giddy. She laughed to herself as she scuttled out of the church and down the street, ducking left and right, just in case Sean should try and follow. When she was certain she'd shaken him off, Abby looked around and gasped at what she saw: the Ponte Vecchio.

She wandered onto the spectacular bridge where shop after shop was crammed into the medieval architecture. It was a dazzling sight, not least because so many of them were fine jewellers. Abby gazed in the windows at the antique brooches made of gleaming enamel, the shell cameos, bright semi-precious stones laced together into a gold bracelet to adorn a nineteenth-century wrist, coral pendants carved into the faces of Roman gods. Most of it was eye-wateringly expensive and Abby gaped, astonished and a little disapproving – why would anyone want to spend so much on one item? Then, in a less ostentatious shop, she saw a silver bracelet set with lapis lazuli and there was something about the intensity of the blue that took her breath away. She stopped and stared. It seemed to be talking to her, something that she tried to dismiss as ridiculous, but she couldn't take her eyes off it. She allowed herself a glance at the price tag and was taken aback to see it was actually affordable. Except it would use up the entire amount she'd brought out to Florence – the whole 150 euros. She'd planned her budget carefully – it was enough to last the whole time she was there. She hugged her bag closer, thought of her purse nestled inside. If she spent the money, she'd have to withdraw more and so eat into next month's budget.

Abby made herself walk on quickly and not look back. The further she got from the shop, the easier it would be to forget about the bracelet. She felt a pang of deep disappointment as she strode along the bridge but then gave herself a stern talking-to. *It'll be worth it. Think of your savings. Think of that early retirement.*

After that she didn't feel much like window-shopping and, in fact, as she debated what to do next, she realized she'd not noticed the evening draw in. The bridge lights were on now and, tummy rumbling, she checked her watch and couldn't believe it had just gone eight o'clock. Dinner was served at the hotel at eight thirty so Abby checked her phone and reckoned on a shortcut to get her back in time.

She headed back over the river, holding her phone out so she could follow the map, and was so busy concentrating on the screen she failed to notice her surroundings change. The tourist-busy streets had disappeared and she was in a narrow alley overshadowed by tall buildings either side. The street lighting was set far apart and the lamps were dim, leaving long stretches of darkness.

It was the quiet that got her attention first. The kind of silence that hung ominously in the air. Abby looked up from her phone and gave an involuntary shiver. There was no one around and she didn't like the sensation of being enclosed by the buildings. She hurried onwards, looking up for the end of the alley so she could break out into the open again, but there was a bend ahead that she couldn't see round.

A clatter sounded behind her, something kicked in the

street, a drinks can perhaps. Abby turned and saw a human figure in the shadows. Shoulders hunched, she quickened her pace, simultaneously tucking her phone into her pocket, out of sight. There was a turning up ahead, another street leading off this one; maybe it would take her back to the main drag. She hurried up to it and was almost there when a man stepped out of that very same turning right in front of her.

Abby jumped. She stopped, her heart hammering. Instinctively she knew the shadowy figure behind her had caught up.

'*Borsa*,' demanded the man in front of her, indicating her bag. He was thin, with sunken shadows under his wired eyes. He kept moving the entire time; desperation seemed to engulf his limbs and he twitched and ticked.

She clutched it tighter, some mistimed sense of justice making her deeply indignant. Why should she hand her bag over to some junkie? She could feel the other man was right behind her but up ahead she could see a main street full of people and noise. Surely she could get to it in time, and even if she couldn't, the very fact she was running for it would scare these two addicts away. They looked like chancers, opportunists who would shrink back into the shadows the minute they might be exposed. She dodged around the man in front and was about to break into a sprint when a white-hot pain seared her shoulder. She found herself stumbling, then falling and hitting the ground with such force her chin felt as if it had been pushed back into her skull. Senses slowed by the pain, she was one step behind the man wrenching her bag off her shoulder and failed to hold on to it. The pain in her shoulder screamed out – or was that her? – and then a crack to her hip made her lose focus and she realized she'd been kicked. She tried to curl up in defence, her hands protecting her head as she cowered at their feet. From her position on the ground she could see her phone had fallen out of her pocket and had skidded across the cobbles. One of her attackers retrieved it and then they were gone, their trainer-clad footsteps running off in the other direction.

She lay there for a while, unable to move. She wasn't sure how to get up; it was as if her body had lost its sense of self-belief, no longer knew how to operate muscles and tendons that it had been controlling for thirty-five years. She felt a warm wetness on her right shoulder and had an overwhelming urge to find out what it was. It was this that propelled her through the pain and paralysis, and she dragged herself up off the street, arching a screaming arm backwards, the agony almost unbearable as she touched blood.

There was a lot. Too much, thought Abby as she began to stumble towards the main street she could still see up ahead. As she broke out of the alley, back into the lights and the fun-seeking tourists, the terror of what had just happened suddenly engulfed her and she was so relieved to see a policeman that she lunged for him, just as he looked up and caught her in his arms.

She had a fractured jaw, severe bruising to the hip and a two-inch stab wound on her right shoulder. She'd been in hospital for three days, and was aware her short break had encroached on the beginning of a new working week. All her other Someone Special companions would have gone home now. She'd half wondered if she'd hear from Sean but no message had made its way to her via the rep who visited to talk her through her journey back to the UK. When the rep left the hospital, after filling in various forms, she burst into tears.

She sobbed silently, not wanting to draw the attention of the nurses. She was used to looking after herself, to not having a guardian to fall back on. She'd prided herself on successfully building her own fortress, on relying on no one but herself. Abby could look after Abby. Except, the first time she fell into trouble, she had behaved pitifully. She hadn't fought back. She hadn't even screamed. She'd just let those thugs do whatever they wanted, let them take her things, and had lain in the dirt, weak and pathetic.

A polite cough drew her out of her reverie. Flustered, Abby wiped her eyes and looked up. A policeman was stood at a respectful distance from the foot of the bed. Abby recognized him as the one she'd collapsed onto on the night of the mugging.

'I'm sorry to disturb you,' he said.

Abby swallowed down the anguish and made herself sit up. 'It's OK,' she said stiffly.

'I'm here to talk to you about the incident the other evening,' said the policeman. 'My name is Captain Matteo Morelli.'

*

She'd given him a description of one of her attackers – the other man, the one who'd thrust his knife into her shoulder, she hadn't seen. Captain Morelli had asked if he could stay in touch while the police tried to pursue the culprits. Of course, nothing came of it. Back in the UK, Abby was left broken. The mugging had changed her. She lost a client at work – or at least, she knew her boss silently blamed her for the client's withdrawal of business. Before she'd left for her trip she'd been at the top of her game. A director with lucrative bonuses, shares in the company. But now she was petrified of everything. She couldn't walk home from the station at night, which put paid to staying late at the office. In fact, she no longer even had the energy for work; she could barely get up in the morning. The whole thing felt so pointless. All that effort, all those savings, and for what? What if she'd lost her life that night in the alley?

The hospital staff had got in touch with Susanna when Abby was admitted, but Abby had fobbed her off with a story of a minor theft and downplayed the physical injuries. She'd made it sound so inconsequential she knew her mother was likely to forget about it fairly quickly. Abby didn't bother telling Ellie at all. She couldn't. She'd spent her entire life proving to her sister and her mother that she was entirely self-sufficient and now she felt great shame at what she'd allowed to happen.

The official emails from Matteo had migrated to a personal address and Abby kept up the correspondence as a distraction from work as much as anything else. But she also got a comfort from them. Matteo was the person who'd been there when she needed help. He was the only one who fully understood what she'd been through. They met up in London a couple of times and then Abby went to visit him on the island of Elba, where he'd been offered a new post. They sat in cafes by the beaches, the skies still blue even in winter, and Abby relished the peace, the tranquil pace of life. People were friendly; the villagers appeared to all know one another and look out for each other. Above all, it seemed safe.

During that trip he asked her to marry him. He also showed her a house he'd found, and when Abby went out into the back garden and saw the pathway to the sea, she felt herself well up.

Abby decided to quit her job. For good. It was the only rash thing she'd ever done in her life. Then she did the second rash thing – she bought the house with Matteo in the fear that she might change her mind about the retirement. Now there was no going back. They moved in together in early spring and Abby told herself she was living the dream.

FORTY-TWO

Abby opened her mouth to scream but no sound came out. She lifted her head off the gravel that was cutting into her cheek and looked up the alley, silently begging for someone to see her. People were passing by on the main street, just metres away, but totally oblivious to her attack. She tried to cry out again and again but her vocal cords failed to vibrate. She was aware of the two men beating her, of the pain and the overpowering sense of helplessness, and then she saw her mother up ahead. Her heart soared – surely Susanna had come to look for her? And despite the fact Abby was unable to cry out, she somehow sensed that Susanna would look straight down the alley and see her. But her mother was facing in the wrong direction. *Turn*, urged Abby desperately, *look around*, but Susanna didn't and then she started to walk away. Panic gripped Abby, along with a sense of total and utter abandonment.

Her eyes flew open. Her heart was thudding in her chest and it took her a minute to understand where she was. She could feel her sweat on the sheets and pulled her damp T-shirt away from her body. Leaning over to the B & B's bedside table, it was just light enough to check her watch.

It was five thirty in the morning. Dawn was breaking and the room's shadows were beginning to slowly lighten. Abby looked across at Ellie's bed.

It was empty.

Puzzled, Abby got out from under the covers. She checked the bathroom but Ellie wasn't there either. Her suitcase was still beside the bed, but her shoes that she'd left by the door were missing.

Abby quickly got dressed and packed up her things. She took both her and Ellie's luggage and quietly carried it down the shadowy stairs. As she neared the ground floor, she thought she could hear a muffled voice, but then it became quiet and she felt she must have been mistaken. *Where the hell is Ellie?*

'Morning,' whispered her little sister as she appeared from somewhere in the darkness at the back of reception. 'You couldn't sleep either, eh?'

Abby jumped in fright. She looked at Ellie, who seemed pale and a little distracted. 'Is that why you came down?'

Ellie nodded. 'I didn't want to wake you.'

Her sister was staring at the bags in her hand. 'I think we should get going,' said Abby, by way of explanation.

Ellie snapped her head up in alarm. 'What, now?'

'Yes.'

'What's the rush?'

'Shush! Don't wake anyone,' said Abby. 'We should go while the roads are quiet.'

Ellie didn't move. She seemed to be searching for something to say.

'You want to stay longer?' queried Abby, a frown appearing on her face.

'No,' said Ellie quickly. She attempted a smile. 'Happy to get on.'

'Good.' Abby hurried over to the desk and opened her purse. Suddenly she stopped. Agonized, she bit her lip.

'What's the matter?' whispered Ellie, her heart racing.

Abby looked up. 'You don't have a five-euro note, do you?'

'What for?'

'The room is eighty-five euros and I only have tens.' Abby saw Ellie was staring at her incredulously. Abby grudgingly put some money on the table. 'Guess Madame will get a tip,' she said, then made her way to the front door. When she looked back, Ellie was still standing in the hallway. 'Well, come on then.'

'Yes,' her sister said and finally picked up her suitcase and followed her.

The sun was lightening the very bottom strip of the sky, a pale blue line flecked with gold. The girls crunched across the gravel and put their bags on the back seat of the car. Then they got in and buckled up. As Abby pulled away, Ellie quietly, anxiously, checked her watch.

'No tolls, remember,' said Abby and Ellie jumped to, retrieving the road map from the door pocket. She concentrated for a moment on their route, directing Abby to the quieter roads. After a few minutes they heard the sound of sirens. Abby urgently looked in her mirrors but the road behind was empty. Then they saw them: two, three police cars on a road running adjacent to theirs, going in the opposite direction.

'I wonder what that's all about?' mused Abby.

'Hmm,' said Ellie, but then the police had gone, their sirens fading into the distance.

They continued to drive, away from Carcassonne. Abby saw Ellie glancing in the wing mirror. After the third time she asked, 'Is there something up?'

'No! Nothing,' said Ellie.

'Only you keep looking behind us.'

'There's nothing there,' reassured Ellie.

Abby frowned. 'Is everything OK? You seem a bit jumpy.'

'Just tired. No sleep, you know.'

Abby nodded and then looked back at the road. 'At least the police have gone,' she said.

Ellie kept silent.

FORTY-THREE

The three police cars, sirens now silenced, pulled up into the driveway of Le Jardin Bed & Breakfast. Police emptied out of the vehicles, running stealthily up to the building, spreading out, covering every exit.

'*Ouvrez cette porte!* Police!' shouted the French chief. His colleague stood by with the ram – he'd give it five seconds before giving him the nod to use it. His team were in position at the back of the building. A window opened a couple of floors up and a bleary-eyed woman leaned her head out, asked what was going on. They ignored her.

The front door suddenly opened. An imperious middle-aged woman in a bed jacket, her long grey hair curled over one shoulder, stood on the threshold.

'Are you the owner of this business?' asked the police chief, in French, as he entered, his team streaming past into the property.

The *madame* eyed him haughtily. 'Yes.'

'We're looking for two English women, mid-thirties.'

'They're on the second floor. Room five.'

The words were barely out of her mouth when the police

chief, accompanied by his colleague, were up the stairs. The door to room five was shut.

'Key,' barked the police chief to the *madame*, who elbowed him aside and, removing a key from a large bunch in her pocket, slid it into the lock.

'Step aside, Madame,' said the police chief and, gun raised, he pushed open the door. It swung open to reveal an empty room.

'*Merda!*' muttered Baroni. She'd been in this house since the early hours of the morning, holed up in the living room. She looked at the English woman with the red face who was sitting down in the armchair. 'You're certain you rang us the minute Ellie called?'

'Positive,' said Susanna. 'I was asleep when she phoned me from the B & B in Carcassonne – like I told you. She said she'd crept downstairs leaving Abby in bed. She's found your gun.' Susanna turned accusingly to Matteo, who was leaning against the wall, listening to Baroni's report of failing to catch his wife and her sister.

'She's terrified,' continued Susanna. 'She begged me to send help. To get there *before Abby woke up*,' she emphasized, this time turning to set her accusing gaze on Baroni.

'We sent the message through immediately,' insisted Baroni. 'As far as I'm aware, the French police responded rapidly. Perhaps Abby woke early.'

'It was five thirty a.m.!' said Susanna.

Matteo looked up at his mother-in-law. 'She has a lot on her mind,' he said pointedly.

'None of this is normal behaviour,' said Susanna, upset. 'My daughter is running across bloody Europe with a bloody gun and dragging poor Ellie along with her and God knows how this is all going to end. But if anything happens to my beautiful girl' – Susanna looked from Baroni to Matteo, her eyes blazing – 'I will never forgive either of you.'

FORTY-FOUR

They were on the move again. Driving, driving. Running. Ellie was following the map, giving her sister directions. To where, she didn't know. She was just heading in the opposite direction to where they'd come from.

Ellie suddenly realized she was having trouble focusing. She looked down at the page again. A jumble of squiggly lines, the minor roads white and ghostlike in contrast to the main red roads they had to avoid. It was easy to lose your way, easy to get snarled up on a route that became like a tangled mess of spaghetti, twisting this way and that, with no way to get back on track.

Ellie had given up checking the mirror to her right. No police cars had followed them. She understood the police they'd seen early that morning had got to the B & B too late. And now the two of them were untraceable again.

'Where are we going?' she suddenly asked Abby.

'Just keep heading west.'

'West is Spain.'

'Is it? Fancy some paella? A bit of flamenco?' asked Abby, breaking into hysterical laughter.

Ellie glanced across. Her sister was losing it. Or had she been like that since they'd set off? Mad? Obsessive?

'Has Jamie called?' asked Ellie.

'I haven't switched the phone on yet. It's only just gone six in the morning, five in the UK.'

'We should check.'

'I will.'

Ellie still wasn't sure if she believed in this Jamie. *Why would Abby need to speak to a criminal lawyer about all this mess if she's planning on doing me in?*

Oh! Ellie's blood suddenly ran cold.

Abby pulled up at a T-junction and waited for instruction. Ellie glanced down at the map but it was blurred. She tried following the map with her finger but the image wouldn't steady. Everything was in double vision. She looked up out of the windscreen. It was the same with the landscape. Two hedges, two electricity pylons, two birds balancing on the wires.

'Left or right?' asked Abby.

Ellie lifted the map closer. It didn't help. She shook it, frustrated.

'Are you OK?'

'It's gone a bit blurred,' admitted Ellie.

'Want me to take a look?'

Ellie handed the road map over and Abby silently checked it, then she gave it back and turned the car left.

'What was all that about?' Abby asked once they were driving again.

Ellie shrugged.

'Do you think . . . ?'

Ellie looked up at her sister. Abby was biting her lip.

'What?'

'It's just a thought . . .'

'Spit it out.'

'You haven't been right since we left on Tuesday afternoon.'

'And?'

'Mum served up. Your first night here. She was alone in the kitchen. You don't think she gave you something, do you?'

Ellie looked over at her sister. Nothing but innocence and concern sprang from her eyes.

FORTY-FIVE

The reporter was one of the best-turned-out women Susanna had ever seen. She wore a navy pencil skirt with a discreet split up the thigh. Her elegant arms were caressed by a fluid silk shirt in a soft pink. At her tanned neck was a single, subtle diamond. Gabriella was in her early forties, but Susanna thought she looked much younger. Her glossy dark brown hair was lifted with copper highlights and her skin glowed. Oh, how Susanna envied her skin, her smooth face. Ashamed of her own, she'd insisted on having her back to the camera and under no circumstances was the cameraman to take any shots of her sunburned face.

Susanna felt insignificant sat in front of this Italian beauty, but reminded herself it wasn't all painful. Gabriella had contacted her asking for an exclusive interview for their cable magazine show, a call that had caught Susanna unawares, and a producer had offered a fee. Something else that had surprised her. The producer had been quite persuasive, Susanna remembered, and she'd concluded that it couldn't do any harm, especially as they'd promised not to broadcast any of the interview until Ellie had been found. They didn't want to get in the way of the investigation and knew that Abby mustn't find out that Susanna was alive in case it made her act rashly.

Susanna had trusted them and invited them in. Matteo had been told to keep out – it was her story, they were her daughters. And it helped to talk about it. She was so desperate for Ellie to be safe and well and she had no one else to confide in. She'd kept the secret of Ellie and Abby's childhood for decades. Matteo was hard to talk to – he was struggling to believe his new wife was temperamental and volatile. It was understandable, but Susanna was losing patience.

'Are you ready?' asked Gabriella in her beautifully accented English.

Susanna nodded. 'Just don't . . .' she began again, nervously.

'It's OK. Paolo will not show your face,' reassured Gabriella. 'Now remember, my introduction will be in Italian and then we will conduct the interview itself in English. OK?'

Susanna nodded.

Gabriella took a breath, then another, a well-practised act of composure. She nodded at Paolo, who'd set his camera up behind Susanna. Then, on his signal, she began to speak.

'It was meant to be a special time, a family reunion between a mother and her two grown-up daughters. One of them lives here, on our beautiful island of Elba; the other has come to visit from London. These sisters have a history of being estranged, after a difficult and painful childhood. There has been a terrible rivalry, where Abby, the older sister, has resented her beautiful blonde baby sister, Ellie,

since birth. Imagine the difficulty for Susanna, the poor mother caught between them, who is here with me today. Imagine her heartbreak when her eldest daughter, Abby, rejects the younger one, Ellie. Then imagine her horror when she discovers Abby tried to murder Ellie when they were children.'

Gabriella paused, her hand fluttering to her chest, then composed herself and continued.

'*Susanna managed to save Ellie's life all those years ago – and we will be talking to Susanna more about that in a minute. But now we have a situation of grave and immediate danger. At this very moment, as we are speaking right now, Abby has kidnapped Ellie and gone on the run with her. They are currently missing, having eluded the Carabinieri for almost two days. We know they have left Italy and made it to France. We do not know where they are now. Meanwhile, their distraught mother, who cannot show you her face due to a terrible accident inflicted by her daughter before she left, is desperate for them to be found.'*

Gabriella turned her gaze from down the lens of the camera to Susanna, where her features softened in empathy.

'Susanna, there is much to talk about here but why don't we start with the most important thing? How concerned are you for Ellie's safety?'

Susanna swallowed; her voice had suddenly dried up. 'I'm desperately worried,' she said. 'Abby has a history of being obsessive and ruthless. She will set her sights on a goal and nothing will distract her.'

'And you think she may have a goal now?'

'Yes, I do.'

'And that goal is?' prompted Gabriella.

Susanna felt her voice catch. She had to say it, however hard it was. 'I think she wants her sister out of the way. Forever. She's always been jealous of her – she still is. Only the other day, here in this house, she was upset that Ellie was getting on well with Matteo.'

Gabriella raised a quizzical eyebrow.

'Matteo is Abby's husband,' explained Susanna. 'I was with Abby when she overheard the two of them talking. Ordinary stuff, you know, just friendly conversation. But Abby hated it. She won't let go. She has everything she could wish for – a nice house, a great life – but she isn't happy.'

'What will make her happy?' asked Gabriella, her voice soft with anticipation.

'Ellie out of her life.'

'And how do you think she will do that?'

Susanna felt tears spring up behind her eyes. 'Any way she can. The most devious, calculating, duplicitous way she can devise.'

'Un-fucking-believable,' cut in an icy voice.

Startled, Susanna turned, realizing too late that she'd revealed the full extent of her peeling face to the camera. Behind her, Gabriella was grappling with the irritation of the interview being interrupted against what looked like a dramatic turn in the story. She signalled for Paolo to continue filming.

Susanna looked up into the eyes of a woman whom she hadn't seen in thirty-seven years.

Her mother's cold, hard gaze made her flinch, and then she spoke.

'What the hell have you done to your face?'

FORTY-SIX

'Turn it off!' shouted Susanna, frantically waving her arms at Paolo until he reluctantly lowered the camera.

'How much are they paying you for this sordid little tale?' asked Kathleen.

'None of your business.'

'You always would do anything for money.'

Susanna bit back the tears. 'That is a nasty thing to say. And it's not true.'

'Really? Working in some tawdry shop selling clothes?'

'I had to get a job.'

'Well, you know why that was.'

'Yes, because you and Daddy cut me off.'

Kathleen gave Susanna a withering stare. 'You had your warnings. We said that man was nothing but a cad and we were right. But you still ran off with him. You made your bed, you had to lie in it.'

It was as if it had happened only yesterday, the way her mother was speaking. Susanna was instantly transported back to the young woman she'd been all those years ago, quivering in front of her mother, buckling under the weight of her disapproval. She took a deep breath, tried to regain her composure, then forced herself to look at her.

Kathleen still dressed impeccably but her blonde hair was now all white. She wore it in a different way to what Susanna had been used to – a more age-appropriate bob that showed off her heart-shaped face. But there was something about her mother's face that shocked Susanna. It was hard, entrenched in bitterness, and for a moment she couldn't understand why. Then it hit her. Her mother was still angry. Her features had been chiselled over the years by a reaction to something that had happened *over three decades ago*.

For the first time in her life, Susanna woke up to just how penetrating her mother's sense of disappointment was. And for a brief second she felt an unexpected flicker of satisfaction, one that withered in fear almost as soon as it had appeared.

'Why are you here?' Susanna asked her.

'Matteo rang me,' said Kathleen, indicating the door, where Susanna saw him standing, leaning against the frame. On the other side of the room, Gabriella was listening, watching, poised.

'I think you'd better leave now,' said Susanna apologetically.

'But we haven't finished the interview,' said Gabriella.

'Get out of my house,' said Matteo, holding the door open. Gabriella weighed up arguing it out but, recognizing defeat when she saw it, she gathered up her things and left the room without even a backwards glance, Paolo trailing behind her. Susanna heard Matteo close the front door after them before coming back in.

'So, are you going to tell me what's going on here?' asked Kathleen.

Susanna quivered but held it together. She mustn't let her mother's voice, that paralysing tone of disapproval, reduce her to a child again.

'Well, Abby has spun a load of lies to Ellie and persuaded her to go on the ru—'

'I know all that,' snapped Kathleen. 'I mean, what are you doing to bring my grandchildren back?'

Susanna stared. 'They're grown women. Not naughty children. Anyway, the police . . . They're searching.'

'And what are *you* doing?'

'I don't understand.'

'Or rather, what *have* you been doing? To drive them away? Because you have a habit of losing your children, don't you, Susanna?'

Susanna felt a rush of blood to her head. She glanced up at Matteo, hoping he hadn't clocked this comment, but he was frowning, looking between the two of them.

'What did you get in contact with her for?' Susanna said to him, as she flung her arm towards Kathleen. 'You had no right bringing her here.'

'I have every right—' started Kathleen.

'Oh, shut up, Mother!' Susanna caught the look of condemnation on her mother's face and she dropped her gaze.

'I phoned Kathleen to try and make sense of everything that's happened,' said Matteo. 'I'm worried about Abby.

Kathleen offered to come over and I saw no reason to stop her.'

'It was quite a shock, hearing Matteo talk about the children – what had happened to Ellie when she was young,' said Kathleen. 'Why didn't you tell me?'

'You'd cut me out of your life.'

'I don't mean for solidarity,' said Kathleen coldly. 'I mean, so I could have kept an eye on Abby when she and Ellie came to stay with me. If it was Abby we should have been keeping an eye on, of course.'

Susanna made an effort to stay composed. 'I'm getting a bit tired of this,' she said. 'Abby is at fault here. She is the one who's hurt Ellie before.'

'So you say. But I'm inclined to think you're lying.'

'I'm not.'

'You want to know why? This isn't the first time, is it?'

Susanna felt herself grow hot. Her heart was trying to fight its way out of her chest. 'You don't know what you're talking about.'

'I think I do. Because Ben left you too, didn't he, Susanna? Died when he was just eleven months old.'

FORTY-SEVEN

Her mother was waiting for her to speak. She had the same look on her face as when she'd impatiently waited for Susanna to recite her times tables or spell a word or tell the time. It was a look that said she expected Susanna to get it wrong. And when she did, Susanna would shrivel inside under the scornful eyes, the look of contempt.

Susanna didn't answer her mother at first. Instead she spoke to Matteo.

'My second child, Ben, died when he was a baby.'

'He was poisoned,' said Kathleen, moving to a chair and lowering herself into it.

'What my mother is saying is true,' said Susanna, 'but not as you are probably thinking. It was an accident, a terrible thing to have happened.'

'He was fed too much salt,' said Kathleen. 'His little body couldn't cope and he had a brain seizure.'

'It wasn't my fault.'

'You were the one who fed him.'

'The police didn't ever charge me. I was in the clear – the whole time. You have no right to speak to me like this.'

Kathleen gave her a hard stare. 'I'm well aware the police

didn't charge you. And at the time I was relieved. For all your faults I couldn't imagine you'd have done something so awful. But now I hear about what happened to Ellie, I think they should have delved a little deeper.'

'You're not being fair.'

'I've had a bit of time to think since Matteo called me. It's amazing the clarity your mind can get thirty thousand feet up in the air – no distractions, just time to piece together what had been staring me in the face all those years ago but I failed to see. And I came up with a theory. That man you ran off with . . . Danny. He was already sleeping with his new woman when Ben got poorly. Was it your way of keeping him at home? Make his son ill so that he felt guilty for going off with someone else?'

Susanna gasped. She'd forgotten how cruel her mother could be.

'Susanna,' said Matteo. 'Can you explain to me why your mother is saying all this?'

Her eyes blazed. 'My son, my beautiful baby, died from a salt overdose. At the time I was pregnant with Ellie and, like with all my pregnancies, I was terribly sick. I could barely function, let alone look after two young children. I would . . . I'd feed Ben and Abby with ready meals – I had no idea they contained so much salt.' She started to well up. 'If I could change it, I would—'

'Pah!' said Kathleen, waving a dismissive hand. 'I'd bet my last pound there was more salt in his body than just from ready meals. You were frightened of being left alone. You'd made a monumental cock-up by getting shacked up with that money-grasping toad and you saw everything slipping away from you.'

'It's not true . . .'

'Stop lying, girl.'

'You don't know what you're saying.'

'But Danny left you anyway, didn't he? His new woman's money was stronger than anything you could do to keep him. Even if it did mean murdering your own child.'

'I didn't murder him.' Susanna was trembling; she rubbed her shaking hands down her sides. This was unbearable, all this pain dragged up again. Everything she'd tried to bury for so long. She closed her eyes. *Maybe it's time to come clean.*

'You just can't bear to be left. Can't stand on your own two feet. Is that why you started on Ellie? You saw her getting a life away from you too? If I'd worked out what happened to Ben, I'd have had those girls taken away from you.'

'You don't know what you're talking about.' Susanna went to leave the room but her mother shouted after her.

'I'm going to call the police! Tell them everything.'

Susanna buckled. Turned back to Kathleen. 'OK, you do that. But first, know what really happened.'

It had the desired effect. Her mother shut up.

'What do you mean?' asked Matteo, in the silence that followed.

'My mother is right,' said Susanna, her voice cracking. 'Ben had more salt than in just those ready meals. But it wasn't me. It was Abby.'

'You little—' said Kathleen.

'No, Mother. It's true. I have never told anyone this, not in all these years.' Susanna started to break down. 'I didn't see it. I couldn't stop it, and then it was too late.'

'Stop what?' asked Matteo.

'Abby added salt to Ben's meals. Over those three days.'

'She was two years old,' scoffed Kathleen.

'It is terrifyingly simple. A teaspoon is enough to kill a child of his age. She was excited at first, at the idea of a baby brother, but when he came along, took up my time, began to crawl, broke her toys, she soon had enough. She would scream at him, and hit him once when he destroyed her Lego.'

Susanna bristled at the sceptical look on her mother's face. *She needs to hear this*, she thought. 'Abby would ask me why I moved the salt cellar off the table when he was old enough to sit with us in his high chair. And I told her. I said it was because salt wasn't very nice for babies.' Suddenly Susanna deflated. 'After he'd died I couldn't work out how he'd had so much. For years I tormented myself, assuming I'd left the shaker within his reach one time and he'd eaten some. But when I saw Abby putting paracetamol in Ellie's milk, it all fell into place. *She* had done it. I'd told her again and again that salt was bad.' Susanna looked up. 'But if you're going to blame anyone, you might as well blame me anyway. I didn't make her feel she could accept him. I failed her as well as him.'

Susanna glanced at her mother. A new emotion flitted across Kathleen's face: uncertainty.

'Call me a bad mother, go ahead. I deserve it. But I am the one who knows my children best. And I'm telling you now, Abby's never changed. And if you don't listen to me, then I am convinced Ellie will be harmed. Argue with me all you like but what if you're wrong? How will you feel then? Because believe me, it's hell having the death of a child on your conscience.'

FORTY-EIGHT

Around them were fields, miles and miles of green that reached far towards the horizon right to the base of the Pyrenees. The lower slopes of the mountains were covered with evergreens, tiny trees clinging like limpets. There were thousands of them, hiding trails and pathways of the national park. Ellie gazed out of the window, wondering if there were people hidden amongst them. Tourists who'd come to enjoy the great outdoors, ordinary people who had nothing more pressing to do each day than decide where to spend their free time, what pleasures to revel in. Maybe there were people there right now, mountain bikes kicking up soil and dust, a picnic in their panniers. She briefly thought of Fredrik – he seemed like a dream now.

A new track came on the radio. It was the summer hit of the year, an upbeat song with a reggae vibe, and it was played frequently. Ellie thought she must have heard it half a dozen times already that morning. Add that to the quota the day before, and the day before that, and she knew pretty much all the lyrics by heart. A summer anthem that, as all anthems did, would bring back memories. Ellie tried to picture the future but came up with a blank. Would she be back at school, helping disinterested teens with the intricacies of natural global ecosystems? It felt like a lifetime ago that she had been in a classroom – an ordinary life that she could no longer grasp.

The car hummed along. The track finished on the radio. The road ahead still beckoned. On and on and on. There had been very few other cars – only the occasional vehicle had passed them. Most likely kept to the motorways and the trunk roads. Certainly no police had materialized. Ellie had a sense of being utterly lost and alone. No one knew where they were. No one was coming to save her. The chance she'd created, the opportunity she'd offered up, had been squandered. Just think, if Abby had stayed asleep for just ten, fifteen minutes more, they would have been caught. They would be in a police station right now, separated. They'd be being interviewed. She'd be safe.

'I need to pee,' said Abby, wriggling in her seat.

Ellie glanced down at the map. It was a little easier to read now; the blurring had abated. There were no towns or villages for miles.

'Layby?' she suggested.

A mile or so on, there was a stopping point. Abby pulled the car in and turned off the engine.

'Won't be a moment,' she said and jumped out. She ran around the car and behind some brush that made a natural cover. Ellie looked in the wing mirror – she could just see the top of Abby's head as she squatted.

In a minute she'll be back, she'll get in the car again. We'll drive off, covering more miles – until what? Ellie hated the not knowing; it made her restless. She found it hard to understand her sister would want to hurt her – but she found it equally hard to dismiss her mother's warnings. The most difficult thing of all was grappling with the idea that her sister had a gun. That cold weapon in her handbag. She tried to reason why Abby might have it. Bears? Ridiculous. Safety? They were in Europe, for God's sake, not Colombia. Ellie couldn't equate the person she thought she knew with this person with a gun. Before now, if she'd seen her sister with a gun, she'd have thought she didn't know her at all.

Which, now she thought about it, she didn't. Not really. And here she was, going along for the ride like a total idiot. Waiting for her sister to show her cards. In the mirror Abby was pulling her shorts back up.

No one is going to rescue me. Ellie got a surge of adrenaline, suddenly furious at being at Abby's beck and call. She turned to the back seat. This couldn't carry on. The not knowing was driving her insane. She pulled Abby's old blue bag towards her, unzipped it. She felt the cold metal in her hands. Then she stepped out of the car and lifted the weapon, just as Abby was walking back towards her.

Abby stopped dead. Ellie looked at her sister, saw fear and confusion spreading across her face. She glanced down at the gun, wondered if she was holding it right. She wasn't sure if she really meant to point it at Abby, but what else could she do?

For a moment, neither of them spoke. Then Ellie thought – as she had the upper hand, so to speak – that she'd start.

'I found this,' she said, waving the gun, noting Abby flinch as she did so. 'What's it for?'

'Jesus, Ellie, put it down.' Abby raised her hands, palms outwards in a calming motion. Then she started to walk towards her, which annoyed Ellie. Her sister was so bloody dismissive.

'Stop!' she instructed. 'Do not move. Do not treat me like an idiot.'

Abby folded her arms, which irritated Ellie further. She raised the gun higher and Abby's face fell instantly.

Good, thought Ellie. *Now you know what it feels like to wonder what's going to happen.* For a brief moment Ellie wondered why she hadn't just asked Abby about the gun, but then in her newfound clarity realized Abby could have simply lied.

'What are you going to do?' asked Abby.

'I just want to know the truth,' said Ellie. 'Why are you driving miles with me, with a gun in your bag?'

'This is silly . . .' Abby had begun to walk towards her again.

'I mean it,' said Ellie, realizing too late the fear had now transferred from Abby and settled within herself. Is that what guns did?

'Put it down.'

'Tell me,' said Ellie, raising her voice. 'What are you doing with this? What's the big secret you're keeping from me?' She aimed this time, properly. Closed one eye and felt the trigger under her finger.

FORTY-NINE

'Ellie, don't do this,' pleaded Abby.

'For once, Abby, not everything is going your way. I am sick and tired of being treated like a lesser individual, the one who can't compete with her oh-so-brilliant sister. You are going to tell me what's going on here.'

'You *know*,' said Abby.

'Was it you?'

Her sister was confused. 'Was what me?'

Ellie made sure she kept the gun raised. 'Was it you who poisoned me when we were children?'

The look on Abby's face seemed genuine enough. It was one of total and utter shock.

'What?' Abby said, her jaw dropping.

'You were jealous of me, Abby, for *years*. I was always the one who got Mum's attention. Maybe some of that stuff still hangs over you. Don't try and deny it,' snapped Ellie, seeing Abby about to open her mouth.

'I wasn't,' said Abby quickly. 'I . . . it's true. Yes, there. You know this. I didn't like you much when we were younger. But as for now . . . what are you suggesting?'

'It's all gone? All that resentment?'

Abby looked awkward. 'We have our moments. But I've never disliked you enough to want to *kill* you, for God's sake. How on earth did you get that idea anyway?'

Ellie watched her. Said nothing.

'Please, will you just put the gun down,' said Abby. 'It's making me nervous. Frightening me out of my wits, actually.'

'Why did you bring it?'

'Um . . . I don't know. Spur of the moment thing. I just saw it there, when I was throwing our stuff together. I was scared. Mum was dead and . . . I don't know, I just felt as if I had to be prepared. For anything. Look, if it makes you anxious, me having it in my bag, then you carry it.'

Don't be fooled, thought Ellie.

Abby kept her expression blank. 'If you kill me, you don't get the money.'

Thrown, Ellie's arms dropped slightly. 'What money?'

'In my will. It's split between you and Matteo.'

'You what?'

'But I should imagine that if you murder me, OK, I'll be dead, but I don't think the law lets you inherit.'

Jesus! Abby had left half of her two-million-pound fortune to her? *Oh my God.* On paper, she was potentially a millionaire. This act of generosity floored her. The idea that her sister had thought of her in such a way was mind-boggling. It left her with a warm glow and Ellie unexpectedly felt her eyes fill with tears.

'If I come towards you, you won't lift that thing again, will you?' asked Abby gently.

Ellie looked down to see her arms had fallen to her sides. She shook her head. She couldn't have used it, even if she wanted to. Suddenly exhausted, the tears started to fall. Abby came over and tentatively embraced her.

'Shall we go?' Abby said softly in her ear. 'I'm certain Jamie will call back today and then we can talk to him and get ourselves out of this mess.'

Ellie stiffened. She was reminded of her earlier fears – and how Jamie would serve to help Abby in defence. Did she trust her sister now? Suddenly Ellie wasn't sure if she'd just been expertly manipulated.

'What if he doesn't? I can't keep on like this, Abby.'

Abby looked at her watch. 'OK, let's give it until this evening. If he hasn't rung by eight, we'll call someone else.'

'Who?'

'I don't know. Anyone. You choose. Use my phone. Google someone. The best person you can find. I'll pay for it.'

There it was again. That same look of genuine care and concern.

Back in the car, Ellie still held the gun in her hand. She didn't want it touching her skin anymore; she found it abhorrent. Should she put it in her own bag? As she hesitated, Abby put a hand over hers.

'I meant what I said. You keep it.'

Ellie dropped it into her bag and pushed it away from her with her feet. Abby started the engine and as she pulled out onto the quiet country road, she exhaled.

'Wow . . . Thank you.'

'For what?'

'Not shooting me.'

Ellie shrugged. 'Welcome.'

'How did you even know how to use that thing?'

'You just pull, don't you?'

'Don't know.'

Ellie looked at her sister. 'You brought a gun and you don't know how to use it?'

'Well, it's not like I've ever needed to find out.'

'Is it even loaded?'

'Not sure. I wouldn't know how to check.'

Ellie pondered. 'I think it was.'

'Really?'

'Yeah. It was heavy.'

Abby looked across and Ellie saw her sister's mouth twitch.

'You could feel the weight of the bullets?' asked Abby.

Ellie frowned. 'What's so funny?'

By now, Abby had erupted into giggles that she was finding impossible to suppress. 'Sorry,' she said, still trying to be serious.

Ellie smiled. 'There was a definite feel of lead, lots of lead.'

Abby was laughing outright now.

'Is that right?' said Ellie, the laughter infectious. 'Are bullets made of lead?'

Abby looked at her and lost control, giddy on the post-adrenaline comedown. Soon both girls were wiping away the tears streaming down their cheeks.

FIFTY

The sun was veering into its mid-afternoon furnace, building on the day's heat to almost unbearable levels. Matteo's mother-in-law had gone for a lie-down several hours ago and still showed no signs of resurfacing. Kathleen had long since left the house. Staggered at the lack of air conditioning, she had retreated to the comfort of her hotel. Matteo suspected she was going to stick around for a while.

Inactivity didn't suit him. He wished he were at work, able to take his mind off these latest revelations.

Abby had a brother who had died as a baby. No, not just died. He had been murdered. And Susanna had covered it up.

It rattled him deeply. Up until now he'd been concerned about his wife's disappearance, yes, but it seemed there would be an explanation. One that would cast his mother-in-law in the less favourable light. At no point had he been fearful. At no point had anyone actually died.

Abby had never mentioned she'd had a baby brother to him. Susanna said she wouldn't have remembered. She'd been so young when he'd died and Susanna had never mentioned him to either of her daughters. She'd also asked

Kathleen not to say anything and Kathleen, not wishing to cause more agony, had complied. Until now.

Matteo needed to get out of the house. He crossed the terrace and took the steps down to the sea. At the platform, a welcoming breeze came off the sea, catching in it the scent of broom from the rocks beside him. He looked at the water rocking gently against the edge; today's clarity was amongst the best he'd seen. Peering over the edge, he could see down four, five metres. Tiny fish flitted against the rocks, searching for food.

Matteo pulled off his shorts and T-shirt and dived in. He swam out, arms circling over his head as he cruised through the water until his muscles began to tire. Then he stopped and looked back at the shoreline. His home was a tiny doll's house on the horizon. He kicked his legs, treading water, knowing there was a great depth below him, a dark unknown, and it felt good to be away from other human beings, an outsider in a watery world.

He tried to think in facts. He was a policeman, after all. A baby had died. Of this he had no doubt. Both Kathleen and Susanna had spoken openly about it. The infant had ingested too much salt and this was the cause of death. Again, neither of the women had denied this. He'd heard stories before of parents – usually mothers – who'd harmed their children in order to gain emotional or financial reward. Fabricated or induced illness, it was now called. There had been a case at work once. A mother had shaved her two-year-old's head and pretended he had cancer. She'd dragged him from doctor to doctor, exaggerating and claiming false symptoms, insisting on tests, manipulating results. She'd been found guilty and the child had been taken away from her.

But Susanna was saying it wasn't her at fault, it was Abby. A jealous older sister who had refused to accept a new sibling. He knew some children could be monstrous towards a new arrival. He also knew they had no real concept of the finality and tragic consequences of death. Toddlers just wanted immediate gratification, order restored. A toddler would struggle with a sense of remorse, would be unable to grasp the extreme overreaction of causing a death to avenge – what was it? – her Lego model being destroyed.

So did he think it was Abby? With a cold jolt, Matteo realized that he didn't know. Doubt sat uncomfortably in his stomach and the calm of the sea left him. He started to swim back, more slowly this time. He climbed onto the rocky platform and sat there, looking out at the water, allowing the sun to dry him off. After a few minutes he heard footsteps behind him and stiffened. He wasn't in the mood to speak to Susanna.

He turned and was surprised to see Lieutenant Colonel Baroni heading towards him, the sun glinting off her shades and her regulation belt buckle. She arrived at the platform, resplendent in her uniform, and looked down at his crotch area. He was suddenly reminded he'd gone swimming in his underwear. He didn't flinch. Let her disapprove. He held position, reclining back on the flats of his hands. Waiting for her to speak. Just then his phone rang in the pocket of his shorts.

'You can answer it,' said Baroni and Matteo bristled. He did not need her permission. Still, he pulled out his phone and saw it was a number he didn't recognize.

Somehow he knew.

'If that's Abby,' said Baroni quickly, seeing the look on his face, 'then you need to find out where she is.'

He almost didn't answer, but the need to speak to his wife was too strong. He swiped right.

'*Pronto.*'

'Hey.'

She sounded subdued, but it was so good to hear her voice he broke into a spontaneous smile. Baroni was looking at him, searching for confirmation. He gave the briefest of nods.

'Are you OK?' he asked Abby.

'Yes, fine. We're both fine.'

Matteo glanced up to see Baroni finishing off writing something in her notepad and thrusting the page at him.

Where is she?

He turned away, but nevertheless asked the question. 'Where are you?'

Abby hesitated. 'Are you on your own?'

His heart stopped. Did he cross over the line?

'Yes.'

He heard her exhale with relief. An exhausted, dispirited

breath. 'A place called Saint-Jean-de-Luz,' she said. 'Almost on the Spanish border.'

Matteo swallowed, weighed down by his betrayal. 'Saint-Jean-de-Luz?' he repeated out loud. 'So you're in France?'

'Yes. The police . . . they've been leaving me messages.'

He started. 'They've got your number? This number?' He turned to Baroni, who was busy on her mobile, searching urgently for something. She looked up at his words, clocked his frown, but simply shrugged at him, then went back to her phone.

'I must've been on CCTV at a retail park. No doubt the guy in the phone shop had to hand over my new number. Although, I'm still not sure how they managed to locate me so quickly.'

Because your sister rang your still-alive mother from a payphone at that retail park, thought Matteo.

'You're probably wondering what's going on?' said Abby.

He let out a strangled laugh. 'You could say that.'

'Susanna – my mother – hurt Ellie as a child. I told Ellie all about it. It ended in a fight. Nothing deliberate,' she quickly added, 'but Ellie pushed Susanna away and she fell. Hit her head. There was nothing we could do. I'm sorry you had to come home to that.' She took a breath. 'What do the police think happened?'

'They don't know for sure.'

'But they suspect foul play?'

Matteo ducked her question. 'What messages have the police been leaving you?'

'Oh, you know: "We can help." "Please contact us." "Let's talk." All the usual.'

Baroni was tapping him on the shoulder. He turned to see her holding up her notepad.

Tell her to go to Hernani. The Palacio Hotel. Tell her you'll meet her there. That you will help.

He pushed the paper away, shook his head angrily.

'Do you know if they're close to finding us?' asked Abby.

'They're not telling me much,' said Matteo. 'What are you going to do?'

'I can't let Ellie go down for our mother's death. It's not right.'

Baroni was tapping him again. More forcefully this time. He turned. She held her notebook out at arm's length. This time she'd written in capital letters and underlined:

ASSISTING AN OFFENDER

She was giving him a long, hard look. *The bitch.* He closed his eyes, knew he'd walked into a trap of his own making. He wouldn't just lose his job; he'd be up in court as well, facing a jail sentence.

'Let me help,' he said, almost choking on the words.

'What?'

'I know that area of northern Spain where you're headed. There's a hotel in a place called Hernani. It's called the Palacio. Go there and wait for me. I'll get to you as soon as

I can. I'll check the flights. I can be there by tomorrow, I'm certain of it.'

'Are you serious?'

'Yes.'

'But your job . . . won't this put you in a really difficult position?'

'I've already lied to them,' said Matteo. *And you*, he added silently, his heart splitting.

Abby was quiet for a moment. 'OK.'

'Turn your phone off now,' said Matteo.

'I will.'

'Or the Carabinieri will be able to trace you.'

'It's OK. I'm going to do it.'

'I'll see you, Abby.'

'See you, Matteo. I love you.'

He nodded. 'Me too,' he said quietly. Then he hung up.

'What was that stuff about turning off her phone?' asked Baroni.

Matteo glared at her. 'She's been doing it anyway, as you already know. Or you would have pinpointed her exact position with that new phone she has, which you didn't bother to tell me about.'

'We weren't certain you'd say the right thing. If you called her.'

'You could have given me the benefit of the doubt.'

But she wasn't listening, she was on her own phone, calling her superiors, requesting a helicopter.

Matteo followed her up the steps, marched past her. He stopped and blocked her path. 'I'm coming too.'

She smiled wryly at him, impatient to get going. 'I don't think so.'

He held up his phone. 'Or I call her right back. She'll pick up the message, you know. And she won't go anywhere near that hotel.'

Baroni paused. Knew she was beaten. 'Fine.' She made to head up the steps again but Matteo called out.

'Why did you come?' he asked.

'Oh. I was going to ask you to call Abby, now we have her number. Only to make sure it all went the way we wanted it to.' She smiled brightly. 'Which it did.'

She turned and walked away. Matteo watched her as she went back into the house. Very soon he would see his wife. Then he would get some answers.

FIFTY-ONE

It had felt so good to speak to her husband. Abby hadn't told Ellie she was going to call him – she hadn't even known herself until the moment arrived. They'd stopped for a break, just a few minutes to use a bathroom, stamp out the fatigue in their legs. Abby had pulled up at a roadside cafe, a place that offered little more than *croque monsieur* and *frites* with a curl of lettuce alongside it.

They'd ordered a cold drink and taken a moment to look at the map, and Abby had seen how close they were to the Spanish border. She'd wondered whether the police knew where they were. If they'd be stopped as they crossed into Spain, Ellie dragged off to a station. Or both of them, actually, for Abby knew she was up to her neck in it as much as her sister.

When Ellie had gone to the bathroom, Abby had risked switching on her phone. She was checking it every thirty minutes just for a few seconds to see if Jamie had rung. There was a message. Her heart raced as she listened to it – but as she'd feared, it was the police, a woman called Baroni. Her third, sympathetically claiming to understand her predicament, pleading with her to call. Abby didn't trust a word she said.

She'd found herself wondering how Matteo was dealing with it all, whether he was helping the Carabinieri. She missed him terribly. She wondered what he was thinking. What Ellie had said had struck home, that thing about not knowing which sister had pushed Susanna. Abby wondered if Matteo thought badly of her, if he thought her capable of cruelty and harm. It made her incredibly sad to think like that and she couldn't bear the idea that he might. She'd also wondered if he knew anything, if the police had confided in him. Before she changed her mind, she'd called him.

The sound of his voice had transported her back home. To their house that sometimes she wondered if she'd ever see again. She could hear the sound of the Tyrrhenian Sea lapping against the rocks and knew he was on the platform. She looked around at the plastic formica-filled cafe and felt a tsunami of homesickness.

When Matteo had offered to help, she'd not known what to say at first. It was the first time someone had offered to ease the burden of what she was carrying alone and she'd felt such a sense of relief, she'd agreed. This was the man who had picked her up after her traumatic attack in Florence, who had held her when the nightmares came night after night. He was the one who'd encouraged her to walk the streets again. He had made her feel safe.

After her call, she hadn't switched her phone off again immediately. There was something else nagging at the back of her brain, something that made her feel off guard. She knew the gun was a Beretta; Matteo had mentioned it once when he'd put it away in the safe. Abby looked around the cafe but there was still no sign of Ellie. She held the phone in her hand and opened up a search page. It didn't take long to google it. In two minutes thirty-nine seconds she had all the answers. She'd watched the video, noting the position of the safety catch, seeing exactly how to fire it. Only when she'd committed everything to memory did she turn off her phone.

A movement made her look up and she saw Ellie come out of the toilets. Abby quickly stuffed her phone in her bag, smiling as her sister approached.

Abby considered whether to tell Ellie about her call to Matteo but knew almost instantly she wasn't going to confide in her. Ellie didn't know Matteo like she did and would likely freak out. Instead they returned to the car and pored over the map together, debating how far they'd get before Abby needed to rest for the night. Abby tried to sound spontaneous as she suggested a place called Hernani.

As they drove off, Abby had butterflies in her stomach. In a couple of hours or so she'd be in a place where she'd arranged to see her husband again. She was nervous the entire drive. As they crossed the border into Spain, Abby half expected to be set upon by a swarm of flashing blue lights, but they drove through without any interruption. She suspected her number plate would register somewhere but defiantly thought she'd be away, lost again in the countryside, before anyone had the chance to act on it.

A warning sign pinged up on the dashboard – a bright orange light in the encroaching dusk. They were low on fuel. Abby didn't want to risk trying to get to Hernani on what was left in the tank.

'We need more petrol,' she said to Ellie. 'Keep your eyes peeled for a station.'

A couple of miles later, a slightly dilapidated service station loomed up ahead. Abby pulled in, noting the weeds encroaching around the edges of the darkening forecourt, the rusty old car abandoned at the back. They were in the middle of nowhere, driving miles between sparsely populated villages; she supposed it didn't get much custom.

She got out and filled the car. Standing with the pump in her hand, she gazed around. There was one other vehicle on the forecourt, a decrepit pickup, being filled by an equally decrepit-looking man. He replaced his pump and went inside.

'I might just go in the shop,' said Ellie. 'See if they've got any mints.'

Abby nodded and then, once the tank was full, followed her sister in.

It was bright inside and Abby made her way over to where Ellie was browsing the confectionery. As she crossed an aisle she didn't see a man coming in the opposite direction and he accidentally caught her shoulder with his own. Both instantly went to apologize, just as her bag fell to the floor. It spilled open and with a tidy thud, the envelope of money fell out, notes fanning themselves as they escaped to the ground.

For a moment, everyone stared. The shop was silent, just the distant murmur of a radio playing, but the money appeared loud, shouty. *Look at me!* it seemed to say, grinning ostentatiously.

Abby looked up at the man who'd bumped into her. He was young, slight, with longish dark hair and low-slung jeans. He caught her gaze, backed away with an apologetic smile. '*Perdón.*'

Abby bent down and quickly retrieved the cash, stuffing it back in her bag. She exchanged a look with Ellie, then went to the till. The older man from the pickup was at the desk paying. The girls waited their turn, and when he was finished he turned and left the shop, the younger man following after him. Abby paid for their fuel and the mints.

As they headed back to the car, Abby noted that it was now completely dark and she wanted to be on her way, to get to the sanctuary of the hotel. She saw the tail lights of the pickup leave the forecourt and disappear from view.

'That was a bit awkward,' said Ellie as she got into the front seat.

Abby nodded. The garage had probably only seen a handful of customers all day – it was bad luck that they had arrived just as there were other people in the shop.

Ellie opened the map. 'Right, back on the road, then there's a left turn about three miles up.'

Abby pulled away from the petrol station. Within a couple of minutes they were back in the countryside, the street lighting gone. Her headlights picked up a rabbit bolting across the road and she was glad to have missed it. It vanished into the thick trees on the verge and was swallowed up into the woods.

The movement caught her eye at just about the same time Ellie screamed. Abby felt the car slide across the road and frantically swung the wheel back, while the hairs on the back of her neck tried to crawl into her scalp. She attempted to flick her head backwards, to see, but her eyes got no further than her sister in the seat next to her.

There was a knife at Ellie's throat. Terror and confusion washed over Abby and she tried to turn, to understand, but—

'Keep your fucking eyes on the road,' snarled a man's heavily accented voice from the back seat.

Petrified, Abby snapped her head back. She could hear Ellie whimpering next to her.

'Don't . . . don't,' stammered Abby.

'Do as I say or I cut her.'

Ellie let out a sound, panic and terror mixed into one.

Abby fearfully flicked her eyes up to the mirror. In the shadows she saw long dark hair and a youthful face. It was the man from the petrol station.

FIFTY-TWO

'I'll give you the money,' said Abby. Her voice didn't sound like her own. It was weak, fearful.

'Turn here,' said the man, ignoring her.

Abby looked skittishly through the darkness, saw her headlights pick out a turning on the right. For a brief second she considered pulling the steering wheel so sharply it would fling him away but she realized the lean of the car and the position of the knife might kill Ellie instantly.

You have to keep calm! You have to think! Her mind was shouting instructions at her but she had no idea how to implement them. The turning got closer and she slowed the car. As she did, she felt a new sickening terror, that of her fight starting to leave her. She changed gear and with the slide of the stick, a penetrating disempowerment began to take hold. *I'm doing what he wants.* No, it was all wrong. Not again. A sense of urgency started up in the background of her mind: *Stop! Don't give up!*

She turned into the road, sped the car up again. Ellie was statue-still on the seat beside her. Abby risked a glance across and saw her sister was white with terror. She was sitting rigid in the seat, her hands gripping the sides. The man's arm was pinning back her right shoulder and his thumb knuckle pressed on her windpipe. The blade was resting on the skin of her neck. Ellie's eyes were locked on some unknown place out of the windscreen; she didn't look back at Abby.

Suddenly the man punched Abby in the face with his spare hand. She screamed and recoiled as far against the driver's door as she could. She heard a mewling sound escape from her sister's throat and understood that, in hitting her, the man had exerted more pressure on Ellie's neck.

'Keep driving,' he snapped.

Abby's face stung. Her jaw felt as if it had been pushed to the other side of her mouth and she tasted blood. She gripped the steering wheel, fighting back tears. She must do nothing to draw attention to herself. She continued onwards, seeing the trees grow denser as they drove further into the woods. Tall pines, thick with green. They were climbing, a sensation that made her sick with foreboding. It meant they were getting further from civilization, from any chance of someone passing them.

Think! Think! She clung to the notion of the money. He hadn't said anything about her offer to take it. Wasn't that what he wanted? Surely, if she could give him the money, then he'd leave them alone? She deliberated bringing it up again. He'd ignored her once but maybe she should say something, tell him how much there was. But she didn't know if it was the right thing to do. She couldn't judge him and she was afraid.

'You can have the money,' she stammered. 'There's a lot. Nearly ten thousand euros.'

He said nothing. The silence grew and in the dark she imagined him on the back seat, watching her. She withdrew into herself, expecting him to slam his fist into her again. She drove on some more. Still he said nothing. It confused her. What was he thinking? What was he doing? She didn't dare look round. The car engine continued to hum as they climbed the winding narrow road, some miles now from the petrol station, their last point of safety.

Abby was suddenly overpowered by a crushing sense of self-reproach. Why hadn't she locked the car? Why hadn't she checked in the shadows of the back footwell amongst all their bags?

'Right,' barked the man and Abby jolted. She looked frantically for the turning, seeing nothing. Then a tiny gap in the trees came up. It wasn't a road, more a track, narrow and steep and overhung with trees. She didn't want to go up there, was resisting it with every fibre of her being.

But there was nowhere else to go. If she drove past it, he would respond with violence.

Abby slowed the car and turned into the track.

FIFTY-THREE

All Ellie could think about was the tiny amount of distance between the skin on her neck and the arteries that pulsated underneath.

He'd barely have to exert any pressure; just a nudge and the knife would slice through, disseminating her blood. There would be no mistake. She'd be dead in minutes.

Suddenly the image of being drenched in her own blood was replaced by another. What if it was her windpipe that was opened up to the elements? What if she was gasping for air, a ragged hole in her neck letting the oxygen escape before it could make its way to her lungs? For some reason this frightened her more and she felt her mind beginning to spasm. She was unable to breathe properly, could feel panic begin to overwhelm her.

Stop, she thought. *You have to stop. Don't panic, don't freak out, don't move*. For Ellie was certain he'd kill her for sure if she began to struggle. He was strong – she knew this by the way he was holding her, never letting up on the pressure across her shoulders ever since he'd grabbed her. She suddenly thought of her mother, of her receiving the news that her daughter had had her throat slit by a random kidnapper, an opportunist who'd seen a pile of euros and would have them, with very little regard to the value of human life. She almost laughed: it wasn't the danger Susanna had been warning her of. Unless . . .

What if Abby had dropped the money deliberately? What if it was a set-up? If Abby had arranged all this in order to get her, Ellie, killed?

You're mad, thought Ellie, squeezing her eyes tight in desperation. *You've lost it; you're traumatized, deranged by fear.*

Who is Jamie? her subconscious demanded, puncturing her attempts at rationalizing her thoughts.

Stop! No, stop, thought Ellie. She couldn't take any more. She had to stop trying to make sense of this nightmare, to unpick her confusion. She had to stop thinking.

FIFTY-FOUR

They'd left Elba quickly – within thirty minutes of Baroni's call to her superiors. They had needed to refuel on the way but it was still only a few hours before the helicopter was passing over some woods just south of San Sebastián, northern Spain. They circled over a golf course where they had permission to land. Matteo looked down, could see the Spanish police car waiting for their touchdown so he, Baroni and Santini could be driven to the hotel in Hernani. As the pilot landed, Matteo exited the chopper and ran over to the vehicle. He ignored Baroni's glare as he took the front seat, leaving her to ride in the back with Santini.

Within twenty minutes they were at the hotel. Baroni took charge at the desk but no one had checked in under Abby or Ellie's names. Neither did the receptionist recognize their faces from the photographs.

Matteo didn't like it one bit. He knew his wife and sister-in-law should have made it by now. Even by going the longest route possible they'd had time to drive the distance.

So where the hell were they?

FIFTY-FIVE

The car rocked as it hit roots and potholes and Abby winced every time, visualizing the flick-knife blade slipping as it pressed on Ellie's throat. They drove slowly along the track for about ten minutes until Abby could see nothing but trees ahead of her. They had come to a dead end.

'OK, stop now,' said the man. Abby put the handbrake on. The car's engine hummed.

'Turn it off,' he instructed.

She did. In turning the key, the headlights dimmed and Abby felt the trees close in on her. The engine ticked as it cooled.

Why were they here? Deep in the woods, miles from civilization? She struggled to think but her brain wasn't working properly, it seemed to have got itself stuck. Then, in a mind-gasping rush, she understood.

He'd brought them here to rob them, yes, take their car too. But he wasn't going to leave them in the woods to find their way back.

He was going to kill them.

She was awash with desperation. *You fool, you bloody fool!* She was now certain that he'd come here because he wanted their bodies not to be found. She was an idiot to have driven here. She'd gone along with what he was telling her, hadn't thought about any of it, hadn't thought what might happen, how she could take back control of the situation. If he'd just wanted to rob them, he would've done it metres from the petrol station. Why hadn't she realized this?

'Leave the key. Get out the car.'

Abby looked back. He was talking to her. She knew she was doing exactly what he asked again, as she slowly opened the car door, stepped outside. *Now's your chance*, she thought. But she did nothing and within seconds he'd got out too and dragged Ellie from her seat as he put the knife back against her neck.

Abby pictured Matteo arriving at the hotel. He couldn't be there yet, but when he did arrive, she'd already be dead. He'd be waiting, thinking she'd changed her mind about meeting him. That she didn't trust him or he didn't matter that much to her after all. It made her unbearably sad.

It was cool in the night air and she shivered. She looked down at her arms, hanging impotent by her side. She felt as she'd done on the ground in a dirty alley in Florence, being kicked – totally and utterly helpless, with a knowledge that her life was in someone else's hands, free for them to do with as they pleased.

FIFTY-SIX

It felt strange, being in the house alone. Susanna had got used to Matteo being around. She'd been surprised when he'd knocked on her bedroom door earlier that evening to explain he had to go out and would be away overnight, maybe longer. She'd pressed him for more detail but he'd been evasive, deliberately so, she thought, citing something to do with a friend. It had sounded highly suspect and it crossed Susanna's mind that his absence was connected to Abby and Ellie, but she had no way of finding out. She'd even called Baroni but had got her answerphone. So far the lieutenant hadn't called her back.

Now it was dark, Susanna could go outside. She took her simple supper of tomato salad and grilled tuna and sat on the terrace to eat. There was something intensely magical about Mediterranean nights: the gently warm air, the sound of crickets with their high-pitched song. In the softness of night, the scents of the garden grew stronger. Hypnotic jasmine hung in the air. Susanna stood at the top of the steps that led down to the sea. It was a full moon and the light glinted off the waves. She thought of her son then, of how small he'd been when he died. Such a tiny little coffin. She was suddenly engulfed by a desire for him to be alive that was so strong it made her gasp. It wasn't supposed to happen like that. So many things in her past that she hadn't meant to happen.

A distant rhythmic banging made her jump. There was someone at the door. Curious, Susanna made her way back through the house.

She stopped for a moment at the front door, suddenly nervous, aware she was alone. Then there was another knock – louder this time – and she jumped. Susanna tentatively opened the door.

It was her mother. Kathleen didn't ask to be invited in, just entered as if it were her right. Not many people said no to her, Susanna supposed. She'd lived a life of believing herself to be a superior breed, had an innate sense of entitlement and expectation for herself and her offspring.

'Where's Matteo?' asked Kathleen as she swept into the living room.

'Gone.'

'Gone where?'

'He didn't say.'

'Something to do with the girls?' Kathleen said sharply.

'Possibly.'

'Don't you *know*? Why aren't you with him, for God's sake?'

'He wasn't issuing invitations. Anyway, he said it was to see a friend.'

'And you believed him?' scoffed Kathleen.

'No, not exactly. I . . .' Susanna trailed off, unsure of

what she was going to say. Suddenly she felt as if she should have pushed Matteo, not been so inadequate and weak.

Kathleen settled herself into a seat. She sat back, appraised Susanna. 'Your own children and you let them despise you.'

Susanna's mouth dropped open in shock.

'Chip off the old block.'

'I don't despise you, Mummy,' said Susanna, feeling an instant need to defend her position, reassure her mother. Even as she did so, her weary internal voice was asking her why. After all these years, could she not tell when she was being manipulated and bullied?

Kathleen made a sound of disdain. 'Are you not going to get me a drink?'

Susanna jumped up. 'Of course. Would you like a tea? Coffee? Or I think there's some orang—'

'Anything.'

Susanna went into the kitchen. As she poured a glass of juice from the fridge, she took a deep breath. *Don't let her get to you*, she told herself, trying to be stern, but when she went back into the living room, her hands trembled as she handed over the drink.

'Thank you,' said Kathleen, then she waved impatiently at the empty chair opposite her.

Susanna knew to lower herself into it. She waited as her mother took a sip of the juice then laid her head back and closed her eyes. Susanna watched her, as a gazelle might view a sleeping lion. After a moment, the glass began to tip in Kathleen's hand. Susanna hesitated, unsure of whether to act, then as it tipped further, she got up, alarmed. She reached out her hand.

'Leave it,' said Kathleen, her eyes still shut.

Susanna froze.

'Sit down.'

She retreated to her seat.

'You can tell me the truth, you know,' said Kathleen. 'I know you poisoned Ben and I know you did the same to Ellie when she was small.'

Susanna looked at her mother's face, old now. She could see the folds on her neck, the lined skin. Despite the fact Kathleen wasn't even looking at her, Susanna was too intimidated to form a robust denial. 'I didn't,' she said. 'You're wrong.'

Kathleen smiled, a mocking, dismissive smile. Her eyes popped open. 'And there I was hoping for honesty, but I can understand why you won't admit it. I didn't treat you right when we cut you off. A lot of what you have become is my responsibility.'

Susanna didn't know what to say, what was expected of her. She stayed silent.

'It was hard for you. Financially.' Kathleen took another sip of her drink. 'I'm well aware of how you survived.'

The knots in her stomach tightened. 'I got a job.'

'Yes, yes, a piddly little thing in a clothes shop. Could've barely kept you in toilet tissue. No, it was your ex-husband's alimony that stopped you going under.'

Susanna's stomach started to churn. She considered just getting up and walking out of the room – knew she should, if she had the courage – but the part of her that despised herself knew she wouldn't be able to do it.

'*He* didn't pay, though, did he? Humiliating enough that he left you because you turned out to be penniless, but for his new wife, the one who'd dazzled him with her millions, for her to be the one who paid your monthly allowance . . . Devastating, I should imagine.'

Susanna sat, writhing in misery.

'If we hadn't cut you off, would he have stayed with you? Was your money good enough? I rather think it would have been.'

'I hate you!'

'Just like a child, lashing out. My God, you're in your late fifties now, surely you've grown up? My fault again, I suppose. I think it's time I made amends.'

Susanna wasn't sure if she'd heard right at first. Not the words – she was familiar with her mother dropping bait in order to manipulate – but it was her tone. It had sounded strangely contrite. A word she would never attribute to her mother. She remained wary. 'What do you mean?'

'When Matteo called me, of course I came to see what's happened to my grandchildren. But I was also curious to see you. It's been so many years.' She paused, portentously. 'Time has slipped by. And I don't have long left.'

Shocked, Susanna sat up. 'What is it . . . ? Cancer?'

Kathleen's eyes flashed in exasperation. 'Goddammit, Susanna, do you always have to be so . . .'

Stupid, thought Susanna instantly.

Her mother pulled herself up short. Took a breath. 'Old

age, for crying out loud. Simple old age. Except there's nothing simple about it.' She sighed. 'It's a great leveller. It gives you a perspective on life that's impossible when you're young. It's why I think it's time we were truthful with one another. Apologize where an apology is due.' Kathleen held up a hand. 'I know I should be first in line. I'm guilty of worse crimes to you than you are to me. But that's why I thought you might understand. How, as a mother, I feel remorse at how I treated my child. I thought we should both come clean, confide in one another. Each of us is guilty of harming our children, albeit in different ways.'

'I—'

'Please, let me finish. I am old and I am tired of dishonesty. I rattle around in that huge house with all my money and I've realized I haven't even been honest with myself. I owe you, Susanna, for past misdemeanours. I have nothing to give to you except what was rightfully yours, all those years ago. It's your legacy. But as I wish to confess, so I think you should too. Strip us both of the blankets behind which we hide our crimes. Take us both back to the beginning. How it should have been.'

Susanna was struggling to take it all in. She shook her head. 'Sorry, do you mean . . . you're going to . . .' She couldn't say it.

Kathleen smiled. 'Give you everything. Yes. When I die, you should have it all. But I can't go to my grave with us like this. Call it catharsis if you like. I'm being selfish. Old age has made me want to atone. Maybe it's what happens when you stare mortality in the face. I think you're more like me than you know. And that makes me feel less lonely.

'So what do you think? I'm asking you to be brave and honest. No judgements. I know it's all because of me anyway. I want to hear what I've been responsible for so I can apologize. It'll be between you and me. And I'll thank you for it. With your rightful inheritance.' Kathleen stood. 'I'm not expecting you to decide now, I realize that's unfair of me. These are big things to admit to.'

She made her way to the front door, Susanna following.

'Let's speak again tomorrow.'

As her mother opened the door, Susanna saw a taxi outside. Clocking them, he started the engine, and Susanna watched as Kathleen made her way over to the car and was helped inside.

She closed the door behind them and collapsed against it.

FIFTY-SEVEN

'*Move*.'

Abby looked up to see their kidnapper was indicating up into the trees. She was suddenly overwhelmed by the smell of pine, its sweetness making her nauseous. Time was running out. He wouldn't have to take them far, just enough of a distance so they were out of sight of the path. It was likely no one came up here anyway; the track had appeared unused and Abby doubted it was a place that saw much human presence. It might be months before anyone found their bodies.

Ellie was staring at her, her eyes brittle with fear. The man had one arm around her sister's upper body, pinning her hands by her side. The other still held the knife at Ellie's throat. Abby saw the blade glint. Light had caught the metal and she looked down to see the yellow warmth from the inside of the car. The doors had been left open and the interior lights were the only brightness for miles. Oh, how she longed to get back inside. Grab her sister and run for it. Slam the doors shut and lock them. Drive like a maniac back down the path, mowing down the monster who had kidnapped them. She knew she wouldn't care if he died, if she killed him. She imagined his body crushed by the wheels, his agony as he screamed out, but she would keep going. The key was waiting in the ignition, dangling. Just a couple of metres separated her from them.

'Now!' shouted the man. 'Fucking move!' Ellie whimpered in terror.

Abby looked at him, saw his fear, his need to get them in the woods. Shaking, she took a step in the direction of the trees. She had to go around the front of the car to do so. He was standing at an opening in the pines, just beyond the front passenger door. Abby continued edging forwards until she was almost around the other side of the car. It was dark and she didn't notice a rock in the ground. She stumbled and reached out to grab the passenger door handle to steady herself. As she did, she saw inside the car, in the footwell.

Ellie's bag.

'Hurry up!' He was getting jittery, dangerous. Abby edged around the door, pretending to limp, holding on to the door frame.

'I've hurt my ankle,' she said tearfully.

'I don't fucking care. Start walking or I cut her throat.'

Ellie began to cry then, gasping out sobs as she struggled to breathe, the man's hold on her tightening, the knife pressing against her windpipe. Abby stumbled again and cried out in pain as she fell against the sill of the car. The movement threw the man and in the millisecond of confusion, Abby twisted and flung her arms into the footwell and into Ellie's bag. She felt the coldness of the gun in her hands and as she turned to face the man she pulled back the slide, disengaged the safety catch and fired.

The noise pierced her eardrums like nothing she'd felt before, disorientating her as it throbbed in her brain. She was aware of her attacker falling backwards, pulling Ellie on top of him. Then Ellie scrabbled away, shrieking and crying, and Abby watched, dumbfounded, as the man lay on the ground, his eyes staring up at the dark sky, the knife still in his hand. Dark liquid oozed swiftly from behind his back.

Abby stared, still in shock. Then she remembered her sister.

'Are you OK?'

Ellie was curled up in a ball, her hands wrapped over her head as she rocked back and forth.

Abby got up, the gun still in her hand. She edged towards the man, her heart hammering. As she got closer, she knew that he could dart out a hand and grab her ankle. She quickly kicked at his hand. The knife scattered away into the damp earth. He didn't move.

Abby went over to Ellie, grabbed her elbow. 'Get up,' she said urgently. 'Get up!'

Ellie stood and Abby manhandled her back into the car. She slammed the door shut, then ran around to the driver's side. Throwing the gun onto the back seat, she started the engine, rammed the car into reverse. Then she let her foot off the clutch and they hurtled backwards down the hill. The car rocked over potholes and roots as Abby desperately tried to keep control.

She looked up, fearing the man wasn't dead, that he would be following, throwing himself onto the bonnet, but the headlights picked up nothing except the dark, empty track. She kept driving, bouncing down the path until she could see the main road in the rear windscreen. She reversed into the road, then turned the car and sped away.

'Are you all right?' she said, glancing over at Ellie.

Her sister managed a weak nod. 'You shot him,' she whispered.

'What, you wanted me to leave him to kill us?'

'No!'

They raced down the road in silence for a while before coming back to the first junction where they'd been forced to turn. Abby looked expectantly at Ellie.

'What?' asked Ellie.

'Which way?'

Ellie stared at her.

'I don't think we should go to Hernani,' said Abby. 'We need to get as far away from here as possible.'

'You're acting like nothing's happened.'

'Plenty's happened but we still have to get away.' She looked at Ellie, indicated out of the windscreen. 'So?'

'Oh my God, you're insane.'

'Just pick a route, Ellie.'

'Um . . . left. Fuck it, left!' Ellie blurted in exasperation.

Abby put the car in gear and pulled away.

FIFTY-EIGHT

Ellie hunched in her seat, hugging her arms to keep out the cold. Except the cold seemed to be coming from inside her. She would shiver uncontrollably every now and then – it wasn't the air temperature, it was the aftershock. How close had death been? It was a question that, if she faced it, she got a sense of fear so great it was as if she was on the edge of a black hole, falling, falling, soundless, meaningless, snuffed out into nothing. She'd gasp, realizing she'd been holding her breath, and try to fixate on something else.

Ellie swallowed and in doing so felt again the tenderness; her throat was bruised. She instinctively lowered her chin, closing up the vulnerable gap where her jugular vein was exposed for anyone to slice through. *Stop it. It's over.* Except that man was lying near the trees, his blood soaking into the ground. And her sister was the one who'd put the bullet in him.

Ellie glanced across at Abby, seeing her focus on the road ahead. Who exactly was she sitting next to? No, she should be grateful. Goddammit, she *was* grateful. If it hadn't been for Abby, they'd both be dead.

'How did you do that?' Ellie asked quietly.

'Do what?'

'You were so brave. So quick. You got the gun.'

Abby gave a small smile.

'He could have killed you. Both of us. I couldn't do anything,' Ellie said.

'He did have a knife to your throat.'

'I know, but even so . . . I was numb. Petrified.'

'I was pretty scared myself.'

'Yes, but you still did it. You didn't give up.'

'It was chance. I saw your bag in the footwell. I just went for it.'

'I'd all but given up, Abby,' insisted Ellie. 'But you . . . you fought back.'

Abby pondered. 'I did, didn't I?' She paused for a moment as it sank in. 'Oh my God, I fought back. I fought back!'

Abby was punching the steering wheel as she spoke, her eyes suddenly alive on adrenaline. 'I bloody fought him. And I won! I won!' She let out a whoop, then threw her head back in a victorious laugh. 'Oh my God, Ellie, you're right. *I fought back.*'

Ellie gave a nervous smile. Her sister's behaviour was a little unnerving. She'd never seen Abby quite so . . . animated before.

'You stood up to him,' she agreed.

Abby grinned. 'I did. I stood up to you, you nasty bastard!' she shouted. 'I didn't let you beat me!'

Ellie yelped as the car suddenly swerved across to the other side of the empty road, then back again. Abby was driving like a maniac, back and forth, whooping and yelling.

'Stop,' said Ellie, gripping the dashboard. 'Please stop.'

Abby hardly seemed to be listening. 'I fought back,' she yelled again and then was suddenly weeping, huge wracking sobs convulsing through her body.

'Abby?' said Ellie in alarm. The car was veering uncontrollably. 'Pull over.'

To Ellie's relief, Abby steered the car back to the right side of the road and slowed until they'd stopped. Tears were still pouring down her face and she was trying to wipe them away but it was as if a dam had broken.

At a loss, Ellie picked up her handbag, rummaged inside. 'Here,' she said, pulling out a tissue and handing it to her sister. 'It's scented. Rose and sandalwood,' Ellie said apologetically, expecting another reprimand about frivolous spending, but Abby just blew her nose.

'Are you OK?' asked Ellie, once Abby had quietened.

'Last year,' said Abby, 'when I was mugged, in Florence . . . it was the most terrifying thing that had ever happened to me. Not because he stole my bag or my phone, or even because I got stabbed. The worst thing was that they stole who I was. Brave, independent Abby.' She turned to look at Ellie, her voice breaking. 'I did nothing when they attacked me. Just lay there. I was too pathetic to even shout out.'

'I'm sure you didn't—'

'It has stayed with me ever since. I knew that if anyone decided they wanted something from me, I wouldn't be able to defend myself. I was a free target. *Come and get it. She won't fight back. Take what you want.*' Abby wiped her eyes with the back of her hand. 'Until tonight.'

Ellie was quiet. Then she squeezed her sister's arm. They sat there for a while in a pensive silence, looking out at the dark road while the moths flitted in the car headlights.

'Is that why you brought the gun?' asked Ellie. 'Because of what happened to you in Florence?'

'Yeah . . . I think so. It was instinct, you know? I just picked it up out of the safe.'

Ellie nodded. 'And there was me thinking you'd brought it to do away with me,' she said lightly. She looked across at her sister. 'I wish you'd told me before. About the mugging. How it affected you.'

Abby shrugged.

'Did you tell Mum?'

'Course not,' said Abby. 'I just told her the bare minimum. Played it down.'

'But why? She's your mother.'

Abby turned patiently to Ellie. 'She and I didn't have that kind of relationship. Not like you.'

'But . . . something big like that . . .'

'No, Ellie. We didn't talk.'

'I'm sorry,' said Ellie. 'It must have been lonely.' She thought of all the times she'd called up her mother to whinge, offload or just have a friendly ear. 'She was a good listener.'

'I could see that. You two were always close.'

'I'd tell her everything. I'd call just to moan about the fact someone had queue-jumped me in the supermarket.'

'Seriously? God, I feel sorry for her now. Was there anything you didn't share with her?'

There was one thing, thought Ellie. Something she hadn't told anyone. Something she guarded with every fibre of her being.

She looked over at her sister, saw her sniff. 'Want another tissue?' she asked. 'I've got lavender and chamomile as well.'

Abby let out a small laugh. 'Sure. Why not?' She blew her nose again, loudly. 'Right. Are you ready?'

Ellie nodded. As Abby continued along the road, Ellie had a sudden realization. That was probably the first time Abby had confided in her. Ever.

Then a second thunderbolt hit her. If her sister was supposed to want to harm her, why had she just saved her life?

FIFTY-NINE

Matteo listened to his wife's phone go straight to voicemail for the second time that night.

'Call again,' said Baroni.

'What's the point? It's obviously switched off.'

'Where are they?' Baroni stomped across the gravel to the entrance of the Palacio Hotel, not caring, it seemed, if Abby and Ellie were to drive in. Except they wouldn't, thought Matteo. They should've arrived hours ago. Santini was sitting on a wall, smoking.

Baroni spun around, fixed Matteo with an accusatory glare. 'Did you call her again earlier? Tell her about this?' She waved her arm at the hotel.

'When was I supposed to do that? I've been with you the entire time.'

Baroni glowered at him, then stared out at the dark road. 'They're not coming. They've either changed their minds or . . .' She shrugged in frustration.

Or what? thought Matteo. That was the trouble. Something had happened to his wife to make her change her plan to meet him and he couldn't think of one positive explanation as to what that might be. Which left him with only a dark sense of foreboding.

SIXTY

Susanna had needed a drink after her mother had left. She'd looked through Abby's kitchen cupboards until she'd found a bottle of wine and then searched in frustration for a corkscrew. The wine was warm so she'd added a handful of ice cubes to the large glass and taken several great gulps. Then she'd laid her hands on the counter and allowed herself to think about what had just happened.

Everything will go to me. It was huge – millions. The house itself was worth five million, the business – well, she had no idea, but it would be another significant chunk. She would never have to worry about money again.

Susanna picked up her glass and made her way outside to the terrace. It was late now and the crickets had quietened. Peace reigned. The stars were out. Susanna stared up at them, thinking what a perfect place this was. How it might now be possible for her to own such a place. To never have to live through a British winter again. To pack in her menial job. She could do anything; she'd never be fearful of what her future held. It was like a fairy tale with a happy ending.

Her mother was sorry. That's what she'd said. She'd actually admitted that she'd been a poor parent, that she'd treated her own daughter badly. Old memories came flooding back and Susanna took another gulp of wine. It was so long ago. She found herself looking at the olive tree next to her on the terrace. Her eyes sought out a branch, quite thin and without any burrs or small twigs attached to it as they hurt so much. It wasn't *too* thin as that was another mistake. If she chose a branch that was too slight, her mother would make her pick another, something with more weight. Susanna instinctively rubbed her fingers against her palms, remembering the lashings. If she couldn't list the capital cities of Europe or recite her times tables. Her mother had said it would focus her attention.

As Susanna had got older the physical punishments had lessened but the control had been tighter. Kathleen had very strict ideas on which friends her daughter saw and boys were taboo. She went to an all-girls private school and wasn't allowed out after nine o'clock at night – even in her late teens. After school was completed, she was brought into the fold of the business, under the tutelage of her father's right-hand man.

Susanna hated it all but was too terrified to change anything. She didn't know how. Once, when she had said she was meeting a friend from school on a Saturday evening, her parents had found out she'd actually gone for a drink with a boy. In punishment for being deceitful, her parents had removed her bedroom door. She had no privacy, not even to get dressed.

Miserable, Susanna could see no way out. Then, one lunchtime, she'd gone to her usual sandwich bar and been approached by a man who was so good-looking he gave her goosebumps. Danny told her he worked in some offices along the street. She told him she worked for her father's business. He'd asked her out, later saying he'd fallen for her the first time he'd seen her. He was the epitome of joy and freedom and his charm was an ointment for her damaged self-esteem. Susanna had sneaked out on dates for three months, always nervous as hell that her parents would find out, as she was certain they'd disapprove of him. Just when she thought she couldn't take the pressure of lying to them any longer, he proposed. They were only twenty, but of course she said yes.

Her parents had been apoplectic, but Susanna knew they couldn't stop her. Not when she felt so empowered now Danny had promised to look after her. Before long she was pregnant. Abby was born and Danny was disappointed at how his in-laws refused to help financially. They struggled on his salary, with Susanna then out of work as she was no longer welcome at her father's company. The early devotion Danny had shown her quickly evaporated and he became more absent, no longer returning for bath time and spending his weekends doing overtime at the office.

Ben came along a year later and Danny was overjoyed at having a son. For a while, to Susanna's relief, things between the two of them got a bit better. Then Danny was passed over for a promotion and they had been counting on the salary increase. It was a real blow. Danny returned to working late and Susanna hated being in the house alone. Worse, she hated the feeling that he was avoiding her. She tried to tempt him back, made sure she didn't complain when he rolled in at ten at night, smelling suspiciously of booze. She still gave him sex when all she wanted to do was curl under the covers and pass out with tiredness. Once, as he climbed into bed, she thought she could smell perfume on him, but when she tentatively asked him about it, he snapped and produced a bottle from his jacket pocket. A gift, he'd said, a surprise he was saving for her. She'd immediately felt guilty but wondered why he hadn't given it to her straight away. She also wondered why he would have sprayed the testers on himself; it seemed out of character to her – he was too image-conscious to put women's scent on his own skin. But by now she was pregnant again and terrified of being left alone. She still had no contact with her parents and was struggling with two demanding children, one of whom had recently been ill.

One day Susanna got home from taking Abby and Ben to the park and found a note from Danny on the kitchen table. He said he 'couldn't handle it'. She tearfully begged him to reconsider when he phoned, but he became embarrassed, didn't want to have anything more to do with her. He wouldn't tell her where he was living and said something vague about staying on a friend's sofa, of it not being suitable for young children. He said that once he was 'settled' he would arrange to have the children for visits. She couldn't argue, not when he sent monthly bank deposits. They kept her afloat – it wasn't enough to feel flush with cash but it kept them with food and clothes and a roof over their head. She often felt guilty that Danny must have been struggling to survive himself – with the amount he was sending, she thought it would be impossible for him to afford his own place.

Then tragedy hit. Ben died and Susanna was devastated. It hit Danny hard too but still he wouldn't come back to her, wouldn't comfort her. At the funeral, Susanna learned why. He turned up, face reddened with tears, clutching the hand of a woman who was a decade older and owned an immensely successful recruitment business. Susanna had always pictured him sleeping on a crusty old sofa, no space or privacy, whereas he'd been living in a six-bedroomed mansion the whole time. She was dumbfounded. All that time he could have taken the children and he hadn't. All that sympathy she'd thrown his way. It had all been lies and she was the fool who had fallen for them.

Soon after, Danny had a new family and they were completely forgotten – except for the monthly deposits, which Susanna knew were paid for by his new, wealthy wife.

All of that misery and shame could be wiped out now. Her mother was offering peace, reconciliation. The only thing she had to do was change her story. Say that it wasn't Abby who had harmed her children – it was herself.

SIXTY-ONE

Dawn broke over the wooded hills south of San Sebastián, the light creeping like tendrils through the trees. A low mist hung near the ground, clinging to its last few minutes before it was obliterated by the growing power of the sun. A buzzing sound came from where the track ended and the pines began. Low at first, hardly impacting on the consciousness; then, going closer, it became louder, more chaotic.

A mass of black flies swarmed, darting in and out, landing on the source of their frenzy.

Matteo stood and looked at the body lying on the track. A man, believed to be in his early twenties. He lay on his back, his face exposed to the flies. They flew freely in and out of his open mouth, landed on the jellied surface of his staring eyes.

Lieutenant Baroni was standing next to Matteo, also looking at the victim of what was clearly a murder. Blood soaked the ground. The forensic team were efficiently cordoning off the scene of the crime. The dog walker who'd called it in was being comforted somewhere down near the road with a strong coffee.

'It's a known criminal,' said Baroni as the Spanish police

busied around them. 'Someone they've had dealings with before.'

Matteo said nothing. He knew she was saving the best for next.

'You think that bullet they pull out of him will match those in your gun?'

Possibly. Matteo's stomach sank like a stone. *Or is it probably?*

Baroni turned to look behind her, beyond the parked-up police cars. 'Tyre marks veering haphazardly from one side of the track to the other. Looks like a fast getaway.' She turned back to him. 'They'll be able to match the tread. Could well be a Fiat 500.'

Matteo could hear the hunger, the relish in her voice. He knew she was like a shark smelling blood, that she wouldn't rest until she'd got the answers she wanted.

Baroni folded her arms. 'So, Matteo, it seems your wife is more dangerous than you thought.'

He wanted to deny it. But the words fell flat on his tongue.

SIXTY-TWO

Ellie sensed light prising open her eyelids. With the light came consciousness and with consciousness came pain. Her right leg felt as if an army of ants were under her skin, crawling up and down it. She tried moving and grimaced, muffling a groan. She opened her eyes, crusty with sleep, and was greeted by the sight of two suns rising over two hills. She blinked until they settled into one and watched as the green on the hill crest turned from bottle to emerald.

They had parked up in the empty layby at about four in the morning, Abby so exhausted she could no longer drive. Ellie looked through the windows of the car, seeing in daylight where she'd spent the night. They were surrounded on all sides by rolling farmland, fields sectioned by trees. Sheep grazed in the distance, small dots of black and white venturing up the hillside. Further away, there was the cluster of red-roofed buildings of a town.

Ellie heard Abby stir beside her. She waited while her sister came to.

'Where exactly are we?' said Abby, rubbing her eyes.

'Not sure. I lost track of the map for a bit while we were driving. When I fell asleep.'

Abby got out of the car and stretched. Ellie took advantage of her sister's distraction to ease herself out. She felt dizzy as she stood and tried to regain her balance while she gripped the car door, her eye catching something on the back seat.

Abby turned. 'Are you OK?'

Ellie smiled. 'Fine. What do you think of our bedroom view?'

'It's beautiful.' She paused. 'I wonder if they've found him yet.'

'Who knows?' Ellie hesitated. 'Should we call it in?'

'You mean, speak to the police?'

'Well . . . yes.'

'And tell them I've murdered someone as well as you? Double arrest?'

Except I haven't murdered anyone, thought Ellie. She wondered about telling Abby then, saying that Susanna was alive. After all, if, as she now thought, Abby was genuinely looking out for her, what harm could it do?

Abby stared pensively at the hills, then shook herself. 'We should get going.' She pointed at a few bushes on the edge of a field. 'Our bathroom?'

'You first,' said Ellie. She waited until her sister was out of sight and then looked back into the car at what had caught her eye. The gun was still lying on the back seat where Abby had thrown it the night before in their quick getaway. There was no need to be afraid anymore. Was there? Ellie looked up and saw her sister was still behind the bushes. She opened the back door of the car, quickly got the gun and put it back in her handbag.

They hadn't been driving long when Abby glanced down at the dashboard. 'Fuel's low again,' she said. 'Going through the night pretty much emptied the tank.'

They found a petrol station and Abby pulled up at the pumps. Wearily she began to fill up. When the tank was full, she got back in the car next to Ellie.

'Do you mind sorting it this time?' she asked. 'Only I feel so tired.'

Ellie felt she could hardly refuse – her sister had paid for everything so far. She tentatively got out and glanced up at the pump, her stomach sinking as she saw the figure on the dial. She crossed the forecourt and went inside. There was no one else there so she went straight to the till and took out her purse to pay.

Please work, please work, she prayed as she typed her PIN into the machine.

A frown appeared on the cashier's face. '*No funciona*,' he said, and Ellie gave a casual smile to hide her panic.

'That's strange,' she said. She made a pretence of looking for cash, knowing her purse was empty. Should she just go and ask Abby? Her heart sank. It was so shameful.

'I'll just get some money from my sister,' she said brightly, indicating through the window at Abby sitting in the car outside.

The cashier looked up, gave a cautious nod.

Ellie left the shop as nonchalantly as she could and got

back into the car. She paused. Now was the time to tell her sister that she was skint and she needed Abby to bail her out.

Ellie took a deep breath, settled in her seat.

'OK, all done.'

Abby, still sluggish with fatigue, slowly started the engine.

Hurry up, urged Ellie silently. She surreptitiously glanced towards the shop and saw the cashier watching them suspiciously.

Abby stretched, pushing her arms up to the roof of the car. Then she dropped her arms down, looked out of the car window. 'Why is that man running towards us?'

Ellie turned her head to see the cashier running across the forecourt. 'Go, go, go!' she shouted.

'What's going on?' asked Abby.

'Just drive!' yelled Ellie, and her sister finally put the car in gear and spun out of the petrol station.

'What was all that about?' cried Abby as they sped down the road.

'Umm . . . my card didn't work.'

'*What?* You drove off without paying?'

'Well, technically, you did.'

'But that's illegal!'

The sun was higher now and Ellie reached into the glove compartment and put her sunglasses on. 'So is shooting someone,' she said.

Abby narrowed her eyes. For a moment, Ellie thought she was going to go nuts. Then the corner of her mouth twitched.

'Oh God, Ellie,' she said. 'You're right, you're right.' She let out a small laugh. 'Don't do it again, OK? We need to get away, not leave any traces. Robbery leaves traces.'

So do dead bodies, thought Ellie.

'Why didn't your card work?'

'Um . . . I'm in a bit of debt.'

'How much?'

'A few thousand.'

'When you say a few, you mean—'

'Eighteen thousand pounds,' declared Ellie suddenly and the car fell silent. Ellie's chest tightened. She felt exposed, as if she was going out into the street naked. She kept her eyes on the road ahead, didn't want to see what she was certain was her sister's gaping look of incredulity.

'Eighteen *grand*?' repeated Abby.

Ellie bristled, felt her cheeks heat up.

'From what?' asked Abby.

She shrugged. 'Gradual build-up over the last few years.'

'Build-up of *what*?'

Ellie snapped her head round. 'Could you stop saying it as if I've robbed a bank or something. And as you're so keen . . . I don't know really. Can't pinpoint anything in particular.'

Ellie felt the car slow and looked up at Abby in alarm. White-faced, her sister pulled over to the side of the road. She seemed detached, was staring out of the window.

'What's wrong?' asked Ellie.

Abby turned to face her. 'You can't account for eighteen thousand pounds' worth of spending?'

Ellie huffed. 'Look, I don't get paid much. I work hard. I need to let off steam sometimes. Look after myself.'

'But that's so much money!'

'It's over years, Abby. I work all the hours I have to give at that school, and my salary barely touches the sides. I feel like I'm going round in circles. OK, so I know I could rent somewhere cheaper, maybe treat myself less often, but I also need to live my life.' She paused. 'You wouldn't understand. I did so little when I was younger. Always ill, always missing out. My world was so small. I feel like I lost something that I'll never get back.'

'But Ellie . . . *Eighteen thousand pounds!*'

The familiar panic fluttered up in Ellie again and she looked at her sister, but then something surprised her. She realized she felt sorry for Abby. At the effect the debt was having on her, and it wasn't even her debt. Her sister didn't seem to have the ability to understand that money could give you choices and experiences as well as security.

'You never know how long you've got on this earth,' said Ellie. 'I guess I always had an underlying understanding of my own mortality from when I was young. You know, always being so ill. I didn't ever tell anyone but when I was little I decided I had cancer. I thought I was going to die. I would go to bed and put a note under my pillow: "I love you, Mum. Bye bye." In case I didn't wake up in the morning.'

Her sister was looking at her expectantly.

'No, I didn't include you.' Ellie shrugged.

Abby blinked and then barked out a laugh.

'Look at last night,' Ellie went on. 'That could have ended very differently. It could have been us lying with our throats cut in those woods. What would your millions do for you then, Abby?'

For once, her sister had nothing to say.

SIXTY-THREE

Matteo was sitting in the back of the police car, alone. He was far enough away from the crime scene to be unnoticed, which was how he liked it, but close enough that he could see what was going on. The tent was now up, covering the body; police and forensics crawled the area.

It was quiet in the car and it gave him space to think. A man lay dead just a few metres from him, shot in the back. There was still no connecting evidence that Abby had done it, or that she'd even been to these woods, but he had a sense of foreboding that later on this afternoon the evidence would start to pile up. The bullet would be the same as those from his regulation police gun, fibres would be found on the corpse's body, Abby's hair might be on the ground amongst the blood and the leaves.

Once all that happened, Matteo knew his wife would be wanted as a suspected murderer. It didn't matter that the piece of scum on the hill probably deserved to die. Abby was armed and would be considered dangerous. When they caught up with her, there would be no softly, softly arrest. They would take her down.

And what about him? How did he feel about his wife

now she was the subject of a manhunt? And what about all that stuff when she was younger? Had she poisoned her brother, attempted to do the same to her sister?

The door opposite him suddenly opened. He looked over to see Baroni slide onto the back seat next to him.

'Have you heard from her?' she asked.

He felt a twinge of irritation. 'No,' he said. 'Otherwise I would have told you.' *Wouldn't I?* He didn't know, and decided to ignore her look of scepticism.

'You made any calls?'

'Again, no.'

'OK. You need to ring her and pretend you know nothing about any of this. Tell her you're on your way to Hernani but you just called the hotel to make sure she arrived safely and they said she never showed up. Ask her if she is OK and where she is right now. Sound like a loving husband. A *concerned*, loving husband.'

He bit his lip to stop himself from saying something he'd later regret. How he hated her authoritarian tone.

'You know that even if she had something to do with this, she's vulnerable. She's not a criminal.' Even as the words left his mouth, he felt stupid.

Baroni looked at him. 'Oh, I think she's very much a criminal. In fact, it seems she's clocking up quite a list of misdemeanours: leaving the scene of an accident, damage to personal property, making off without payment, murder, and now . . .' – she paused and he felt himself tense – 'it seems they've driven off from a petrol station without paying too. This morning. Caught on CCTV,' she added, in case he questioned it.

Matteo felt her watching him.

'So, are you going to call?' she prompted. 'Only, her sister might thank you for it, before she gets hurt too.'

He glowered. 'Her phone will be switched off.'

'If it is, leave her a message. Tell her how much you want to see her, that you're worried about her.'

Matteo looked up the hill, saw Santini strutting about, champing at the bit to get involved.

'Don't shut me out, Matteo,' said Baroni. She glanced up at Santini with a flicker of a frown. 'It's in your wife's best interests.'

Matteo took out his phone and dialled Abby's number. As he suspected, it went straight to voicemail. He turned his back on Baroni.

'Abby, it's me. I know you didn't make it to the hotel. What's happened? I want to help. I'm here for you. Call me as soon as you can.'

He hung up, just as a white zipped-up body bag was carried down the hill, right past the car window. He looked away.

A phone rang. Matteo jumped, but it was Baroni's.

'*Pronto*.'

She listened for a while and Matteo saw her face flicker with interest. She clocked him watching her and got out of the car so she could continue the call in private. Matteo frowned as she walked away, deep in conversation.

SIXTY-FOUR

They'd been driving for two hours and not seen one police car. A cautious sense of security began to creep its way into Ellie. Maybe the man hadn't yet been discovered. Maybe the cashier in the petrol station hadn't reported their theft. Or maybe he had but the police were too stretched to deal with it.

The sun had strengthened and Abby had lowered the roof. Driving with the heat of the sun and the wind against her skin made Ellie feel incredibly alive. They were a part of the rising hills, the winding roads. She could reach out a hand as they brushed past trees. Kites wheeled overhead, searching for prey. The landscape was within them as they were in it. They went miles on empty roads, passing through tiny villages, avoiding the major highways and towns.

'It's beautiful, don't you think?' asked Ellie.

'Um-hum.'

'You go to many places with Matteo?'

'Not really.'

'You don't want to?'

'It's not that,' said Abby. She shrugged. 'He works.'

'But the weekends?'

'It's not always easy to fit around his shifts. And when he's on nights . . . well, he sleeps in the day.'

Ellie looked at her sister. 'You could go someplace on your own?'

'It's not the same, is it?'

No, thought Ellie, *it isn't*. 'But don't you get . . .'

'What?'

'Bored?'

Abby gave a small laugh. 'Bored? Course not!'

'How do you fill your days?'

'Plenty of things. There's loads to do.'

Ellie went to open her mouth.

'And don't ask me to list them all because I'm trying to drive.'

Ellie recognized denial when she saw it but kept quiet.

A tiny hamlet, barely marked on the map, suddenly became a small cluster of shops and houses. It was quiet, just a few locals going about their daily business.

'Shall we stop?' asked Abby. 'I could really do with a coffee.'

They pulled up on the edge of a small square dotted with orange trees. Their dark, waxy leaves gleamed in the sun, the fruit beginning to ripen. A stone basin sat atop a raised wall, above which was a gargoyle's flattened face, water pouring from its open mouth.

The girls left the car and made their way over, splashing water onto faces, necks and under armpits. Refreshed, they found themselves drawn to the shops, and joined a crowd of locals in a bakery. The queue inched forward incredibly slowly, each customer a regular and enjoying a full conversation with the staff. Ellie began to feel dizzy in the heat.

'Do you mind if I just get a bit of fresh air?' she asked Abby.

She stepped out of the oven-heated shop and, seeing that the other side of the street was in shade, crossed over. She came face to face with a boutique and her eye was immediately caught by a dress in the window. It was elegantly simple, falling just to the knee with a deep V-neckline. But it was the colour that made it: a blue that equalled a cloudless August sky. Instinctively she glanced at the price tag, then winced. Three hundred euros. She gazed at it wistfully, knowing how it would look on her, knowing how much she already loved it.

'That's not bad, actually,' said Abby, from behind her. 'Flipping heck!'

Ellie turned to see her sister staring goggle-eyed at the dress, or, more accurately, its price tag.

'Here,' said Abby, handing over a fresh coffee. 'You weren't seriously thinking of buying that, were you?'

'Have you forgotten our little escapade at the petrol station?' said Ellie. 'I was going to dash into the shop, grab it and do a runner. Joke,' she added, seeing Abby's face.

Abby appraised the dress, considering it properly. 'It's nice. But three hundred euros? Would you actually spend that much on one item of clothing?'

'If it looked amazing, then yes.'

'You're nuts.'

'Thanks.'

'Welcome. It won't cost anywhere near three hundred euros to manufacture.'

'Course not.'

'And that sort of money would keep you going for at least a couple of weeks of retirement.'

'But I'm not retired,' said Ellie tartly. 'You're taking all the magic out of it.'

Abby looked at the dress again and pulled a face – part amusement, part puzzlement. 'Magic?'

Ellie grabbed her sister's arm, led her up to the window. 'Look at it. The design, the fabric. Look at how it's going to swish around your legs. Look at that colour. Instant holiday. It's not about the cost. It's the fact that when you put it on you'll feel as if nothing in the world can bring you down.'

Abby nodded. 'Wow. But not convinced. There's always something in the world to bring you down.'

Ellie went quiet. 'Tell me about it,' she said.

'What's up?'

Ellie looked at her sister incredulously. 'Are you serious? "*What's up?*" What are we going to do, Abby? How are we going to get out of this? We are in so much shit, I don't even know where to begin.' She started laughing hysterically. 'Oh my God,' she said. 'What's up? *What's up?*'

'OK, OK,' said Abby, 'I get it.' She indicated over to the square. 'I was going to see if Jamie had called back. I've left my phone in the car . . .'

'I'll just hang out here a bit,' said Ellie, deflating. She took a sip of her coffee. 'Until you've finished your call.'

Abby went to retrieve her phone and, once she'd switched it on, saw she had a message. Heart thumping, she dialled into the mailbox. But it wasn't Jamie, it was Matteo. As she listened to his voice, she felt herself well up. She swallowed down her emotion, now certain of two things. One, the police had found the body. It was in his voice, the way he sounded so careful, while trying not to be. The other thing she was certain of was that, despite his plea, she couldn't call him back. She knew that on some level, the police were controlling what he said. This hit her like a punch to the gut and she got such a pang of loneliness she had to lean against the car, catch her breath.

Abby didn't want to keep the phone on too long, but there was one other thing she wanted to do before she switched it off. It felt very strange typing her name and the word 'murder' into the search engine. The news report came up and she recognized the man from the photo. Then she saw herself and Ellie staring out from the screen – that same photo from the restaurant. It had only been three days ago but it felt like an eternity.

Hands shaking, she hurriedly turned the phone off. Abby felt sweat beading on her forehead. She wiped it away with the back of her hand, forced deep breaths to calm herself. She looked around the square for faces, someone who might be watching her, about to report her. But apart from an elderly lady pulling along a shopping trolley on wheels with a rustic loaf sticking out of the top, there was no one.

They don't know where you are, she told herself, then repeated it, her internal voice more stern the second time.

And anyway, that man would've killed them. Surely that gave her some sort of defence?

How long did she have? she wondered. Until the police caught up with her? Because no matter how much she might be able to explain all her actions away, she just didn't want all this to stop.

Not yet.

Abby made her way back over to the shops but she couldn't see Ellie. She must have gone for a wander somewhere. Abby didn't mind. It would give her a bit longer to compose herself. She sat on the wall outside the boutique, the dress staring her in the face.

After a couple of minutes, Abby got up. She opened the door of the shop and stepped inside. She stood there, feeling the air conditioning soothe her hot skin, smelling the sharp, welcoming tang of new clothes. She went up to the window and reached out a hand to touch the dress.

'*¿En qué puedo ayudarle?* Can I help you?'

Abby turned to see a dainty woman with stylish glasses smile at her.

'This is a nice dress,' said Abby.

'Would you like to try it on?'

Abby looked back at it. 'No,' she said. 'Thank you. But I would like to buy it.' She felt an involuntary flutter of anxiety but fought it back.

The sales lady was surprised but appraised her customer professionally. 'I have your size here,' she said, plucking one of the same dresses off a rail.

'I need two,' said Abby.

'Two?' The lady's professional stance was slipping. This was unusual indeed.

'Yes.'

'The same size?'

Abby nodded. She stared, feeling slightly sick as the sales lady wrapped each dress in tissue paper and placed them in a paper bag.

'That'll be—'

Abby thrust some cash at her. If she heard the amount said out loud, she wouldn't be able to go through with it. Other than her properties, she'd never spent so much money in one go in her entire life.

She saw Ellie returning from further down the street. 'I got you a present,' said Abby, then plunged her hand into the bag and pulled out one of the tissue parcels.

Ellie frowned, then as she opened it her mouth dropped. 'I don't understand . . .'

'Nothing in the world can bring us down,' said Abby, pulling out the second dress. She almost laughed when she saw her sister's expression, except she was still recovering from the purchase.

'Oh my God, Abby,' said Ellie, stunned. 'Thank you.' Abby smiled as her sister threw her arms around her.

They put them on in the car. Two sisters in two blue dresses in a red Fiat 500, on the run through Spain.

SIXTY-FIVE

2002

It was as bad as she'd expected. A scraped pass in English and maths and a C in geography. Everything else was a monumental fail. It was certainly a far cry from her sister's ten A* and A grades a few years ago. Abby was at university now, doing a degree in economics at Manchester, where she was on track to receive a first. She came home only occasionally, preferring to spend her term breaks in Manchester, working in her local bar.

Ellie tried not to mind about her grades. She stood amongst the crowd of students in the main hall, each of them clutching the piece of paper with their future written on it. Most of the teenagers were celebrating, eyes shining as they hugged each other, peering over at one another's results. Ellie knew her mother was waiting for her to call to announce the news. Might as well get it over with. She left the main hall and found a quiet spot outside the front of the school. Her mum was working in the boutique but had promised to answer, even if she was with a customer.

As Ellie relayed the sum of her total life's work to her

mother, she felt her bravado crumble. By the end, she was reduced to tears.

'Don't worry,' said her mother quickly, 'life isn't all about university. Look at that Richard Branson – he didn't even finish school and he's a billionaire.'

'I don't know what I'm going to do, Mum,' said Ellie, through her tears. 'I'm just not very clever.'

'Rubbish,' said Susanna, but Ellie recognized a desperate consolation when she heard it. 'You just had a difficult start in life, that's all.'

My illness. Her bloody illness. If she hadn't been sick for all those years when she was younger, things would have been so different.

After a year of helping out in her mother's boutique, she decided to take a gap year off. She had longed to go travelling ever since she was small, inspired by all those years being holed up at home clutching a sick bucket. Her mother had a small amount of savings that she gifted to her and Ellie took off to Southeast Asia. She found she could make her money stretch a long way as the cost of living was so low and, because she was good-natured and pretty, other travellers were keen for her company. It was the first time Ellie had really experienced a carefree life. In Indonesia, while she was volunteering at a sea-life sanctuary, diving in the ocean to count and monitor species of tropical fish, it didn't matter that she was an academic failure.

Ellie loved what she did and worked hard, so they offered her a paid job. The salary was barely anything but Ellie didn't care. While she was working with the other staff protecting the turtles at laying season, she forgot all about her disastrous childhood, the years of feeling like an outcast, of not fitting into school life, of longing for her older sister to take some notice of her.

A year passed quickly and then, in one of her mother's emails, Ellie heard that Abby had graduated with her predicted first-class honours and had landed a management trainee position with a prestigious shipping firm in London. For a moment Ellie got a pang of homesickness, although when she delved deeper inside herself, she knew it was more than that. Abby had a good job, one with prospects and the potential for dazzling rewards and status. As much as she loved working at the sanctuary, Ellie was under no illusion that it was a permanent fixture. Neither was she going to get rich working there.

She managed to hang on for another year, then some of the funding dried up and she had to leave. She returned to the UK on a cold, wet November morning, aware that it would be as difficult to find a job as when she'd left with her pathetic GCSE grades. Nine utterly broke months later, after scores of rejections, she managed to get accepted onto a teaching assistant training programme – back at her old school which she'd left as a pupil only a few years before. The pay was laughable, but at least it was something. Ellie was deeply relieved and allowed herself a treat to celebrate. Something she'd never usually have, as it was so expensive – but this was a special occasion – she bought a bottle of Laurent-Perrier Rosé, feeling dangerous but deserving. She put it on her new credit card, telling herself she'd pay it off when she got her first pay packet in a month's time. That evening, she and Susanna sat out in the late August sunshine, in the tiny garden in Redhill, and toasted her future.

'To success!' said Susanna, holding up her flute.

Ellie smiled and touched her mum's glass with her own.

'I knew you'd make it,' said Susanna proudly.

'It's not CEO of a multi-national corporation,' said Ellie, but she couldn't help feeling a little bit pleased with herself. It was a well-known fact that teaching assistants were paid a pittance, trainee ones even more so, but after all these months, she'd got herself a job. She finally had reason to feel a sense of achievement.

Two days later, Ellie and Susanna received an email from Abby. She'd written to tell them she'd completed her trainee programme and had been offered a manager position within the company. Ellie tried hard to be pleased but later she secretly googled and found her sister's job on the company website. Her eyes were immediately drawn to one thing and one thing only: the salary. It was over four times what Ellie had been offered in her new role. And it was only Abby's first real position in the company!

Ellie suddenly got a massive wake-up call. The chasm between herself and her sister was widening ever further – Abby was going to be a corporate superstar, commanding six-figure salaries and travelling all over the world for business. Ellie would be lucky if she was offered a proper teaching position. She tried her best not to mind, but it was impossible.

Susanna was as supportive as ever. 'You had a different start in life. That illness. You've done really well.'

Ellie nodded, used to the platitudes. 'What was it? My illness?'

A shadow crossed over Susanna's face. 'They never found out.'

SIXTY-SIX

Susanna hadn't slept well. Her night had been invaded by dreams. She'd had a sense of attaining intense wealth, of knowing she could afford anything she set her gaze on. But what would ordinarily have given her a blast of pleasure instead made her wake in panic and fear. She'd risen early, showered and dressed, all the while thinking about her mother's proposal. It was an ugly one, that much she recognized, but people had done worse for money and there was the ever-present question of survival. Susanna was aware she wasn't getting any younger.

She continued the morning with routine tasks in the hope it might distract her. *Don't think about the money, just get yourself some breakfast.* But as she chopped a melon, she imagined the large kitchen at her mother's house. She washed the plate knowing she had the opportunity to never wash a dish again. Instead she'd be able to employ someone, a cleaner who would make chores a thing of the past. *But it's all wrong*, she constantly reminded herself. She'd have to confess to those heinous acts. A mother who harmed her own children – who could ever forgive such a thing?

When Kathleen knocked on the door, Susanna had been in a state of pent-up expectation for several hours. She stood aside to allow her mother to enter the house.

'We're going out,' said Kathleen.

Susanna saw the taxi behind her in the drive, engine still idling.

'What?'

'A picnic. Come on, it's all arranged.' Kathleen turned and went back to the car.

Susanna hovered for a moment, then with a sense of unease got her bag.

'I can't be outside, remember,' she said, pointing at her face as she got into the back. Her mother was sitting next to her, dressed impeccably in linen culottes and a short-sleeved blouse.

Kathleen waved a hand dismissively. 'Don't worry about that. I've got it all sorted.' She removed her sunglasses and fixed Susanna with a warm smile. It was so unusual, Susanna found herself looking away.

'We're going to have fun,' said Kathleen. 'A bit of mother and daughter time.'

Susanna was unsure how to react. This new, maternal Kathleen was alien to her. She'd go with it for a while, as it was sure to wear off before too long.

They drove inland, then west, up into the hills along winding roads that revealed mind-blowing views of the island.

'Where are we going?' asked Susanna.

'It's a surprise,' said Kathleen, and she looked so pleased with herself, Susanna left it at that. She stared out of the window, drinking in the beauty of the island, wondering if her mother was going to bring up the previous night's conversation. But Kathleen stayed silent, seemingly entranced by the views herself.

Maybe she's waiting until we're alone, thought Susanna, glancing up at the driver. This wasn't an ordinary cab; Kathleen had managed to secure a luxury sedan, perhaps through her hotel.

After a while they turned off the mountain road along a private lane marked with a sign so discreet that Susanna didn't catch it, except for a glimpse of some understated white and grey lettering. It had seemed elite, expensive, and then up ahead a low, elegant, modern retreat emerged from the pine trees.

'This is our first stop,' said Kathleen, getting out of the car. 'I thought you could do with a bit of special care.'

As Susanna walked into the reception of the spa, it took her breath away. A sense of peace and calm hummed through the air. The decor was refined and professional; clean lines softened by luxurious fabrics. The woman on the desk stood to welcome them, an unpretentious glow of proficiency about her.

'They'll give your skin the proper attention it needs,' said Kathleen, and Susanna was so overwhelmed by this act of kindness she felt tears spring up.

She didn't see her mother for the next two hours. Instead, the girls with their healing hands applied the gentlest of creams and care, and when she was shown the results in the mirror, for the first time in days she looked like her old self.

As they left, her mother nodded with approval at Susanna's appearance. 'That looks better,' she said.

A woman in white trousers and a neat white tunic led them through a door to the outside. Susanna involuntarily flinched, expecting sunshine, but the walkway was covered with a long pagoda, laced with pink bougainvillea. They stopped in a secluded area set with tables, under a white canvas canopy. Each table was set apart from the others by small palms and potted olive trees, giving the impression of being alone in a personal dining space. Kathleen and Susanna were directed to a table at the front with views down the mountain towards the sea.

'And now for our picnic,' declared Kathleen.

Susanna wasn't sure what she'd been expecting – perhaps some nice sandwiches and fruit – but instead a wicker basket was placed on a stand beside their table and they were left to discover the contents themselves: potato and rosemary crispbreads, sliced salami and hams, fresh tomatoes and olives, tiny milky mozzarella balls, little dishes of truffle-infused honey, pieces of pecorino cheese. They ate, the ever-present mountain breeze keeping them cool.

Susanna had said very little since she'd been taken into the womb-like calm of this retreat and she was aware her mother might be expecting something.

'Thank you,' she said, 'for doing all this.'

Kathleen waved her thanks away. 'Just a small thing, a token.' She paused. 'Considering how much I have to make up for.'

Susanna tensed. Now the subject had been touched upon,

she knew her mother was waiting. But Susanna felt her insides curl in apprehension and she kept quiet.

When it became clear her daughter wasn't about to speak, Kathleen continued. 'We should've still given you money, when you got married. Certainly after your divorce. You always think making the point is the most important thing, sticking to your beliefs. Then when you get older . . . well, who cares? What good did digging my heels in do? Who gives a shit, quite frankly? It was petty and I'm sorry your father and I couldn't see past our outrage.'

It made Susanna nervous. Her mother's admission was extraordinary. She thought back to the years and years of struggle and loneliness, the feelings of abandonment.

'Do you' – she had to pluck up the courage to say it – 'do you still think less of me for going against your wishes? For marrying Danny?'

Kathleen looked at her and Susanna forced herself to hold her mother's penetrating gaze. 'He wasn't the best choice, was he?' said Kathleen. 'But I understand. You probably couldn't wait to escape from us. I don't blame you, actually. Anyway, Danny's not really the issue. It's Ben and Ellie and what happened to them.' She paused. 'You must have been desperate.'

Susanna swallowed. Was this how easy her mother thought this was going to be? Hook her in with a sympathetic question and she'd capitulate into a confession?

'I've told you, Mother, I didn't give Ben and Ellie anything. It was Abby. She was fiercely jealous of her siblings from the minute they were born. I think her father's absence had a lot to do with it.'

Kathleen smiled. 'I understand why you feel the need to continue denying it. Fear, certainly. Not just at admitting the truth to yourself but also of what you think I might do with the information. The answer is nothing. It's not going to help anyone if you go to prison for killing your own child. Not now. When it comes to Ellie, well, she obviously already knows one of you was out to get her. But you two have had a good relationship since. I'm certain she'd forgive you.'

Susanna sighed. 'There's nothing to forgive.' She was unsettled by her mother's insistence and looked out at the view. A villa was perched on the edge of the hillside, its outlook directly facing the sea. It was one of those idyllic places you saw in travel magazines.

Kathleen followed her gaze. 'Beautiful, isn't it? Imagine living somewhere like that, waking up to the ocean out of your window every morning.'

Susanna stiffened.

'Timing's not right, obviously. I haven't even kicked the bucket yet. But it's all possible.' She waved a hand out towards the view, an infinity of blue. 'Anything would be possible.'

Then Susanna felt her mother lay her hand over her own.

'I just want to know what I caused,' said Kathleen, 'what my actions have ultimately been responsible for. I want to look my sins in the face. There's nothing to be afraid of. Whatever you've done, I'm not going to let you down again.'

Susanna turned to her then, saw the imploring expression on her mother's face.

'It would be a brave thing to do,' said Kathleen, with genuine reverence. 'Braver than anything I've ever done.'

Susanna felt a glow of recognition, a taste of the parental approval she'd craved her entire life. She yearned for more – to have the sense of inadequacy, the knowledge she'd been a disappointment, taken away forever. All she had to do was meet her mother's open arms and allow herself to melt into them.

SIXTY-SEVEN

Susanna lifted her glass of sparkling water and took a sip, mainly to buy some time.

'You're trembling,' said Kathleen.

Noticing her hand, Susanna immediately put the glass back down on the table.

'No need to be nervous,' said Kathleen. 'I can't tell you how much better I feel for coming clean. I hope my apology has made you feel vindicated,' she added, checking Susanna's face for a reaction.

Vindicated? Not really, thought Susanna. Sad, yes. Unnerved, certainly.

She suddenly realized something. She was now responsible for her mother's peace with the world before she died. And her mother had put her in that position. It didn't seem fair. Susanna felt a tightness across her chest, a pressure she hadn't wanted.

But if she admitted to these crimes . . . did it even matter? If Kathleen was going to keep it a secret, then she could say anything and in the same breath secure her future.

That would make her feel vindicated, she thought. After

all these years, actually getting the windfall that was her rightful inheritance.

'There's something else,' said Kathleen, 'that you might not have thought about. If you tell me what you did, then of course the money is yours. But after you there's Abby and Ellie. It'll go to them. So in a way, you'll also get to make amends.'

'Why don't you just leave it to them in the first place?'

'Because I don't owe them.'

Susanna looked at her mother, saw the watery eyes, the fadedness of her, and marvelled at how such an old woman could still have such a hold over her. She pictured a moment in the future, a time when she got a call from some hospital saying her mother had very little time. Would she be so weak that she'd no longer have the reach and power to make Susanna feel so belittled?

'You never met Ben,' she said.

'What?' Kathleen was wrong-footed by this change of topic.

'My son. You didn't ever meet him. He died at eleven months and you never made the effort.'

Kathleen was rattled. 'That's because I made mistakes back then. I told you.'

'Nor did you come to the funeral.'

'Your father was away on business. I couldn't face it alone.'

'Liar.' As soon as the word came out of her mouth, Susanna's heart started to race. Her mother looked as if she'd been physically assaulted. She even raised a papery hand to her cheek. Buoyed by this rare upper hand, Susanna spoke again. 'You simply weren't interested,' she said. 'He and Abby were too young at the time for you to want to bother with them. It was only when my children got older, when you felt you could have a hand in shaping them, making them what you felt was worthy of being your grandchild, that you paid them any attention.'

For once, Kathleen had no comeback. It was strangely satisfying, but only in a temporary way. Like eating fast food you'd craved for ages and then regretting it. *That's enough*, thought Susanna. *You've had your say.* It was something she hadn't thought she had in her, to speak to her mother like that. But she wasn't about to set fire to this new bridge Kathleen had built between them. And anyway, she couldn't afford to.

SIXTY-EIGHT

It was strange being on the other side of the desk. Matteo sat facing the two Spanish detectives, feeling the invisible wall of authority that ran across the middle of the tabletop. At the side of the room, Santini sat on a chair, which he occasionally tipped against the wall. Matteo could feel his eyes boring into him.

He wasn't under arrest, simply 'helping them with their enquiries'. The way the phrase was put, it sounded as if they were all in this together. But Matteo knew better than that.

They'd started by asking him about his job, what it was like working for the Carabinieri, comradely questions designed to make him feel part of one big police club. He'd had a few questions of his own, chiefly, where was Lieutenant Colonel Baroni? He hadn't seen her since she'd got out of the car at the murder scene that morning, when she'd taken that call. The detectives had claimed not to know much, except that she was in the building somewhere. Matteo had learned that she'd got herself a lift back to the station before him and he suspected her rapid departure had something to do with the telephone call she'd received in the car.

One piece of information the detectives had been very forthcoming with was the news that the bullet had been extracted from the victim and it matched those in his police weapon. He'd somehow known this to be the case but nevertheless it still hit him like a punch to the stomach. Of course, he had pointed out there were other Berettas like his out there, but they all knew the bullet was probably from his gun. Also, they had no knowledge of who had actually pulled the trigger, but Matteo had a strong sense he knew which of the two sisters it was. Which meant his wife was a killer.

The lead cop, Detective Carlos Vila, had recently ordered fresh coffees and the questioning was about to continue. He was a tall, lanky man and the froth from his coffee caught in his moustache.

'We'd like to ask you a little bit about your wife, Señora Abby Morelli,' said Detective Vila. 'You live together, yes?'

Matteo nodded. 'In Elba.'

'It's a house you both own?'

'Yes.'

'And Señora Morelli, does she have a job?'

'No.'

Detective Vila raised an eyebrow.

'She's retired.'

'Retired? At' – he checked his notes – 'thirty-six? This is a very nice life!'

Matteo shrugged. He didn't need to discuss Abby's financial circumstances with this man.

'And how is it, living with Abby?'

'It's fine.'

'She good company?'

'The best.'

'Does she have any history of violence?'

Matteo bit down his irritation. 'Of course not.'

Detective Vila glanced down at his notes again. 'Except for this accusation from Abby's mother, Susanna Spencer. That Abby harmed her sister as a child.'

'You've got it the wrong way around,' said Matteo, ignoring the niggling disquiet in his gut. 'It was Susanna who harmed Ellie.'

Detective Vila watched him for a moment, then nodded. 'How well would you say you know your wife?'

'Extremely well.'

'Enough to predict her behaviour?'

'None of us can predict what other people will do.'

'Like shoot someone?'

'You don't know it was her.'

Detective Vila smiled. 'No, we don't. You're right. But let's assume for now it was. Your wife and her sister had a very lucky escape. The man who was killed – he is a nasty piece of work. We have wanted to nail him for some time. We believe he had kidnapped a woman before. Robbed her and then murdered her. So it could be self-defence. It's very possible. The thing is, we need to know more about that. About who your wife is.' The detective paused. 'So you say you know her pretty well?'

'I've just confirmed that.'

'How long have you been married?'

Matteo made himself stay calm. 'Three months.'

Detective Vila gave a look of surprise. 'Four months? So, you are newly-weds!'

'But we've known each other for a year.'

'A year? Still not very long, is it?'

'It's long enough.'

'OK. So you saw each other regularly during that year?'

Matteo wondered if he already knew. If he was deliberately winding him up. 'Not at first, no. She lived in the UK and I lived in Italy.'

'So how often would you say you saw each other? Every week? Every month?'

'We met in July last year. We started dating in September. We'd see each other one, maybe two weekends a month. We got married this April and Abby moved to Italy. I don't see what relevance this has to anything.'

'You're right. The most important thing is that we find your wife. Before anyone else gets hurt.'

'She's not on some killing spree,' snapped Matteo.

'Let's hope not.' Detective Vila let his comment hang in the air.

Matteo held his gaze for as long as he could. He didn't want to believe Abby was responsible for any of these terrible crimes. Three acts of violence that had reared their ugly heads in the last three days.

But he was a policeman. He'd been trained to be attentive, thorough. His whole being was telling him to look further, deeper, beyond his agonized emotions, and face up to the very real possibility that the truth was something he wouldn't like one bit.

SIXTY-NINE

Ellie lay back against the seat and closed her eyes, still filled with a sense of wonder at her sister's generosity. Her hands rested on her lap, the new blue fabric under her palms. She felt the warm breeze on her skin as it rushed over the car and thought how she could just fall asleep. The coffee Abby had given her earlier hadn't perked her up; in fact, if anything, after she'd drunk it, she had felt decidedly unwell. Not wanting to complain, she'd kept it to herself and gradually the feeling had passed.

As the sun created a kaleidoscope of colours on her closed lids, she wondered if she should come clean to Abby about Susanna, admitting their mother was alive. But however she tried to phrase it, it sounded like a betrayal. She'd kept it secret so long and had spoken to Susanna on several occasions. It was all such a mess and for the first time in ages she was feeling completely relaxed. She didn't want to ruin the moment. She felt herself dozing and made a conscious effort to sit up and open her eyes. It wasn't fair to sleep when Abby was driving all the time.

She looked across at her sister and smiled. There was

something uniquely bonding about them both being in the same clothes. It united them, made them a team. Except it wasn't that, not really, Ellie knew.

It was the last few days. What they had been through. She thought back to her mother's warnings but couldn't connect the Abby her mum was talking about with the one sitting here in the same blue dress as her own.

'I've been thinking,' she started tentatively, 'when all this is over, maybe we could spend more time together?'

Abby glanced across. 'What, in a jail somewhere? Cell-mates?'

The smile slid off Ellie's face. Trust Abby to ruin it. Or was she just avoiding answering the question?

'You don't seriously think that's how this is going to end, do you?'

'Might,' said Abby. She looked back to the road. 'We're coming to a junction.'

Ellie glanced down at the map. 'You do realize we're running out of road.'

'Are we?'

'Only a hundred or so miles and then we fall into the sea.'

'What?'

'Well, would you look at that . . .' exclaimed Ellie, as she stared at the map. '*If you don't go while alive, you must go after death.*'

'What are you talking about?'

'That's the saying,' said Ellie. 'At the Vixía Herbeira cliffs. Some of the tallest in Europe. If you don't visit while you're alive, then after your death you'll be reincarnated as one of the animals that inhabit the area.'

'We'd best go then,' said Abby. 'I do not have plans to return to this earth as a rabbit.' She saw a sign up ahead: five kilometres to the next village. 'First, shall we stop for a bit of lunch?'

SEVENTY

'OK,' said Susanna. 'I did it.'

Kathleen slowly put her drink down. 'What did you do?' she asked.

'I gave salt to Ben, paracetamol to Ellie. I made them ill.'

'Why did you do that?'

Susanna frowned. 'Everything was crumbling. You'd disowned me. Danny was having an affair. I . . . needed to feel I had worth. I enjoyed making them better. Looking after them.' She paused. 'I was ill myself.'

Kathleen nodded but said nothing. Seconds ticked by.

Susanna grew agitated. 'Well?' she eventually burst out.

'Yes?'

'You've got your confession. Aren't you going to say something?'

Kathleen closed her eyes. 'You want me to congratulate you?'

'No . . . I . . .' Susanna felt her grasp on the situation slipping.

'Write you a cheque?'

'What are you talking about?'

'So I had a hand in the death of my grandson,' said Kathleen. 'At least that's what you told me.'

'Because it's true!'

Kathleen opened one eye. 'Is it? Only, the correct thing to say would've been, "I did it but I don't want your money." Then I could have given it to you. But now' – she shrugged – 'I don't even know if you made it all up just because of greed. After all, it's not the first time you've sold your soul for money, is it? I'm disappointed,' she said flatly.

Susanna stared at her mother, steely-eyed. She barked out a laugh. 'Disappointed,' she repeated. 'Well, guess what? It goes two ways. Except I'm not disappointed in you, I'm disgusted.'

'You watch your mouth.'

'I cannot believe you are using the death of my son as a bargaining chip. Actually, I think I knew all along what you're capable of. I allowed myself to go along with this charade to prove to myself just how manipulative you are. Well, thank you, Mother, for showing me yet again that I should have nothing more to do with you.'

Susanna got up from the table.

'Sit back down. I haven't finished,' said Kathleen.

'We're done, Mother.'

'We are not. So, are you lying to get the money or not?'

Susanna looked back at her aged mother and knew it would be the last time she ever saw her.

'You'll never know,' she said, and turned and walked away.

SEVENTY-ONE

Ellie and Abby had feasted hungrily on the tapas laid out before them at a small restaurant in a tiny village lost in the north-western Spanish countryside. It was quiet and there had only been a couple of locals still remaining – elderly people sitting out the front with a coffee, idly chatting away to each other, passing the time of day.

Perhaps even better than the food had been the promise of a hot shower. Abby had seen a sign for rooms upstairs and she'd paid the owner for the use of one for a few hours. Ellie lay on clean sheets with washed hair, as her sister took a turn freshening up. She felt her eyes closing. The comfort of the room and her full stomach wove a calming magic that allowed her to pretend everything was OK for a moment.

It was funny how life unexpectedly spun you around until you were going in a completely different direction . . . This trip could have all been so different. She could have still been in Elba, diving off the rocks into the Tyrrhenian Sea at the bottom of Abby's garden. She might have met a handsome Italian man. Or maybe she would have met Fredrik a different way and they'd be in the south of France together – or perhaps she could have joined him on his Camino de Santiago pilgrimage. There was something quite peaceful about the idea of following a trail to free yourself of your troubles. Ellie wondered where he was, how he was getting on. She looked across at Abby's bag on the floor; then, driven by curiosity, she got up. She could use the phone. He'd left a message once – maybe he would again?

Ellie took Abby's phone and dialled her own number. She had a message. The corners of her mouth lifted as she heard his voice again. He was now in Spain and wondered how she was doing. He was well into his pilgrimage and if there was any chance of it, he'd love to speak to her before he went back to Norway.

Ellie's heart gave a flutter of excitement. Should she call him back? There wasn't any point really. They'd exchange a few words, then that would be it. He'd go home to Norway and their paths would never cross again. Except it would be nice to hear his voice. If only for a few minutes . . . The shower was still running. Soon Abby would be out and then any opportunity would be lost.

Before she talked herself out of it, she called him. He answered after three rings.

'Hello?'

'Fredrik? It's Ellie.'

'Ellie! It's so good to hear from you.'

He sounded relieved to hear her voice. 'I got your message,' said Ellie. 'How's the pilgrimage?'

'I'm taking a day off to rest the legs.'

'Congratulations.'

'Thanks.' He paused. 'How's the road trip?'

'OK. Good!' enthused Ellie.

'Where did you get to?'

Did it matter if she spoke the truth? Ellie couldn't see a reason not to. 'Spain.'

'Oh wow, you too. I thought you were avoiding me,' said Fredrik teasingly. 'You didn't return my last message.'

'Oh. It's not that. Long story.' The conversation hit a lull and Ellie felt the need to bridge the gap. 'So you're off to Norway soon?'

'In a couple of days.'

Back to normality, thought Ellie, feeling irrationally sad that he was leaving.

'Hey, you don't fancy hooking up before I go, do you?'

Her stomach flipped. But of course she couldn't. It was impossible.

'Spain's a big place,' she said, as an excuse.

'Depends,' said Fredrik. 'Where exactly are you?'

'North-west,' said Ellie.

'Me too,' said Fredrik. 'Whereabouts?'

She didn't want to say. 'Oh, I don't know. A small village somewhere.'

She could almost hear Fredrik's mind turning over and felt bad about what would seem like a brush-off. She liked him, didn't want him to think she wasn't keen.

'You *are* avoiding me,' he said with a smile.

'Honestly, it's not that.'

There was an awkward silence.

'So, have you seen much on your travels?' asked Fredrik.

'Some beautiful scenery,' said Ellie, relieved to change topic. 'The Camargue was amazing. What was your highlight?'

'Fixing my fifth puncture in a day.'

Ellie laughed.

'I've run out of patches. I'm at a hostel, waiting for one of the guys here to get back from the nearest village – he offered to get some more for me.' He paused. 'I'm kind of at a loose end.'

'It's difficult . . .' said Ellie. 'You'll be miles away from me anyway.'

'We don't know unless we look at the map.'

Ellie smiled, bit her lip. 'OK, I'm in a village called Baleira.'

'Baleira, Baleira,' repeated Fredrik. 'I'm just looking for it.' He suddenly laughed out loud. 'Are you serious? That's so close to where I am! Come on, just for a short while?'

'Honestly, I can't. We're kind of on the move.'

'I can get in a taxi. Be with you in under an hour.'

An hour. She could spare an hour or so, couldn't she?

'I've got pictures of Antibes . . .'

Ellie smiled. It was funny how life was always unexpectedly spinning you around, she thought as she arranged to meet Fredrik in the bar downstairs in – she checked her watch – less than an hour.

Fredrik hung up his mobile and placed it sombrely on the desk in the police station. Shrugged.

'It's all arranged?' asked Santini.

'I said I would, didn't I?' said Fredrik.

Lieutenant Colonel Baroni saw Santini narrow his eyes and quickly jumped in. She smiled at Fredrik in what she hoped was a reassuring manner. 'Excellent. I thought you handled that really well.' She kept her excitement at bay; it was essential he didn't back out of their agreement.

'And you say she had nothing to do with the shooting? That man?'

'It's her sister we want. Obviously the news report didn't specify where our suspicions lie – the press don't know. I want to thank you again for getting in touch.'

'Like I said, I recognized the photos. I was worried.'

Baroni smiled at him again. 'I'm glad you cared enough to call. We need to protect Ellie. And you're the one who can lead us to her sister.' She stood up. 'The car's ready.'

She indicated the door and Fredrik followed her out of the office.

'Remember,' said Baroni as they walked down the corridor, Santini bringing up the rear, 'there are going to be several vehicles watching. You'll be miked and we'll be able to hear everything. She may lead us to Abby straight away, but if not, I want you to keep her talking.' She placed a hand on Fredrik's shoulder. 'She may well be scared of her. It's a good thing you're doing. Ellie's the innocent one here.'

She led Fredrik out of the building but faltered as she saw Matteo waiting, leaning against a wall. Quickly, she took Fredrik over to the unmarked car and opened the door for him, but not quickly enough. Matteo, spotting her, came running up, pushing aside Santini's outstretched arm of obstruction.

Baroni swore under her breath.

'Going somewhere?' asked Matteo.

'Don't interfere with my investigation,' said Baroni in a low voice. She deliberately kept her tone pleasant; there was no need to alarm the witness.

Matteo indicated Fredrik. 'Who the hell is this?'

'Never you mind,' said Santini.

Fredrik looked from Matteo to Santini, curious at the obvious tension between them. 'Fredrik Andersen.' He held out a hand.

Baroni stepped between the two men and nodded towards the inside of the car. A driver was sitting in the front, waiting for them. 'We need to get going,' she said firmly and put her hand on Fredrik's arm, guiding him into the vehicle. Then she got in next to him, Santini sitting up front. Before she could close the door, Matteo bent down, held it open.

'Are you going to see Abby?'

'Remove your hand, please,' said Baroni.

'That's a yes, isn't it? Where is she?'

'Want me to do something, Boss?' asked Santini, watching carefully.

Baroni looked at Matteo and spoke calmly. 'You need to remove your hand immediately or I'll have you arrested for obstructing this investigation.'

Furious, Matteo knew when he was beaten. He took his hand from the car and Baroni pulled the door shut. Within seconds they were away.

SEVENTY-TWO

Ellie lay on the bed, waiting for Abby to come out of the shower. She was alternately buffeted between a sense of liberation at meeting Fredrik and nerves at telling Abby. Wondering how best to phrase it.

The bathroom door opened and her sister came in, towelling off her hair.

'That felt so good,' said Abby.

Ellie nodded. Maybe she'd build her up to it slowly. *Abby, I think we can afford to take a bit of a breather, don't you? Just for a couple of hours?*

'What the hell is that?'

Ellie looked up to see her sister stock-still, staring at her bed. Or rather the phone on her bed.

Damn, she'd forgotten to put it away!

'What's going on?' asked Abby.

'I just spoke to Fredrik,' said Ellie, smiling. 'He left me a message and so I just called him back. You're never going to believe this – he's really close by! I'm going to meet him for a drink.'

Abby's jaw dropped. 'You what?'

'Oh, come on, Abby. It'll only be for an hour or so. He's

going back to Norway, so chances are I'll never see him again.'

'Have you lost your mind?'

Ellie bit her tongue. It was important she stayed calm. 'No, Abby, I haven't lost my mind.'

Abby picked up the phone, held it out. 'You need to call him right back. Tell him it's not happening.'

Her sister's face was set firm, not just in her decision, but in a conviction that, as usual, Ellie would do what Abby wanted.

Well, not this time.

She sat up on the bed. 'I'm not going to do that, Abby.'

They were locked in a stalemate. Abby glanced down at the phone. Frowned.

'There's a voicemail,' said Abby. 'Did it ring while I was in the shower?'

Ellie shook her head. She watched as her sister listened, then saw Abby's face crumple.

'What is it?' asked Ellie.

Abby didn't answer; instead she urgently dialled a number, then swore and threw her phone on the bed in frustration.

'What's happened?' asked Ellie.

'That message was from Jamie.' Abby could hardly contain her upset. 'Jamie tried to call. While you were on the phone to Fredrik.'

'Oh.'

'And now he's unavailable. He's just got on a plane to Thailand and his phone is switched off.'

'Thailand? What's he going there for?'

'It's the summer holidays, Ellie! People are going away, having a nice, relaxed time. And now our only help is not contactable for thirteen whole hours.'

Ellie bit her lip. 'I'm sorry.'

'For God's sake!'

'I've apologized.'

'This is typical of you,' said Abby.

'What?'

'You were always allowed to do whatever you wanted, no matter how it affected anyone else.'

'For goodness' sake, Abby, I just want to meet up with a friend . . .' – she paused; she hadn't known him long enough and knew Abby would call her on it – '. . . ly man that I get on with.'

'Fancy, more like.'

'That too,' said Ellie hotly. 'What of it?'

Abby cut her a furious look and Ellie waited for her sister to explode. She could see her wrestling with her anger, trying to stay in control, to be the grown-up one.

'There was another one, you know,' said Abby coolly.

Ellie was thrown. 'Another what?'

'Thing I used to do. To wish you dead.'

'There was more than one?' said Ellie, aghast.

'I'd fantasize about going into your room at night and putting the pillow on your head and then sitting on it.'

'Well, thanks very much.'

Abby just threw her a look of daggers and stalked out of the room.

SEVENTY-THREE

2008

Abby was aware her eyes were bloodshot through lack of sleep and her hair was a mess as she'd run out of time to wash it after finishing off an urgent report for her boss, due at six o'clock that morning. It was one of the drawbacks of working for an international company where deadlines were set by time zones.

She was late. It had been a hell of a day and she'd finally escaped the office with nineteen minutes to get to Westminster Pier – a journey that took twenty-five minutes. Now, seeing the pier ahead of her, she broke into a run, praying the boat wouldn't go without her, and wondered if the others were already on board. She and Ellie had arranged a rare evening together. They both had new boyfriends – they were on the fourth or fifth date and Ellie had decided they should all go out together, for reasons that Abby now couldn't remember.

Lungs bursting, she clattered down the gangplank onto a long, wooden boat where calm, relaxed people populated the decks, holding aloft flutes of fizz in the summer evening sunshine. She thrust her ticket at a man in a bow tie, while another man handed her one of the flutes. As she took it, she saw one of the crew untie the ropes – *that was close*.

Abby climbed the steps onto the upper deck, looking for her sister and the boyfriends, wiping the film of sweat from her brow as she did so. She noticed Ellie first – or rather her hair, its golden strands catching in the sun. Her sister was talking animatedly to Abby's boyfriend, Jon, and beside him, another man whom Abby took to be Rory.

Abby took a deep breath and automatically fluffed her flat brown hair out. She raised a hand and caught Jon's eye, and he broke away and came to greet her. His linen shirt and shorts and his feet clad in deck shoes made Abby suddenly feel hot and overdressed in her grey work suit. He leaned in to kiss her and she clamped her arms by her side as she caught the whiff of something unpleasant from her armpits.

'Hard day?' asked Jon.

'Didn't think I was going to make it,' said Abby, laughing. 'How about you?'

'I was lucky. Finished at four,' said Jon and Abby noticed he seemed to have already had a couple of drinks.

Ellie came over, leading her boyfriend by the hand. 'Hi, Abby. This is Rory.'

Rory broke free from Ellie and held out his hand. Abby was still clutching her briefcase and her glass, so a handshake became an awkward nod and a raising-of-glasses sort of greeting. She was struck by how normal he looked – average, if she was being unkind – and it surprised her. Ellie usually attracted the good-looking type.

Abby turned to Jon. 'I guess you guys have already met . . .'

'Jon's been telling us about his work with London Harlequins,' said Ellie enthusiastically. 'You didn't say he was a physio for one of the best rugby teams in the country.'

Hadn't she? Abby couldn't remember. And since when did her sister know anything about rugby teams and which were the best?

'So, has everyone had a good day?' she asked, suddenly noticing a pile of shopping bags near Ellie's feet.

'Spent a fortune,' said Ellie. 'But it was a lot of fun. Got the most amazing dress.'

She was already looking amazing, thought Abby. That was one of the upsides of working in a school – her sister had the summer off and had acquired a golden tan from the freedom of days outside. She was wearing a blue cotton dress and looked relaxed and carefree. Jon was on her other side and, in his blue shorts and white shirt, they looked as if they were the couple and Abby in her suit was with Rory in his grey trousers.

'Then Rory and I met for a cocktail before the boat,' said Ellie, and Abby was reminded of how Rory was a teacher and had the same extended holidays.

'Nice,' said Jon. 'I was hanging around like Billy no-mates.'

'If we'd known, you could've joined us,' said Ellie warmly.

Abby smiled, but it felt uncomfortable across her lips. She

glanced at the two men but neither seemed embarrassed. Abby chided herself: she had to get out of this stressed, corporate mood; her little sister was just being friendly.

'Hey, there's the OXO Tower,' exclaimed Ellie as they passed the landmark. 'I can recommend their watermelon mojitos.'

'Blimey,' said Abby. 'Must've cost a bit, going in there.'

'It was a one-off,' said Ellie. 'And the view was amazing.' She lifted her arm and waved up at the tower. 'Hello, lucky people enjoying your mojito cocktails!' She looked at Abby. 'Hey, you should come,' she said, 'maybe a girlie night out one day?'

'Bit pricey for me,' said Abby lightly. 'What are they, ten quid each?'

'Thirteen,' said Ellie, and Abby winced.

'Abby's just bought her first flat,' said Ellie.

'Oh yeah?' said Rory. 'Congratulations.'

'She's taken advantage of the recession and the drop in property prices.'

'Amazing you managed to pull together a deposit,' said Rory admirably.

Abby shrugged. 'Saved.'

'Hard on a teaching assistant's salary,' laughed Ellie, but Abby thought she caught a note of resentment. *Might be easier if you didn't shop so much or spend thirteen quid on a drink*, she thought, and then immediately hated the way it made her feel.

'Hey, look,' said Jon. 'Is that St Paul's?'

They all turned to face the other side of the river, and up

ahead loomed the familiar dome of the cathedral. It glowed in the soft evening light, its stateliness a direct contrast to the modern gleaming Gherkin which they could see further downstream.

'What a great city we live in,' said Ellie. 'Or at least I will do soon.'

'What do you mean?' asked Abby, surprised.

'I'm finally moving out of the parental home. Found a flat in South Wimbledon.'

'Wow,' said Abby.

'Renting, of course.' Ellie gave a resigned sigh. 'Except the rent's the same as a mortgage.'

'Maybe we'll all win the lottery one day,' said Jon. 'Then we can buy penthouses on the riverfront and retire early.'

At that, they all raised their glasses in solidarity. Although Abby smiled along with them, she hugged her secret to herself. It was something she'd told no one, but that was her quiet dream. Not to buy a penthouse but to retire early. That was why she was working every hour she could, to climb the corporate ladder as fast as she could. She lived on a strict budget that would shock some students and saved every penny she could spare. It made her feel safe.

The band started up and Ellie grabbed Rory's hand. 'Come on, let's dance,' she said, refusing to take his protests seriously.

Abby felt Jon's arm rest on her shoulders. 'You fancy it?' he asked, but she didn't. She felt tense and strait-laced and she still hadn't put her briefcase down. She suddenly had a sense of the evening floating out of her grasp and she took a deep breath. Maybe this double date thing had been a mistake. After all, she still didn't know Jon all that well herself. They'd met at a work function – she had been at an event with clients at the rugby and Jon had also been in the corporate box. Perhaps it would have been better if they'd gone for an intimate dinner tonight, just the two of them. She looked wistfully at the shore but there was no chance of that. She was stuck on this boat whether she liked it or not.

'Do you mind if we just stay here a bit?' she asked.

'Course!' he said enthusiastically – *too enthusiastically*, thought Abby, and she found herself questioning whether he really wanted to.

She fixed on a bright smile. 'So, have you done any physio today?'

'Yes.' He smiled. 'I do it most days.'

Because he's a physiotherapist, you idiot, thought Abby.

'Have you been watching any of the Olympics?' he asked her.

Oh God, she knew this question was going to come up. She'd mentally filed herself a reminder to watch some now she was dating a sports specialist, since it was something that was bound to interest him. But work had taken over and she hadn't got around to it yet.

'Not much,' she said vaguely. 'Work,' she explained.

'Not even Usain Bolt?'

Everyone was talking about Usain Bolt. 'I saw him on the news,' she said, and after a pause, Jon nodded.

The silence was broken by the sound of a loud ring. Abby

tensed. It was coming from her briefcase which was down by her feet. She knew who was calling.

'Go ahead. Answer it,' said Jon.

'Sure?'

He nodded and she pulled her phone out. As she suspected, it was her boss. She turned away to take the call, listened to how a potential client in the Far East needed a document first thing Monday morning, so that was her weekend gone. She felt Jon tap her on the arm, and he indicated he was going to get them both fresh drinks. She nodded distractedly. Once she'd jotted down what was needed, several minutes had passed by. God, she needed that drink now. She looked around for Jon but it took her a while to see him, and then she did: he was dancing with Ellie. The track was something that even in that moment she knew she'd never, ever forget: the Arctic Monkeys' 'I Bet You Look Good on the Dancefloor'. They did.

Rory came up alongside her, sipping from a pint. 'So, what do you do?'

'I'm a business analyst,' said Abby. 'For a shipping company.' She was met with a blank face.

'Sorry, I don't know what that means,' said Rory.

'No one ever does,' said Abby, but she wasn't in the mood to explain.

'The Globe,' said Rory, pointing, and Abby looked over at the circular white and black-beamed building with its thatched roof.

'Give me now leave to leave thee,' said Rory dramatically. '*Twelfth Night*,' he explained.

Abby looked at him.

'Sorry, English teacher.' There was an awkward pause, then he saw her empty glass. 'You look like you need a top-up. I can go . . .' Rory indicated the bar. But then Ellie and Jon looked up and waved, and the track ended and they came over, laughing and hot. Jon gave Abby a long, lingering kiss on the lips – but it still didn't surprise her when he called up three days later to cancel their dinner date, saying it had been 'fun' but he 'wasn't ready for a relationship'. It had hurt like hell.

A month later, Abby was walking to the train station, heading home from work. It was eight o'clock and the sky was almost fully dark. A man walking towards her kept looking at her and then away, back and forth. She edged to the side of the pavement and considered crossing the road, but it was too late.

'Hi,' said the man, and then she recognized him.

'Hi,' she replied, with great relief that it wasn't some weirdo. 'Rory!'

'How's things?'

'Yeah, good. Good. I work nearby. Office is over there.'

'Oh. Cool. I've been out with some mates,' he said, waving vaguely to a row of pubs. 'Well, it's nice to see you,' he said, making a move to carry on.

Abby smiled, amused by his apparent hurry. 'You too.'

She waved as he made to walk off, but then he suddenly turned back. 'Got to say, it's pretty forgiving of you.'

The smile hadn't left her face. 'What?'

'Or is it open-minded?'

'Sorry. I don't know what you're talking about.'

'Ellie. Your sister. Dating Jon.'

Abby felt as if she was falling. She was aware she was staring at Rory, her smile now rigid on her face.

'You knew, right? Oh shit.'

She snapped out of it. 'Course I knew,' she lied. 'Yeah. Look, I'm going to be late. Train to catch.' She turned away. 'Nice to see you,' she called out before hurrying on, tears filling her eyes.

SEVENTY-FOUR

Ellie almost wavered as she walked down the stairs to the small bar, where legs of cured ham hung in the windows. It wasn't as if she knew Fredrik well – this meeting had been agreed in a moment of madness, an escapist interlude from the last few days where her perspective on life had been picked up and thrown in the air. In fact, *what the hell* seemed a perfectly good motto by which to live right now, and thinking this strengthened her again as she walked in the door.

She saw him immediately and her stomach flipped, not with apprehension but with excitement. He looked over and she was gratified to see his eyes light up, and knew she'd done the right thing. He was over to her instantly, buying her a drink, and they found a table tucked away at the back of the room.

'Thanks for agreeing to meet,' said Fredrik. His tan had darkened and when he smiled the cracks along the sides of his eyes seemed even whiter.

'It's a nice break from the road trip,' said Ellie.

'How was France?'

'Good,' she replied, knowing she couldn't tell him anything.

'And now you're in Spain!'

'We just kept on going,' said Ellie.

He nodded. There was a pause in the conversation where Ellie thought he was making a conscious effort to relax.

'You look great,' said Fredrik. 'That dress suits you.'

Ellie glanced down. 'It was from my sister. A gift.'

'Nice gift.' He spread his hands out. 'Where is she?'

'Who?'

'Abby.'

Ellie tilted her head. 'Abby?'

'Yes, that's right, isn't it?'

'Sure. I just don't remember telling you her name.'

He smiled. 'You did. When we met at the fountain.'

Ellie thought back. She couldn't recall doing so, but it didn't matter. She shrugged. 'Honest answer is I don't know. We had a bit of a falling-out.'

'Sorry to hear that. Nothing serious, I hope?'

She shook her head. 'Oh no. Just spent a lot of time together the last few days. Got a bit on top of each other, you know. She's gone out for some space.'

'You two close?'

Ellie laughed. 'She's hated me for most of my life.'

'How come you've ended up on a road trip then?'

'It's a long story.'

'I'd like to know.'

Ellie shook her head. 'No . . . I've only got a short while

and then Abby will probably be back, rounding me up again. Do you have any siblings?'

'I'm an only child.'

'What was that like?'

'I hated it. I was lonely my whole childhood.'

'I had a sister but I was lonely too.'

'I had this imaginary friend,' said Fredrik, leaning conspiratorially towards her. 'Aksel. Whenever I did something wrong, I used to blame him. Aksel broke the cup. Aksel took the chocolates from the cupboard. Aksel shaved off the dog's fur with your razor, Daddy.'

Ellie laughed, incredulous. 'You shaved off your dog's fur?'

'I wanted to see what it looked like underneath.'

'Wasn't the dog . . . cold?'

'I didn't do all of it. Just a patch.'

'Oh, that's OK then.'

He looked contrite. 'Yeah . . . poor thing probably was a bit chilly. We lived in a small town north of Trondheim. It was January. There was a lot of snow.'

'Lucky it was Aksel who got the blame, not you.'

'Yeah . . . except my parents didn't believe me.'

'No!'

'I know! Hard to fathom, eh? Especially as I described Aksel so vividly. He would just never show himself when needed. What about you?'

'What about me?'

'Did you have an imaginary scapegoat to take the blame for your innate awfulness?'

'I was a good girl,' said Ellie, smiling smugly. 'Never did anything wrong.'

He laughed. 'The perfect daughter, right?'

Ellie paused, reflective. 'I was definitely the favourite. It was obvious. Which is why I don't understand . . .'

'What?'

She looked at him, wondering whether to say. These few minutes were probably the last she'd spend with him and then she'd never see him again. 'My mother did something bad to me as a child. I've only just found out. But I don't have the whole picture.'

'Have you asked her?'

'Not yet.'

'What do you want to know?'

Ellie thought. What *did* she want to know? 'She always acted as if I was the apple of her eye. So why did she do that to me? I'm not saying she should have done it to Abby or anything but . . . she loved me.'

'Call her.'

Ellie shrugged.

'Honestly. Don't leave it,' he urged.

'How's the pilgrimage been?'

He was amused. 'That's OK if you want to change the subject. The pilgrimage has been good.'

'How come you've managed to take so much time off to do it? Do you work?'

'I have a very demanding job in Oslo. Long hours. It's a job I love.'

'So . . . ?'

'I resigned. Or at least I told them I was coming out here. If they didn't like it, they'd have to fire me.'

'Wow, strong words.'

'It was necessary. I'll be sad to finish it.' Fredrik paused. 'My dad came out here earlier this year. He got to the half-way point – about two hundred and fifty miles – but then went back home. He said he'd been feeling a bit unwell. He called and asked me to go home and visit – he needed some help around the house.'

'Something's telling me you didn't?'

'I was in the middle of a project. I didn't want to leave. I made a half-hearted promise to spend time with him in the summer, maybe even join him on the rest of his pilgrimage.'

'But he's not with you . . .'

'He died in June. Got diagnosed with pancreatic cancer and was told he had three weeks to live.'

Ellie bit her lip. 'I'm so sorry.'

'So that's all I had left. Three short weeks.'

'You mustn't feel bad.'

'I can't help thinking about all those times I didn't go home. This year wasn't the only time. I just enjoyed my life, did what I wanted.' He took a deep breath. 'So I decided to get myself out here. Finish his pilgrimage. You want to see my route passport?'

'Of course.'

'Every time you get to a hostel you get a stamp.' Fredrik pulled a folded cardboard booklet out of his pocket, worn and curved from use. He opened it up and ran his fingers along the first stamps, each a different design. 'Most of these are my dad's.' He moved his finger along. 'And these are mine. Now I'm doing it I miss him even more. Do you know what I mean?'

Ellie nodded and felt a little part of her heart tie with Fredrik's. She wanted to put her hand on his but wasn't sure . . . *What the hell*, she suddenly thought and felt his warm skin under hers. 'I miss my mum,' she said softly. 'I know she's not dead or anything,' she added quickly, feeling embarrassed at him thinking she might be comparing her situation to his own tragedy, 'she's just not the person I thought I knew. I've lost that person and I'll never get her back.' Fredrik turned his hand over so he could link his fingers through hers, and Ellie felt as if she was fused to his rough palm. The point where they touched was all she could focus on, as if a current was running through them. And she knew he was feeling the same thing.

'Got a dad?' asked Fredrik.

Ellie shook her head.

'So that makes us both orphans,' he said.

She smiled at him.

'You're a survivor, Ellie, I can tell.'

'Takes one to know one.'

Ellie looked at her hand, still clasped by his. *What the hell.*

'Fredrik?'

'Yes?'

She had to do it quickly or she'd lose her nerve. So she leaned in to kiss him. He hesitated for a tiny moment and then kissed her back. They pulled apart, eyes locked. *So what next?* thought Ellie. This felt like her moment, space and time that belonged only to her. She was aware of its fleeting nature, how it would drift away from her unless she grabbed it with both hands.

SEVENTY-FIVE

In the back of the surveillance van, Baroni sat listening to Fredrik and Ellie. She was flanked by two techie cops, who monitored a bank of screens that held views from the cameras fitted to the two unmarked cars parked at strategic parts of the village. One was directly opposite the row of buildings where the B & B was nestled in between the village hall and a delicatessen. Other screens were showing the views up and down the main street.

So Abby had gone off in a huff, thought Baroni. It must have been a while ago as none of the police had seen her leave. It was only a matter of time before she returned. Baroni knew she just had to remain patient. Unless Fredrik could find out where she'd gone. He seemed to be doing a good job at gaining Ellie's trust – and maybe Ellie knew more than she let on.

Baroni suddenly realized she could no longer hear voices. She looked across at her colleagues but they shook their heads, as puzzled as she was. Baroni reached for her radio.

'It's gone quiet,' she said to Santini, who was in the

unmarked car parked on the street outside the B & B. 'Any sighting outside?'

'Nothing,' he replied. 'It's clear.'

Baroni frowned. They must still be in the B & B. So what were they doing?

SEVENTY-SIX

Abby stared out of the wooden window frame that captured a view of the road. Not just any old road but the road that led out of the village. She'd been drawn to it ever since she'd arrived, gazing out, wishing she was in the car, driving away, deep into the countryside. She didn't like staying still too long. It made her tetchy and anxious.

She would have walked that road if she could; in fact, after she'd stormed out on Ellie she'd got as far as the end of the village and then realized that unless she wanted to leave without her sister, she had to stop and wait for her. The last building on the street was a tiny cafe – Rosa's – run by a lady whose age was hard to determine. She had the look of belonging to where she lived, as if she'd been in the village her entire life. In the lines of her face was written her story, visible and intriguing and yet indecipherable. She had been friendly when Abby came in for a coffee, placing a homemade biscuit on a plate, even though Abby hadn't ordered one. Then she'd gone back behind the counter and was sitting watching a tiny television screen, on which Abby could just make out horse racing, the volume turned low.

Abby checked her watch. She'd give Ellie an hour maximum, then she'd walk into that bar and tell her sister that unless she wanted to be left behind she'd better get herself back to the car. Abby sighed. She recognized self-pity in amongst her frustration. If she was honest, a little part of her was . . . not jealous, but with Ellie meeting up with that Norwegian man, Abby was reminded of how much she missed Matteo. She could do with an hour or so out of this situation herself, sitting in a bar being distracted by something fun. Having something other than her current predicament to torment her mind.

'Another coffee?' The ageless lady had appeared at her shoulder.

Might as well, thought Abby. She nodded and watched as the lady took her cup and, moving slowly across the cafe, went to make her a fresh drink, then walked slowly back again.

'*Gracias*,' said Abby.

'You are here on your own?' asked the lady.

'No. My sister is up the street. In the bar. With a . . . friend.'

The lady gave a knowing smile and Abby blushed as she realized how she'd sounded. Petulant, almost.

'I am Rosa,' said the lady. 'Like the cafe.' Without invitation Rosa took a seat at the table.

'I have seen you staring out of the window,' said Rosa.

'It's a lovely view,' replied Abby, non-committal.

'You don't want to sit with your sister and her friend?'

Abby shook her head. 'Three's a crowd.'

Rosa nodded. 'He is the wrong man for your sister. You are protective of her.'

'It's not that. It's just . . . we had plans. And instead she's gone to meet him.'

'Doing what she likes, eh?'

Abby smiled.

'Little sister?'

'How did you know?'

'It is always the same. I too have one. Carmen. She never did any wrong. My mother forgive her everything. Even when she cut my doll's hair!' Rosa laughed. 'I was so upset but Mama told me I should not have left the scissors on the table. It was my fault.'

'It's always our fault,' said Abby.

'And she is five years younger, so she never had to do any chores.'

'Mine neither,' said Abby. 'My mother would let her play instead. Or watch TV.'

'Carmen would never get told off.'

'Ellie always got sweets when she fell over.'

'But at least they got the old clothes. When we had grown too big for them.'

Abby laughed. 'True. Where is your sister now?'

'I kill her.'

Abby froze.

'Joke.'

'Oh my God.'

'Sorry. But sometimes you feel like it, no?' Rose mimed encircling someone's neck with her hands.

Abby shrugged.

'So who is this man that your sister is with?'

'Someone we met in France. We're on a . . . road trip,' said Abby. 'We bumped into this guy a few days ago. He's also travelling. Been cycling the Camino de Santiago trail.'

'How nice that they arrange to meet up again here in Spain.'

'No, it wasn't like that. We actually thought we'd never see him again. Then Ellie gets a message from him – turns out he's only down the road. It was a total coincidence . . .' Abby trailed off as her brain started to wake up, see the cliff she'd been wandering towards in the fog. 'Oh my God.'

'Is everything all right?' asked Rosa.

Abby stood. Quickly got some money out of her purse and put it on the table. 'Yes . . . I need to go.' She tried to maintain a calm demeanour. 'Thank you, Rosa. The coffee was wonderful.' Then she hurried out of the cafe, dread seeping right through her. Knowing it wasn't a coincidence at all.

SEVENTY-SEVEN

Baroni heard a muffled sound that she couldn't quite identify. She pushed the headphone in close to her ears, straining to hear more. What *was* that? And where was her plant? Why wasn't he speaking? Why weren't either of them speaking? It was making her nervous.

She looked across at her techie guys and saw a grin slowly creep across the face of one as enlightenment dawned on him.

'What is it?' she asked quickly. But she didn't need to wait for an answer as she heard distinctive heavy breathing. Heaving breathing interspersed with kissing. It was still muffled but now she'd identified it, she knew it could be nothing else.

What the . . . ? Where was the mike? It obviously wasn't still on his body. Baroni grimaced. Fredrik must have removed it, and by the muffled sound, he'd hidden it under something.

The radio burst in. 'Any more from the suspect?' asked Santini from outside.

The techie guy answered: 'They can't speak. Too busy eating each other's faces.'

A bark of laughter came from Santini. 'Serious? The dirty bastard.'

'What a player, eh?'

'Can't trust those Scandis to keep their dicks in their pants.'

Baroni did her best to ignore them. Damn Fredrik – this was definitely not what they'd discussed. What the hell did he think he was playing at? She tried to clear her head, to block out the other officers so she could think, but they were like a pack of hyenas.

'Quiet!' she barked.

This elicited raised eyebrows but Baroni hardly noticed. She got up and moved over to the screens. On one of them, a young woman was hurrying down the road towards the B & B. It was Abby.

Baroni's heart began to race. She pushed the button on her radio. 'Suspect in view.'

SEVENTY-EIGHT

'On it,' said Santini, all attention now, his voice coming up on Baroni's radio.

'She's coming down the main street, north to south, towards the B & B,' replied Baroni. 'She'll be in your sight in about thirty seconds.'

'Got her!' said Santini. 'I am exiting my vehicle.'

Baroni watched on the screen and saw what Santini could see – Abby was nearing the B & B. She wasn't alone on the street, though; a large group of women with their young children were pouring out of the village hall. In moments, they had surrounded Abby: kids, prams, teddies, mothers.

'I can still see her,' said Santini.

'No,' said Baroni. 'Wait.'

'I've got her in my sights.'

He what? Baroni scanned the screen but Santini wasn't far forward enough to be on camera and she couldn't see what he was doing. 'Do you have your weapon?' she barked.

'Directed right on the suspect,' said Santini.

There were dozens of children around. What was he

thinking? Baroni watched and waited, mentally urging the young mothers to move on. They laughed and talked and attempted to cajole their children along in an orderly fashion. It was like watching people trying to herd cats.

'Get back in your car,' said Baroni.

'I can get to her,' said Santini. 'Make her hand herself in.'

'I said return to your vehicle!'

There was silence. *Jesus!* Baroni had no choice but to yank off her headset and exit the van. She jumped into the road and up ahead saw Santini pressed low to the road, his gun raised at the crowd ahead. Somewhere amongst them she caught a fleeting glimpse of Abby.

'Lower your weapon immediately,' she said into her radio. 'I am right behind you and that is an order.'

Santini flicked his head back and sullenly dropped his arms. Furious, Baroni searched again for Abby, but she'd gone. She marched back to the van, looked at the screens as the mother and baby group subsided.

She grabbed the radio. 'You see where she went?'

'No,' said Santini. 'You should have let me intercept,' he said sourly.

'Maybe she went into the B & B?' said the techie cop.

Merda! It was time to find out.

SEVENTY-NINE

Abby stopped dead as she entered the bar of the B & B. It was empty. She looked around again, even though it would have been impossible not to have spotted her sister and Fredrik the first time. The place was tiny and there was nowhere to hide. Then she clocked two empty glasses on a table and somehow she knew they were theirs. So where had they gone?

Abby's eyes moved upwards, towards the ceiling. Surely not . . . ? She decided to check, just in case, and then if they weren't there . . . well, she'd have to think again.

As she climbed the stairs she wondered if she should make her tread heavy, let them know she was on her way. She cringed at the thought of catching them mid-act. Reaching the landing, she looked over to the door of the room. It was closed, as she'd left it when she'd stormed out earlier. She edged closer. Stood outside the door and leaned her head towards it. She was about to try the handle when a sound came from the room, like a piece of furniture being knocked or something, and she knew someone was inside. She placed her hand on the door handle.

EIGHTY

Ellie perched on the edge of the bed, Fredrik beside her, hands gentle, lips soft. Then she felt him pull away. 'I can't,' he said, so quietly she barely heard.

'What?' Ellie sat up, surprised.

'I'm sorry.'

She looked for a ring, saw bare fingers. 'You're married?'

'No.'

'Girlfriend?'

'No . . .'

'So what's wrong?'

He put his finger urgently to his mouth. 'Shush.'

'Why are we whispering?' whispered Ellie.

He looked so wretched then, she began to get worried.

'I'm really sorry, Ellie. Look, why don't we leave here? Together.' He looked across at the bags on the floor. 'Grab your suitcase and come with me.'

'What do you mean? The Camino?'

'Or something. Just away from here.'

'But what about Abby?'

He shrugged awkwardly. 'I don't think she should come.'

'You mean, I should just leave her?'

'I think it would be for the best.'

'The best, how?' Ellie saw how agitated Fredrik was. It unnerved her. She pulled down her dress, which had hitched itself over her thigh. She knocked the bedside lamp as she did so and Fredrik put a hand out to steady it.

Then something caught Ellie's eye. The door handle was slowly turning.

'Someone's trying to get in,' she whispered, pointing.

Fredrik grabbed her hand, pulled her off the bed towards the side of the room. He stood in front of her, making sure she was hidden behind him.

Ellie watched as the handle became still, the person on the other side unable to gain entry. She knew she'd locked the door when she'd come up with Fredrik. Then she heard the sound of the key going in and turning. Ellie tensed as Fredrik held her behind him, then the door slowly opened.

'Abby!' exclaimed Ellie, pulling away from Fredrik. 'You're back.'

Her sister was cutting Fredrik a malevolent look. 'Who sent you?' she demanded.

'Sorry?' said Fredrik, but Ellie detected a note of dissembling in his voice.

'Was it the police? Because don't tell me you just happened to be passing the exact same village as the one we are in, because it's bullshit and you and I both know it.'

'What's going on?' asked Ellie, bemused. 'Abby?' She looked at her sister who was staring out Fredrik and couldn't understand Abby's level of hostility. 'Why would Fredrik have anything to do with the police?'

'He's going to tell us,' said Abby. 'Aren't you?'

Ellie looked to Fredrik for affirmation that her sister had got the wrong end of the stick but no such affirmation came. In fact, he looked distinctly uncomfortable.

'They said you have a gun,' Fredrik said coolly to Abby. He put a protective arm out to Ellie.

Ellie's mouth dropped open. 'What? Who said, exactly?'

Fredrik turned to her. 'I'm sorry, Ellie. I saw the news article. About the shooting. I recognized you from the photos and I contacted the police.'

Ellie's face fell as she began to realize the true extent of his duplicity.

'I didn't want to lie but . . .' He saw he wasn't getting through. 'She's got a gun,' he repeated.

Ellie slowly stepped away from him, the news still sinking in. She walked over to her bag, unzipped it.

'I've got the gun,' she said.

He flinched, eyes agog, and she put it away. Her shoulders fell.

'We need to get out of here,' said Abby. 'Now.'

She grabbed the bags and, making sure Ellie was following, went to the door. Then she stopped. 'They're outside, aren't they?' she said to Fredrik.

He nodded.

'Shit!' She looked wildly around the room.

'I can help,' said Fredrik suddenly.

'I think we can do without your help,' snapped Abby.

'No, seriously.' Fredrik went over to the window, opened it. On the floor below was a balcony. Steps led from the balcony down to the gardens, beyond which was the car park. Abby could see the red Fiat from where she stood. It was tantalizingly close – but still a world away.

A loud scraping sound distracted her – she turned to see Fredrik heaving the bed over to the door. Then he ripped off the sheet and ran back over to the window.

'Let me tie this around you,' he said to Abby.

'I don't think so.'

'It's the only way.'

Abby narrowed her eyes. 'You'd better not be messing me around.'

She let Fredrik tie one end of the sheet around her middle. Then, on his instruction, she climbed out of the window onto the sill, as he had the other end of the sheet wrapped around his waist to support her.

'Use the drainpipe,' said Fredrik, and Abby reached across and grabbed it with both hands and then lowered herself down. She untied the sheet and Fredrik hauled it back up.

'Ready?' he called, holding her bags at the window. Abby nodded and he dropped them onto the balcony.

'Now you,' Fredrik said to Ellie.

She hesitated.

'Hurry,' he pleaded.

A loud noise from behind made Ellie jump: a hammering at the door.

'Open up! Police!'

Ellie knew she had no choice. She tied the sheet around her waist and looked down to see her sister urgently waiting.

'Was any of it true?' she asked Fredrik. 'All that stuff about your dad?'

'Every word,' he said.

There was no time to say anything more as Ellie could hear a battering ram being hurled against the door. The last she saw of Fredrik's face was as he pulled up the sheet. He gave her a small smile, then Abby was urging her down the steps and across the garden. They raced to the car, throwing their things in. Abby started the engine and they sped away out of the village.

In seconds, in the wing mirror, Ellie could see two unmarked cars chasing them, blue lights flashing, sirens wailing.

'Shit,' said Abby as they raced over a small bridge, landing hard.

Winded, Ellie grabbed the dashboard. This was it, surely.

'They're going to get us, Abs,' she said.

'Over my dead body,' her sister replied.

'Maybe we should just hand ourselves in. Deal with the consequences.'

Abby looked at her, aghast. 'Are you joking? No. This is not how this ends.'

She pushed the car even faster and Ellie clung on. The country lanes were narrow and they hurtled around corners, blind as to what was coming on the other side. Spartan trees and bushes lined the road, beyond which fields stretched into the distance, dotted by the odd farmhouse. Abby had managed to gain a bit of distance and for a few seconds they lost the two cars behind them. They neared a turning and, without warning, Abby flung the car left, into an even narrower road. She continued at speed, both girls watching anxiously in their mirrors.

'Have they gone?' asked Ellie urgently.

'I don't know, I don't know,' cried Abby.

Then they saw the police cars hurtle past the turning.

'Oh my God,' said Abby, not quite believing what she'd witnessed. 'We did it. We got away!'

Ellie broke into a smile. 'They didn't see us.'

Abby punched the air. 'Yes! *Yes!*'

'Maybe you could tell me next time you spin around a corner so I can make sure my stomach comes with me,' said Ellie.

Abby was laughing, buoyed by their success.

'Where did you learn to drive like that, anyway?'

'Never driven like that before in my life. God, that was fun,' Abby added, surprised at herself.

'Fuck,' said Ellie, suddenly sombre.

'What?' Alarmed, Abby glanced in her rear-view mirror. There was nothing.

'I thought I saw—' Ellie stopped abruptly as they both glimpsed a police car gaining on them.

'Oh my God,' wailed Abby, putting her foot down. 'Where did he come from?'

Up ahead, a farmer was opening a gate leading from his field into the road. Behind him was a herd of russet-coloured cows.

'Abs!' said Ellie, pointing.

The farmer hadn't spotted them. He continued to push

the gate until it was wide open. Then the first of the cows walked towards the road.

Abby checked her mirror. The police car was even closer. *She couldn't stop.* She hit the heel of her hand on the horn, one long, continuous blast. The farmer looked up, saw them hurtling towards him and his herd. He put his arms out, tried to halt the cows but now they were moving as one, a mass of blood and bone heading for the road.

Abby drove as fast as she could, Ellie squeezed her body into itself and they raced past the herd, inches from hitting them.

Without speaking, both girls looked in their mirrors. Behind them, the police car had come screeching to a stop, his path blocked by two dozen cattle.

Abby whooped ecstatically.

Ellie knew it would be several minutes before the police officer could resume the chase. He'd never catch up with them. There was no sign of the other car. They'd got away.

'I love cows!' yelled Abby.

Ellie looked across at her sister. She'd never seen her so high. She'd never seen her so *alive*.

EIGHTY-ONE

Ellie held the payphone receiver to her ear, her hand damp with sweat. They had stopped at a roadside cafe; Abby was stretching her legs and Ellie could see her walking up along the edge of a nearby field, a small figure in the heat haze. Ellie had claimed she was tired – which was true – and instead had plucked up the courage to do what had been burning away at her since her time with Fredrik.

His words echoed in her ears as she listened to her mother's phone ringing. *You're a survivor*. Then Ellie heard her mother pick up and the operator asked Susanna if she would accept a call from Ellie Spencer. She heard her mother's gasp of acceptance and then the operator connected them.

'Ellie!'

'Hi, Mum.'

'Tell me what's happening. Are you OK?'

Ellie took a breath. Composed herself. 'I'm fine, Mum.'

'Where are you?'

'Spain.'

'*Spain?* Whereabouts?'

'Mum, I need to ask yo—'

'Is Abby still with you? Did you find the gun?'

'Mum! Please. Stop interrupting. Yes, I found the gun. You were right.'

'Thank God!' said Susanna, deep relief in her voice.

'At least, you were right about Abby having taken it,' said Ellie.

Susanna paused. 'What do you mean?'

'Last night, Abby and I were held at knifepoint—'

'Oh my God!'

'Mum. Please let me speak. A man climbed into the back of our car when we were at a petrol station. He made us drive up into a forest. He forced us out of the car, was about to take us into the trees. He had a knife to my throat the whole time.' Ellie found she was shaking with the memory. 'He was probably going to kill us. Which is why Abby shot him.'

Ellie waited for a reaction but her mother was silent.

'Mum?'

'Yes. I'm here,' said Susanna quickly, her voice steeped in shock. 'Shot him? You mean . . . he's dead?'

'Yes.'

Her mother was silent again.

'Mum, he was about to slit my throat,' said Ellie, emotional. 'If Abby hadn't done what she did, both of us would be lying dead in the woods. But do you see what I'm saying? *Abby saved my life.*'

Susanna was taken aback. 'What?'

'You told me she hated me, that she was dangerous. You told me she did that awful thing to me when I was young.

But she saved me. Without Abby I'd be dead.' Ellie paused. 'Which means I think it was you, Mum. You were the one who poisoned me, like Abby said all along.'

'Now hang on a minute.'

'Please, no more lies. I just want to know why you did it. Actually, I don't want to know that. I need to tell you something. You robbed me of my childhood. Do you realize that? You took something from me that I'll never get back. And what I really want to know is, do you feel bad for what you did?' Ellie's voice cracked. 'All those times sitting watching while I cried as a doctor performed tests on me . . . the hours and hours of feeling I was missing out when I was kept home from school . . . the terrible sense that I was left behind, that I was a failure. What about all those things? Do you ever regret it?'

Susanna mustered a deep breath. 'Ellie, you need to listen to me.'

'Mum, stop.'

'Please. I beg you.' Susanna waited and, when Ellie said nothing, she continued. 'This man she shot. You say he had a knife to your throat at the time?'

Ellie frowned. 'Yes, I told you.'

'So he was restraining you? He was close to you?'

'Yes, he had his arm around my neck.'

Susanna inhaled. 'So how do you know Abby didn't miss her original target?'

'You what?'

'Was there anyone else around?'

'No . . .'

'No witnesses?'

'No.'

'So are you sure she was aiming at the mugger?'

Ellie recoiled.

'I'm so sorry, darling,' said Susanna, her voice barely audible. 'I only say these things because she's dangerous. You need to get away from her.'

'You're wrong, Mum. She saved my life.' Ellie was suddenly triumphant. 'If she wanted to get rid of me, why didn't she just shoot both of us?'

'I don't know. She's a control freak. I have no idea what she's really planning. She's always been secretive, you know that. She'll have some hidden agenda, some big plan, that you can be sure of. Are you still feeling unwell?'

'Yes . . . But—'

'I knew it! You've got to be vigilant. You need to watch your food, your drink.'

Ellie looked up towards the field, where Abby was still walking.

'Mum, Abby's not poisoning me. I'm not going to be swayed. I wish you'd just admit to what you did.'

'I can't watch you get hurt by her. I'd never forgive myself.'

'She's named me in her will, did you know that? Left me half her fortune.'

Susanna paused. 'She said that?'

'Yes. A million quid. Why would you bother leaving someone a million quid if you didn't at least like them?'

Susanna was silent for a moment. 'I don't know, Ellie. Now, listen to me. You have to do whatever it takes.'

'Mum, I'm not going to *do* anything.'

'Don't ignore me. It's too important. You have to stop her.'

Ellie exhaled loudly. 'What on earth are you talking about?'

'Do I need to spell it out? You have to get to her before she gets to you.'

Shocked, Ellie was silenced for a moment. 'What are you suggesting . . . ?'

'You know. Deep down, you understand.'

Ellie hung up and backed away from the phone in case her mother tried to call back. She wrapped her arms around herself, dumbfounded at her mother's strength of belief. Then she looked up at Abby, a small dot near the field. Her sister turned and waved. Ellie raised her own hand, then watched as Abby walked back down the track.

EIGHTY-TWO

Susanna swore under her breath. She knew it was pointless to call back; Ellie wouldn't answer.

She sat down in the living room chair and tried to think what to do. She was so worried. The message just didn't seem to be getting through. Her favourite daughter was out there somewhere in the Spanish countryside, completely under Abby's spell.

A thin line of perspiration broke out on Susanna's forehead. Somehow she had to get to Ellie, convince her she was telling the truth.

But how?

Susanna opened up her phone again, googled the number Ellie had called from. It was located somewhere in northwestern Spain. Susanna couldn't tell exactly where, so she zoomed out and it was then her heart stopped. She remembered a child's atlas from decades ago, a journey around Europe's biggest, longest, highest. She looked again at the red pin in the map, marking the position of the payphone from which her daughter had just called her. It was instinctive, as true as a mother knowing her child she'd nursed from ill health.

Susanna knew where Ellie and Abby were heading.

EIGHTY-THREE

Matteo sat in a utilitarian plastic chair in the front office of the police station. Waiting. He'd stay there the entire day and night if that's what it took. An hour ago, Baroni and Santini had stormed through the doors, with that Scandi guy, Fredrik Andersen, in tow. Matteo had been on Baroni in seconds but she'd refused to acknowledge his presence, much less answer his questions. Matteo knew that right now Fredrik was being debriefed – or having his head ripped off, if the Carabinieri's mood was anything to go by.

Matteo glanced up at the clock, watched the hands tick on. He'd managed to glean from some of the more friendly local staff that Fredrik had been a honey trap but he'd switched allegiance halfway through the operation. He also knew that sooner or later, Baroni would have to let Fredrik go and Matteo was not going to leave his post until he saw that man walk past.

The door that led to the offices and interview rooms opened. Out stepped a tall blond man. Matteo leaped to his feet.

'Fredrik?'

He stalled, then recognized Matteo. 'Oh, hey. Look, I'm

done with answering all the questions. Like I told the lady back there, I don't know where they've gone.'

Matteo nodded. 'But you saw them?'

'Sure . . .'

'And how were they?'

'Doing OK, considering.' He frowned. 'Hey, should I even be talking to you?'

Matteo flashed his ID. 'Captain Morelli, Italian Carabinieri. You said, "considering". Considering what?'

Fredrik appraised Matteo. 'You know, you cops should maybe cut them a bit of slack. They've been through a lot.'

'How was Abby?'

'Yeah, she seemed OK. Fierce.'

'Fierce?'

'Yeah, like someone you wouldn't want to mess with. Gotta have some sympathy for her husband.'

'I'll bear that in mind.'

'What?' Fredrik frowned, then it clicked. 'Oh! That's *you*? Right!' His eyes widened. 'She's married to a cop? Whoa. She is one dangerous lady.' He raised his fist and gave Matteo's arm a friendly punch. 'Respect.' He indicated the door. 'Hey, it all right if I head off? Got a pilgrimage to finish.'

'Just one minute. Are you sure you don't know where they're heading?'

Fredrik laid a palm on his chest. 'I swear.' He paused. 'I just kind of hope they get away. Even with you being Abby's husband.'

Matteo watched as Fredrik walked down the front steps, the door shutting behind him.

He sighed. Where was his wife? The longer this went on, the worse it would be – for all of them. And Baroni had shut him out of the investigation, so he had no idea what she was planning next. His phone rang. Matteo looked at the screen. It was Susanna.

'Hello?'

'Matteo, I have heard from Ellie.'

He straightened up. 'Did she say where she was?'

'No.'

'But where did she call you from? A payphone?'

'It makes no difference whether I have the number or not. She'll be gone by now.'

'But we'll be able to locate her from the last . . . How long?'

'I can do better than that,' said Susanna. 'I can tell you where she's going.'

'Where?' he demanded.

'One condition,' continued Susanna. 'You speak to Lieutenant Colonel Baroni and get me there too.'

EIGHTY-FOUR

Ellie was saddened by her mother's continued denial of what she'd done. Perhaps she was deluded – couldn't even admit it to herself. As the car flew past the fields, Ellie wondered about her desire to hear remorse in her mother's voice. It felt so important to hear those words. *I'm sorry. I wish I hadn't done it.*

But then what? Even if her mother had repented, it wouldn't change anything. It wouldn't give her back her childhood. She'd still be the same person she was today. Actually, she wasn't the same person. She was dealing with even more loss: that of their relationship as mother and daughter. They'd been so close, had shared so much. Ellie had thought her mother was her rock. How wrong she'd been. Susanna was a weak woman.

Suddenly Ellie knew she'd never get an apology from her mother. She could spend the rest of her life waiting and hoping, that hope turning to resentment when a sorry never materialized.

She stared out of the window, tried to put it from her mind.

'You OK?' asked Abby.

'Fine.'

'Only you don't look it. You look like someone who's just been dumped.'

'I think, under the circumstances, it is currently hard for me and Fredrik to maintain a relationship.'

'You don't half pick 'em, Ellie.'

Ellie bristled. 'Hang on, he just helped us escape.'

Abby pulled a face.

'Admit it. If it hadn't been for Fredrik, we would've been in the back of a police car by now.'

'It was Fredrik who got us nearly caught in the first place!'

'Right, pull over,' said Ellie.

'What?'

'Let's get this sorted once and for all.' She tugged on the steering wheel and, alarmed, her sister slowed the car until they stopped on the side of the road.

Ellie turned to face Abby. 'I am sorry.'

'For what?'

'Jon.' Ellie saw her sister stiffen. 'You still seem to have an issue with it so I want to clear the air.'

'An issue? *An issue?* Well, I think I'm entitled to have an issue.'

'It was ages ago.'

'You stole my boyfriend from me.'

'It wasn't like that.'

'I would really find it a whole lot easier if you would just admit the truth,' said Abby.

'You'd already broken up. You'd dumped him!' said Ellie. 'Told him work was making it difficult to find time for a relationship or something. He was gutted, as I recall,' she mused.

'I *what*?'

'You broke up with him,' repeated Ellie. Abby was looking at her incredulously. 'Right?'

'He broke up with *me*,' said Abby.

'Seriously? That is not what he said.'

'You'd better not be lying . . .'

Ellie put her palm on her chest. 'Swear on my moth— my life.'

'The bastard . . .'

The two sisters were quiet for a moment as they contemplated this change in history.

Ellie thought for a moment. 'I didn't feel good about it,' she said. 'I was envious of you, of your job, your new flat, how everything seemed to be falling into place . . .'

'I was working like a lunatic. I would fall asleep the second I got home.'

'It didn't look like that. Not from the outside. It looked like you were succeeding in everything. Again. Jon made me feel as if I had the right to be at your level as well. Except it was weird. I only met him twice. And no, for the record, I didn't sleep—'

'Blah blah blah blah,' said Abby suddenly, drowning her out.

'What's up?'

'I don't want to know.'

'That I didn't sleep wi—?'

'BLAH BLAH BLAH BLAH! Too much information.'

Ellie laughed.

Abby shook her head. 'God, to think all this time . . . Hey, for the record, it is still not cool to date your sister's ex.'

'Don't know why I bothered. He was boring. Always on about various muscle groups and how important it was to do daily exercises.'

'He was, wasn't he? Hey, did he get you doing those weird squat things?'

'You mean, with your legs bent out a bit?'

'Yes!' Abby laughed and pulled away, back onto the road.

Ellie looked across at her sister and for a moment her vision swam. Abby became two until Ellie blinked and held her head still. She was sick of feeling unwell. Ever since they'd left Elba, it had been getting steadily worse.

Recognizing she was also hungry, she reached for her bag, where she had a bar of chocolate stashed. Inside, Ellie saw the gun. She stared at it, recollecting that she had handled it, that both her and her sister's prints were on it. Ellie found herself wondering, if it had been Abby who'd had the knife to her neck, and she had been the one driving, whether she would have been able to pull the trigger and save them both. Would she have had the guts? She wasn't sure, and anyway . . . She stopped, her mind whirring, suddenly struck by something. Neither of them knew how to use it – they'd even laughed about it. And yet . . .

'Abby?'

'Yes?'

'You know yesterday, when we were laughing after I pointed the gun at you?'

'That sounds weird, but yes?'

'And how we said we didn't even know how to use a gun?'

'Yeah . . .'

Ellie shrugged. Where was she going with this? 'Just . . . you seemed to make it work quite easily in the forest.'

Her sister looked at her. 'I checked,' she said flatly. 'Looked it up online when you were in a shop or something. I can't quite remember.'

Ellie looked at her curiously.

'I guess I was intrigued. Why, you want a lesson?'

Ellie shuddered. 'No, thank you. In fact, I don't even want it in my bag anymore.' She picked it out between her thumb and forefinger, holding it at arm's length, then turned to put it on the back seat.

'Better not leave it there,' said Abby. 'In case we get stopped.' She saw her jacket on the seat. 'Put it in my pocket. We'll get rid of it someplace.'

Ellie leaned over and, taking Abby's jacket, tucked the gun inside the pocket.

'Junction,' said Abby.

Ellie quickly turned back to the map on her lap. 'Right,' she called. As they turned, she got out the chocolate bar and, breaking it in half, handed one piece to her sister.

They drove on.

EIGHTY-FIVE

Susanna stepped out of the helicopter, holding her hair tight against the downwash from the rotors. As she walked across the field, away from the chopper, she could see Lieutenant Colonel Baroni heading towards her, her face set in a humourless expression. Further back, Matteo was waiting by a police car, his arms folded.

'Now for your side of the bargain,' said Baroni, as she approached. 'And this better be good.'

'Thank you for bringing me here,' said Susanna. 'You may have just prevented a tragedy from happening.'

Baroni was impatient. 'Where are they?'

Susanna looked grim. 'I will tell you exactly.'

EIGHTY-SIX

They could see teasing glimpses of blue as the car rose over a hill, or when the trees thinned to reveal the horizon.

'Oh my God,' said Abby, leaning forward to peer through the windscreen. 'Is that what I think it is?'

'The Atlantic,' said Ellie.

They continued in silence, looking out for the sea, which became more visible as they got closer, passing rocky outcrops, trees misshapen by years of westerlies blowing off the ocean, until the single-track road came to a natural halt.

Abby stopped the car and turned off the engine. Both girls stared ahead. Land had ended. They were on the edge of an enormous cliff, the ocean spread out before them. Far out to sea, the horizon stretched until it blurred into a blue haze. A breathtaking drop below, the waves battered the edge of the rock. Gulls wheeled on thermals, soaring, looking for all the world as if they were in their own playground.

'Vixía Herbeira, six hundred and twenty-one metres – that's nearly six times the height of the White Cliffs of Dover,' quoted Ellie.

Abby looked at her sister. 'Is that *the* cliff? The *if you don't visit in life, you'll visit in death* cliff?'

'Yep.' Ellie saw Abby staring in wonder. 'Now, for God's sake, don't do anything crazy. No *Thelma and Louise*.'

Abby was puzzled. '*Thelma and Louise*?'

'Yes, you know, the movie. Driving off the edge.'

'Why did they do that?'

'To evade capture. To be free. Don't tell me you've never seen it.'

'I didn't really go to the cinema.'

'Good God, Abby, it's ancient. It came out in the nineties.'

'I never had cable either.'

'It would be on normal TV. Please tell me you watched TV.'

Abby was indignant. 'Of course I did! I'm not a freak. Just not that often. Too tired or at work. Must have missed our friends Thelma and Louise. Were they sisters?'

Ellie smiled to herself. 'Might as well have been.'

'OK, Louise,' said Abby. 'I'm not going to drive off that cliff.'

'I think you're probably Louise,' said Ellie. 'The level-headed one. The one who was strong, who led all the time. The achiever.'

'You've achieved,' said Abby.

Ellie let out a small laugh.

'Of course you have. You've lived your life to the full. Travelled, had experiences I've deliberately deprived myself of.'

'But you had the high-flying career.'

'Not the life, though. You may have had a stunted childhood being wrapped up in cotton wool but you sure made up for it.'

Ellie pondered, eyes lighting up as this new revelation sank in. Maybe she had.

'Who are you calling stunted?'

Abby smiled.

'Looks like we've reached the end of the road,' said Ellie.

'Yes.'

'We've come a long way.'

'We have,' agreed Abby.

'Seems a long time ago we were swimming in the sea at your place.' Ellie thought back to the house they had left, the simple life Abby had carved out for herself. There would be no going back. 'I'm sorry I messed up your retirement.'

Abby was quiet for a moment. Then suddenly her face broke into a huge smile. 'Are you kidding? These last three days. They've been the best of my life.'

'Seriously?'

'I was too young for retirement anyway.' Abby nodded towards the cliffs. 'You want to get out?'

'Sure.' Ellie opened the door and the wind immediately caught it. A chilly blast filled the car. 'It's cold out here,' she said.

'Take my jacket if you want,' said Abby as she got out of the car.

Ellie leaned over and grabbed it. As she stepped onto the cliff, she pulled it on.

She walked as near to the edge as she dared. Then she leaned into the wind and felt the physical freedom of the seabirds as they soared. She didn't see Abby step behind her, lift her hands.

'Look at that,' said Ellie in awe, as she saw a gull swoop through the air. She turned then, saw Abby's hands just behind her shoulders, at exactly the right position to push her off the edge. She wouldn't stand a chance; the shock and the loss of balance would make her stumble right over.

'Abs . . . ?' Ellie said in a scared voice.

Abby's face broke into a grin. 'That's my third.'

'What?'

'Idea. From when I was little. I was going to push you off a cliff.'

'Oh my God.'

'Not now, obviously.' Abby lowered her palms.

'Are there any more?' asked Ellie. 'Only, if we could get them out of the way now, that would save me having any more heart attacks.'

'You'll have to wait and see.'

'Oh, come on.'

'No.' Abby smiled and turned away.

'There's something I need to tell you,' said Ellie.

'Sounds serious.'

'Kind of . . .' Ellie took a deep breath. 'It's about Mum . . .'

'What about her?'

How did she explain? Abby was looking at her expectantly but then they heard the sound of sirens squealing, tyres screeching to a halt. Both girls looked back to see several police cars blocking the road, dust rising into the air. Doors flung open and police officers exited at speed, crouching down behind their vehicles, guns raised.

'Oh my God,' said Abby.

'Are they pointing those things at us?' asked Ellie in shock.

'I don't think it's the seagulls,' said Abby.

'Step away from the car with your hands above your head,' ordered Baroni, through a loudspeaker. She crouched down behind the door of the police car, watching intently, alert for any sudden moves. Santini was in another vehicle to her left. He got out, raised his weapon.

Susanna was sitting in the back of the car. She'd had strict instructions to remain there, whatever happened. She looked through the windscreen, could see her two daughters up ahead on the cliff edge. Suddenly she didn't want to do as she was told. She opened the car door and, getting out, she stood tall.

'Get back in the car,' snapped Baroni, but Susanna ignored her. She could see Matteo standing by another one of the police cars, but this was her moment, her children. She stepped forward, disregarding Baroni's increasingly furious demands.

Abby blinked, unable to take in what she was seeing. 'Oh my God,' she faltered. She looked over at Ellie, saw her guilty face.

'That's what I was about to tell you,' said Ellie, biting her lip. 'Mum's not dead.'

'Are you joking me?' said Abby. 'How . . . ?' Lost for words, she just stared at her mother, who was slowly moving towards them.

'This is your last warning,' said Baroni. 'Move away from the vehicle with your hands raised in the air!'

'I think we'd better do as she says,' said Ellie. She slowly stepped away from the car. Abby had no choice but to do the same.

'Move further away from the vehicle,' ordered Baroni and both girls started to walk away from their car, towards the police, their hands above their heads. The police edged towards them, their weapons still raised.

'You need to arrest her,' said Susanna, pointing. 'Abby. She's the one who's dangerous.'

Abby's mouth dropped open.

'She's been saying it's you,' said Ellie quickly. 'The whole time. You're the one who hurt me as a kid. She's been saying you've tried to poison me on this trip. Hiding stuff in my food.' It pained her to admit to this, to see her mother again. She had loved her so much. Ellie felt the ground spin. She stopped still, regained her balance.

Abby looked at her mother and was shocked to see the distance in her eyes. It was as if Susanna was looking at a stranger, someone she had no connection with. Abby was suddenly filled with an incredible anger. She had tried so hard to make her mother love her. She hadn't deserved any of this. She dropped her arms by her sides, started to walk towards Susanna, slowly at first, then faster.

'Stop right there!' yelled Baroni but Abby kept on going.

Susanna stood absolutely still.

'Has she got the gun?' Baroni asked her colleagues urgently. 'Can anyone see if the suspect is armed?'

'Can't see,' said an officer agitatedly, his gun aloft.

Santini stayed conspicuously quiet. He raised his weapon, holding Abby in his sight-line.

'Abby!' Matteo stepped forward in desperation but was immediately held back by another officer.

Susanna didn't move, waiting for the inevitable to happen. Just a few more seconds, then Abby would be cut down by the police and order would be restored.

EIGHTY-SEVEN

Abby's eyes blazed as she approached Susanna. 'You gave her something, didn't you? That night at my house when you helped cook. She's been ill ever since we left.'

'I swear I didn't,' said Susanna, innocence cast across her face. 'It's not true,' she insisted loudly to the police.

'You're lying.'

'It wasn't her,' cried out Ellie but her voice was weak and got lost in the wind.

Susanna stood in front of her eldest daughter and held her head high. 'If I had, it would have worn off by now,' she said, 'and if anything, Ellie's been getting worse.'

Matteo saw his wife falter. *Jesus*, he thought, *she's right*. His mother-in-law was right. Which meant . . . He looked at Abby.

'You know it's true,' continued Susanna. She lowered her voice. 'And you know you were always jealous of her.'

'Get your hands up!' shouted Baroni to Abby.

'With good reason,' said Abby to Susanna. 'You ignored me. Ellie was always your favourite. Why did you do that, Mum?' She looked at her mother, searching her face for an answer, but Susanna was inscrutable.

EIGHTY-EIGHT

Ellie continued to look at her sister, horrified. Abby had to stop moving; she had to do what the police were saying! In desperation, Ellie's hands fell to her sides and, as they did, they brushed against the pocket of her jacket and she felt something hard and weighty. She froze – *the gun!*

Awkwardly, she moved her hands away.

She didn't notice Santini clock her movements, see her nervousness, her fear. She didn't see his eyes light up, as he instinctively understood what she'd felt in her pocket. She didn't see him swing his arms so that his weapon pointed at her instead of Abby.

EIGHTY-NINE

Susanna waited. Surely it was only a matter of seconds now? The police suspected that Abby was armed and there was no way they'd let her keep on coming at them. She half wondered about provoking Abby into launching at her, just to get to the end of this nightmare. Maybe she should say something that would cause Abby to make a sudden movement. Then it would be over. Susanna would deny anything Kathleen claimed – that 'confession' she'd made would never stand up. If she could just silence Abby then Susanna knew she'd be safe forever and no one would ever find out what she'd done.

'She doesn't care for you, you know,' said Susanna.

Abby frowned. 'Who?'

'Ellie. She's been talking to me this whole trip.'

'You're wrong. We get on now, we're close.'

Susanna shook her head. 'You never have been and you never will be. I'm sorry about that but it's the truth.'

Susanna turned to smile at her younger daughter and as she did so she caught sight of Santini pointing his gun in a different direction to all the other cops. She frowned, trying to understand, then it all happened so quickly. She was distantly aware of Abby lunging for her, Baroni shouting a warning. But Susanna wasn't even looking at her eldest daughter; she was staring at Ellie, who was rushing towards them – not to her, Susanna, but to Abby – with fear and love etched across her face. Susanna reeled around to see Santini, his gun at eye level, and in a split second she knew what he was going to do. She screamed out in denial, throwing herself at her favourite daughter. There was a blinding pain, then she fell to the ground.

NINETY

The world seemed to slow down. Ellie was aware of a deafening bang, an explosive sound that made her ears ring and suddenly left her feeling as if she was watching everything from a distance. Her mother was lying on the ground next to her, blood seeping from her back. Ellie felt dizzy . . . *Must not fall*, she thought and tried to right herself. Abby was gesturing at her wildly, trying to get away from the police, but they pinned her hands behind her back and restrained her with handcuffs. Ellie knew that if she tried to walk towards her she would tumble. The ringing in her ears just wouldn't go away. She closed her eyes for a moment but felt herself sway so opened them again. The policewoman who'd held the megaphone was now on the ground next to her mother. She'd rolled her over, was pushing on her chest, but Ellie knew she was dead.

Her mind suddenly swirled and she couldn't focus properly. In despair she tried to grab hold of something, but there was nothing but thin air and she collapsed to the ground.

EPILOGUE

Eight months later

'Trust you to take the best position,' said Abby. Holding a tray with two glasses of iced lemonade she'd just brought from the house, she looked down at her sister, lying on a lounger beside the Tyrrhenian Sea. Ellie had already made herself comfortable in the shade, cast by the new umbrella that Matteo had put up before he went to work. The other lounger was in full sun.

'I need the shady one, the heat worsens the MS,' said Ellie.

'I thought we weren't meant to wrap you in cotton wool?' said Abby, but she spoke lightly as she placed the tray down on the rocks and handed her sister a drink.

'I forbid it,' said Ellie. 'But I'm allowed the occasional perk. Just don't ever make a fuss, OK?'

Abby held her hands up. 'I promised, didn't I?'

'I didn't even want you to know . . .' mused Ellie. 'I didn't want anyone to know.' She'd kept her illness secret ever since she'd been diagnosed with multiple sclerosis nearly two years ago. It was only when she'd been taken to hospital after that fateful day on the cliff that it had all come out. 'I'm normal,' she continued. 'Not the ill person. Never again.'

'Course.' Abby lay back on the other lounger and started to apply sun cream.

Ellie could see her sister glancing over every so often; she knew Abby was plucking up the courage to ask something she'd been dying to confront her about for months. She'd been skirting around the subject, knowing Ellie didn't like to discuss it.

'Do the doctors know?' asked Abby casually. 'How you got it?'

Ellie smiled wryly. Her sister already knew the medical professionals couldn't say how she'd developed her illness. This wasn't the real question. Better to deal with this once and for all. 'If you're asking whether I got MS as a result of what Mum did to me when I was younger, the answer is no.'

'Is that what the doctors said?'

'There's no credible scientific link. That's enough for me.'

Abby nodded. 'How do you like the sunbeds?'

Ellie ran her palms over the soft padded cushion. 'Spectacular. What I can't get over is the quality. You really splashed out, didn't you?'

'I thought I'd celebrate. Seeing as the Spanish justice system decided it wasn't in the public interest to prosecute me.' Abby felt a shiver, despite the sun. That night in the woods still made her wake up in a cold sweat every now and then. She would never forget how close it had been to ending differently.

'Thank God,' said Ellie.

'Plus, I didn't want . . .' Abby trailed off.

'What?'

'As you once pointed out, the rocks are hard. Can play havoc with my joints.'

Ellie raised her sunglasses and narrowed her eyes as she looked over to her sister. But Abby had her eyes closed: the picture of innocence, no mollycoddling in sight. As it happened, Ellie felt fine and had done for some time. In fact, she'd been in remission for seven months now. The doctors had said that there was every possibility that the remission period could last for years. Of course, Ellie also knew it might not. Moving out here had really helped. Maybe it had even bought her some more time, time she was intending on making the most of. She'd given up her full-time job in London and had a less stressful role working at a local language school teaching English. It paid enough to rent a small place and get by, and with some careful managing, she was slowly paying off her credit card debt. Once, Abby had offered to help, but now Ellie couldn't stomach it. She refused and made it clear she didn't want her sister to bring it up again. It had surprised Ellie how much her independence had meant to her.

'This is nice, isn't it?' said Abby.

'What?'

'You know.'

Ellie smiled. She did know. She and Abby together. Sisters.

'Just think,' said Abby pensively, 'if it hadn't been for

Mum, we wouldn't have been apart for all those years. She was determined to keep us apart, too. Would have succeeded if she'd convinced everyone it was me who did those awful things when we were children.'

'Don't let it get you down, Abby.'

'You're in a very forgiving mood.'

'What's the point otherwise? I know she lied about you, said terrible things, but she was scared. If the truth came out about what she'd done to me, then the police might have reopened the case into Ben.'

Their grandmother had sent Ellie and Abby a letter. In it she'd spoken about the brother they'd never known had existed. She'd also told them about the confession she'd got out of Susanna – a confession that, when given to the police, was enough to make them leave Abby in peace.

'I wonder what Ben would have been like. If he was still around,' said Ellie. 'What would he be doing? Where would he be?'

'He'd be here. With us,' said Abby firmly.

Ellie smiled. She liked this new inclusive sister. She knew there was a truth in what Abby was saying – and the two of them had lost decades that could have woven a very different story. Yet those years were gone. And now Ellie dared to think about a possible future. A future that, because of her illness, currently had an unknown limit on it. But at least she *had* a future. Ellie knew that policeman's bullet had been meant for her.

'If it hadn't been for Mum,' she said, 'we wouldn't be together now.'

She glanced over at Abby, who nodded. 'You're right.'

Ellie looked out at the Tyrrhenian Sea, at how it met the horizon. The light held the promise of a new season and the sky seemed to go on forever. Her eyes travelled over the ocean and the clear blue water near to her rocked in the sun. There was such beauty in nature. In life. Their mother had done an awful thing to both of them. But Ellie knew you had to live in the moment, right here, right now.

'If it hadn't been for Mum, we wouldn't *be*.'

ACKNOWLEDGEMENTS

A huge thank you to all the wonderful readers who have decided to pick up this book and take it home with them or download it into their hands. You are always who I think about most when I have a new book out, and your support and kind words mean more than you can ever know.

Trisha Jackson and Jayne Osborne, my fantastic editors, thank you for helping to shape this book and for your continued guidance and enthusiasm. It means a tremendous amount.

Mel Four, the minute I clapped eyes on your jacket design, my heart sang. It's outstanding – thank you so much.

Samantha Fletcher, your eagle eyes saved me more than once. I am indebted to you. Huge thanks also to Lorraine Green for saving countless other blushes. There's a whole team of people who work incredibly hard to get a book published and I am also extremely grateful to Eleanor Bailey, Ellis Keene and Rebecca Lloyd.

Gaia Banks, my wonderful agent, who has the rare and precious ability to give just the right advice at exactly the right time. Lucy Fawcett and Alba Arnau for your psychological insight – into the characters, not me – and putting your thoughts so succinctly. Big thanks also to Joel Gotler and Markus Hoffman.

The Coulsdon girls – Gabriella Ferri-Marshall, thank you so much for your insight into all things Italian; and Anna Stimson, yet again you have been my police 'rock'. I would also like to thank the staff of the Public Relations Office of the General Command of the Carabinieri, who patiently answered question after question on following an investigation in Italy and beyond. And a special mention for Di Oakley who helps spread the word.

My family, as always, for your incredible support: Mum, Rhys, Dad, Sally, Ettie, Neil, Tina, Leila and Brandt.

And, of course, Jonny, Livi and Clementine, who put up with all my crazy working hours. I couldn't do it without you. The adventure continues!